# The Prom Dress Killer

A Detective Al Warner Suspense

by

## George A Bernstein

Award winning Amazon top 100 author

GnD Publishing LLC

**GnD Publishing LLC**
Palm Beach Gardens, Florida 33418
www.GnDpublishingllc.com
info@GnDpublishingllc.com

Publisher's Note: This is a work of fiction. Names, characters, and incidents are a product of the author's imagination. Locales and public names are sometimes used for atmospheric purposes and may have been altered to meet the demands of the story. Any resemblance to actual people, living or dead, or to businesses, companies, events, institutions, or locales is completely coincidental.

Cover Design by Paradox Book Covers

Ordering Information: Quantity sales. Special discounts are available on quantity purchases by corporations, associations, Bookstores, and others. For details, contact the publisher.

**The Prom Dress Killer**/George A Bernstein
1st edition

**ISBN 978-0-9894681-6-9**

# *The Prom Dress Killer*

**S.L Menear, Award-winning Author:** The master of suspense is back with another unique murder mystery that kept me captivated with every thrilling turn of the page. Like *Death's Angel* and *Born to Die*, *The Prom Dress Killer* features Al Warner, a relentless homicide detective, called "The Hero" for ridding South Florida of many deadly criminals. Warner faces the most difficult case of his career in this desperate rush to stop a madman from killing more innocent young redheads and possibly destroying everything Warner holds dear. A must read.

# *Death's Angel*

**Midwest Book Review: December, 2015 Magazine:**
"A masterfully crafted suspense thriller from beginning to end, *Death's Angel* is a terrifically absorbing read and very highly recommended."

**(Five Star)** K. Lintneron 12/14 A Keep You Up All Night Read. After reading Death's Angel, it is easy to see why George Bernstein is a top selling writer on Amazon. The story is ripe with suspense and action. All of the characters are excellently developed and bring the story to life with dialogue that feels natural and never forced. Death's Angel breaks out of the formulaic police procedural/serial killer genre and excels above its peers. Al Warner could easily be the next Alex Cross.
A thrilling murder mystery with a surprise ending no one will guess!"

**Born to Die** - 5 **Stars - Readers' Favorite**, By Tracy A. Fischer.
"Whoa! Just, whoa! That's exactly what I thought when I got to the end of the fantastic new book by author George A. Bernstein, **Born to Die**: A Detective Al Warner Suspense. This book grabbed me from the very start and had me obsessively reading all the way through until the very end.

I loved Born to Die. Loved. It. How's that for a review? Well, it's definitely how I felt about this book. As a great reader of mysteries, it's difficult for me to find one in which I can't figure out "whodunit" much before the book is over, but this plot had me stumped. Author George A. Bernstein has done a fantastic job in creating realistic and interesting characters, a fascinating and sympathetic story line, and a simply great read in general! I highly recommend this book to any reader who loves mysteries or just loves great fiction, and I am very much looking forward to reading more from this very talented author."

# DEDICATION

Thanks to my critique team and buddies: Sharon, Fred, Richard and Tina. These four experienced authors help me sharpen my skills to make this novel the best it can be.

And to my ever-suffering wife, Dolores, who steadfastly rereads all my works, over and over, providing pointed and merciless editing comments.

And to all the cops out there, making the world a safer place. We need more real-life Al Warners.

# The Prom Dress Killer

# PROLOGUE

" ... The Captain listened, but not hearing anything, he began to grow uneasy, throwing stones again a second and also a third time." Helen Weitz glanced at her daughter's eager face, and then continued reading from "A Thousand and One Nights."

"His men didn't hear because they were dead, right, Mommy?" Shelly asked, snuggling deeper into her mother's lap.

"That's right, sweetie. When Marjaneh discovered the thieves in the barrels, she protected Ali Baba by pouring hot oil on them."

"Good. They wanted to hurt him. So, what happened next?"

Helen found her place, skipping a few lines, and began reading.

"Much alarmed, he went softly down to the yard, and smelt the hot boiled oil, which sent forth a steam out of the jar. Hence he suspected his scheme to murder Ali Baba, and plunder his house, was discovered. Examining the jars, one after another, he found all thirty-eight of his gang were dead."

"I bet he ran away then, huh, Mommy?"

Helen stroked her six-year-old daughter's hair and lifted her to sit next to her on the bed.

"Yes, he did, honey. There's more to the story, but it's time for bed."

"Was this the last story Shahrazad told the Sultan? Was it the thousandth night?"

"Yep, it's the last one in the book. Because she kept telling new stories each night, leaving him wondering about the next, she stayed alive."

"Cool. She was a smart lady. What happened then?"

"Well, according to the legend, the sultan fell in love and no longer needed to kill her like his other wives. I suppose they lived happily ever after. She, and the things he learned from her stories, helped him defeat his nasty brother, who was trying to take over his kingdom."

"Yea! It's an old story, isn't it?"

"Yes, pumpkin. They were a bunch of legends, passed down from storyteller to storyteller for many years. It was finally put into a written collection over a thousand years ago."

"Wow! And still so interesting. Old stuff is still good today. Right, Mommy?"

"Yes, my darling," Helen said. "You never know when things learned long ago may be important to you now." She slipped Rochelle under the blanket festooned with dancing bear cubs and skipping lambs, tucking it around her neck. The girl's auburn hair scattered like a shimmering halo on the pillow. Helen planted a butterfly kiss on her forehead and tweaked her daughter's small nose.

"Sleep tight, munchkin, and pleasant dreams."

"Un-huh," Shelly murmured, already drowsy. "I'm Shahrazad ...."

# 1

"Why are you not properly dressed, Camille?"

"Audrey! I keep telling you, my name is Audrey!"

"Stop being foolish, Camille." Feet spread, fists planted on his hips, he would have seemed menacing, except for the expressionless, smooth round face ... and he was so short.

"I don't know where you got those silly clothes, Camille, but they're just not proper for my lady. You must change into what I've set out for you."

"Audrey, Audrey, Audrey! Will you stop calling me Camille? My name is Audrey, goddammit!"

Audrey Williamson's anger had trumped her fear. This pint-size jerk had snatched her right out of the Miami Library parking garage. A sickening sweet smell, probably chloroform, still clung to her clothes.

She shivered. She should have been more careful, with some lunatic out there, kidnapping young redheaded women. But this nut, who she suspected was a lot older than the kid he appeared, never physically threatened her or seemed dangerous. Still didn't, despite having kept her locked in this simple, windowless bedroom for two days.

He's made no sexual advances ... so far.

*If he tries that I'll kick the shit out of him.* Hollow bravado. If she were so cocky, why hadn't she already attacked him and made a break for it? A broad-shouldered yet trim fitness nut, long triathlon-hardened legs stretched her to a height two inches above his.

Still, despite being no more than five-six, he was thick limbed and muscular. He somehow intimidated her with his placid face and complete impersonal disdain.

Whatever he craved from her, they would get to it eventually. She shuddered again and wondered what that could be?

She had no idea why he was so insistent she wear this stupid little girl prom outfit. If it were to dress up for sex, she might just play it safe and give in. She'd occasionally enjoyed rough, sometime even physically dangerous sex. An aura of jeopardy was an aphrodisiac to her.

If that were it, just get it over with so she could go home. It'd still be rape. Let the cops deal with him later.

Audrey Williamson wasn't terribly worried about her safety. She was a sharp evaluator of guys who rarely misjudged their motives, and she was certain this one wasn't the serial killer doing those other gals. He had some other agenda, somehow connected to this Camille he kept talking about.

*How is it he doesn't know I'm not her?* Once he realized she wasn't that girl, things would change. He'd probably let her go, unharmed.

Catching his dark eyes, Audrey bit her lip and shivered slightly under his cold stare as the first tendrils of doubt wound its icy fingers around her mind. She'd never misjudged a man before.

She had not yet realized this would be the first ... and last ... error she would ever make.

# 2

"What d'ya got, Jack?" Al Warner asked, as he settled his lithe, hard muscled six-foot frame on the corner of his ex-partner's desk.

"Not much, Al. The criminalists swept the entire area of the parking lot, but they didn't come up with anything." Jack Harris flipped through his notebook an shook his head.

"We know for sure she was snatched in the lot?" Warner asked.

"Yeah. Security cameras picked her up, entering from the library. There're two cams on every deck, but unfortunately, Miss Williamson was parked where there was no real coverage, and we never saw her leave."

"Terrific!" Warner said. His fingers gently probed the spot at the back of his skull, more itchy than tender now, under the mat of thick curly black hair.

"That whack on the noggin still bothering you, Al?" Jack asked.

"Nah, not really. Just habit. Good thing I got a hard head." Warner picked the crime scene report from Harris' desk.

"Yeah, lucky for you. Not so lucky for the guy who beaned you ... or his two nasty partners." He grinned and delivered a little punch to Warner's arm. Harris marveled at the steel hardness of his friend's forty-year-old body.

"Easy, there, bud," Warner said, his lips ticking upward. "So no video of the snatch ...?"

"If it was one. I ain't so sure." Harris stood and came around the desk.

"The third redheaded gal to go missin' in the last three months? No longer a coincidence, Jack." Warner self-consciously dropped his hand from another visit to his itchy scalp.

"If it's the same perp," Warner continued, "which now seems damned likely, we got five, maybe six days to find her alive. This guy's got a timetable, and he sure doesn't waste much time between vics. He drops one in an alley and has usually swiped the next within two weeks, max.

"Did the cameras at least pick up auto traffic in and out? We need something, Jack." He levered himself off the desk and started to pace.

"Sure, they got every vehicle coming and going. Problem is, we don't have an exact timeline when she went missing. She left the library at about five p.m., and we got no shot of her leaving the garage."

"Let's review the tapes, startin', say, at four-thirty, through about six. Look for the same vehicle comin' and goin' durin' that time. He had to drive in and out. Maybe we'll get lucky," Warner said.

"Okay, boss, but he coulda followed her there and just waited for her to come back."

"Good point. So look for her arrivin' about three p.m. ID the next three or four vehicles behind her, and then look for one of them leavin' right after we think she was snatched."

"That's kinda thin, boss ... and it's gonna give me a lot of sore eyes."

"What else we got, Detective? Put one of the techs on it, if you're gettin' too old," Warner said with a mischievous grin.

"Shit, you think I'd leave something like that to some nerd punk. I got a bottle of Murine."

"Yeah, I figured. So get your lazy ass in gear. Let's try to find this gal before the sands run out. I'm gonna zip by the parkin' lot again, just in case we missed something. Her car been towed to the lab?"

"Yep. The Tech boys are about done." Harris returned to his desk and tilted his chair back. "I thought you might wanna take another peek at the scene. It's still taped off, all the markers in place, and we got two full-time blues on the spot, so nothing gets disturbed."

"Okay. Give me a copy of your interview notes of the lot's attendants, and get on that film ASAP." His voice raspy, he leaned forward, balancing on his arms, fingers spread like claws braced against the top of the desk.

"I don't want a third pretty young corpse, all dolled up in a fancy prom dress, lyin' in an ally somewhere. Not the goddamned Angel of Death, all over again." Warner's face contorted, as he slammed his fist down hard enough to spill the pencil container.

"Easy, boss." Harris pushed away from his desk and stood. "We're doing the best we can, with what little we got."

"Well it's not fuckin' good enough." Warner straightened and caught himself from reaching for his last head wound again.

"I'm goddammed sick and tired of serial-killers around here. Three in the last three years is three fuckin' too many! Let's get this bastard before this last gal becomes his third vic, and before he takes a fourth."

"We're doing what we can, Al. He's gotta make a mistake soon. I just hope we can do it this time without ya catching a bullet or rock off the noggin. Ya gotta stop playing those sympathy cards."

Warner glared at the smaller man, but couldn't contain laughter that bubbled up, erupting like a ruptured dam ... which in a sense, it was.

"Goddammed little shit! You always know how to cool my fuse when it gets too hot."

Harris grinned. "Someone's gotta chill ya out. You're the best cop I know to solve these things, if ya don't get too emotional about the vics. Never knew a detective who cared as much as you do, boss."

"Thanks for the bucket of cold water, Jack. I get too wound up and I could miss something. Can't afford to do that, 'cause this perp's on a serious mission. I'm pretty sure bodies of pretty young redheads are gonna keep pilin' up if we don't nab 'im soon." He rolled his shoulders and flexed his neck, easing his tension.

"Anyhow, get on that film, and get one of the techies to help. Two sets of eyes are always better. I'll be back in a couple of hours. I'll wanna go over the patrol canvas reports, too."

"Gottcha. Is Doc Guttenberg working on a profile?" He circled his desk.

"Not yet. I'll see Eva tonight and see if she can come up with something that might help."

"Right. That's real tough duty!" Harris grinned. "At least you two getting together is one thing good coming outta the last caper."

Warner smiled. "Always lookin' for the silver lining, huh."

"Gotta be some perks in this job. I'll call ya if anything comes outta those videos."

Warner nodded, scooped up the file from Jack's desk, and headed out of the Miami-Dade Homicide Department. Something had to break, but time wasn't on his side.

It never was, with a nut out there, killing innocent victims. Three years ago, it was teenagers. A year later beautiful young women ... almost including Sharon. Now this nut — just sixty days after he snagged the perps with all those SIDS infants dying ... and him getting bopped by a small boulder on the noggin in the process.

It's redheaded women this time, meticulously groomed and dressed to the nines. Each smothered, dying peacefully while apparently in a chloroform daze. It looked like the Unsub didn't want them to suffer, but that seemed at odds with him laying them out in dark alleys like so much trash.

He hoped Eva could come up with something other than the killer seemed conflicted over his vic's care. If nothing else, the lovely doctor would at least manage to drain off his tension.

He grinned, in spite of his anger. How was he so lucky to have that beauty love him? He thought briefly of Sharon, who fled to Buffalo after her near deadly encounter with the Angel of Death. And then that blonde angel, Casey, consumed by the SIDS deaths of all those baby boys. That case eventually brought him to lovely Dr. Eva Guttenberg ... and how lucky was that!

Will love last this time? He didn't give it freely, and was too hard-case to receive it back very often. He had already used up a lifetime of opportunities, and he didn't want to screw this one up.

He unlocked his gray Dodge Charger coupe, slid in, and tossed the file onto the passenger seat. He lingered, eyes focused on some distant, invisible spot. Fingers tap-danced on the leather cover steering wheel as he considered the current serial lunatic.

This psycho wanted something specific from these girls, and when they couldn't feed his need, he discarded them, cleaving to some unique, personal ritual. Then he went hunting for another. That they were in their twenties and redheads of similar size and build had a special meaning, but so far nothing else had conjoined these gals except age group and hair color.

He sighed and fired up the engine, enjoying the rumble of its power.

"Better figure it out soon," he mumbled, "or more bodies are gonna start pilin' up. We're one or two redheads away from city-wide panic." He shifted gears and drove out of the police lot, shaking his head.

They needed a break ... and soon.

# 3

Rochelle Weitz did a graceful pirouette and toe-danced across the rust-colored shag carpet of her living room floor, clutching the white paper against her modest breast. Her hair swirled around her head like a ruby crown and her slate gray eyes sparkled with joyous moisture.

"I passed!" She thrust the paper high overhead, spun again, and dropped into a ballerina's curtsey.

"Shelly Weitz, *licensed* real estate associate." Not only had she passed the state licensing exam, but she did it with an impressive score of 92. She must have aced the math section, which had been her major concern. Little math was required to obtain her Literary Degree at the U of Miami, and she never thought of herself as an expert.

Unfortunately, that degree, with her side major in Creative Writing, only led to a dead-end job at the local paper, North Miami News, as a copy editor. She'd hoped it would provide an opening to publish her short stories, but that seemed less and less likely.

With the country's long stagnant financial woes and the dwindling fortunes of much of the Fifth Estate, opportunities were drastically limited. Shelly saw little apparent future in news journalism. Over lunch, always dependable Mom suggested she go for a real estate license. Houses and apartments were always on the market, regardless of the economy.

"With your personality and attention to detail," Mom said, "you'll be a great agent and you can make a nice income. And it'll give you time to work on your short stories."

Shelly loved writing and thought she was a pretty good short-story author. She loved them as a kid, with Mom reading from *The Thousand and One Nights* and an O'Henry anthology. She was especially fond of *Ali Baba,* and O'Henry's *Ransom of Red Chief.*

Shelly had splurged on a local 3-day writers' conference in Orlando where she attended several inspiring classes. She garnered some real heartening comments from two New York agents. Both encouraged her to consider writing a novel, but that was a distant dream. First she needed a real job.

Well, now that she had her real estate license, she would visit NMB Realty, just a few miles from her apartment in North Miami Beach. Any agency would gladly accept your "shingle" as an independent agent, but she wanted to work in an office, to really learn the ropes. Lisa Howell, the managing broker, offered her a part-time job, once she passed the exam.

Part-time meant a salary, less the usual tax and FICA deductions, but no benefits like health insurance. Shelly didn't care. Once she got her foot in the office, she was confident she'd earn her way into full time associate status. She might eventually go for her Broker's license.

She wound her way into her second bedroom that she'd set up as an office ... a place to create exciting fiction, and soon to work real estate deals. She scanned the ivory-colored walls, searching for the ideal spot to display her newly-to-be-framed test score results and a proud copy of her Associate License.

Somewhere prominent.

# 4

Shelly eased onto her black leather executive chair ... her one indulgence, and it *was* second hand ... and flipped open her laptop, clicking on the *Word* icon. She opened the directory and selected *Untitled Story 6*, which quickly blossomed on the screen. She squiggled closer to the scarred old mahogany five drawer desk she'd snagged for a song at a recent yard sale.

"Gotta cut over three hundred words somehow," she muttered, as she studied the LED screen.

*How in the hell can I write a good short story in two thousand words or less. That gives me maybe eight pages to create interesting characters, develop visual locations, and arouse tension before the climax. Those are what they stressed in the seminars: tension for your protagonist, then more tension, and then even more tension on top of that!*

Damned tough to do in the less than the two pages she can devote to building reader anxiety, but no one is interested in a casual stroll on the beach ... unless there's a killer shark in the surf!

Her cell phone trilled to the opening of Beethoven's 5th, and snatched her thought away from her computer. It was Mom's ringtone.

"Hi, Mom," she said.

"Hi, Pumpkin. How're you doing?"

"Great." She paused and sucked in a breath. "I got my results."

"Results? What ... oh, your Real Estate Licensing Test scores?"

"Yep."

"And? Are you going to keep me guessing?"

"Just heightening the suspense, like a good author. " Shelly snickered. "I got a 92."

"Wow! That's terrific. I told you you'd be a natural at this. Have you told Ms. Howell?"

"Not yet. It's late. I thought I'd call her tomorrow. Meantime, I'm trying to cut three hundred words out of my new short story."

"Really? Why?"

"It's the *Short Fiction Monthly* contest rules. Two-thousand words, max. Some short story contests are only 500 words." She punched the "speaker" button on her phone and laid it on the desk.

"That seems so ... arbitrary," Helen Weitz said. "How do they come up with such a thing?"

"I don't know, Mom. I think they're trying to teach us how to write tightly, with nothing unnecessary. It sure isn't the *Arabian Nights* you read to me as a kid. Or even O'Henry."

"No. Those were real storytellers, weren't they, Pumpkin."

"Yeah. That's what really got me into this." She leaned back and folded her hands in her lap. "I love telling stories. Anyhow, I still got to find a way to chop three-hundred words out of my Number Six, and come up with a grabber for a name."

"Okay, sweetie. I won't keep you. You're going to call the real estate agent tomorrow?"

"Yep. First thing. I need to get started making some money."

"Good. How soon do you think you'll be able to start there?"

"Don't know. Maybe right away. Ms. Howell said she needed someone to clean up their filing. I'll be on rotation for walk-ins, and I'll have to start scratching for some listings. Tell all your friends. I'll need whatever help I can get."

"Of course, Pumpkin." Helen hesitated, a soft cluck echoing in her throat.

"What, Mom?"

"It's nothing, Shelly. It's just that ... it's just ...."

"C'mon. I know that worried sound. What's bothering you?"

"It ... oh, just be careful, baby. You're all I have, and I worry ...."

"Jeez Mom, it's only an office job."

"I know, but you'll be taking people out. People you don't know. And there's this guy who's snatching and killing young girls. Two redheads so far, like you. And I just heard a third has just gone missing."

"Yeah, it's scary. But I'll be careful. The office vets every client to see they're legit buyers or sellers." She picked up her phone, cancelling "speaker."

"I wish you wouldn't worry so much, but I know that's your job as a Mom. I promise to be careful."

They said their good-byes, and Shelly turned back to her writing.

She wondered, in a corner of her mind, how thorough that vetting really was.

# 5

Audrey Williamson sat on the creaky twin bed and fingered the lacy hem of the little pink and blue party dress. It looked like something a teen would wear to a prom.

Maybe if she stopped being so stubborn and donned the damned thing, this nut job might be happy and let her go. But then again, maybe not.

*I wonder what's got him so fired up over seeing me in this? And why does he keep insisting I'm this Camille?*

She jumped at the sound of footsteps, then a key scraped in the lock.

*He's back, and he's going to be pissed I haven't changed.*

The door opened on very squeaky hinges. She flashed to the old radio show her folks had loved, *The Inner Sanctum*. Their intro was a creaky door opening very slowly. This little story she was trapped in had started to get just as eerie. Maybe it was time to get really worried.

Her abductor silently slipped inside. This guy seemed to move without a sound. She hadn't heard him sneak up from behind when he surprised her in the parking lot.

"Ah, Camille. Still not properly dressed?"

"Damn it, I keep telling you, my name is Audrey?"

She probably should give in. Let him live his fantasy, but she was too obstinate. She wouldn't let him intimidate her despite the fact he already had. She refused to accept he scared her.

[18]

"Don't be foolish, Camille. How can I expect to present you if you refuse to dress appropriately? They won't understand."

"They?" she said, shaking her head. "Who are 'they'? I'm not interested in them. I just want to go home."

"But you *are* home, my darling." He took her by the arm, and then gently squeezed her shoulder.

Audrey peered into his eyes, and then pried his fingers away.

*Maybe I coulda made a break. Try for a karate chop on his windpipe, but what would he do if I missed? He really hasn't shown any signs of wanting to hurt me, but he's got me trapped here. Maybe if I ...*

"Look," he said, his eyes narrowed, his thin lips compressed. "We've got things to do and places to go, and you *must* be dressed for the part. I'm running out of patience."

"I ... I don't know what you *want* from me. I'll dress up for you, if you'll just let me go. My family's got to be very worried."

"Your family?"

"Yes. My mom; my dad; my brother. You seem like a nice man who must have confused me with someone else. So please think of them. I miss them. They miss me. Please!"

"Your family," he repeated. "My Camille has no family. Not anymore."

"See. I told you. I'm not this Camille you're looking for. Please, let me go!" She took his hands, her eyes pleading.

"I see." He disengaged her fingers and cradled her face between his hands, searching her eyes.

"No, you're not Camille, are you? It's been so long, and I thought ...."

"No. No, I'm not. I kept telling you." Her lips tweaked into a tentative grin. Maybe he would finally get she's not this Camille. Was he going to let her go?

"You look so much like her. How could I have made that mistake again?" He stared at her, arms akimbo.

*Again?* Audrey studied his frowning face. *Again?*

*What does he mean, again?* Perspiration sprang up across her forehead, despite the damp, musty coolness of the room, and tiny goose bumps skittered across her scalp and neck. For the first time, real fear washed over her. She began to tremble.

*I'm not his first? Jesus, maybe he is that guy who ....*

"Yes. It seems I've erred. I'm sorry. It's time I set you free."

"Oh thank you. Thank you so much." Her voice cracked with tension. "I promise I'll never tell anyone." *At least until I get outta here and find a cop. This guy is certifiable.*

"It's too bad you bought this lovely outfit for nothing." She fingered the lacy sleeve of the gaudy little dress.

"Oh, don't worry," he said, his face again an impassive mask. "This lovely will not go to waste." He removed an mp3 player from his pocket, setting it on the night stand, flicking the ON button. A man and a woman were singing a duet, a lovely ballad.

"That's pretty," she said, rising to leave.

"Natalie Cole and her father, singing 'Unforgettable.' It was my mother's favorite. I always play it for Camille. It's our song."

He held up a hand. "Just a moment more. I need to get your things, and then we'll go."

He departed, moving in no hurry, but returned in less than a minute He shouldered a huge, empty duffle bag, and a tray containing a plastic bottle and rags.

"Those aren't my things." Her eyes were brimming.

"Ah, but you'll need them for the trip we're going to take."

Shrugging off the bag, he popped open the bottle, soaking a large rag with liquid.

"Here we go, my dear. Audrey, you say? Time to exit, Stage Left."

# 6

Al Warner lurched awake and swatted the air in front of his face. But it wasn't a fly attacking him. It was the unrelenting buzz of his cell phone, vibrating on his nightstand. As he scrabbled for the insistent critter, he glanced at the LED crystals of his alarm clock: three-ten. Never good news when the phone beckoned in the middle of the night.

"Yeah, this is Warner. What's up?" His voice husky from sleep.

"Sorry to wake you, Al," Captain Santiago said. "Sounds like you were coming out of a bad dream."

"You mean like after Leordano? No, I *was* dreamin' but I lost it. Something about water." He swiveled to sit on the edge of the bed.

"No nightmares, though?"

"Nope. They seemed to die with the Angel of Death. But I know ya didn't call at three a.m. to check on my sleep, Cap. That usually means a murder. Another redhead?"

"Good guess, Detective. Audrey Williamson. The woman we thought was snatched from the Miami Library lot."

"Dressed to the nines, I bet." Warner slipped into slippers and clicked on his night lamp. He scrounged for a pad of paper and a pen.

"Yep. A baby-blue, lacy prom dress." Santiago said.

"Who found her, and where, this time?" Warner asked.

"In an alley off 82nd St, near Lake Arcola. A patrol car found her after neighbors complained about some street dog that wouldn't shut up."

"That's quite a ways from the last drop," Warner said as he scribbled notes on the pad. "She looks nicely arranged and peaceful?"

"Yeah. One different wrinkle, with her hands across her breasts, cradling a single red rose."

"Well, maybe we'll learn something new from that. I'll be out the door in three minutes." Warner's hand absently rubbed the X-shaped scars on the right side of his skull, hidden under the mat of curly dark hair. A year and a half since the second wound, but it still itched.

"Who's securin' the scene?" he asked, his phone on speaker while he dressed.

"Harris should be there by now. The M.E. and the Crime Scene Unit are about ten-minutes out."

"The Hawk?" The nickname for Maurice Gold, the chief of Forensics, as much for his sharp-eyed probe into evidence as his inordinately large, hooked Semitic nose.

"Of course. Who else, on something like this?"

"Good." He hurried into the kitchen where he plucked a chocolate donut, an apple, and a foam cup of cold coffee from the fridge. "We ain't got much on this mug, and I don't want to miss something because of a mishandled scene."

"You and me both, Al. Get over there and work your magic. The county's going to be in an uproar, with another serial bastard out there so soon after Dedios."

"Yeah." Warner paused. "When are we gonna bring in the Fibbies, Cap? This is right up their Behavioral Analysis Unit's alley."

"I know, I know, but it was you who put away the Angel of Death, without any real input from the BAU."

"That was pure luck. Better safe than sorry. I'd call 'em, Captain. The more heads we got on this, the better."

Captain Santiago sighed. "Yeah, I guess. The brass never likes having the Feds steal our thunder on these big cases, though."

"I know. But young redheaded women's lives are more important than who gets credit for the takedown. Whatever this perp's lookin' for, it ain't gonna stop at three vics."

"Unfortunately, I'm sure you're right. I'll see what I can do."

"Okay. I'm on the way. I'll keep ya posted, after I've gone over the scene. Hope we find something this time, but I ain't too optimistic. These crazy bastards are always damned careful ... at least in the beginning."

"Yeah," Santiago said. "I just hope we don't have to fill too many body bags before he makes a mistake."

"Me too, Cap. Me too. I should be on the scene in about thirty. Talk to ya later."

Warner clicked his phone closed as he slid into his Dodge Charger.

*Here we go again.*

*Damned nut-cases, killing women. Where the hell do they come from, and why do they love Miami?*

# 7

Warner skidded his Dodge coupe to a stop just outside the yellow-taped-off alley entrance. He was out the door, striding toward the crime scene before the engine had grumbled to a complete halt.

The narrow blacktopped passage was lined with lidded plastic and galvanized steel trash cans and two dumpsters. Not a lot of litter. While this was a primarily an African-American and Cuban community, it wasn't a ghetto.

A cluster of uniformed and plain clothes cops hovered fifty-feet down from the opening, close to the south wall. They were scanning the ground, loosely circling outward from a small man, crouched next to what appeared to be the victim.

The Hawk had arrived and had begun the painstaking collection of evidence. The M.E. hadn't yet made an appearance.

"What d'ya got, Moe? Please give me something solid."

"Ahh, The Hero has arrived," Maurice Gold said, "and impatient, as usual."

"I wish you'd drop the hero shit, Moe. It's been almost two years since Leordano."

"Okay, Detective, but you keep upping the legend. Anyhow, I just got here. Even a genius like me takes a while to put things together."

Warner chuckled. "Sorry. Didn't mean to rush ya. But I'd sure like to finally get something on this bastard. This *is* victim number three from our newest loony?"

"Yes, it appears that way. They're calling him The Prom Dress Killer. I'll need some time to confirm a few facts, but the MO is his."

"Yeah." Warner dropped to one knee for a closer look. "Pretty thing, all dolled up, ready to party. He really spiffs 'em up, doesn't he?"

"Yep, and I'm pretty sure it's all done postmortem. Wherever he imagines they're going, she's doing it from the other side."

Warner studied her eyes and, saw the signs there. "Suffocated again, huh?"

"Looks that way," Gold said. "The M.E. will tell us for sure. You can still smell the chloroform on her ...."

"So no defensive wounds?"

"Don't see any," the Hawk said. "Doesn't seem to want his honeys to suffer, so he puts them to sleep first. It's a new one on me." He laid a hand on the detective's shoulder.

"Anyway, my guys are scouring the area, and we'll examine her for anything that might give us our killer's DNA. Maybe a loose hair or a scrape of skin under her nails."

"Okay," Warner said as he rose, "but DNA ain't gonna give us much unless he's in the system for something like a sex crime. How about prints?"

"C'mon, Detective! We'll check every hard surface: her belt and buckle, her shoes, even her finger and toe nails, since he *did* dress her. We find anything, you'll be the first to know."

"Okay, okay. Don't get touchy. We're all under a lot of pressure here. This is our third serial loony in less than three years, and it's starting to wear on me."

"I know, Al." The Hawk grunted and massaged his lower back. "Never knew a cop who really cared about the vics as much as you. Most guys are desperate to solve the case. For you it seems personal, like you want to get revenge for their victims."

"Yeah, maybe. It really rankles me, seeing pretty little gals like her, lying on the coroner's slabs, all because some nut job's got an agenda we ain't figured out yet."

A hand tapped Warner on the back.

"Hey, Al. We gotta stop meeting like this."

Warner pivoted, finding a short, wiry man rocking back and forth on his feet.

"Hey, Jack. Didn't see ya there."

"Been scouting the alley with the Crime Scene Unit guys," Jack Harris said. "So far, not much to see. Looks like a simple, clean drop. Not even any useable tire marks."

"No surprise. The people here keep the area pretty clean. Our best hope is the Hawk can lift something useful off the vic, but I ain't holdin' my breath."

"Yeah," Harris said. He look up the alley. "These clever bastards seldom leave much for us."

"You got uniforms canvassing? Be nice if somebody saw something."

"I got six working the neighborhood, but so far, *nada*."

"Using African-Americans?" Warner glanced back at the M.E., who'd just arrived, supervising the bagging of the body. "These people are more likely to talk to one of their own."

"Sure. Three blacks and two Cubans. Covering the bases."

"Okay. I'm gonna look around a bit, and then might as well head back to the station. I ain't gonna get any more sleep tonight."

"Right," Harris said. "I'll hang around here until CSU finishes up before I come in. Just in case they turn something up."

Warner nodded, and then started up the alley, hands in his pockets as he scanned the blacktop. He often saw things others missed, but he wasn't holding out any hope.

He sighed. *Gotta get some rest next day or so. Got the third camp startin' up, and I gotta be fresh.*

The boot camp he and four of his cop buddies ran for troubled teens demanded more time and energy then he had to spare right now, but the five of them were committed to trying to make a difference with wayward kids that held some promise.

But rest was a rare and precious commodity when they had a motivated and deadly maniac to snare.

Somehow, he'd have to work it out.

# 8

Shelly Weitz settled behind the three-foot wide faux-cherry topped desk and adjusted her snug cotton plaid skirt. Mental note: wear looser fitting clothing, and opt for comfort over style.

Her fingers skimmed the smooth mica surface as she deposited her cell phone and vinyl-covered notebook within easy reach. She fluffed her auburn hair that hung in loose waves just below her shoulders. She scanned the walls, wondering where they would hang her freshly minted license that proclaimed Rochelle Weitz was a fully accredited Associate Realtor.

Shelly had arrived at office, centered in a six unit strip mall, five minutes prior to its opening, intent on making a good first impression. Her three-year-old silver Toyota Rav4 looked totally appropriate, nestled between a Dodge minivan and a Lexus 350 sedan.

She glanced up as Lois Howell, the brunette licensed broker and owner of NMB Realty, approached.

"Glad to see you, Shelly."

"Thanks, Ms. Howell. I really appreciate the opportunity ...."

"It's Lois, dear" Ms. Howell interrupted. The average height, lanky, hazel-eyed woman, was tastefully dressed in a gray wool skirt and white, short-sleeved blouse.

"Everyone's on first names here," she said. "You *do* realize your position, for now, is primarily clerical? That's the only job in real estate that earns a salary. Associates work on commission."

"I know Ms. ... Lois, but I *am* licensed, so can't I ...?"

"Yes, of course you can still earn commissions: bringing in listings or handling walk-ins if no other agents are available. But your first job is answering the phone, filing, doing on-line searches for other agents. Things like that, getting your feet wet and learning how we do things here."

"I understand," Shelly said, forcing herself to hold the other woman's gaze. "But I really do want to get into actual sales, too."

"Look. You're a bright young lady, and I'm sure your time will come soon enough. Meanwhile, a salaried job, providing regular income, should be appreciated right now. Commissions, especially for a newcomer, can be tough to live on."

"Yes, of course. I'm just so eager to show what I can do. Meanwhile, I'll be the best clerk you've ever had." Shelly extended her hand.

"That's why I hired you, my dear," the broker said She smiled and accepted the handshake. "You're an impressive young woman. So, to start, grab that pile of folders on the next desk, and file them in the 'Active' drawer. Check each first to verify we have all the contact info on those that are buyers. I believe only two go into 'Listings.' Can you find everything?"

"Yes, ma'am. I spent an hour here last week, getting the lay of the land, so I wouldn't be wasting any time today."

"Fine. I knew hiring you for this was a good idea. It frees the agents to work the deals. So, I'll leave you to it." The older woman pivoted on three-inch black leather heels, and strode off toward her private office.

Shelly sighed and picked up the stack of folders. She slid in behind her new desk and fanned the files across its top. She scanned them for a moment before she opened one to check its contents.

It was for a middle-aged couple with a pair of preteen kids, searching for a modestly priced house near good middle and high schools. It looked like the husband was a corporate transferee, and she supposed they weren't sure any move was permanent.

Shelly knew just the area in North Miami Beach, east of I-95, in the 170's streets. With the right house, the kids could be in biking distance to both Beaches Middle School and North Miami Beach High. The area was dominated by three-bedroom, two-bath ranches. If they were *her* clients, she'd find them something in no time.

She slid that file to the corner of her desk and started scanning the rest. She found only one that needed more information ... whether they preferred a ranch house or a two-story ... as she filed them away. She called the clients on the one errant file and confirmed they wanted a single story, three or four-bedroom house with a pool. She made the appropriate notations, and slipped the folder into the "Active" drawer, where it would await an agent's involvement.

Finished filing, Shelly glanced at the last folder, still perched on the corner of her desk, silently calling her. She snatched it up and moved to a computer, where she pulled up her agency's listings. They had four in the general area she knew would be of prime interest, but only two met their client's parameters. Selling one of NMB's own listings doubled the commission to their company over one from the Multiple Listing data base, where they shared the commission with the listing agency.

She printed out the two likely candidates and attached them to the files with a sticky note explaining what she'd done. She hoped whomever was assigned the file would appreciate the work she'd done for them.

The balance of Rochelle Weitz's first day was spent answering the phone and pulling data from the computer for various agents.

[30]

Most were pleasant and appreciative of her help. A few were short tempered and brusque.

One agent, Oleg Karlov, called and asked her to research a listing in North Miami, but she couldn't find anything at that address. When she called him to report failure, he said she had transposed numbers, so she tried again ... with the same frustrating results.

She heard a suppressed snicker after the third apologetic call, and she remembered Ms. Howell referred to him as "our Russian-American prankster." Shelly realized she was the butt of some good-natured hazing, so in the spirit of joining in, she went into a complete "description" of the property.

"I found it, Mr. Karlov. It's a four-bedroom, three-bath Tudor, with an office and den. Listed at 2850 square feet."

"Huh?" he said, after a ten-second pause.

"Yep," she continued. "Taxes are $2,635, and it's got a $350,000 first mortgage that's in default. The appraisal's a half mil, so if you've got a buyer, he may be able to steal it."

"What? Are you sure you've got the right property?"

Shelly's grin faded as Lois Howell walked up.

"Is that Karlov?" she whispered.

Shelly nodded.

"Good." Lois gave her a thumbs-up. "Serves that joker right."

"Look," Oleg said, his voice intense, "who's holding the mortgage? I do have a guy ...."

Shelly's uncontainable laughter erupted, cutting him off.

"Un-huh," he said after a small pause. "Turned the tables on me, didn't ya, kid?"

"Sorry, Mr. Karlov, but it only seemed fair. I hope you're not ...."

"Angry? Me? Never. Just a little first day hazing. You and me, we're going to get along fine. First newbie smart enough to snag me in my own trap. Next time I call, it'll be a real job."

Shelly hung up and was rewarded with gentle applause from the three agents in the office.

She grinned.

She was becoming one of "the gang."

# 9

He slid his battered 2006 gold Dodge Caravan into a spot far from the sprawl of stores. Sawgrass Mills was one of the largest outlet malls in America, and it hosted virtually every major designer brand. He knew the odds were small, but something told him he might find her there in one of the high end stores: maybe Saks or Nordstrom's. Or possibly Coach, because she was so enamored with handbags.

He sauntered across the Macadam lot, hands thrust into pockets of his gray cargo pants. He wove through a maze of vehicles, their drivers distracted as they edged along in search of *the* store.

At five-foot-six, he was a stocky, bland-faced guy. A Miami Marlins ball cap was pulled low over short light brown hair. He was a non-descript young man, unnoticeable in any crowd.

Fingers nudged the canister of chloroform in his right lower pocket, and he sighed. Even if he found Camille today, it was unlikely there'd be an opportunity to bring her home. Like all the pretenders he'd mistaken for her, she probably wouldn't come willingly, uncertain of his intensions. She wouldn't remember how he adored her ... worshiped her very existence. No, he'd have to remind her of the love they'd shared ... before she disappeared.

Why was she so elusive? And *why* was his memory of her so blurred that he confused those other women with her? The look-a-likes. Redheads like Camille. The seemed like her in every way, but were *not* her … not even close, once he uncovered their duplicity.

Well, he sent them to the ball anyway, properly dressed and ready to party. Too bad he couldn't join them, but his mission was Camille, not some opportunistic double. He left them forever asleep, awaiting their black coach for a trip to eternity.

He approached the Designer Wing, a pedestrian cul-de-sac, lined on either side by every major fashion outlet shop. He'd wander through each, seeming to browse while he scanned the shoppers as he searched for his prize. If she were there, he would trail her and assess his opportunities. Although unlikely he could reunite with her today, he'd at least learn what car she drove. He'd follow her to where she lived. Then he'd devise a strategy.

The stores were crowded—mostly women. Lots of elegantly attired South Americans that strutted around in heeled leather boots and swirling flowered skirts. The air was replete with yammered Spanish as they scoured the stores for bargains. Many of the clerks were Latinas, too. Miami had become a third-world country, all to its own.

One of the staff sported Camille's luxurious auburn-red hair but the object of his search certainly wasn't a Cuban. Camille was elegant and educated, and spoke high school French, not Spanish.

He gave a small head shake and sighed, then wandered out of Chanel, the delicious odor of Number Five wafting after him. He angled right, onto the walkway and into the next store: Prada.

Two hours later, he lingered in the still humid shade, just outside the double glass doors of Saint John. He idly scanned the foot traffic, no longer expectant.

No Camille today, but he wasn't dissuaded. Disappointed, yes. He'd had a strong sense she would be there, and he had diligently scoured every likely shop, but to no avail.

# THE PROM DRESS KILLER

It was possible he'd just missed her, but that seemed unlikely. If she *were* shopping today at Sawgrass Mills, he would have found her.

No, he had to take his hunt elsewhere. He'd already covered much of the western part of Miami, so it was time to move easterly: downtown Miami, Miami Shores, North Miami, and maybe even South Beach.

He grimaced at the thought of that glitzy Miami Beach enclave, filled with "beautiful people" and dilettantes. Would a woman as classy as Camille even debase herself by associating with such a tawdry group? She certainly was gorgeous enough to fit in, but it wasn't her style. Still, he'd comb that white-sand strand anyhow. Every glimmer of a lead would be followed—no venue left unexplored. He was certain she was somewhere here in south Florida.

He *will* find her, and make her see they were destined to be together. He will not be denied, certain she would see the Karma in that, too.

Miami Beach and Miami were his next targets. He stroked his chin. Or maybe the northern towns: North Miami and North Miami Beach. He may take some time to cruise through that area before he committed to a more intensive hunt in the south.

With diligence he would find her.

He was sure of it.

*Patience. Patience is my friend.*

He sigh again as he strode off towards his mini-van, parked a good ten-minute walk away. An unsuccessful but not wasted day.

The net was shrinking.

# 10

Warner's Dodge Charger idled up the narrow access road, now about two miles north of the Tamiami Trail, as he search for the sign. They hadn't run a camp since last fall, and the Everglades wilderness had swallowed up the landscape.

There it was, finally, partially overgrown by weeds and sawgrass. He pulled into the rutted, semi-obscured lane, parked, and retrieved a machete from the trunk. After three minutes of vigorous hacking, sweat-drenched, he'd cleared the entrance and the sign:

DADE COUNTY BOOT CAMP FOR TEENS

Now the twenty-seven delinquents couldn't use "I couldn't find the place" as an excuse. Not showing up today was a return ticket to Juvie.

He returned to his coupe and edged it down the bumpy dirt path. Luckily they'd found this dry savannah in the usually swampy 'Glades. No gators to contend with here, but snakes, especially rattlers, were a concern.

First job, once they got all the kids organized, would be to clear the lane and cut away overhanging branches. Mosquitoes and horse flies would be their major challenge. That effort would have to last for the eight-week duration of this session.

A quarter-mile up the path, he slid into the main compound, a dry, grassy clearing. A green panel truck was being unloaded by two of his comrades: Darnell Franklin and Jorge Ignacio. Hector

Carrera, who was ten minutes behind Warner, would man the entrance, so no one would miss the turn-off, and Ben Ellison would bring out three of the boys, kids with no families to help them.

Two-hours later, three ten-bed canvas barracks tents, a staff tent, and a canvas covered and screened meals area were in place, and all but two of their "campers" had arrived. That duo ... and their parents or guardians ... were going to learn the lesson for being tardy.

Warner stood on a four-by-eight wood platform with Detective Hector Carrera, a Narco from Little Havana. He was Al's first recruit into the "Fearsome Five." Warner conceived the DCBC and took on the four other volunteer cops, all detectives, to run this often unrewarding effort to salvage troubled teens before they were completely lost in the gangs.

Warner's eyes swept the disparate gaggle of youths that milled around the trampled grass parade ground—mostly Latinos and African-Americans. Only two were Caucasian.

"Okay, listen up." He spoke into a hand-held bullhorn. "My name's Detective Al Warner. This is Detective Hector Carrera. You'll meet the other three volunteer detectives as we go. Now, form into two lines in front, and we'll get started."

Grumbled curses ebbed through the crowd as the boys, there not of their own volition, found some semblance of two ragged rows.

"Knock off the bitching and straighten those lines," Hector called out. "One arm spacing between you and the guy on your right, and move it. We're not real patient guys, here."

"Let's get the pleasantries outta the way," Warner said, "and lay down some ground rules. You're all here because ...."

He was interrupted by the growling arrival of a tricked-out gold and red Trans Am, rumbling into the clearing. The engine revved, eliciting two backfires before dying. A lanky light-skinned Latino, about seventeen, and a much darker fifteen-year-old exited the hot rod, both grinning.

"Aww, ya started w'out us. Tsk, tsk," the smirking older boy said.

"Yeah, we did," Warner responded and nodded at Jorge Ignacio, one of the Five, who approached from behind the new arrivals.

"But don't worry," Warner continued, "we're gonna finish before you, too. Give Detective Ignacio your keys. You're supposed to be driven here by someone else. No one has their own wheels while relaxin' at our camp. And you're gonna learn the consequences of arrivin' late. I don't think you'll do it again.

"Now form up on that back line, and we'll get started ... again." Warner surveyed the restless, shifting mass of teenagers, and then began once more.

"I started to say, you're here because a Juvie judge thought there was a slim chance this camp could make a difference in your life. We call this a camp, but it's no picnic. For the next eight weeks, you're here from six p.m. Friday evenings to eight p.m. Sundays. You're gonna work harder than I expect you ever have before. We'll run, do exercise and have classes. We're gonna try to teach you self-respect," grumbles and a few cat-calls echoed from the group, "and maybe a way to straighten out your lives." He stared at them, his mouth a tight slit.

"Rule number one: when you're out here, no talkin' unless we talk to you first. And let's get something straight. Ego and swagger don't equal self-respect. That's just bravado, and we don't tolerate it here.

"You don't like how we do things, you can leave ... and finish your time in Juvie detention. You might survive there, but I guarantee you're gonna be in the big house not long after. You'll be lucky to live past twenty-one, but that's your choice. Stick it out here, you gotta follow the rules. No second chances. Break 'em and you suffer the consequences."

"You don't know shit 'bout our lives, copper," someone shouted from the crowd.

"You deaf? Didn't he say no talking'?" Ben Ellison, a homicide detective from North Miami, grabbed the black teen across the back of the neck.

"Let it go this time, Ben," Warner said. "Seems like we hear that same bullshit every camp, so let me set you straight.

"I was raised in a little town north of Chicago. My dad was a nasty drunk who beat my mom with a bullwhip, and tried to get me, but mostly I was too quick for him. We lived hand to mouth, and I got into plenty of trouble. I was goin' down the same road as you punks, until a coach and a local cop decided to teach me better. I was tough, but they never quit on me, and I finally learned not to quit on me, either. Without them, I probably woulda been sucked into the gangs, dead by twenty-one." He paused, fingers findi8ng his X-shaped scars on the side of his head.

"Hector, here, rafted in from Cuba with his mom when he was five, barely makin' it alive. His little brother drowned during the voyage while his dad rotted in a Cuban prison. There was plenty of pressure on Hector to join the gangs in Little Havana, but his mom and his grandpa expected more from him." Warner gestured at the three other cops, standing behind the lines.

"Darnell, Ben and Jorge, behind you there, all had to fight the odds to turn out straight. Luckily, they all had good role models ... an uncle, a teacher and a priest ... who got 'em on the right track." Warner hesitated, his dark eyes sweeping over the small crowd.

[39]

"We're all volunteers here," he continued, "doin' this 'cause we're tired of bustin' you punks, time and again ... or lookin' at you in a body bag. We do it on our own time, at our own expense, with a few donations from some judges and other cops. No city or county money. Just us."

Warner's eyes probed the restless group of teens. "So you can be bitter and feel sorry for yourselves ... or take this chance to make the break and become the guy some judge felt you might be.

"I'll be frank," he said. "Usually about half of you don't make it. Those guys end up at Raiford ... or on a coroners slab. The others start to realize that there's something else out there other than the gangs, drugs and murder.

"Those guys shun the streets, start studyin' in high school, and several have gone to college ... some on full scholarships. They've discovered there's more to life than bein' a gangbanger. It's all up to you now. Fuck up here and you got no one to blame but yourself.

"That's a lot more talkin' than I usually do, so it's time to get started." Warner picked up a lined pad, with the names and summaries of each "camper."

"You that hero cop, ain't cha?" someone shouted from below.

"No heroes here. Just five guys tryin' to make a difference. Now were gonna start by cleanin' up the entrance and roadway into camp. Pullin' weeds, trimmin' branches, fillin' pot holes. We got loppers and trimmers and *every one* of those will be accounted for when we're done. Ben's got some mosquito dope to ward of the bugs. You're gonna see plenty of those little critters, especially as we get into summer."

Grumbling and quiet curses rumbled across the group.

"Want something to bitch about? No dinner until that's finished. See Ben, back there, for repellant and a pair of canvas gloves. We expect the gloves back." Warner's glance found

Darnell Franklin, an Overtown detective and one-time all-county running back for Glades Central High.

"Darnell. Take charge of our two late arrivals. Show 'em why it pays to be on time."

The African-American detective grinned, nodding. "My pleasure, Al. A two-mile run and fifty pushups should make the point."

"You crazy, man?" the older Latino shouted.

"Gonna be doing them right with you, punk. Or you can go back to Juvie Hall and await trial. I hear the ADA is charging you as an adult. Tasty piece like you won't last long in Raiford."

Five hours later the five detectives sat on their folding army cots, recapping the day.

"What d'ya think, Al?" Hector asked. "Any winners here?"

"Hard to say so soon. Always some who see the light. Damned problem is those who don't, and end up back on the streets."

"Yeah," Jorge said. He stroked a chin laced with a dark, two-day stubble. "I know that older kid, ChiChi, that Darnell ran into the ground today. He's too hard baked and full of hate to ever make it. Don't know why the judge even sent him here."

"You never know," Warner replied. "You guys remember Carlo Delgado?"

They all nodded.

"Never had a tougher nut to crack than that *muchacho*," Hector said, grinning.

"Well, he graduated high school Suma cum Laude, and he's in college on full scholarship. He straightened out his two little brothers, and they're doin' well in school, too. He's become the role model to them that we were to him."

"You mean that *you* were, Al." Hector patted him on the shoulder. "You became the father that kid never had. You still talk to him, don't ya?"

"Yeah. He calls, nearly every week. Point is, ya never know who's gonna come out of the pack as a positive leader. Make ChiChi your project, Jorge, and maybe you'll get a surprise."

The conversation wound down, and they turned in. With a six a.m. start in the morning, even these tough, fit cops needed their rest.

Partners covered their cases while they were out on bivouac, with requests not to call unless the end of the earth was imminent.

So far, on three previous eight-week camps, none of the detectives had ever been bothered with the outside world. And in the process, they'd managed to turn around the lives of thirty-two of the seventy-four kids they'd run through their little boot camp.

Less than half, but it was a success that was becoming noticed in departments throughout south Florida.

Warner had been asked to speak to several, outlining their procedures and accomplishments.

# 11

"NMB Reality. How may I help you?" Shelly Weitz was poised at her desk with a lined pad and a ballpoint at the ready. She was alone at the office for the first time in the nearly two weeks she'd worked there.

"Hi. My name is William Crozier." The voice on the phone was deep but clear. "We've just moved to South Florida and purchased a business in North Miami. We're renting for now, but would like to find a house there or in North Miami Beach."

"Of course. We'd be happy to help you with that," Shelly said in her most professional manner. "I'm the only realtor in the office at the moment, but if you'll give me your information and an idea of what you're looking for, and a price range, I'll have someone call you within an hour. We're the perfect office for the area you're interested in."

"Yes," Crozier said. "You've been well recommended by a neighbor. So, we're looking for a four-bedroom, about three thousand square feet. Preferably three full baths."

"Okay, perfect. Price range? And do you prefer a ranch or two-story?" She scribbled notes on the paper tablet.

"Four to five hundred thou, and either one or two-story works for us, but we'd prefer the Master on the ground floor. And we need a good high school reasonably close by."

"Well, both North Miami Beach High and North Miami High are A-rated schools, so you'll have a large area to pick from."

"Fine. Here's my contact info. I haven't bothered with a land line, but this one is always available" He rattled off his cell phone number, which she noted on the white pad. Later she'd enter them on the computer and print out the prospect sheets.

"Thanks very much for your efficient help, Ms ....?"

"Weitz. Rochelle Weitz, but everyone calls me Shelly."

"So, thanks again, Shelly. I'd like you to be my agent. As professional as you seem, we'll get along just fine."

"Thank you." She swallowed and her heart began the Tango. "And I *am* an agent. Just in the office alone for the moment, but if you'd like one of the more experienced ...."

"No, no one else. I think you'll do fine, so as soon as you get some relief, give me a call. I've got a year's lease on this apartment, and my wife and two sons aren't joining me until the school year ends in Jersey, so it's not like I'm under the gun. Once we've narrowed the field, she'll fly down for the final choice. She'll be the one spending most of the time there."

"Right," Shelly, said, with a chuckle. "Keeping the lady happy makes everyone's life easier."

"You can't imagine how important it is for me to keep my lady happy." His voice was soft, the words measured.

The conversation ended with some traded pleasantries. Shelly sat, beaming. Her first client! Lois had to let her work this one because it was the client's request.

Shelly hurried to a computer and searched the agency's own listings for the area. There were two, one in North Miami and the other in North Miami Beach. Both seemed to meet Crozier's requirements.

After printing them out, she logged onto the Multiple Listing Site, and looked for at least three more. The agency's listings were preferred because of the higher commissions, but she wouldn't lose the sale as Buyer's Agent because she didn't have enough properties to show.

After an hour's work, she had four more addresses that all looked good, although one was a bit higher than Mr. Crozier's top price. She'd show that last, only if necessary.

She had organized each listing into separate file folders when Lois Howell arrived, trailed by a pair of clients, all hurrying into her private office. They were apparently filling out an Offer Sheet on a property they'd visited.

Shelly was excited to tell Lois about her first client, but that would have to wait until the broker was finished with her own customers.

# 12

He backed the gold Dodge Caravan into an open spot on Seventh Street, just west of the park, and after locking it, slipped three quarters into the meter. That gave him ninety minutes to finish his canvas of the South Beach area.

He'd just finished three days of cruising Miami Gardens, North Miami and, especially North Miami Beach. He uncovered some interesting leads yet to be confirmed, but he was determined to scour the south county as well. He would pursue both as the opportunities presented themselves.

He sauntered across Collins Avenue, the main Miami Beach north-to-south thoroughfare, as bumper-to-bumper vehicles awaited the green light. He was headed for Lummus Park and Beach Boardwalk, which stretched from below Fifth Street all the way to Lincoln Road. This famous site, South Beach, was lined with restaurants, bars, clubs, and hotels.

This was *the* spot for the rich and beautiful, trendy haunts for dilettantes, actors, models ... and predators on the hunt. Many of those were seeking sex or publicity connections.

He was a different type of stalker. Although Camille certainly had the qualifications to lounge here, he was pretty certain it was beneath her to mingle with such tawdry trash. Still, he would be thorough and careful, in case he'd misjudged her. He was a patient man, and time was on his side.

# THE PROM DRESS KILLER

He strolled along the boardwalk, gently buffeted by the warm, salt-laden breeze, as he wove among the pulsating mass of bikini-clad women, thonged men, and occasional skateboarders. He grimaced at the blatant display of skin, disgusted by how many overweight, flabby humans exposed their grotesqueness with scanty outfits.

Of course, beauties abounded as well, with many, he suspected, cosmetically augmented. Some, in an earlier time, may have aroused his lust, but he'd buried that old passion ... and the desire to punish them ... under his current resolve: Camille.

He cruised in and out of several eateries and pubs, swamped by aromas of grilled fish, fried food ... and stale sweat ... while he surveyed the crowds both inside and on their open verandas, but there was no sign of her.

He strode off the walkway onto the warm, yielding sand and eased his way toward the gently singing surf. Shrieking white gulls strutted along the water line, scavenging for food, while a young boy collected bits of sea shells. Brown bodied muscle guys jogged along the firmer footing of the wet shoreline, closely appraised by women, young ... and not so young ... that lounged beneath broad, striped umbrellas.

The pungency of sea air and beached Sargasso weed, flavored with a whiff of decayed fish, inundated his senses. Beaches were *not* his favorite places.

He sidestepped to avoid two statuesque beauties as they trotted by, breasts shamelessly bobbing, barely restrained by flimsy bikini tops. The blonde trailed long blue-nailed fingers across his shoulder and back as she slid by.

"Hey, shorty," she said. "You're kinda cute. C'mon," looking back over her shoulder and tossing her head, lemony hair swirling as she continued away. "I might be available later." The smile carried heated promise.

He spun around and watched their curved, nearly naked butts, his eyes hard dark pools, lips creased in a tight, bare smile. His fingers closed into crushing fists as he struggled for control.

A vision edged into his mind ... his mother, nearly naked, sprawled on her knees, lustrous auburn hair cascading over her face. He would crouch in a corner, fingers shielding his eyes, a frightened eight-year-old, as his father taught her discipline, shouting that her immorality required constant punishment.

*No! Not this time.* He wouldn't let his old ways cloud his hunt for Camille. A woman like that, so confident of her looks .... maybe even a professional. He might teach her proper behavior some other time. But not today.

She called him "Shorty," but in high school his nickname was "The Smiling Irishman," or just "Smiley," but he wasn't Irish, and he rarely smiled. He never found it as humorous as the kids did. And the boy who first labeled him never called him Smiley again. He'd learned, even at that early age, how persuasive he could be.

Smiley shook his head and turned away, and continued up the beach, his balled hands thumping against his thighs.

"Camille!" he muttered, jaw clenched. "Where are you?"

Eighty minutes later, he'd returned to his Dodge, his latest quest not surprisingly unfulfilled. It was late afternoon, so he decided to idle along Seventeenth Street, just in case she was there. He would park in one of the many lots and patrol the pedestrian path along Lincoln Road and stop in one of the numerous eateries for dinner.

If nothing turned up, he'd recross Biscayne Bay via the MacArthur Causeway, back to downtown Miami and scout possible venues along Brickell Avenue. Not likely Camille would be out and about there in the evening, but it would give him a chance to plan the next day's search.

He'd scratched off the Little Havana area of South Miami from his grid, certain it wasn't in her comfort zone ... unless she was cleverly doing the unexpected, to foil his quest. But why hide from the man who loved her, and whom she loved in return?

He'd have to think about that. And then there was follow-up to do with someone he'd spotted in North Miami Beach. But one thing at a time.

*Patience. Patience is my friend.*

# 13

Shelly surfed the MLS listings for north Dade County, while Lois was still involved with her clients. They apparently phoned in their offer after they filled out the tender sheet and now awaited a reply from the seller.

Tiny bells jangled as an older, well-dressed couple strode through the doorway, and scanned the room. Shelly didn't recognize them, but she'd only been at the office for a short time.

She smiled. "May I help you?" she said as she rose and slipped around her desk.

"Possibly," the suntanned man said. "We just finished lunch at Marcello's and saw your sign."

"We're new to this area," the shorter, equally bronzed woman said. Her diamond tennis bracelet and five-carat ring sparkled in the filtered sunlight. Both appeared to be in their mid-fifties and fit.

"We're looking to possibly buy if there's something in a gated golf and tennis community nearby."

"Right," the man added. "Southern Miami is getting a bit too Latin for us, but we really don't want to get as far from work as Boca Raton."

"Well you've stumbled upon the right people to help with that," Shelly said and extended her hand, to be shaken by both.

"I'm Rochelle Weitz, but everyone calls me Shelly. Let's sit over here," She gestured toward a sofa and two chairs poised around a low rosewood coffee table, "and you can tell me what you've got in mind." She gathered a pad of paper and a pen from her desk.

She struggled to suppress tremors at the thrill of possibly landing two clients in the same day. They settled on the sofa, with Shelly on one of the chairs.

"We're Jon and Marcia Ingram," the man said. He wore lightweight gray slacks and a white collared knit shirt. The woman was clad in a light pink tennis skirt and matching Fila blouse.

"We live in Kendall and belong to Kings Bay Country Club there," he continued. "We never expected to feel like a minority in this country, but the area is getting so Cubanized that we've become uncomfortable."

"It's not that they're unfriendly," Marcia said, giving a small wave of her well-manicured hand. "But when it's hard to find a restaurant or store where they speak decent English ...."

"Anyhow," he continued, "we've decided to move farther north, and buy into a residential country club so Marcia doesn't have to travel for golf or tennis, as long as it's not too far from my Coral Gables law practice."

Shelly made notes on her lined pad as they spoke.

"It sounds like either Aventura or the new Miami Gardens Golf & Tennis Club would be a perfect fit, depending on whether you want a house or an apartment, and your price range."

His answer was interrupted by the ringing phone. Shelly glanced at Lois's office as that door opened and emitted the broker and her clients.

"Excuse me a moment," she said. "I have to get this." She plucked up the receiver.

"NMB Realty. Can I help you?"

"Rochelle Weitz, please," an unfamiliar clipped male voice said.

"This is she," she said. Who might this could be?

"This is Officer Don Martini, North Miami Police. I'm sorry to tell you, your mother has been in an auto accident."

"Ohmygod!" her voice a choked whisper. "Is she ... she's not ...?"

"No, it's not critical, from what I hear," the officer injected. "Pretty banged up but not life-threatening. I'm not sure how serious it is, at this point, but she was conscious and alert."

"What ... what happened?" A traffic accident? Her mom was an especially careful driver.

"Looks like a teen, high on something, ran a red light. Her car's pretty badly mangled. She's at Jackson North Medical Center's Emergency Room."

"Okay. I'm on my way, as soon as I tie something up here."

"I'm sure you're anxious," the officer said, "but I understand your mom is sedated and resting quietly. Is there anyone else I need to inform, or will you ...?"

"No, no one. My dad's in California, and they've been divorced for ten years. I'll let him know later, but he's too ill to travel, anyhow. Thanks for calling. I gotta get going." She hung up before he could respond.

"Excuse me a moment," she said and jumped up, searching for her broker. She spied her near the agency's exit and over hurried there.

"Lois. Lois!"

"In a moment. I'm finishing up with these happy buyers. We just ...."

"I don't mean to interrupt," Shelly panted as she fought to calm herself, "but my Mom's been in a bad car accident, and I've gotta leave."

"Oh, of course, my dear. Whatever you need." She turned to her clients. "If you'll just hang on a minute, I've got to attend to an emergency. Then we can finish up on your purchase."

"Certainly," the woman said. "Do what you have to. We're in no special hurry."

"Thanks." She turning back to Shelly. "What do you need from me?"

"The couple at my desk, the Ingrams, are looking to move up from Miami. They're interested in a golf and tennis community, which would probably be Aventura or Miami Lakes Golf and Tennis. I think the latter would be an easier commute for him to his offices in Coral Gables. I was just signing them up as their Transaction Agent when I got the call. I don't know exactly what they're looking for, house-wise either."

"Not a problem, sweetie. I'll handle it. Anything else before you go?"

"Yes. I signed another call-in when you were out ... the Croziers. The information is on my desk, and I've already pulled several listings ... two of ours and some from the MLS."

"Been a busy girl, haven't you? Good work. I'll see to everything. You go to your mother. That's the most important."

"Thanks, Lois." Shelly turned, and then glanced back over her shoulder. "These are *my* clients, aren't they, Lois? I hope to be back in time to show the Croziers and the Ingrams around. They said they were in no real hurry, and Mister Crozier specifically asked for me."

"Really? Two weeks in and already making a rep, huh? Don't worry, Shelly. No one's going to poach your clients. If we make a sale, the commissions will be yours."

"Great. Thanks again. Now I gotta go." She hurried to her desk and snatched up her shoulder bag. Jon Ingram stood, offering his hand, as she started to apologize for rushing off.

"No problem, Ms. Weitz. Family comes first, especially in an emergency. Marcia and I like your style, so we'll leave our info with your boss. Call us when you get back. Meanwhile, we'll drive around the area, getting out feet wet, so to speak. May even stay up here for a few days."

"Swell," Shelly said. "I should be in touch no later than day after tomorrow ... I hope. Depends, I guess, on how badly my mom is hurt."

They shook hands, and she sped out of the office, angling toward her Toyota, parked in the rear of their lot.

*Damned Florida drivers. Everyone thinks it's the old people ... the retirees ... but it's the kids who ... Oh, what the hell. Just hope Mom's not too badly hurt. No one here to care for her but me.*

She slid into her car, cranked the engine, and was quickly on her way to the hospital in North Miami. She knew they had a great Trauma Unit there. Jackson had a well-earned reputation for excellent care and cutting edge technology.

She hoped her mom was just a bit banged up and didn't need anything exotic in the way of care. Luckily, Mom had her Teachers' Union health insurance, so whatever it was, it should be covered.

That self-assurance did little to ease her tension.

# 14

Warner's key scraped quietly out of the deadbolt. He eased the door open and slipped softly inside. He made a lopsided grin.

*Like a thief in the night,* but he didn't want to awaken Eva if she'd taken advantage of a few quiet moments to grab a quick nap.

The scrabble of clawed paws echoed in the hallway, as Buff, his rescued golden retriever, skidded around the corner. A soft chuff resonated deep in his throat as he slid to a stop, dropping into a "sit." He offered a paw of welcome. Warner chuckled, scratching behind drooping ears. He could never imagine why anyone abandoned this beautiful, intelligent animal.

The odor of some delectable concoction wafted out from the kitchen, along with the quiet scraping of a skillet on the cook top. Eva was clearly awake and puttering over dinner.

Casting aside unnecessary stealth, he strode toward the aroma and the sounds of a chef at work. Buff trailed at heel. Warner entered what could at best be called a studio kitchen, and spied the tall, auburn-haired beauty, busy with her creation.

"You're the eternal optimist, Eva," he said with a chuckle.

"Oh, Al! You startled me. I wasn't expecting you for at least another thirty minutes." Her wide, full-lipped mouth split into a whimsical grin, her green eyes twinkling.

"I was making something special for dinner and wanted to surprise you." She shed her oven mitt and dried her hands on a flowered apron as she circled the breakfast bar and moved into his open arms.

"No progress on the case, so I bugged out early. Glad I did. Smells yummy." He wrapped her slender body close against him, his face buried in the thick fragrance of her silky mane.

She giggled. "Me or the meal?" A lobe of his right ear found its way into her mouth, while her long fingers gently patrolled his hard-muscled back.

"Both, I guess," he said. "And I *am* surprised ... constantly. You totally confound me, woman."

"Really?" She leaned back, and the corner of her lips tugged upward. "And why is that, Detective?"

"Ever since that day in your office when you suddenly said I had to see another therapist," he tilted her chin and his lips lightly brushed hers, "because you'd fallen in love with me. Wow!"

"That was over a year ago, darling, and you were in the midst of that SIDS mystery ... and, as I remember, hooked on a blonde nurse named Casey." She was unable to maintain her fake pout.

"Yeah. But that didn't work out, and you were my backup plan."

"Backup plan? Me?" Her eyebrows arched, her attempt at a stern look dissolved into a grin.

"Don't play innocent, Miss Headshrinker. I guess I shouldn't really be amazed that you understood what I was goin' through, and waited it out."

"It was a confusing time for both of us, Al. We each had a lot to work through." She wiggled deeper into his grasp. Her head snuggled into the crook of his neck.

"I know. I guess that's why I'm still checkin' to see if I'm awake. I'm an everyday guy, with a lot of hard bark on me, who never expected to be loved ... ever since I was just a kid. Especially by a beautiful, smart, educated woman like you,

Doctor Guttenberg." Their lips connected and their tongues lightly danced together in something more profound than just passion.

She drew back, panting. Her fingers caressed his cheek.

"There's nothing 'everyday' about you, Al. You're the most compassionate tough guy I've ever known. And, by the way, a tender and skilled lover. I've never been happier."

The next kiss flowed with heated passion. He scooped her up, lips and tongues still tangled, their hearts galloping to William Tell.

"Dinner," she gasped. "Still on the stove."

*Let it burn.* He flashed back to an almost identical moment, thirty months ago, just moments before his surprising deadly confrontation with the Angel of Death.

*Not this time.* Supporting Eva with one arm as she dangled, hands clasped behind his neck, he edged into the kitchen. He slid the veal cutlet filled skillet over and switched off the burner.

"There," he murmured. His mouth worked across her neck and ear. "The only thing left burnin' now is me."

"Me, too, darling," her voice a choked whisper. "Definitely me too."

# 15

An hour later they were savoring an Argentine Malbec over plates heaped with veal scaloppini, sautéed mushrooms, and roasted baby sweet peppers. She had slipped into one of his cotton long-sleeved shirts; he into boxers and a T-shirt.

Perched on stools at the breakfast bar, she regarded him from the corners of her eyes. Despite the heated urgency of their coupling, the sex had been drawn out with tender teasing as he slowly fanned the flames of her passion to a shuddering climax. Two, actually, the second, in even greater intensity, quickly followed the first.

No man had ever played the fiddle of her ardor as expertly as Al Warner. At first it was scary almost as much as thrilling. She was one of only four people knowing details of his hidden past even he was unaware of.

Those lost memories were what thrust him into her care while in the grip of PTSD during the end of the Angel of Death investigation and its incredible conclusion. She finally succeeded at putting behind her any reservations from that fiasco, first born at the deadly end of the Baby Butcher serial killer case.

This was the *real* Al Warner now. She loved this wonderful, sensitive, caring guy, and he seemed to love her too. His lost past appeared well secured in an impenetrable mental vault that would probably never be opened. Best *that* stayed sealed, for everyone's sake.

"Something botherin' you, Eva? Ya look perplexed."

"No." She covered his hand with hers. "Just thinking how fate brought us so blissfully together. How about you?"

"Haven't been this happy, ever. Even though I loved Sharon, we were polar opposites on crime and punishment. Cops versus Public Defenders, I guess."

He raised her hand and kissed it softly on the palm. "I'd be as excited as a pig in shit, if it weren't for this new loony, killin' young redheads. I brought home the files to see if something pops out, away from the constant rumpus of the department."

"You have no leads on the killer, Al?"

"Nothin' concrete. Kinda hoped my psychologist lover might come up with something."

"Hasn't Special Agent Dalwin done a profile yet?"

"They're workin' on it," he said. "His BAU team is crackerjack, and they're reviewin' everything, but so far it's all still pretty thin."

"These women are all decked out in little party dresses?"

Warner nodded, then opened the file and fanned out photos of the four victims.

"Hmm," she mused. "These dresses look like what teenagers might wear, not adult women. Did they seem new to you?"

"Good point." He spun two photos and studied them through narrowed eyes.

"Yeah, you're right. While I don't think they were shabby or worn, I doubt they were brand new, either. Good catch, Eva."

"So, if they're not new," she ran fingers through her auburn locks, eyes distant, "they either came out of someone's closet or were maybe bought at a resale shop."

"Wow! You nailed it, beautiful. I'll get the troops out, checkin' all those shops. Big job, county wide, but if we can turn up a repeat buyer ...." He gave her a hug and planted a kiss on her forehead.

"And I'm guessing whoever this killer is," she took his hands in hers, her voice filled with eager excitement, "it's a teen girl he's fantasizing about, not a woman. Maybe thinks she's an adult now, and he's a bit uncertain what she looks like today. I'm guessing he's a white male, probably under thirty."

"Jeez, great insight. I'll get this to Agent Dalwin. His team's just gettin' started. Maybe you've helped 'em get off on the right foot. Don't know if this'll get us any closer to our Unsub, but the resale shop idea gives us the first real shot at findin' him."

Warner grabbed a few more bites of his dinner, and then jumped off the stool. He pulled her into his arms for a short heated kiss.

"Hope you don't mind, babe, but I'm gonna run back to the office with this. I love ya." A quick kiss and he was gone before she could respond.

She sighed. Their quiet evening alone had evaporated. She'd learned one thing, however. Make love first before starting any conversation. She couldn't suppress a chuckle. If they had waited until after dinner, she'd be returning home horny as hell.

She packed up the leftovers in covered Pyrex bowls and put them in the fridge. The dishes rinsed and in the dishwasher, she checked to see if she'd missed anything. Then she fed Buff, and gave him the few minutes he needed in the postage-stamp sized back yard, not knowing when Warner would return.

Satisfied there was nothing else to do, she locked the door and strode down the townhouse steps, heading for her Jag convertible, still awash with the glow of their lovemaking.

Life had never been so fulfilling.

# 16

Shelly shoehorned her silver Rav4 into a spot made narrow by a carelessly parked Lincoln SUV. Unfortunately, nothing else seemed available within proximity to the Emergency Room, so she'd risk possible parking lot rash. The spot was so cramped she could barely escape her car.

Finally free, her purse slung over her shoulder, she sped for the entry doors. She brushed away a sheen of perspiration, unsure if it was early arriving summer heat or tension. Her mom was the center of her world.

Shelly hurried through the entrance as the automatic doors swished open. She scanned the bustling room, spying what appeared to be a registration desk. The air was rife with the stench of stale sweat and strong chemicals.

Her nose twitching, she hitched her shoulder bag higher, and approached a nurse talking on the phone. The woman, dressed in blue scrubs, held up a finger before Shelly could say a word.

"Okay, I got it," she said and scribbled a note on a yellow sticky note. "I'll get this to the attending. Anything else?"

Shelly danced from foot to foot while her fingers drummed on the counter. The nurse still signaled "wait" with her upraised palm, smiled at her, and shrugged.

"Yes sir," she said and hung up and scratched an additional notation on the yellow slip. She glanced up at the clearly impatient young woman and asked, "May I help you?"

"I'm looking for my mother, Helen Weitz. She was in an auto accident, and the police ...."

"Weitz? Yeah, I saw her ...." She ran a finger down a chart. "Yep, just went into surgery; compound fracture of her left leg. Should be an hour or so. There's a waiting room over there." She pointed up the hall.

"The officer who called said she was badly banged up. Is there anything else ...?"

"Nothing noted here," the nurse said. "I don't see anything else scheduled for her. You'll have to ask the doctor when he comes out. Now I've gotta get this," waiving the yellow slip, "upstairs. There're vending machines, TVs, and magazines in the lounge. Get comfortable and relax. Your mom's gonna be okay." She hurried off, leaving the desk momentarily vacant.

*Relax? How the hell am I supposed to do that?* A small tear trickled across the swell of her cheek. She wandered down the white-tiled hallway and found the waiting room nearly overflowing with a disparate mass of humanity. A Latino teenager, noting her distress, offered her his seat. People of all ilks supported each other in times of crisis, and what could be worse than awaiting news of a sick or injured loved one?

She nodded thanks and slumped onto the chair, cradling her leather shoulder bag on her lap. She sighed and rummaged around inside, snagging her Android tablet. Shelly powered it up and stared blankly at the screen, unable to organize her thoughts. She blinked several times, shook her head, and sighed. She then began entering notations on the afternoon's activities. It *had* been an exciting day, with two new clients of her own ... until that scary phone call.

Well, all she could do now was wait, and that wasn't something she was good at. She groaning and tried to bury herself in her work, but her thoughts were constantly fractured by visions of her mother, trapped in the mangled car.

Time trundled by on boggy feet.

¤ ¤ ¤

"Weitz? Someone here for Helen Weitz?"

Shelly twitched, her eyes struggling open. Despite the uncomfortable chair, she had dozed off. A stumpy fortyish woman wearing wrinkled surgical wear and a white face mask dangling below her chin hovered in the doorway, her eyes sweeping the room.

"Here," Shelly croaked. "I'm Rochelle Weitz, her daughter." She lurched from her chair, wobbling for a moment before gaining balance. She glancing at her watch and shook her head.

*Jeez, nearly two hours.*

"Oh, good," the woman said, and held out a hand in greeting. "I'm Doctor Dinato, your mom's surgeon."

"Oh, thank god. I've been worried sick. How ... how is she?"

"Doing quite well, under the circumstances. It was apparently quite a nasty accident. She suffered a compound fracture of the left femur, two broken ribs on the left side, a badly strained wrist, and, unfortunately, a moderate concussion."

"Jesus!"

"It could have been worse. I understand it took twenty minutes to extract her from the wreck. Good thing she was in her seatbelt, or she may have been killed. Kind of unfair that the punk who hit her had only minor bruises and a few small cuts."

"The officer said he was high on something," Shelly said.

"Looks that way. We're running tox screens for the police, and I heard he's been arrested."

Shelly shuddered, blinking away tears. "So, my mom ...?"

"Right. The leg required surgery, and I inserted two pins. It's in a cast now, and should heal fine. There was a lot of damage to the bone, however, and it may end up a quarter inch short."

"Won't that cause a problem walking?"

"Only barefooted. Orthotics can give her the required lift in her shoes. She *is* going to be in some pain for a while, so she'll get a prescription for pain meds."

Shelly nodded, tears pooling, as she fought the urge to hyperventilate. "What about her ribs?"

"They were simple fractures. We don't wrap them anymore. They're mostly uncomfortable rather than dangerous. I'm more concerned about the concussion," Doctor Dinato continued. "She'll require bed rest at home for several days, and she'll need to take it easy for at least two weeks."

"Je-e-e-sus. Thank god for her teacher's insurance plan. She can have someone with her during the days while I'm at work."

"That's good. We're going to keep her here for a day or two, to be sure there're no complications or infections after the surgery. She'll see a neurologist again before she's discharged, for concussion protocol. Once she's cleared, she'll be good to go."

"Thank you so much, Doctor." Shelly gave her an impulsive hug. "When can I see my mom?"

"She's still in recovery. Probably about an hour. We'll move her upstairs into a regular room and you can visit her there. Someone will come out and tell you when and where. Now, I've got another patient." She patted the younger woman on the shoulder and hurried away.

Shelly sighed and turned back to the waiting room. A seriously obese woman had commandeered her seat and seemed uninterested in giving it up.

*She probably needs it more than me. Think I'll go to the cafeteria for some dinner. It's going to be a long wait.*

*Poor Mom. I hope they roast that damned kid's butt.*

She turned and found an orderly for directions.

# 17

The gold Dodge van cruised slowly north on Brickell Avenue, as the driver scanned the walkways. Maybe he should park so as to have more time to look around. Camille could well be working in the business districts of Miami. She was a clever girl and surely went on to higher education ... maybe an MBA or legal degree.

How had he let her escape him, all those years ago? He was so busy developing his craft ... obsessed with teaching proper virtue to those girls that deserved of his efforts ... that he missed their senior prom. He had promised to take her, but he'd been so consumed with teaching that young slut, Jenny, discipline, he'd been late for their date.

Totally embarrassed, he had rushed to her home to beg forgiveness, but she was gone. Her parents, who never approved of him, wouldn't say where ... despite using all his skills to convince them. What a waste!

He had watched from a distance as the Evanston Police showed up to their house, hoping they might lead him to his love. Surely she'd come home to say a final goodbye to her mom and dad, but she never showed. It was two weeks before he was certain she'd left town.

She'd often talked about going south: collage in Atlanta, and maybe a career in South Florida. It took only three foolish imposters in Georgia before he realized she must have bypassed that metropolis for the less hectic sunny climes of the Sunshine State.

So here he was, getting closer, certain he was nearer than ever to success. Time now for boots on the ground.

He pulled into one of the numerous multi-level parking structures that dotted the downtown Miami office district and backed into a narrow slot on the third level. Better to have the rear unexposed just in case he stumbled across Camille and was able to "convince" her to join him.

After two fruitless hours of wandering the canyons of Miami's office district, he wondered if this was a waste of time. The better part of yesterday was lost in Miami Beach, although not entirely without ancillary promise.

He visualizing the brazen blonde jogger on the beach and resolved to revisit there once Camille was back where she belonged. South Beach was rife with women that needed to learn discipline and morality. He was a masterful educator of those things, with myriad successes in Chicago and Atlanta. South Florida offered many opportunities to repeat those lessons.

He paused, arms akimbo, at the curb at Brickell Avenue and SE 7th Street, glaring at the towering concrete buildings, many festooned with elaborate murals, mostly of things nautical. This busy strip housed much of the Miami area legal offices and corporate structure. He had patrolled the streets and scoured the lobbies, always subjected to security scans. Not a problem, as he'd left all his "tools" in the van, quickly retrievable should the opportunity present itself.

Where to go next? He was drawn to increased sounds from the nearest building as a persistent trickle of secretaries, clerks, and executives began flowing out the doors. Glancing at his watch he realized it was lunch break time. He scanned the walk and saw similar exoduses from other buildings.

As the flow of humanity burgeoned, his eyes narrowed. He shuddered and an electric charge trilled across his spine, raising the hairs on his neck. He slid quickly to one side and arched his neck, straining of a better view.

Red hair! The right shade and height, bobbing along between two large males. He scurried ahead, weaving through the growing crowd, desperate for a better look. He slipped off the walk onto the grass and strode along, eager but cautious. The small group hesitated at the curb to await traffic as he hurried ahead, seeking a better vantage point. Her face. He needed to see her face.

As if hearing his thought, she turned and grinned at the young man beside her.

His breath caught as his heart hammered on his ribs.

*Camille!*

*I've found you!*

# 18

Al Warner slouched back from his desk and glared at the papers strewn across its scuffed oaken surface. While seeming haphazard, they were actually arranged in an order only he fully understood.

The left edge of the desk supported four overlapped files, each containing the forensic details from the four murders. They were thick with data, none of which told him anything specific about their Unsub: who he was and what were his motives. Warner had scoured those files dozens of times with no substantive rewards.

Directly in front of him lay a half-dozen unruly stacks, each growing by the hour, detailing the searches for where the party dresses may have originated. Jack Harris and Rafael Olvida, his two best detectives, were spearheading that effort, which had recently expanded into Broward County.

So far, that hunt hadn't turned up much, either. It was a huge landscape of resale stores, many trendy but some not. Then there were auctions, where older clothing was often sold. And many of those could be accessed online, and were often out of state. Even yard and garage sales were a possibility, but there was no reasonable way to check those out. It was like searching for a specific straw in a barn full of hay, but those four outfits had to come from somewhere. Did this lunatic have a stash of others in line for his next vics?

Possibly.

The right side of the scared oaken surface was strewn with three folders filled with backgrounds of each deceased redhead. Warner had shuffled those like peas in a shell game, scouting for some plausible connections besides hair color.

*What is it about these gals that drew his deadly attention?* Other than hair color, similar body size and shapes, and age, there were no other connections he could dredge up.

*He huntin' women with red or auburn hair within a specific age, height and physique parameter that makes 'em prey. He's lookin' for someone specific, but I don't think he remembers exactly what she looks like, which is strange.*

He glanced across the room at the white Murder Board, displaying photos of all the victims ... portraits they'd secured from friends and/or family, as well as crime scene shots of their final resting places. He pushed away from the desk, rose and moved in for a closer look.

The expansive board was typically crosshatched with erasable marker lines that connected and intersected notations on times and places, and data any of the detectives working the case felt may be important.

This particular board was surprisingly sparse, considering the number of body bags they had acquired in the last three months. So far, the crime scenes, the forensics, the background checks, and hours and hours of canvassing had produced almost nothing.

"You think staring at it'll expose some hidden clue, Al?" Captain Santiago had materialized at his right shoulder.

"No such luck, Cap. Just tryin' to get a feel of where we are on catchin' this nut."

"And ...?"

"Nowhere close, unfortunately. He hasn't given us much so far. Ed Dalwin and his Behavioral Analysis Unit are preparing their profile. They've been delaying, hoping for something new to make it more viable, but that was pissin' in the wind. It ain't gonna us tell anything we don't already know or suspect."

"Which, other than pretty young redheads dying, is damned little, Detective."

"Unfortunately true." Warner groaned softly, swaying to and fro on from foot to foot, eyes sweeping across the Murder Board, desperate for something ... anything ... to ignite a spark.

This was their third serial killer in three years, and the first two hadn't provided the slimmest clue to their identities until the very moment of their violent ends ... both at his hands.

His fingers found the X-shaped scars, hidden beneath the thick mat of curly dark hair on the right side of his skull: the reminder of how close he'd come to dying at the hands of each of those two madmen during those final deadly confrontations.

"Those wounds still giving you trouble, Al?"

"Nah. Just habit. Gotta go now." He sigh and he flexed his broad shoulders, and then returned to his desk where he gathered his badge and 40-caliber Glock from the drawer. Time for the BAU's profile, but like those other two killers, they had little more than nothing on who he was and how to find him.

Another clever and careful loony, not making mistakes. Warner shivered as he slipped on his shoulder harness, covering it with his lightweight mocha sport coat.

This bastard won't make life any easier for them than had the other two, who had made zero mistakes until their very last moments. And those errors had cost them their lives while nearly taking Warner with them ... both times.

Maybe the boys from the FBI had figured out something he'd missed this time.

He doubted that.

# 19

He edged the Dodge Caravan backwards, close to the curb, lowering the driver's side window and killing the engine. A warm, salty breeze ruffled his honey-colored hair. How lucky that Buick pulled out just as he arrived opposite the towering office building where Camille apparently worked.

He glance at the meter and saw thirty minutes remained. Probably enough time, as they should soon be on the way to lunch at one of the many cafes that peppered the Brickell Avenue area.

He rummaged through the contents of the scuffed brown leather satchel that rested on the passenger seat, verifying all was ready: rags, a canister of chloroform, duct tape, a stun gun, zipties, and a black hood. Prepared for any eventuality.

He eased back against the beige leather-trimmed seat, his eyes fastened on the building across the bustling avenue. The hum and rattle of traffic on the busy thoroughfare was almost mesmerizing.

Probably too crowded to take her now, but he would be ready in case of a lucky opportunity. This was his second day of scouting, but he had not yet managed to follow her all the way home, wherever that was. That's where it would probably happen. He was determined to make today *the* day. His usually abundant patience had deserted him.

He tensed, suddenly erect, as the doors of the building burst open and emitted a surge of men and women, hurrying off on their midday break. He scanned the swelling crowd, sure her auburn hair would signal her presence.

And there she was: Camille, draped in a tailored light blue knee-length skirt and a matching silk short-sleeve blouse. She marched along, laughing and in animated conversation with two taller men, garbed in dark suits. Probably attorneys, like her. He raised the window, grabbed his satchel, and exited the van, locking it.

He dart between the busy auto traffic and crossed the street, drawing a single angry blare of a horn. He wove among the pedestrian crowd as he sauntered after the threesome who were striding south, deeply involved in happy discourse. Something good had happened in her life. She giggled, her eyes riveted on the taller of the two men— suntanned face, straight longish black hair, athletically built, and probably considered handsome.

Smiley ground his teeth, his mouth a knife-slit crease, as he watched her hand run possessively down his arm, taking his hand. They continued on as their joined arms swung with their gait, their shoulders brushing together.

He growled, fists balled, beating against his thigh. This was wrong. Camille was his, not to be shared by some interloper. He would have to correct that ... show her how she has erred. And maybe teach that cocky intruder proper restraint while he was at it. He was very good at those kinds of lessons.

He lingered by a street light, watching as they paused outside an open-air Greek bistro, clearly of conflicted opinions as to where to dine. Finally the other guy, sandy haired and rail lean, shrugged. Camille glanced over her shoulder, catching his stare. Their eyes locked together for a moment, then she turned and they disappeared inside.

THE PROM DRESS KILLER

He hesitated, then sighed. There was no recognition in the look. He headed back toward his van. There'd be no opportunity to return her to him that afternoon to rekindle those memories, but he'd come back at the end of her work day. Maybe then ....

He grimaced. Attorneys often worked long hours. He may be in for a lengthy vigil. But he was usually patient. He had discovered where she parked her Honda sedan and had scouted a great observation point where he could see either her departure from the office building, or her arrival at the parking lot, should she come from a different place. Either way, he'd be ready.

If he were lucky, he might find an opportunity to take her by her car. That had become his preferred modus operandi. If not, he'd follow her home, determined not to lose her this time.

Whatever it took, he'd be ready. He'd become impatient of this game of hide and seek. He inhaled a slow, deep breath.

*Patience. Patience is my friend.*


Smiley hovering in the shadowed portico of the deserted office building and glanced at the LED dial of his watch: Six thirty-five. His eyes scanned between her building down the street and the parking structure where she stored her car while at work.

*Why is she working so late?* Serenity had been a bulwark of his quests, but it was beginning to wear thin. Camille had played this game long enough. No more dancing in the shadows.

Shifting from foot to foot, he flexed his shoulders and struggled to remain calm. Tonight was the night. He ignored the thinning traffic, humming along Brickell Avenue. With the work day finished, many had left for home.

So where was Camille?

His gaze was drawn to the doors of her building, which began disgorging small clusters of men and women. The remnants of a late office meeting? Possibly her ....

There! Lustrous auburn hair ... and then Camille, on the arm of that same interloper from lunch. Where were they going? Not to her car, it seemed. They strolled south on Brickell, past the garage that housed her green Honda Accord.

He shouldered his leather satchel and slipped out of a shadowed doorway, pacing their progress from his side of the divided avenue. With the man's arm around her waist and her head nestled against his shoulder, they were in no hurry.

His fists, flexed into iron balls, thumped against his thighs, his short nails biting into his palms. Heat flushed his face, and his heart tattooed against his ribs. Smiley was not smiling.

*Camille is mine, you bastard. Hands off ... while you've still got hands.* He sucked in several slow breaths and struggled to calm himself. Anger clouded judgment and impeded effectiveness. He eased his pace, hanging back, again calm as he watched them approach a tavern. Just before they entered she pulled her companion to an abrupt stop, paused, and then pivoted quickly on a three-inch spike heel. Her eyes raked the walkway behind her and caught him as he turned away. He glimpsed her auburn eyebrows knitting together as she tugged on the man's sleeve.

His back to them now, he crossed the street and observed their reflection in a large plate glass window. They were entering the pub, but Camille's eyes were still focused on his back.

He returned after he circled the block and spied them through the window, clinking beer mugs in apparent celebration. Commemorating a legal victory, it seemed. She appeared happy now, unconcerned about whomever she thought may have been following them.

They were clearly out for the evening. He'd have to wait.

A hundred feet down the street was a small grassy glade with a bench, where he settled and watched, patience again his friend.

# 20

Shelly slid her silver RAV4 into the Patient Pickup drive, spying her mom sitting in a wheelchair. Jumping out, she ran around to help with the front passenger door. The candy-striper volunteer positioned the chair, and he helped Helen Weitz hobble up. She winced as Shelly and the aide settled her onto the front seat, adjusted in the fully-back position to accommodate her left leg cast. Shelly secured her mom's seatbelt and planted a quick kiss on her cheek while the aide deposited a pair of crutches in the Toyota's cargo hold.

"You okay, Mom?" she asked.

"Yes, sweetie." Said through tightly pressed lips. "The leg's throbbing a bit, but I'm glad to get out of here."

"How about your ribs? The seatbelt too tight?"

"No," she sighed, "I'll manage, as long as we don't hit anything. I don't think I could take another pop in the face by a damned airbag again."

Shelly chuckled. "I'll drive carefully, Mom. Promise." She waving to their helper as she accelerated smoothly, pulling away.

Twenty minutes later, they drove into Helen Weitz's driveway. Shelly retrieved the crutches from the cargo bay, and then steadied her mom as she crawled out of the SUV and onto their support.

Hovering close, with one hand on her mom's arm for added reinforcement, they made their way through the French door and into the family room. Helen eased herself onto a maroon leather easy chair  and winced as she positioned her leg on the low padded cowhide ottoman.

"Does it hurt bad?" Shelly asked as she rummaged in her purse for the prescribed pain meds.

Helen nodded, grimacing. "I'll live, no thanks to that maniac who slammed into me."

"Yeah, well he's in jail, awaiting charges. Hopefully they'll give him more than just a slap on the wrist. Here, take these," offering two hydrocodone tablets. "Doctor Dinato says you have to keep the pain in check."

Helen looked at her daughter and frowned.

"I know, Mom. You hate meds, but this is necessary. The day nurse will be here tomorrow, and I'm telling her not to take any crap from you."

"Okay, okay." Helen chuckled. "I promise to be a good girl. I don't want you worrying about me while you're at work. So, tell me about these new clients you got. How's that going?"

"Swell, so far. Miss Howell offered to show them around while I was involved with you, but both couples said they'd wait for me."

"I'm not surprised. You've got a knack. People love you. But I hope you're being careful. A realtor can be an easy target when showing a house alone."

"I know. Mr. Karlov said he'd come with me the first time, but these are middle aged people. I don't really feel threatened."

"Okay, but it's still my prerogative to worry. There's some lunatic out there kidnapping and killing lovely young redheads, just like you."

"Yeah, scary, isn't it. I hear the FBI is here now, too. We've got that local hero ... Detective Warner, I think ... on the case. I read he stopped the last two killers, and solved that case with the SIDS babies last year, so they'll get this nut sooner or later."

"I hope so," Helen said. "Just be careful and stay alert. Maybe you should carry a can of pepper spray, or something."

"Good idea, Mom." Shelly didn't admit she was already so armed. Mothers like making important contributions.

"So, here's the remote for the TV. I've fixed up the guest room down here for you so you don't have to deal with stairs. I'll sleep in your room. I picked up a baby monitoring system, so you can call me if you need me for anything. I'm going upstairs now to change the sheets."

"A baby monitor?" Helen's grin was whimsical.

"Yes." Shelly turned back, chuckling. "You're my baby girl until you're on your own again. The nurse will be here tomorrow at eight, so I can get back to work."

"Sounds good. Or at least, the best we can do, under the circumstances. Umph!" Helen grunted as she changed position.

"I'll be back down in a couple of minutes. Then I'll run out to Whole Foods to pick up some dinner."

"Okay." Helen sighed and clicked the TV remote. Just in time for the six p.m. news.

As usual, they started with a brief weather report. Partly cloudy with a forty percent chance of rain.

Always a safe forecast in South Florida.

# 21

Al Warner lounged against the wall near the podium of the Squad Room, awaiting their arrival. Special Agent Ed Dalwin and his BAU team were about to publish their profile for the nut the press had labeled "The Prom Dress Killer."

Unfortunately there wasn't going to be anything really substantive in their findings. Very little that might help them nab this unusual psychopath. So far he'd made no mistakes to help them in their hunt.

Warner glanced across the room, filling with a full cross-section of the department, as well as representatives from Broward and Palm Beach Counties. This would be the third full-scale Tri-County manhunt in the last three years, twice for a guy intent on killing young women, and once for a murder of teenagers.

He hated serial-killers, not only for the deadly damage they caused, but especially for the heartbreak they dealt to so many families in the wake of their atrocities.

Leordano, the Baby Butcher, who sliced up innocent teenagers that thought he was their friend. Dissecting them while alive and conscious.

Then a year later, Angie Dedios, the Angel of Death, snuffing out some of South Florida's hottest young women.

Those were two elusive maniacs that provided few clues to their identity, and only luck and his quick reactions ended their reigns of terror. This new nut was no less clever.

Heads of uniformed officers, plain-clothes detectives and undercover cops all swiveled as Dalwin and his troop entered from a side door, striding across the raised platform.

Warner pushed away from the wall and joined them in his role as chief homicide detective. Ed Dalwin nodded to him, gave a small shrug, and muttered, "Not what we'd hoped, so far."

"Yeah, I know," Warner replied, and then he addressed the room.

"Okay, you guys, settle down. Special Agent Dalwin's team is ready to give their profile on our newest loony. This won't take long. I appreciate seeing officers from Broward and Palm Beach County. Our Prom Dress Killer hasn't ventured up there yet, but if history teaches us anything, you know he's coming ... unless we get him first. So, give the people from the BAU your attention. No one does it better." Warner turned to the tall, sandy-haired man at his left, and nodded.

"Ed, it's all yours."

"Thanks." Dalwin was joined by statuesque blond Inga Yeager and linebacker-built African American Ansel Whitehead ... his top profilers. Dalwin's gaze swept the room as he began his briefing.

"We're looking for a white male, probably between twenty-two and thirty. He projects a mild, non-threatening physical appearance, allowing him to approach these women without setting off the warning radars. His victims are slim, attractive redheads, all about five-foot-six, which shows he's looking for someone particular. He probably believes these girls *are* the specific person he's searching for. He's a patient stalker, clearly psychotic, and has a distorted view of who he's hunting and exactly what she looks like."

"Once he realizes he's made a mistaken ID," Agent Yeager said, "he kills them, but does it painlessly and with minimal physical trauma. This indicates he loves the woman he's searching for, and probably believes she loves him too."

"Fitting them out in prom-type dresses," Agent Whitehead continued, "suggests his last contact with this woman ... more probably, girl ... was as a late teen, in high school. We suspect it was someone he wanted to take to a Junior or Senior Prom, but failed in that attempt. If in fact he is in his twenties or thirties, he may have been searching for her for years, and probably in other states too.

"So reach out to your contacts in neighboring states," he said. "Look for unsolved murders that are similar. He may be evolving, so his MO may have changed somewhat, but the basic bones should still resonate."

"Meanwhile," Ina, the Germanic blond agent pitched in, "I'll be casting a wider net, searching the NCIC data bases to see if we can link him to other deaths. If we can trace him back to the beginning through that national data base, we may discover who he is."

Dalwin said, "I wish we had more at this point, but there hasn't been much to work with. Like many of these psychos, he's careful and clever.

"Detective Warner and Metro-Dade Homicide are leading the local investigation, so route anything through him, no matter how trivial it seems. Detective, anything to add?" He looked at Warner.

"Thanks, Ed. One more thing. These fancy outfits he dresses them in aren't new, so we're canvassin' clothing resale shops, thrift stores and auction houses to see if we can find out where he's gettin' them. It's a small needle in a very big barn full of hay, but maybe we'll get lucky. If you guys from Broward and Palm Beach can do likewise in your counties, it'll speed things along. Any questions?"

Ben Ellison raised a hand. He was a homicide detective from North Miami Beach, and one of Warner's partners in their Dade County Boot Camp for troubled kids.

"You're saying he's looking for the girl who may have jilted him in high school, but he doesn't remember what she looks like? Pretty damned weird."

"It's probable that's what he thinks happened," Agent Dalwin answered. "There's a good chance the date to the prom was a figment of his warped mind. The girl may never have even been aware of his interest. That's not uncommon in a dissociative mind, where events are massaged to meet a perceived need."

"And because the whole thing is manufactured by a psychotic mind," Agent Yeager added, "she's probably remembered more by what he wished her to be than what she really looked like."

"So she probably had auburn or red hair, about 5'6", slim and attractive," Agent Whitehead pitched in, "but her actual facial features are unclear to him. That's what has sparked this trial-and-error abduction routine."

Agent Dalwin ran a hand through his hair, nodding, "Despite his victims' probable denials that they're not whomever he's searching for, it takes several days before he's convinced."

A hand went up. "Why doesn't he just release them if the vic's not who he's looking for? Why kill them? Psychos like him aren't usually worried about getting caught."

"Good question," Whitehead said. "His killing seems like a natural, remorseless thing for him. So, there's an excellent likelihood he's killed other women before, not just redheads. The MO would be different. No party dresses, and possibly with more violence. There may have been some new stressor that started him looking for his high school dream girl. Whatever, this is certainly his main focus now."

"Okay, guys," Warner stepped forward. "This is what we got. I know it ain't much to work with, but it'll have to do for now. Your main task right now is tryin' to find where he's gettin' the dresses. That seems our best chance to get a lead on him, 'cause he sure ain't makin' any other mistakes. And you can be damned sure he's huntin' another redhead as we speak. So let's get to it."

The rumble of conversation and the shuffle of feet echoed in the emptying squad room. Special Agent Dalwin and his BAU team left the stage the way they came in, heading for their temporary quarters, where they would comb through the data they'd acquired, trying to find one previously missed nugget.

Al Warner aimed for his own desk, intent on calling his troops in the field. He hoped to have some news on where this clever psychopath as acquired the outfits he eventually dressed his victims in.

He wasn't rift with high hopes, but it was all they had to work on for the moment.

# 22

Smiley returned to the bench after he retrieved a light hooded rain jacket and his Android tablet. He hunched over the device, tapping randomly at the keys whenever the door to the tavern opened.

Camille had noticed him earlier in the day but showed signs more of concern rather than recognition. In fact, she seemed spooked, which was strange. Regardless, he'd opted for camouflage until he could make her see who he really was. She'd been dining and drinking for over two hours, so he expected her to head for her Honda soon. Tomorrow was a work day.

Of course, when he reunites with her this evening, she won't have to worry about work in the morning. They'd be very busy catching up on lost time.

She'd never have to work again.

He glanced up as noise and light spilled from the restaurant, and two people came into view. Camille and her companion (he *couldn't* be her boyfriend!) paused in the dim shadows and shared a lingering kiss. He watched, battling surging heat, his strong, thick fingers flexing and clenching. Rage must be contained or it could lead to mistakes ... and he *never* made mistakes.

*I warned you about putting your hands on my girl! You may have to be taught a lesson.* But that's for later. First he had to bring Camille home.

The embrace finally ended, arms linked together, they started toward him and the multi-story garage behind, where she'd parked her car. He bent over his laptop, the jacket's hood concealing his face as he pretended to surf the Internet. They passed him without notice. It took all his resolve to keep from leaping upon that brazen interloper and rescuing her right there.

*Patience!* Patience has always been his friend. *Patience!*

He peeked past his hood, and then rose to follow them, the tablet returned to his satchel. His fingers explored the bottle, rag and zip-ties nestled inside. Everything he needed was there.

His pink-tipped tongue swiped across dry lips as he watched them saunter along the walk, the man's arm circling her waist. Smiley realized his eagerness had drawn him too close, so he slackened his pace. As if sensing his presence, she swiveled her head, lustrous auburn hair shimmering in the glow of silver moonlight, and tugged on the man's arm, turning him.

He hitched his satchel higher and turned away, strolling across the street, seemingly headed for a street level parking lot, one of several dotting the landscape of the office district. The man had taken a few steps in his direction, but noting his apparent destination, he paused, said something to Camille, and they continued along their route to her car.

Except their course took them into another small street lot, not the multi-level garage that housed her Honda.

*What the hell are they doing?* It was already after nine. She should head home to get some rest before tomorrow's work day ... something that wasn't going to happen.

He hurried to his Dodge van, parked two hundred feet down the street. He didn't want to lose her again, once she headed for home ... if that's where she was going tonight. He gritted his teeth, his face flushed. She wouldn't dare go with that jerk ....

As he slipped inside his van, his eyes narrowed. He snarled and pound his fists on the wheel. She planted a kiss on his lips

[84]

before she entered the passenger' seat of his Mercedes sports coupe. She *was* leaving with him.

Maybe they were headed to another bar or club before she started for home. If not ... he mulled possible alternate scenarios, none of which pleased him. He sucked in a slow, calming breath, then another.

*Patience! Patience is my friend. It's only a matter of time. If not tonight* ... He fired up the ignition and pulled away from the curb, following Camille and the brazen interloper as they headed off to the southwest .... Kendall or Coral Gables? Not likely another watering hole.

Lips pressed so thin they were almost invisible, his knuckles white around the steering wheel, he struggled for his usual serenity.

*Patience.*

*Patience is my friend.* The mantra echoed repeatedly in his head, easing his tension.

An hour later he was en route home. He had followed them to the man's townhouse in Kendall, and they'd disappeared inside. Lights flicked on, and then off, as they made their way through the house, ending in what he guessed was the bedroom. Camille was clearly spending the night with this ersatz lover. Not likely they would make the forty-minute drive back to her car that evening to where it still lingered in the Brickell Avenue garage.

Peace had once again descended over his soul. Tomorrow was another day. If the evening were a repeat of tonight, he'd already devised a plan to deal with that. Camille would be his ... finally ... one way or the other.

All those imposters he'd dealt with in the past ... but this time it *was* her.

At least, he thought it was. He'd been certain ... but still wrong ... before.

That other girl he'd seen while cruising around farther north ... she also looked so much like Camille. But he'd been uncertain then, and now he'd found the real one here. He gripped the steering wheel so tightly his knuckles looked bleached.

Smiley shook his head, lips turning down. Why had he been mistaken so many previous times? It was her face that sometimes seemed unclear.

He eased his stranglehold on the wheel and nodded to himself. This time he'd gotten it right. He was sure this *was* her, and he was going to take her away from that handsy clod. After tomorrow, that guy was never going to paw his girl ... or any other ... again.

Camille would finally be his. Together again, now forever. His mouth twitched into a bare, tight smile as pink tongue caressed narrow lips.

*Patience.*

*Patience is my friend.*

# 23

Al Warner shoved through the entrance of his office, causing the door to boomerang off the wall.

He shrugged out of his beige sport coat, tossing it on the worn navy vinyl couch, and then unhooked his shoulder holster. That, with his Glock secured inside, went into his lower left desk drawer, next to two fully loaded spare clips nestled there.

He sank down on his leather chair and rolled close to the desk and dropped his head into his hands, elbows braced against its scarred oak surface.

*Burnin' too many candles at both ends*. He groaned softly.

Jack Harris slid through the doorway and paused as he regarded his boss. "You look like something a cat wouldn't even bother dragging in, Al. You had a whole weekend to get some rest. What's up?"

"Ya always know how to lift a guy's spirit, Jack," Warner muttered, the corner of his lips ticking up. "In case you forgot, me and the boys are runnin' another teen boot camp. That was our second weekend."

"Oh, yeah. I *did* forget. No rest, huh?"

"You kiddin'? Between our newest serial maniac who's given us nothin' to work with, and a bunch of surly teenage punks lookin' to push the limits, there wasn't much time for sleep."

"How's that going?" Jack asked as he settled in one of the chairs. "That's a great thing you guys are doing. Bet it's pretty frustrating, huh?"

"Not a strong enough word, Jack. These are all pretty smart kids, who could make it outta the ghetto and have a real life ... instead of an early death. Two have already washed out in only the second week. One's on the way back to Juvie Hall, but the other one's goin' to Raiford. He's goin' in as a scared punk, but he'll come out ... if he survives ... as a hardened criminal."

"Too bad, but all you can do is give 'em a chance. The rest is up to them."

"Yeah. The successes mostly outweigh the disappointment. Some are tougher nuts to crack than others.

"Anyhow, enough of that. Anything happen on our search for where this new nut's buyin' his pretty little dresses?"

Jack shrugged. "Not so far, but we still got a long way to go, chasing down all the possible outlets. Agent Yeager got a hit on NCIC on three vics in Atlanta that might fit his MO. Dalwin's sending a team up there to check it out. Sure sounds like our guy."

"Shit. Hope they come up with something tangible."

"Problem is," Jack said, "that's gonna expand our possible sources for the dress buys. If he's been killing redheads out of state, he may have brought dresses with him."

"Maybe. But remember, we think he's lookin' for a specific gal. He's not just tryin' to off redheads, so why stock up on prom dresses? I doubt he's expectin' to keep gettin' it wrong."

"Good point, boss. So he's probably buying them here, maybe one at a time. So we keep looking."

"Right. So get on your troops, and be sure they're not slackin' off. It's been two weeks since we found the Williamson girl. This bastard's gonna take another gal soon. We're on the clock."

"I'm on it, boss," Harris said as he levered himself out of the chair and tossed off a casual salute.

"And check with the Broward and Palm Beach sheriffs," Warner said. "Keep a fire lit under them, as best you can. They're not gonna be happy if they start findin' dead fancy-dressed redheads on their turf."

"Gotcha," Harris said as he hurried from the room.

Warner slouched back in his chair, fingers drumming on the desktop. They needed a break but he wasn't too optimistic. Maybe Agent Dalwin's BAU team would turn up something in Atlanta. A little nugget that would point them in at least the right general direction. This perp had been killing over a wider area than first thought. Warner wondered if there were other cities before Atlanta where he'd plied his deadly trade?

The BAU profilers felt there was a fairly recent stressor that set him off chasing redheads. They believed killing women may not be new for him, so everything has become more complicated.

He was jerked from his musing by the warble of his phone.

"Homicide. This is Detective Warner."

"Hey, Al. Ya made it back alive." Hector Carrera chuckled.

"Yeah, barely. Where'd you disappear to, Hector?"

"Chi Chi's mom never showed, so I drove him home. Kinda lucky, 'cause it gave me some one-on-one, and I think he's starting to listen."

"Good work. You get him on your side, it could turn the whole camp around. He's a natural-born leader."

"Right," Hector said. "When you got through to that Delgado kid two years ago, he brought the whole camp under control."

"Carlo's our best success, but I think Chi Chi's got all the makin's of another one. Keep in touch with him, even before the next camp. He's gotta know he can call you for anything, Hector. These boys are starvin' for a *real* male role model."

"Wilco, Al. Meanwhile, I got the boys out here in Little Havana scouring the resale shops, looking for the dress buyer."

"Good work, but there's been no Latino component to these murders. I don't think he's searchin' on your turf, but it doesn't mean he's not buyin' the dresses there."

"Right. So I was just checking in. See ya next weekend, unless we turn up something on our Prom Dress Killer."

Saying their good-byes, Warner rose and made his way to the Murder Board. Feet spread, arms akimbo, he scanned its white surface, patched with photos of the faces of their victims and their bodies at their "dump" scenes.

The board was streaked with black, blue and red markers, connecting photo and data blocks. He glared at the hodgepodge, as if he were daring it to belch out one fresh lead. But there was nothing new since Friday.

He sighed, and his fingertips absently found the X-shaped scars under the thick matt of curly dark hair.

*Fuckin' frustratin'. This nasty bastard's gonna take another gal any day now, and there's nothin' I can do about it.*

*I hate waitin' for another fuckin' murder so I can dig for clues.*

*This nut better give us something to work with soon, or the whole Tri-County will be in an uproar again, barely a year after the Angel of Death did his dirty work. Seven dead beauties then before I got lucky ... if ya call a slug off the noggin "lucky."*

He grunted, spun on his heel, and headed for his office. He would go over everything they had from scratch. Like a new pair of eyes. There's gotta be something there they've missed.

He shivered an goose bumps scattered across his scalp. He knew it would take at least one more snatched ... and probably dead ... redhead to have any shot at snagging this deadly loony.

*What a way to run an investigation!*

# 24

Shelly nudged the door of her silver SUV with her rump, closing it as she hiked up the shoulder strap of her tan leather attaché case. She paused an scanned the small parking lot off the alley behind the NMB Realty offices.

Sucking in a nervous breath, she struggled to quell a persistent sense of unease. There was no apparent danger there ... no one lingered between the cars of their small strip mall. No one meaning her harm ... despite an unshakable sense she'd been followed.

*It's those kidnappings and murders of redheads. I'm such a drama queen.*

They had all been taken in South Miami, not North County, where she lived and worked. Still, it paid to be cautious, since she was a perfect fit for the kinds of women this nut was taking.

She expelled a soft breath and her lips ticked into a wry smile. She shook her head and strode toward the office's rear entry. The most dramatic event in her current life was her mom's accident, and that finally seemed under control.

Shelly placed her attaché case on the corner of her desk and settled onto her chair, swiveling slowly to and fro. Her thoughts drifted to her mom, who, for two more weeks, was in the capable hands of a home care therapist. Mom was already making her way around her house with the use of crutches or a wheeled walker. The worst of the pain had subsided, and it appeared she was on the way to a full recovery.

Thank god. What a scare that was.

Shelly was happy being back at work. She had two clients, only one of which she'd met in person, and she wanted to start showing them homes.

The Ingrams had left a message with Ms. Howell, her broker, that they had returned to Kendall but they planned another visit that weekend. With Friday just two days away, she'd call them and check their schedule so she could set up a tour of houses in the two country club communities they had discussed.

She checked her notes and called William Crozier's cell phone. He was, so far, just a phone contact who said he was there without his family, which may make it easier to schedule appointments. He answered on the fourth ring.

"Yes?" Sounding distracted.

"Mister Crozier?"

"Yes. Who is this?"

"Rochelle Weitz. The realtor you called at NMB Realty about 10 days ago."

"Oh, yes. I was wondering what happened to you," he said.

"I'm so sorry I didn't get back to you sooner. I left a message on your voice mail that my mom was in a serious auto accident, and I needed a few days to get her settled back at home."

"Ah, yes, I remember now. I've been ... busy with a project down in Miami, so no harm done by the delay."

"Thanks. I didn't want you to feel I've neglected ...."

"No problem, Rochelle," said with a chuckle. "Shelly, isn't it? I could never find myself upset with a lovely redhead."

"So, would you like to make an appointment to see some houses up here, so we have something to show your wife when she ...?" She glanced at her notes. Had they met? No, she was

[92]

certain of that. A chill skittered down her spine. How did he know she had red hair?

"Well," he interjected, "as I said, I'm rather tied up with a project that I've been working on for quite a while. Concluding that successfully may have a serious bearing on where I ... we ... intend to live."

"Okay. I understand."

"I've Googled your office's web page, and I'm impressed. If things conclude, uh ... unfavorably ... down here, I'll definitely pay you a visit."

"Thanks. I'll be available whenever you've got the time," she said. "If you decide on another area, let me know, and maybe we can recommend a good realtor in that area. While all realtors are created equal, some are created more equal than others."

He chuckled. "Paraphrasing Orwell's 'Animal Farm,' are we?"

"Yep. I love reading those old stories, especially ones with a moral."

"And I love hearing them," he said. "We'll have to compare notes, once we get together."

"Of course." She relaxed. He wasn't really blowing her off. "Let me give you my personal cell number so you can reach me at any time. A good realtor is always available to meet your schedule."

"Good. I'm confident you *are* that good realtor too. So, let me have that number."

Shelly rattled it off, and they said their good-byes. She slouched back in her chair, legs splayed out, twirling a pencil. If he decides on another area, maybe they can earn a referral fee from his broker.

*Damn. My first client. I hope he decides to end up here.* She moved to the MLS computer and started to research properties she might tour that weekend with the Ingrams, still bothered by how Mr. Crozier knew she was a redhead? There is that guy out there, killing ....

*Oh, he said he Googled our office page.* She typed in "NMB Realty" to see what came up on that popular search engine.

There they were. She clicked on the link, and after the site loaded, she clicked on the "Our Realtors" tab. Up popped color photos ... including hers, auburn waves framing her face ... with short bios of the five agents from her office. A simple explanation, as usual, to debunk imagined fears. Mom had taught her the perils ... and joys ... of an active imagination. It *was* a definite plus when you're a short story author.

She smiled, turning her attention back to her property search, never considering that sometimes simple explanations might just be wrong.

# 25

Smiley awaited their departure, parked on the street outside their offices. When he spotted them exiting together and heading for the guy's car, he took off for the man's townhouse. He parked around the corner, out of sight, taking no chance his van might be recognized.

The locks were easy for anyone with the skills and the right tools. He slipped inside, easing the door closed, beating them to the interloper's home by at least five minutes.

He reengaged the locks and quickly reconnoitered the six-room abode, tastefully appointed with high-end modern furniture and expensive knickknacks. Apparently even associate attorneys made enough to live expensively. He stiffened at the sound of voices and a quiet giggle, just outside the door.

They're here.

He hurried into the bedroom and edging behind the closed door, he readied his tools. With some luck, he'd meet them separately. If not, he'd still manage the scene. He cocked his head at the sound her high heels clickity-clacking across the hardwood floor as they entered the home. His lips tipped into a grim semblance of a smile.

"Camille. We'll soon be together again," he whispered softly.

"I've gotta pee, Chris," she said. "Too much coffee."

"Okay. I'll get a bottle of Merlot and meet you in the bedroom."

Smiley tensed, preparing the sedative-soaked rag. The door opened as she hurried into the room. He moved behind her and shouldered the door closed. She turned at the sound.

"Chris, I'll just...." Her eyes flared at the sight of the man snatching her shoulder, drawing her into his arms.

"Camille, my darling," he whispered.

She shoved her hands in his face, struggling to twist free. Her attempted scream filled her lungs with chloroform from the cloth he shoved over her nose and mouth. Her attempt to knee him and twist free were quickly quelled by the anesthetic, silencing her with little more than a soft 'chuff.'

"We're together again, Camille," he whispered in her ear as she sagged into his arms, unable to struggle. He eased her onto the bed and brush auburn locks from her face and straightened her skirt.

"Take your time, babe," the man called from the other room. "I'll have two glasses poured so the wine can breathe a bit." His feet padded across the floor toward the door.

Smiley hurried into the closet and withdrew a hard case from his cargo pants. It held just what he needed next.

The guy entered, a wine bottle and two glasses in hand, and paused. Confusion wrinkled his brow.

"Jeez, Elke, that was quick. You're not falling asleep on me are you?" He jerked to a stop and started to pivot at a scraping sound. The bottle and glasses clattered to the floor when a short but powerful man bear-hugged him and pinned his arms to his sides, followed by a sharp sting in his neck. He twisted, trying to break free, lashing out with his foot and trying to knee the man holding him. The glasses on the floor shattered as they tromped back and forth, fighting for balance.

He began to collapse as the sedative Smiley injected in him took hold. The Prom Dress Killer cradled the man's sagging body, not wanting to chance a fall leading to a deadly concussion from a piece of sharp-edged furniture. This guy was going to live to regret putting his hands on another man's girl.

He retrieved another hypo from his hard case, injecting Camille with sedatives. The drugs would ensure no interruption while he completed all his tasks there.

Once they were both resting quietly, he dragged the man into the bathroom and slid him into the tub, lying face up.

"Now for a lesson you'll never forget," he said. "You'll never put your hands on another man's woman again." He opened his bag and readied all his tools, everything in order. He wouldn't rush and not do the job right. The tiled bathroom provided an ideal work place, with no fear of setting off the fire alarm. He wasn't yet ready to draw attention to his activities.

Twenty minutes later, he paused at the bathroom's doorway, surveying the results of his efforts. The gush of blood had been confined mostly to the tub and was quickly choked off.

Satisfied, he slipped out the side door to retrieve his Dodge Caravan, backing it up to the garage. He gathered up Camille an rolled her into a six-foot rug he'd brought. Working around the Mercedes coupe parked inside the narrow one-car stall, Smiley eased her into the carton, nestled in the rear of his van.

He gathered up his supplies and deposited them on the floor of the front passenger seat, and closed the overhead garage door. No need to wipe down the scene. He'd worn comfortable vinyl gloves throughout.

Once clear of the neighborhood, he dialed a number.

"911. What is your emergency?"

"I'd like to report a home invasion in Kendall. There may be injuries." He gave the address, and then hung up, despite the operator's request for his name and plea to remain on the line.

*Not a chance.* He chuckled without humor as he removed the battery from the disposable phone. They weren't going to be able to trace *that* call.

Easing to a stop at a red light, he glanced over his shoulder at the back, where he'd removed all of the van's rear seats. The carton for a fourteen-inch memory foam queen-size mattress filled most of the floor. Good cover, should he be stopped for any reason by the police.

Smiley was meticulous at insuring his Dodge minivan displayed no infractions that may draw a nosy cop. No broken lenses or tail lights out, turn signals working, and license plate clean, with a current tag sticker. And cruise control was always set to the exact speed limit.

Even if he were stopped, there was no reason to suspect Camille was sleeping, snug as the proverbial bug in a rug inside that roomy carton. Chloroform had put her down, and a mild sedative would keep her there for at least another hour. More than enough time to get her home and settled. Once there, he'd again partly muddy the plate to partially obscure the numbers, just to be safe from discovery.

On I-95 now, he headed north, whistling softly to himself. No one else was awake to hear.

Camille was finally coming home, just in time for the prom. He hoped she liked the dress he'd selected for her.

She was going to be the Queen of the Ball.

Smiley did something rare for him. He smiled.

But there was no humor in his eyes.

# 26

"Warner. My office."

Al Warner glanced away from the crime scene photo he was studying, then groaned.

"Be right there, Cap." He rose and stretched, rubbing the crick in his neck, then strode from his office. Sounded like something was up.

A moment later, he entered his boss's office. Santiago lingered by the rear wall, arms crossed, staring out the window.

"Have a seat, Al. I need your opinion on something."

"Okay, shoot." Warner settled onto one of the two armless chairs fronting his captain's desk.

"I just picked up on a strange new case."

"Something to do with our Party Dress nut? How come I didn't ...?"

"It's not a homicide," Santiago said, dropping into his own chair, "but my gut says there may be a connection to your current lunatic. He ran a hand through curly dark hair.

"It's just weird enough," he said. "A young male attorney was found with both hands amputated ...."

"What? Cut off? He didn't bleed out?"

"No. The perp cauterized the wounds. CSU thinks he may have used a propane torch. The perp apparently wanted him to live like that."

"Jesus! That's damned sadistic. How did they find the vic? Doesn't seem like he could call 911."

"That's what seems strange to me. The perp must have been waiting for him in the apartment. Apparently knocked him out with a sedative before taking his hands. As if he didn't want him to suffer during the amputation. Then someone ... the perp, I think ... called it in."

"Weird. But why do ya think this is connected to our Prom Dress loony, Cap?"

"He left a message, pinned to the vic's shirt: 'Because you can't keep your hands to yourself.' And the CSU says there was evidence of a woman there. They're bringing that in, whatever it is."

"Okay, maybe." Warner's fingers found their way to the X-shaped scar under his thick thatch of hair. "What did the vic say?"

"Nothing yet." Santiago rolled a pencil between his fingers. "He's still out. Doc said he woke up, saw his stumps, and faded out again. I'd like you to check out his office, talk to his co-workers, and learn if he was seeing someone. Maybe another redhead? What d'ya think, Al?"

"I think it's worth a shot, Bob. Certainly, if this guy was datin' a redhead our perp thought was his prom date, he coulda done this. I'll get on it. You got an address for his office?"

"Right here." The captain slipped him a piece of paper with a Brickell Avenue location scribbled on it. "I hope I'm wrong about the girl, but our killer is overdue to take another vic. Take your partner."

"Jack's out, chasin' prom dresses. I'll take Olvida. If there's no connection to our guy, you can turn it over to the detectives."

"Okay. Keep me posted."

Warner nodded, and then hurried back to his desk, signaling for the lanky, dusky-skinned detective, Raphael Olvida, to follow him.

# 27

Forty-minutes later, Warner and Raphael Olvida were ushered into the walnut-paneled offices of Samuel Burns, a partner at Williams, Burns, Klass & Cooper.

The attorney rose to meet them and waved them into plush leather sidechairs.

"What can I do for you, detectives?" He settled back into his executive chair, fingers steepled together. "I hope no one here has transgressed in the eyes of the law."

"Not to our knowledge," Warner said. "We're just tryin' to gain some information about an employee or two. I presume you know Chris Shultz?"

"Of course. One of our rising young stars. Has something happened ...?"

"In a minute. Do you know if Mr. Shultz was datin' someone? Maybe a serious relationship?"

"What's this about?" Burns' eyes narrowed. "We don't mix into our associates' private lives unless there's some sort of blatant impropriety."

"We're not allegin' that. Just lookin' for information. Did he have a girlfriend? Someone maybe serious?"

Burns sighed, easing back in his chair. "We discourage associates dating, but have no strict rule against it. They were advised of the potential conflicts, but they said they were in love."

"So there was a girl? Someone in the office?"

"Yes. Elke Sorenstan. Another promising young attorney. I knew it would cause trouble. What have they done?"

Warner glanced at Ralph Olvida, and then turned back to the frowning partner. "Ya got a photo of Ms. Sorenstan?"

"Certainly." He punched an intercom button. "Julie, will you retrieve a photo of Elke Sorenstan and bring it in?" He turned back to the detective. "Are they in trouble?" he asked again.

"Possibly. Let's see the photo and then I'll tell you what I know."

A few moments later, the secretary delivered a laptop with a photo of four young people displayed.

"From their victory celebration after the Unger verdict."

"This is Ms. Sorenstan?" Warner asked, pointing to an attractive redhead, hoisting a toasting beer mug.

"Yes, that's her," Burns said. "So ...?"

"Has she shown up for work today?"

"I don't know. Let me check." He stared at Warner, eyebrows arched. A moment later, he'd hung up his desk phone.

"No, at appears Elke hasn't checked in yet today. So ...?"

Warner sighed, easing back in his chair an rubbed his eyes.

"You've heard about this Prom Dress Killer? The guy kidnappin' young redheads?"

"Yes, but ... ohmygod." His eyes bulged. "You mean ...?"

"Yeah, I'm afraid Ms. Sorenstan may be his fifth victim."

"And you think Chris has something to do with this? I can't believe ...."

"His only involvement may be dating this girl at the wrong time," Olvida injected. "Our killer seems very possessive about his redheads, and probably didn't like Mister Shultz touching her."

"We can't tell you much more at this time," Warner said, placing a quieting hand on his partner's arm. "It's just become an open investigation. Does Mr. Shultz have any local family? He's at Jackson Memorial, if you're interested."

"He was injured?" The attorney was making a note on a lined yellow pad.

"In a sense," Warner said, rising. "Seems our lunatic amputated both his hands."

"What? Good Jesus!" Burns slapped a hand over his mouth.

"We're sorry about your people," Olvida said, glancing at Warner, giving a small head shake. He usually had more tact that that. They rose to leave.

"We're gonna do our best to catch this nut and save Miss Sorenstan," Warner added. "I promise you, I'm gonna get this guy."

They pushed their way through a small crowd of people that had gathered at the doorway, clambering for answers.

Something they had very little of at the moment.

# 28

He studied her for a moment, then squatted and smoothed her auburn curls, draping them over her bare shoulders.

Lustrous as fine silk, glistening after her recent ... and last ... shampoo. Why had she so vigorously resisted a shower in preparation for the prom? His lips thinned, turning down, as he inspected the darkening bruises on her upper arms.

He hadn't wished to hurt her, but like all those others impersonating Camille, she had rejected him. This was the first one he'd actually left marks on. He was more careful than that.

*Damn! How could I be so wrong, five times in Florida, too? Camille and I were in love, going to the prom ... was it really over seven years ago?*

He knelt at her legs, first adjusting the frilly white lace of the dress's hem, then straightening a wrinkle in her hose.

*Do girls even wear nylons anymore? Doesn't matter. She'll look so nice when she gets to this last dance.* He sighed.

She'd meet the ten other imposters he'd sent ahead of her, all waiting for their chance to dance with him. Which one might be voted queen of the prom? And how to choose among them, all looking so much alike.

Alike, but none of them Camille. He was saving her coronation for the *real* Camille, once he found her. Only she deserved to rule.

Smiley rose, and hands clasped behind his back, circled the supine woman, her once rosy complexion now paling and cold.

# THE PROM DRESS KILLER

The bare-shouldered aqua-green dress, slashed with magenta and ivory swirls and trimmed in alabaster lace, was one of his favorites.

He'd been overcome almost to tears when he discovered it nestled among the things he'd packed for Camille. He'd thought he had carelessly given it to one of the early imposters. It should be worn only by the *real* Camille, but he had no others, and this poor foolish girl needed to be appropriately clad to attend the prom tonight. Despite her brazen duplicity, she deserved that proper respect.

All in the name of the real Camille, wherever she was.

He nudged a leg with his toe, sensing stiffness. Good. She would be more easily carried as she became rigid, keeping her carefully adorned attire from disarray.

Time to arrange for her to find a ride in that long, black limousine that the police would provide for her. He positioned his mp3 player on the dresser, the strains of the silky-voiced father and daughter crooning 'Unforgettable' filling the air.

A chance for one last dance.

"Ah, Camille. Where are you," he murmured.

He hunkered over the steering wheel of his van, elbows wedged against the spokes of the wheel, his head cradled in his hands.

What to do now? He'd left the last imposter waiting for her ride to the prom. He hoped her chauffer arrived before weather and animals disheveled her appearance. She really looked beautiful, resting peacefully on that bench, awaiting her chariot.

Now what? Somehow he had missed Camille again, mistaking another pretender for the woman he longed for. He adored her so, but had such a fuzzy memory of her face. All those that had confused him had the same burnished coppery hair, the same height and body shape, and, he'd thought, the same face.

[105]

But he'd been wrong! Eleven times now. Three in Chicago, three in Atlanta, and now five here in South Florida. His fingers prowled over the tender spot on his right temple, where, in frustration, he'd struck himself repeatedly.

He needed to regain his sense of peace.

*Patience. Patience is my friend.*

The familiar mantra rolled through his mind and calmed him. He could do this.

He'd gone nearly five years after he completed his first futile search for her. But she had vanished, and he'd abandoned that hunt, instead opting to teach other brash and clueless women proper care and morality, just as his father had with his mother. Lessons he excelled at delivering.

Then almost three years ago, that brazen redheaded Chicago hussy reignited his passion for Camille, setting him off on this so far fruitless quest.

But now he was certain she was here, and he would find her. He was *not* going to make another error. He slipped his scuffed leather wallet from his pant's cargo pocket and extracted the creased and faded print from an inner fold. Camille, clipped from their 2008 Senior Yearbook.

He'd carried it with him all these years, holding her close. He studied the scratched and washed-out portrait, struggling to visualize her face, no longer clearly recognizable in the photo.

He thought of the redhead he'd seen in North Miami Beach. He'd been so drawn to her, he'd almost suspended his quest for this last girl. That was clearly a blunder he was going to rectify.

Sighing, he straightened and fired up the Dodge's engine. Better not rush things. That's how mistakes are made. It won't take long to finish combing Miami and North Miami. Just a few neighborhoods left to visit.

*Patience. Patience is my friend.*

But somehow, in his gut, he knew things would finally be right when he got to North Miami Beach. Maybe he *should* stop wasting time and just skip the center of the county, and head north now.

Something to consider.

Calm and resolute, he whistled softly as he drove off.

# 29

Rochelle Weitz slouched against a pillar in the entrance portico, lingering in its shade, as she followed the departure of the maroon Infinity sedan. She pushed away and strolled toward her Toyota SUV as the big car turned onto Country Club Drive, heading out of the resort complex.

The Ingrams seemed enthusiastic about this mini-mansion, the fourth house they'd visited that day. Marcia was especially taken by the large kitchen, with its dark cherrywood cabinets, granite counter tops, and island prep sink. Apparently, despite all their wealth, she preferred to cook more often than eat out.

Jon Ingram spent nearly twenty minutes prowling around the spacious home office. With its TV and Internet outlets and loads of custom cabinetry, including a sprawling built-in mahogany executive desk, Shelly could imagine the wheels turning over how much work he could do here at home, rather than constantly traipsing down to his offices in Kendall.

She grinned, thinking of a fat commission, as she slipped into her silver Rav4, folding and storing the windshield sun screens. Despite the sun lingering behind a raft of marshmallow-like cumulus in the western sky, after ninety minutes at this last stop of the day, her car would have been an oven without them.

Shelly fired up the engine and cranked the A/C to full bore, loitering for a moment while the car cooled, reviewing her day.

She'd arranged viewing of two houses in each of the two country-club communities, starting with Aventura, which she felt was their least likely choice, and ending in the Miami Gardens Golf & Tennis Club. She'd saved the best for last—a four-bedroom, five-bath beauty, nestled close to the seventh green of the Nicklaus-designed championship golf course.

Despite Herculean efforts to restrain their enthusiasm, with the sellers hovering nearby, Shelly knew this was the one. Her share of the agency's three percent commission on a two-million-dollar sale would net her a year's living expense.

And she still had hopes of making a sale with Mister Crozier, whom she hadn't heard from for almost a week. That seemed more likely to be in the range of their more usual three-hundred to six-hundred-thousand dollar listings. She'd have to make a follow-up call to him, to see what was going on.

In the meantime, she expected to hear back from Jon Ingram by this evening or tomorrow with an offer. She slipped the Toyota into gear and started back toward her office, eager to discuss the day's progress with her boss, Lois Howell. Maybe get some pointers on how to present the Ingram's offer to the Miami Gardens real-estate agent. Shelly knew she still had a lot to learn.

¤ ¤ ¤

Four hours later, Shelly was on her way home, floating in a near haze of rapture. The Ingrams had arrived at the NMB Realty offices just two hours after Shelly had returned. With Lois' guidance, they executed an offer of $2,100,000 for the last house they'd seen. Lois had called the listing agent, giving them just twenty-four hours to accept, inventing an urgency based on another house competing for their business.

Shelly had intended to call Mr. Crozier to check on his interest, but they were so swept up in preparing a purchase offer for the Ingrams, she never got the chance. She'd do it from home that evening, which may be a better time, anyhow.

She had no idea how much things *were* coming together.

# 30

Al Warner stood, his feet slightly spread, his left hand jammed in a pocket while the other unconsciously explored the X-shaped scar, hiding under a thick patch of curly dark hair.

Snatching his hand away from his right temple, he rolled his shoulders, struggling to release tension. He glowered after the receding black coroners van ... 'the meat wagon' ... as it disappeared around the corner, ferrying the prom-dress decorated remains of Elke Sorenstan to her last dance.

Warner groaned and flexed his shoulders again against a persistent knot at the base of his neck.

*That's half the promise broken.* He didn't save the lovely redhead, but he damned well intended to keep the other half of the pledge he'd made to her boss ... to catch this bastard, and hopefully get that done before another beauty died. He was fed up with deranged nuts snuffing beautiful women on his beat. First the Angel of Death, and now, a little over a year later, this crazy.

Maybe they finally caught a break this time. The girl's arms were bruised, apparently from a pair of strong hands restraining her. These were perimortem injuries, so she'd struggled with her captor before he chloroformed her. Hopefully he left some trace and useful DNA that might put a name or face on their killer. The lab techs would scour her remains, looking for hair or skin cells ... anything to give them something to work with.

[111]

He glanced back at the six cops searching the area with strong flashlights, hunting for anything that might give them a lead. The body dump was in a small secluded park. A jogger found her reclining on a bench, hands clasped across her breast, clutching a red rose. She seemed so peaceful, he almost moved on, thinking she was napping. Then the red hair and the elegant gown awoke a memory of the news stories, and he called 911.

Warner shrugged. He doubted they'd come up with much. This bastard, like so many others of his ilk, was very careful. The bruising was an unusual slip. He glanced at the green LED on his watch: 2:20 a.m. He yawned, stretched, then pivoted and headed toward the team of searchers, supervised by Detective Olvida.

"Find anything, Ralph?"

"Not yet, Boss. You know these guys never leave us much."

"Yeah, well keep at it. Someday we may even get lucky. I'm gonna bug out. Try to catch a few Z's, and I'll see ya back at the station around seven."

"Okay. Who's gonna make the call?"

"To the family?" Warner cocked his head to the right. "You want the job, Ralph? I'd be happy to delegate ...."

"No thanks, Al. You're Chief Detective. I defer to you."

"Yeah, I know. I've had to make too many of those, the last two years. It ain't fun."

"No kidding. I remember that Gannon gal, the first Angel of Death vic. Didn't the mom faint or something?"

"Yep. It's not the kind of call you expect. Nothing prepares you for something like that. Anyway, we'll see what we got when we gather the team in the morning," Warner said.

"Get Dalwin to assemble his BAU posse too. This gal was killed a lot quicker than the first four. Maybe our perp is getting restless, and he'll finally make a mistake."

Warner spun on his heels, heading for his Dodge. Get a little rest, and maybe something will pop out later.

He sure hoped so.

# 31

Warner lingered at his breakfast nook, following Eva as she puttered at the cook top. She was sexily adorned in one of his red-checkered flannel long-sleeve shirts that barely hung half way down her thighs. He grinned as she expertly flipped over two eggs, sizzling in the ceramic coated skillet.

"Why am I not surprised?" he said, chuckling.

"What?"

"That you're so damned good at everything. You handle that pan like a chef."

"Actually, I was a short-order cook in college, earning some extra bread, if you pardon the pun."

"Good one. But I thought you were on scholarship."

"As an undergrad at Michigan, but they only offered a partial for their master's and doctorate programs."

"You did all three there?" he asked, rising and sidling up against her back.

"Yes." She sighed, reaching back, caressing his cheek. "The tuition was reasonable, and I loved the campus."

"But how'd you manage the cold in the winter? I'm from Illinois, and I know what it's like."

"Yes. Damned cold." She plated the eggs next to four strips of crisp bacon and a crunchy pile of hash browns. Moving the pan off the burner, she pivoted, draping her arms over his shoulders.

"And no handsome tough guy like you to keep me warm. Where *were* you, Al Warner, when I needed you?" She snickered, edging against the hard sinew of his broad chest as her fingers danced across the back of his head and neck. The kiss was sweet temptation, their tongues fencing.

"Wishin' I was somewhere like this, I guess," he murmured, nipping at her ear.

"Huh?"

"Where I was," he swept her up, one arm under her knees, with hers hooked around his neck, "doubtin' I'd ever be loved by a woman like you, darlin'."

"Oh, yes. Loved, Al. Very loved. Unbelievably ...." Her words stifled by his insistent lips as he rushed into the bedroom.

"Looks like I'm gonna be late for work," he mumbled as they tumbled together onto the still unmade bed.

They lay intertwined, her neck wedged into the crook of his arm, auburn hair a fiery halo spilling across the beige sheets. His fingers trailed like butterfly wings across the planes of her body and the swell of her breasts. At thirty-eight she had a firm elegant figure most twenty-two-year-olds would kill for, the rewards of nearly daily Pilates and yoga classes at the Fit & Firm gym. Eva was as dedicated to staying trim and strong as he was.

"Gotta go, babe," he said, brushing a kiss across her cheek.

"Breakfast is cold, Al."

"I don't care, 'cause everything else was hot. Meanwhile, I got a killer to catch."

She sat up as he swiveled to exit their love nest and trailed her nails along the rocky swell of his arm.

"Call me when you start home, and I'll whip up something for dinner," she said.

"Wilco. You got patients today?"

"Yeah, a pretty full schedule. Should be wrapped up by four, though."

"Look," taking her hands, pulling her to her feet, "I want you to be careful. This prom dress nut is killin' woman that look a lot like you, so ...."

"But they're all at least ten years younger than me, aren't they?"

"Yeah, but you *look* that young, so just be cautious if you're takin' on any new male clients in their late twenties to mid-thirties."

"Okay, but I'm not really worried. All but one are established patients."

"It only takes one, darlin', so just be safe. I don't fall in love easily, and I don't know how I got so lucky. I lost the only other two women I've ever loved, but neither were killed. Well, Sharon almost, but I stopped that bastard. Things ... good and bad ... come in threes, it seems, so just be careful. Promise?"

"I promise." She pecked him on the tip of his nose. "Now go catch that bad guy, so you can get back to the plain old drug and gang murders."

He chuckled as he donned his sport jacket. One quick heated kiss, and he slipped out, pausing to ruffle Buff behind the ears. He refreshed the dog's water and dumped two cups of kibble into his bowl. He was rewarded with wet slurps on his hand and cheek. A moment later he was out the door.

He trotted across a narrow strip of grass, retrieved the newspaper and propped it against Mrs. Gerber's stoop. A small daily chore to ease her arthritic joints.

Then he was in his Dodge coupe, heading for his office, hoping forensics had turned up something on this deadly lunatic. If they didn't catch him quickly, he'd have another redhead locked up sometime soon, playing out his deadly fantasy ... whatever that was.

Maybe the BAU team would come up with something more specific as to motive. Something that might point them in the right direction.

They desperately needed a break.

# 32

Shelly Weitz slid her silver Toyota close to the curb and killed the engine. She hesitated, fingers curled around the leather covered wheel, surveying the house. Mister Crozier was nowhere in sight.

*Damn. Wish he'd come to the office first.* Her client had called yesterday to set up some viewing appointments, but that morning he called back to arrange to meet her at the first house. He was apparently running late on some other appointments.

There was something a little creepy about the whole thing. She'd asked one of the male agents, Oleg Karlov, if he'd go with her, since Crozier was someone she'd only talked to on the phone. Her mom's admonishment about caution buzzed in her head, thinking about some nut killing redheads.

Oleg had agreed, but at the last moment, was sidelined by clients of his own, making an offer on a house. That took precedence over chaperoning a nervous newbie agent,

So Shelly stiffened her resolve and made the journey alone to the first of four houses they were to visit that day. William Crozier didn't *sound* threatening, and she was packing a can of pepper spray, just in case.

Sighing, she exited her SUV and hurried up the walk and into the covered entrance cupola of the two-story colonial. She checked her notes and punched in four-digit on the lock box hanging from the door knob. The metal cover slid off and she retrieved the front door key just as she heard someone striding up the path behind her.

Turning, she observed a short, somewhat stocky youngish man, sporting a charcoal blazer, khaki slacks, and a Chicago Bears ball cap pulled down, half covering his eyes. He had one of those baby faces that made it hard to judge his age.

"Mister Crozier?"

"Yeah. Shelly?"

She nodded, shifting her laptop to her left hand. The other one was quickly in her jacket pocket, lightly curled around the small can of pepper spray. He didn't look deadly, but ....

"Your web site picture doesn't do you justice," he said with a chuckle, but without a smile. "Sorry to have to meet like this, but some things came up at the last minute. I've been very busy chasing down some business leads that didn't pan out, and ...."

"That's okay," she said, forsaking the canister and taking his outstretched hand. "We prefer to register people at the office first, but since your morning was apparently so hectic, we can do it afterward." He seemed reluctant to release her grip, but eventually she slipped her fingers free.

"That'll work," he said, shoving his hands into his pockets. "You said you've lined up four houses that should meet our needs?"

"Yes." She craned her neck, scanning the street, a tremor of refreshed angst scampering across her scalp. "I don't see a car. How did ...?"

"Yeah. I got screwed up on the address. It's parked out back in the alley, while I searched for the right house."

"Okay. No problem." She forced calmness she didn't feel into her voice. This guy gave her the chills, but she was a professional, wasn't she?

"So this is our first stop," she said, "a four-bedroom, three-bath colonial. The master's on the first floor, the other three bedrooms are upstairs." She held the door open, and he brushed lightly against her as he entered, sparking shivers down her spine.

They traversed the house and she pointed out features as the moved through the living room, family room, kitchen, with its granite counters and hardwood maple cabinets, the hexagonal-shaped breakfast room with wide views of the fenced lushly landscaped back yards, and finally, the master suite.

Despite her best efforts, she couldn't seem to avoid his insistent contact. It bordered between inappropriate and downright creepy. She gritted her teeth, trying to avoid the hand at the small of her back as they trudged up to the second level to view the remaining three bedrooms.

She dodged and weaved throughout the second floor, evading as best she could his determined attempt to corner her, as she highlighted details of the three upper-floor bedrooms.

The tour completed much quicker than she had hoped ... this *was* an ideal residence for his needs ... she hurried out the front door and onto the walkway. Turning, she snatched a quick breath and forced authority into her voice.

"So, what do you think? This house seems perfect for your family, and the price is well within your budget."

He stood, eyes taking her in, his hand again jammed into his pockets, his face expressionless.

*Doesn't this guy know how to smile? A real weirdo.*

"I don't know. This wasn't quite what I planned. You say you've got three more to see?"

"Yes. All within easy access to the schools, as you requested. But if this doesn't suit you ...."

"I didn't say that, but I want to see what else you've got to offer. We can go together in my van, and I'll bring you back here when we're finished."

"No. No, that's alright. I always have my car, in case of an emergency. My mom, you know. She's still recovering ...."

"Oh, right. A car accident, you said. Well, we can go in your car, if that's better."

"No, we usually drive our own cars. You'll just follow me in your vehicle."

He grimaced, but no way was she going to be alone in a vehicle with this creep. She'd rather lose the sale.

He sighed and shrugged. "Okay. Meet me at the west mouth of the alley." But he didn't move. His gaze swept over all of her, lingering finally on her face.

"What? We've got to get going if we're going to finish all four houses this afternoon." His stare injected a chill into her bones.

"It's just that you remind me of someone. Another redhead. Almost a twin. Were you ever in Chicago?"

"No. I thought you were from the east."

"Chicago suburbs through high school. I was wondering ...."

"We can talk about it later. I've gotta lock up. Get your car and I'll meet you around the corner when I've finished."

"Okay." He shrugged again. "I'll figure it out." He strode off the stoop and around the side of the colonial, heading for the back and his parked vehicle.

A breath hissed out between her teeth, releasing tension she hadn't realized she held.

*How did I end up with such a weirdo?* She trotted up to the front door, depositing the key in the lock box and sealing it.

Entering her Toyota, she called the office as she drove to the rendezvous with Mister Inappropriate. Maybe another agent could meet them at their next stop. Just checking up on the rookie as an excuse.

Unfortunately, no one was available to rescue her.

Shelly was on her own.

# 33

Shelly glanced in her mirror, verifying Crozier was following close behind. He drove a surprisingly old minivan for a guy looking for upscale housing.

Returning her attention to the road, she crept along at the 35 mph speed limit, struggling with what to do next.

She shivered, reliving his constant attempts at physical contact. Her scalp crawled as if mice feet were tiptoeing across her auburn tresses. She had dodged and weaved for the nearly forty minutes they had spent in that lovely house as she struggled to avoid the persistent pawing, the rubbing, and the leers.

Now they were on to the next property, and she didn't want to face him alone again. She thought of the recent news of another redhead murdered by some delusional loony ... dressing them in party dresses. Girls who looked a lot like her. She shivered, her back now ridged with a mountain range of goose bumps.

She shook her head and sighed. Not likely Crozier was that guy or he would've tried to grab her at the first house. Would her little canister of pepper spray be enough to save her? What a scary thought.

Both her mom and Lisa Howell had admonished her not to display houses alone. Women sales agents working solo had occasionally been attacked while showing a residence. Not usually murdered though. Raped, mostly ... but that was certainly bad enough.

Shelly grimaced, grinding her teeth as she came to a resolution. She would *not* go into this next house with Handsy Andy without backup. She dialed the office again, seeking advice.

"From what you're telling me," Lois Howell said, "I don't want you there alone with this pervert, or whatever he is. I can be at your next stop in ten minutes, so stall him. Plead inexperience, or something, but stay locked in your car until I arrive."

"Thanks, Lois, but shouldn't a man ...?"

"Both guys are in the field. I'm licensed to carry. My 9mm S & W is a pretty good pacifier, and I'm not afraid to use it, either."

"Okay," Shelly said. Her breath seeped past clenched lips. "I hate inconveniencing you like this, but he scares me."

"As well he should. That's what your broker is for. Better to lose a sale then end up in the hospital ... or worse. Meander around the neighborhood a bit to delay things. I'm on the way. I'll try to beat you to the site."

"What'll I tell him, when he sees you there?"

"Don't worry about that. I'll say I'm just checking up on how my newest employee is treating our clients."

"Okay. Sounds good. That's what I'll say if we arrive first. That you called and told me to wait for you."

"Right. See you in a few."

Shelly disconnected and exhaled, first realizing how very tense she'd been. Her whitened knuckles regained their color as she eased her strangle hold on the steering wheel. Everything would work out just fine.

She turned north off of 163rd Street for three blocks, and then back west, circling the location of the next house on her list. Her cell phone rang, and glancing at the Bluetooth display on her dash, she saw it was Crozier.

"Where are you going? You're driving in circles."

"Sorry, I got distracted by a call from the office, and I missed my turn. We'll be there in a few minutes."

"Anything I should know about?" His voice was soft and measured. Was he angry?

"It was my broker. She's joining us at the next house. Sort of a quality check on my work. I'm pretty new at this, you know."

"I think you're doing just fine. We've established a real rapport. You don't need her."

"Not my choice. She's the boss, and she told me to wait for her before going into the house."

"That's not necessary, Shelly. I think …."

"Look, it's her office and her listing. If she wants to handle it, then she will." Her voice had taken on an unintended sharpness.

"Jeez, I'm sorry. I didn't mean to make you angry."

"No, it's me that should apologize." She shook her head, disgusted at her outburst. He is a client, creepy or not. "I just don't want to do anything to anger my boss. You understand?"

"Sure. Sure. I just thought … well, I like you. You remind me of a girlfriend back in high school. Anyway, when your broker arrives, I'll tell her what a great job you're doing. Okay?"

"Yes. Fine. The house is on the next block. We can wait in our cars if Miss Howell isn't there yet."

"Okay. Whatever you say. I don't want to get you into any kind of trouble."

"Thanks," she said and disconnected the call.

The ranch-style home loomed ahead on her right, and she slid her Rav4 up to the curb. He parked, twenty feet behind.

She left her engine idling so she could have A/C. It wasn't so hot out, but she was reluctant to open her windows for a breeze, with Mr. Inappropriate lurking about. And she was teed up and ready to get away if things suddenly got dicey.

# 34

The three of them stood in the shaded portico of the two-story Tudor, the last of the properties visited that strange afternoon.

"So, what do you think?" Shelly asked, looking first at Crozier, and then glancing at her boss.

The broker had lingered in the background, allowing the young agent to run the last three showings with little of her own input. Bill Crozier had been a perfect gentleman throughout.

"It's strange, because I was prepared to want a ranch house. I like the idea of not climbing stairs, but the first one you showed me, and this one, seems perfect. And with both masters and dens on the first floors, stairs are less of an issue."

"Well," Lois said, edging forward, "they're both great houses. I do believe the seller of the first one may be more willing to dicker on price, however."

And, Shelly knew, it was NMB's listing, which doubled the commission if they made the sale. She studied his chocolate eyes, no longer spooked by his earlier behavior.

"Are you ready to make an offer?" Lois asked.

"Are you kidding?" He grinned. "I'm not suicidal. My family's still up north. I picked up this old van to get around while here alone, and to help with the move.

"I'll fly Debbie down next week for two days to look at them both. Might be a good idea to find a couple of others to view, too, in the unlikelihood she passes on these. However, I'm pretty sure she'll love that first house ... especially that kitchen and back yard."

"I think that's a good plan. The wife should always know *everything*," Shelly said, "To avoid marital problems."

Crozier paled and did a little shuffle, jamming his hands into his pockets.

"So if we're finished here," Lois said, "we'll let you go, and you can call Shelly when your wife arrives so we can set up the visits." She waived a hand toward his van, unprepared to abandon her agent until this strange man was on his way.

Crozier nodded and turned to his young agent. "I want to thank you for this afternoon. You really did a great job of picking the right kinds of properties for us."

He extended his hand, and after a minor pause, she took it for a formal, unthreatening shake. Then he shook the broker's hand and turned to leave. Glancing over his shoulder, he made a parting comment.

"Miss Howell can be proud of your professionalism, Miss Weitz. You're an excellent agent." He strode off as the two women exchanged glances.

Shelly's lips ticked up. "He didn't seem nearly so dangerous after you arrived, Lois, but I'm glad you came along for the rest of the afternoon."

"Me too," she replied. "He may have not caused any real trouble, but a female agent is better being safe then exposing herself to possible rape ... or worse. Driving over, I was thinking about those five young redheads that were murdered recently."

"Yeah. That occurred to me too."

"I saw the last victim's photo on TV last night. She could almost be your twin. So I want you to be doubly careful. You're never to show any properties alone. And I mean *never*. That's not a suggestion. That's an order, from your boss. Get it?"

"Yes ma'am, I got it." She chuckled. "I don't need any convincing on that subject. I'll be careful."

"Good," Lois said as they exited the portico, heading for their cars.

¤ ¤ ¤

Shelly was waiting at the intersection with 163ʳᵈ Street when her cell phone trilled. The Bluetooth display on the Toyota's dash showed it was William Crozier calling.

"Mister Crozier? Was there something else you needed?"

"No. Well, I guess, yes. I need to apologize."

"Apologize? For what?" She knew "for what," but was astonished that he might too.

"When your broker showed up ... the looks she gave me ... I suddenly realized how crass I'd been acting. Jesus, I was actually trying to grope you. I'm mortified at my behavior."

"Yes, well I must admit it made me a bit uneasy."

"Look, there's no excuse, but I hope you'll give me a moment to explain."

"Certainly." Spying an opening between oncoming cars, she darted onto the busy avenue, heading west. "I'm listening."

"Thanks. Remember I said you reminded me of a girlfriend from high school? That was only partly true. You remind me of someone I *wished* were my girlfriend: Helen Pearl. I used to think of her as 'The Ruby and the Pearl.' I'm a nostalgia junkie, and I loved the old Nat King Cole songs. It kinda fitted, with the red hair and the name.

"She was every guy's heartthrob ... gorgeous and sensual, at least in our fantasies. We were in many classes together, went to the same parties, ran in similar crowds, but I was always too shy to ask her out. She dated mostly upper classmen."

"The high school dream girl, huh?" she said, chuckling softly to herself.

"Right. Anyway, we were all in love with her. And she was a really nice gal. I realized years later that she probably liked me, based on the friendly contact we had throughout frosh and sophomore years, but I never mustered the courage to ask her for a date."

Shelly pulled into the alley behind the real estate agency, parking in their lot but not exiting her car. She let the engine idle to keep the Bluetooth phone connection active.

"Anyway," he continued, "when I saw you, images of Helen swarmed over me, and I guess all the years of restrained desire just got the better of me. I'm totally embarrassed that I allowed it to get so out of hand."

"Well, like I said, it did make me uncomfortable. Female agents have been attacked and raped when alone on sites. And then there's this lunatic who is murdering redheads that look a lot like me. Frankly, I was getting scared."

"Jeez, I'm so ashamed I put you through that."

"Well, it's all water under the bridge now. Let me know when you want to schedule appointments with your wife. Just so you know, I *will* be accompanied by another agent or Miss Howell, by her orders. I'm not allowed to show houses alone, at least until they catch this serial killer."

"I understand." He paused, and she could hear him breathing. "May I ask a favor of you ... and act of kindness, I hope."

She shrugged, eyebrows knitting together. What now?

"What is it?"

"I want you to be our realtor. To show us the houses and everything. I just hope you won't mention to my wife anything that happened earlier today. Debbie would kill me if she thought I was still obsessing over Helen Pearl."

"She knows the story?"

"Yeah. We were all in school together. All the girls were jealous of Helen."

"Don't worry. I have no reason to bring it up. Have a good evening."

She sighed and ended the call.

*Men! Who can figure them?*

She locked her car and headed for the office.

# 35

He turned into a Publix lot, and slid the minivan into a parking slot shaded by a large live oak tree. The engine was left idling, the A/C whirring away in deference to the gathering heat of a late spring afternoon.

Smiley slouched against the slightly reclined driver's captain's seat, arms folded across his chest, as he surveyed the comings and goings of busy shoppers. His lips tightened, turning down, as he massaged a small tick at the corner of his right eye.

*Damn. This is getting me nowhere. I'm cruising all the probable spots, but how likely is it that I'll see her wandering across a supermarket's or mall's blacktop, pushing a shopping cart.*

Even if he'd found the right venue, she could have passed by ten minutes before, or an hour later. He'd cruised all the best shopping areas in Miami Shores, Biscayne Park and even the Bay Harbor Islands with "no joy," as his pilot dad would say.

He had become uncharacteristically impatient, not allotting anything near sufficient time to do the job professionally. And this *was* a task at which he usually excelled.

So why the rush? He exhaled noisily, cupping his hands behind his head, elbows spread wide. Well, Bal Harbor was his last stop on the four-day swing. It seemed a possible locale for Camille ... upscale and trendy, but he'd not found her there.

North Miami was the next village on the map.

Sitting forward, powering the electric seat into driving position, he tightened his jaw. He was going to bypass that town and go directly to North Miami Beach. He shook his head and grunted, determined to delay no longer.

He had forced himself to follow his grid search pattern, despite *knowing* where Camille was. Uncertainty had fueled his delay after his last failure. Eleven times now he'd mistaken other women for his redheaded love.

He'd almost lost control, struggling to restrain violence bubbling inside, when the last girl, who insisted her name was Elke, proved to be another fraud. Had he known all along she was an imposter, sure in his heart he finally *had* found his love, seeing her entering that real estate office on 163rd Street?

But at that time he was sure this last girl, this Elke, was Camille, so he had centered his efforts and considerable talent on her ... and was *wrong* again. Too damned many fuck ups.

He massaged his eyes, a small whimper escaping his lips before he backed out of the parking slot, and exited the lot, heading for home.

It was after six and his stomach was grumbling, seeking the solace of an Outback hamburger, smothered with sautéed onions and mushrooms. Maybe he'd treat himself to that big fried onion they specialized in. He craved comfort food to settle his soul and prepare him for his final quest.

It may take a few days to relocate Camille in North Miami Beach, and then devise a ploy to get close enough to convince her to return to him. He was flooded with confidence. They would be together again, finally preparing to go to their prom.

He sighed, remembering how beautifully he'd adorned his last error. The loveliest, and last, of all his elegant outfits.

He would have to buy Camille an appropriate prom dress.

# 36

Al Warner hurried down the steps of his townhouse, the corner of his lips ticking up in a lopsided grin.

*Gonna be late again. Every time Eva sleeps over I can't seem to get outta the house without an early morning diversion. I guess I'd better set the clock thirty-minutes earlier.*

He retrieved Mrs. Gerber's newspaper, hurrying back up his neighbor's stoop, to save her arthritic bones the steps.

Strange. Yesterday's paper was still nestled where he'd left it the morning before. He paused, glancing at his watch. He had this serial lunatic to catch, but it was unlike Adele to leave the day's events unread. Sighing, he resolved to delay crime-fighting for a few minutes to check on his eighty-seven-year-old widowed neighbor.

He punched the bell button, setting off a cascade of musical chimes. Thirty seconds later he repeated the act, but no one appeared at the door.

He cast indecision aside and withdrew a small leather zippered wallet from his gray cargo pants pocket and extracted his lock-pick set. Forty-seconds later he was inside the Gerber foyer, his gaze sweeping the living room and den. Both empty.

He glanced at the stairway and realized her lift chair was parked at the top. She would never descend without using her power ride. He strode to the base of the stairs.

"Adele? It's Al Warner. Are you up there?"

"Adele?" he called again when she didn't reply. He edged up the stairs, conflicted over invading her privacy or helping a friend in need. She'd been the grandmother he never had.

"The hell with it," he muttered and bounded upward, taking two at a time. He hesitated outside her bedroom door.

"Adele? It's Al Warner." He strained to hear, but nothing. "Are you okay?" Still nothing.

"I'm comin' in," he said, and then pushed through the ajar door. She wasn't on the bed, which was rumpled, with all the bedding pulled down the far side. Circling around, he spied her lying on the floor in a crumpled pile, tangled in the covers.

He dropped to his knees, feeling her neck for a pulse. Good. She was alive and delivering a reasonably robust heartbeat. Pale blue eyes fluttered open.

"Detective. Nice to see you." Her voice was thready, but her lips edged into a smile.

"Are you okay? You gave me a hell of a start."

"I don't know. Yesterday, when I tried to get up, my legs seemed numb." She paused, panting, and closed her eyes for a moment. Her eyes slitted open. "I got tangled in the sheets and fell out of bed. I guess I passed out."

"You've been like this since yesterday mornin'?"

"I guess," her voice a bare whisper. "If you say so."

Warner dialed 9-1-1 on his cell phone and requested an ambulance. Next he called Eva, still at his townhouse, asking her to come over to tend to Mrs. Gerber. He had to get to work, but he wouldn't abandon his elder neighbor without someone to watch over her until the paramedics arrived.

He worried she may have had a stroke.

Ten minutes later, he was heading downtown, just as he heard the warble of the EMTs coming from the opposite direction.

Time to get back to catching their elusive Prom Dress Killer.

¤ ¤ ¤

Warner's cell phone trilled as he pushed through the doors of the squad room. He checked the caller ID.

"Eva. What's up?"

"They've got Adele in a private room and are running tests. There's no indication of a stroke."

He spotted Jack Harris slouched against a desk, staring at the Murder Board, and he headed toward him.

"So, any diagnosis?" He regretted any distraction from the killer he was hunting, but he really admired that old lady, and they'd come to share a warm bond.

"Well, it may be sort of a chicken or egg thing. It looks like her legs may have tangled in the blanket as she was trying to get up. She remembers falling off the bed, and they think that may have caused a lower disc problem, pinching a nerve."

"Okay. Look, I'm up to my ears in alligators here. Can you stick around until you know what they think? She's got a son in New Jersey, but there's nobody local. Get his number and call him. She's a sweet old gal, and I'm sorta her go-to guy here."

"Of course. I don't have any patients until this afternoon. I'll stick around, and once we have a diagnosis, I'll call him."

"Thanks babe. I ... you know. I don't know how ...."

"It's okay, Al. You don't have to say it. I love *you* too. Now go catch a killer. I'll take care of this end."

"Thanks." He pocketed his phone and turned to Harris.

"Any news ... good or bad, Jack?"

"Nah. The street cops and some of the detectives are still scrubbing the area for shops that sell those kinds of fancy dresses. So far, we've found two sales, but both checked out for kids actually going to a prom."

"There a lot of shops for that frilly stuff?" He resisted his recent habit of exploring his head-wound scars.

"Forty-eight in Dade County so far. No count on Broward or Palm Beach, but they're still looking in both those counties, too."

"Right. And they're leavin' contact info, in case our boy shows up later?"

"Yeah. We're handing out fliers at every store on what to look for, so it ain't outta sight, outta mind."

"Good job. So far this is our only shot at him. We don't want it to fall between the cracks."

Warner pivoted and staring at the sprawling white magnetic board, festooned with photos of victims and crime scenes. Scrawled red and black marker notes, lines, and arrows, struggled to make connections where there really were none.

"Who *are* you, you crafty bastard?" Warner muttered.

"He's an enigma, for sure," Harris said, joining his boss.

"Thanks to the BAU ... and Eva, too... we got a pretty good idea of the who and the why for his pool of vics, Jack. But not a single damned inklin' of who *he* is or where he came from."

"But despite that, Al, no matter how strongly we caution the public, some pretty young redhead's gonna be careless enough to be his next toy." Harris scratched his considerable nose.

"Unfortunate." Warner sighed. "But probably true. And we got zip chance of catchin' him until that happens. I just hope, whoever she is, she's smart enough to play his game long enough for us to nab him before he sends her off to his imagined prom."

"It's a shitty way to run an investigation, boss, waiting for ... almost *hoping* for ... another vic."

"Ain't that the truth," Warner said with a grunt as he turned away and headed for his office.

# 37

Shelly Weitz rapped the file on her desk, neatly stacking the sheets before stapling them together. She slipped the slim pack into a folder labeled "Ingram," and laid it on the right side of her desk.

Their bid of $2,150,000 in reply to the seller's counter of $2,250,000 had been accepted, subject to the usual buyer's inspection. That was finishing up now with no serious problems uncovered. The Wind Mitigation scrutiny was positive, the mildew tests were negative, and everything else seemed to be falling in line. A few minor things here and there, falling well within the thousand-dollar limit.

All the check-ups were scheduled to finish tomorrow, and the closing was tentatively set for next month, five weeks from now. Since this was NMB's listing, the agency would split most of its six-percent commission with her, after the one percent deducted for the listing agent: a whopping $53,750 to Shelly on her first sale.

She grinned. She could finally afford to move out of her tiny studio apartment and into something nicer ... maybe even a townhouse. Even at twenty-five-hundred a month, she'd still have over a year's worth of living expense cash to work with.

Now Debbie Crozier was arriving on Friday, and if she loved the same house her creepy husband had ... another NMB listing ... Shelly might be pocketing another twelve-thousand in commissions. No wonder good realtors (something she already considered herself to be) lived so well. She was going to set up a mutual fund account—something conservative—where she'd lay aside expected federal income tax expense to hopefully grow during the year, awaiting next April 15. This would be the first time she earned enough to actually owe taxes.

She swiveled to and fro in the like-new black leather executive chair she'd bought on sale at the local resale shop, her first indulgence. Her gray eyes probed, unfocused, a future beyond her current visibility.

She was striving to acquire two new listings, one from a friend at the gym and the other from one of her mom's neighbors. Both were moving out of state and Shelly had caught them at their early decision-making time. Listing agents make commission, regardless of who sells the property.

A small head shake dragged her into the here-and-now. Her mom was finally getting around pretty well on her own. Shelly had lingered there, unwilling to trust the full-time nurse without supervision. But it was time to move back to her apartment, and start the search for new, more comfortable digs.

Rolling up to her desktop computer, she accessed rental listings from the MLS site. She had decided to rent first, to see how she liked living in a townhouse, before she invested in a purchase.

Entering a few parameters, including a North Miami Beach/North Miami location and a maximum rental of twenty-five-hundred per month, she scrolled through several opportunities, printing out five. She'd cruise past those after work, checking out their exterior condition and the neighborhoods, before setting up appointments for viewing.

Her excitement at finding more comfortable living space was momentarily tamped down by an eerie feeling of being followed. She never actually saw anything suspicious. Well maybe once when she thought she glimpsed a van that looked like Crozier's. Hard to believe he'd be stalking her, though, with his wife arriving in two days.

Oh hell. He'd made her so jumpy she was seeing things around every corner. Still, there was that lunatic killing redheaded girls, which was plenty enough to make her edgy. She'd read that a lot of likely-looking possible victims were dying or bleaching their hair. No way would she let some nut make her change who she was. She'd just be as vigilant as possible.

She sighed and gathered her papers, cramming them into her briefcase, adjusted the three file folders on her desk into an orderly stack, and then headed out the back door. She was having dinner with her mom tonight and they were going to a movie ... her mother's first night out since the accident.

Tomorrow was Thursday, her day off, and she'd begin her search for a new place to live. She only had two months left on her current lease, so the timing was perfect.

¤ ¤ ¤

Parked across the street in a dry-cleaner's lot, he watched her through the large plate-glass window as she packed up and started toward the agency's rear entrance. He wouldn't be able to tell which way she left, but Smiley suspected she was headed to her mom's house.

Camille was such a devoted daughter. He had no idea her mother lived in South Florida now. In fact, he had no inkling her mother lived at all. He was pretty sure he'd settled that, back in Chicagoland. Maybe this was a step-mom of sorts, someone to provide succor after the "tragic" demise of her birth parents.

Whatever, this woman didn't have to suffer if Camille came with him willingly. Following her was no problem, since while she was at work he planted a tracker on her Rav4 and a remote Bluetooth mic that would monitor any of her in-car phone conversations. She used her cell phone in the car a lot, so he'd always be privy to her plans. He'd be able to plot a perfect opportunity to bring her back to him.

And this *was* Camille. He'd never been surer of anything. His tongue darted across his lips, ticking at the corners of his mouth. He could almost taste her kiss.

Finally! They'd be together again, and they could attend their long-denied prom: The king and queen of the ball.

He'd have to make time to find an appropriate dress for her. Something classic and more beautiful than any he'd wasted on all those pretenders. He may make the trip to that shop he passed in Jupiter, while on his way to Miami. It was all the way at the top of Palm Beach County ... an eighty-mile drive ... but he'd noticed some quality dresses in the window. And he'd made it a rule not to shop near where he 'worked.'

He wiggled in his seat and adjusted his pants as he grew hard. God, this was so exciting.

Starting the van, he switched on the tracker viewer, locating the LED-lit red blip moving across the mapped streets on the screen.

*Camille. I'm coming for you. We'll be so happy again.*

He put the Dodge in gear and started after her, in no particular hurry. He'd await the perfect time to make her his again. A few days at most.

His unaccustomed grin was not a thing of beauty.

# 38

Shelly sat at her kitchenette counter, studying her laptop's screen, making notes.

Thursday was her day off from the office, a rare chance to sleep in. After a leisurely breakfast of a pair of eggs over easy, three strips of crisp bacon and one of her homemade buttermilk biscuits, she'd spent two hours working on her novel.

She was a hundred pages in, and to her surprise the intended romance had morphed into a time-travel thriller. A best-selling author speaking at the writers conference in Orlando last fall, had said the characters of a novel often take over the action, taking it to places the author never expected.

That certainly had happened to her currently untitled work, and it was damned exciting. She had revised her story outline and envisioned the next ten chapters, and she was as eager to see where they led as any future reader might be.

But now she'd taken a break to research available rentals, looking for new, more comfortable digs. The Ingram sale was finalized, with all the inspections passed and the twenty-five per cent down payment ensconced in NMB's escrow account. Their mortgage had been preapproved so there was no pending impediment to final closing in less than four weeks.

Last weekend Mister Inappropriate's wife had arrived, and she loved the same house he had. The Crozier's subsequent bid was accepted after a pair of counter offers, so there was another twelve thousand bucks just around the corner. In three months she'd already earned about seventy thousand in commissions and had landed the two new listings she'd been after. Those were bound to up her earnings total sometime later that year.

She was zeroed in on finding a townhouse to rent. Shelly had scrawled on a yellow-lined pad four likely listing: addresses, basic apartment info, and leaser's (all other realtors) phone numbers. She'd make appointments using the Bluetooth in her car while running errands that afternoon.

She chuckled as she closed and packed her laptop in the copious shoulder bag she used as a purse. She was a young woman in a techno world who still loved the feel of pen and paper.

Everything would eventually end up in the computer as a permanent record, but she'd refine it the old-fashioned way.

# 39

His chortle was soft and mirthless, as he laid aside his iPad after successfully recording Camille's cell phone conversation with three realtors about rental listings for four townhouses.

*Foolish girl, wasting your time. You'll be living with me soon. No need for any other home, but at least I know where I can find you now.*

She had set several appointments for Sunday, using her alias, Rochelle Weitz. Where did she come up with such a name? Rochelle wasn't bad, but not nearly as classy as Camille. Was she trying to hide from him? He had no idea why. They were soul mates.

Smiley had entered the parking lot of a five-store strip mall. It was late afternoon, and many shops were preparing to close. Better hurry. He exited his van and strode toward his objective: *A Bit of Nostalgia*, the clothing resale store he'd noticed while driving by last month.

A tinkling bell announced his entry and drew the attention of a fiftyish balding man with bushy gray sideburns and a waxed handlebar moustache. Playing the part, Smiley guessed.

"Can I help you?" he asked, setting aside some hangered shirts he was carrying. "I was about to close, but I always make time for clients."

"Thank you. I won't be long. I'd like to see that fancy dress in your front window."

"Dress? Which one?"

"The pink and blue. Sort of a party dress. It's for my sister."

"Ah, yes. I know the one." He retrieved a ring of keys from under the counter. "For a special occasion?"

"Yeah. Her Senior Prom. But she doesn't know it yet."

"Aha. She has a secret admirer, huh?" He unlocked the sliding glass panel and reached inside.

The short, muscular man nodded.

"Kind of early, isn't it? The proms aren't usually for another two months," the older man said.

"I like to be prepared, and she isn't able to afford the dress on her own. I love these classic outfits instead of those sleek modern things the kids seem to wear nowadays."

"Yes. Obviously I agree. That's why my store deals exclusively in classy retro clothing." The man held the dress up for Smiley's inspection. "A beauty, isn't it? Absolute classic sixties."

"Yes. How much?" He retrieved a fat envelope, stuffed with cash, from his beige cargo pants pocket.

"A hundred-twenty-five, and since you seem to be paying cash, I can waive the sales tax. Good for both of us."

"Yeah," he said counting out six twenties and a five.

"I'll write you a receipt." He was pawing through papers behind the counter, looking for his pad.

"Not necessary," Smiley said, glancing up and finding the clerk staring at him.

"Okay. Whatever you say." He glanced again at a paper on the low rear shelf, and then back at the young man across the counter, and seemed to have trouble swallowing. "So, if that's all, I'm really late in closing. I've … I've got some place to be." A light dew of perspiration blossomed on his forehead and bald pate.

"Thanks for your help. Camille will love this." He started toward the door, watching the man's reflection in the plate glass, reaching for his phone. Hearing three distinctive dialing beeps, Smiley paused at the exit and sighed.

"Oh, one more thing I just remembered," he said, pivoting back. "Can I see that hat?" pointing toward a lacy creation on a display shelf.

The salesman hesitated, and then lowered the phone. "Of course. Another classic." His voice quavering, rising an octave.

He circled the counter, moving to the rack, taking a quick glance at Smiley who was close behind. As he extracted the bonnet, Smiley reached over his shoulder, grasping his chin with his left hand and the back of his head with his right. A sharp twist resulted in an audible crack, and the unfortunate clerk slumped to the floor, his neck broken. A quick and painless death.

"What was it you read that made me suddenly so interesting?" He hurried to the door, locking it and displayed the "CLOSED" sign.

On a shelf behind the counter he found a flier asking owners of stores such as this to be on the lookout for someone fitting him to a "T:" a man in his twenties or thirties who may be purchasing classic prom-style dresses.

The police knew more than he expected. Knew he may be looking for another dress. *Well, no matter. My search is over. This is the last dress I'll need, now that I've found Camille.*

He lugged the man behind the counter, out of sight from the street. He then rifled the cash register and snatched some costume jewelry from the display cabinet. Making this look like a robbery should cover his trail.

He froze, balanced on the balls of his feet, head cocked to one side, listening. There was someone ... *oh shit* ... he snatched up the phone. The clerk had hung it backwards and it was still transmitting. Snarling, he ripped out the connection. A 9-1-1 call would bring the cops, even with no one talking. Maybe even quicker because of that.

He scurried around the shop, wiping down anything he thought he may have touched.

Searching the eves, he spotted a surveillance camera. Hurrying into the back, he found an office where the recorder was stored: an old style VHS with a cassette tape, which he snatched out and pocketed. He checked to see he'd done whatever he could, then was out the back door, carrying the dress, covered in a long plastic bag.

There may be security cameras in the parking lot, but the best he could do was to keep his head down and move quickly. Luckily he'd smudged his license plate with mud. He'd been at this for years, and no one had found him out yet.

He exited the lot, racing off at five over the speed limit, just as he heard the warbling song of fast approaching squad cars.

Safely away with his prize.

He was untouchable.

Or so he thought.

# 40

Tinkling door chimes announced a tall, lanky, almost skeletal man, ducking under yellow crime scene tape as he entered the shop. He mopped his brow and receding forehead with a maroon handkerchief, and muttered in a squeaky sing-song voice.

"Damned summer coming earlier and earlier every year. Must be close to ninety already." His fingers brushed a pencil-thin salt-and-pepper moustache and the scant Van Dyke decorating the narrow chin on his hatchet face.

"The cold morgue doesn't prepare ya for the heat, does it, Doc?" a chunky Latino said with a chuckle, as he rose from behind the jewelry counter. His sport jacket lay across the glass-covered cabinet. His collar was open with the tie tugged down.

"You don't look any more comfortable than me, Detective."

"No, it's hot for sure. They got the A/C jacked up now, so it should be okay in a few. Meanwhile, let me show ya what we got." He motioned Doctor Magilly, the Palm Beach County Sheriff's M.E., to the narrow space behind the counter.

The proprietor's body was sprawled across the limited floor space, requiring almost ballet grace to avoid disturbing the corpse. His head lay swiveled at an unnatural angle.

"Looks like the COD is a broken neck," Detective Nogales said.

"Well, his neck is clearly broken, but it's yet to be determined if that was the cause of death, or an aftermath to it. I don't jump

[144]

to conclusions, Felipe, no matter how obvious it may seem. Was this a robbery or something else?"

"You know I don't jump to conclusions either, Doc."

"Touché." His soprano giggle was almost feminine. "No one has moved the body?"

"Nope. I was able to fish out his wallet to confirm his ID: Anton Braun. He owned this store with his oldest son, Gustav."

"Young Mister Braun has been notified?"

"Jupiter PD's on it, but so far, no joy. Seems like he and his wife are outta town."

The M.E. withdrew a thermometer he'd plunged into the corpse's liver, jotting the results in his notebook.

"How cold was it when you arrived, Detective? The A/C was running?"

"Yeah, set at seventy-eight, so just comfortable. You got a TOD for me?"

"Based on body temp," the M.E. glanced at the thermometer, tweaking his moustache, "I estimate five to seven p.m. last night."

"That makes sense. The perp comes in at closing time. Maybe fakes a buy, then kills the guy and cleans out the joint." Detective Nogales straightened from leaning over the display case as a Jupiter PD detective came in from the rear of the shop.

"Any luck with surveillance tapes?" Nogales asked.

"Sorry Detective. He had an old-style machine, but the VCR cassette was gone. Forensics is dusting for prints, but it all looks wiped down. Maybe we'll get lucky, but ...."

"Figures," he said, glancing at the ME, rising from examining the body.

"I've done my prelim." He signaled to two men with a gurney. "Load him up and get him to the morgue. I should have a

COD later today. The obvious seems the most likely at the moment."

"Well, robbery seems the most likely here, too. Not the usual stick-em-up approach, I'm guessing. Looks like he faked a buy, like I said." The detective nodded toward the disabled phone.

"Braun must have suspected something, 'cause he managed to dial 9-1-1, but then the perp somehow distracted him. The phone was live and the 9-1-1 operator heard everything. The perp fakes another buy ... something about a hat from what the operator heard on the phone." He gestured at two feathered and flowered bonnets scattered across the floor next to a wall-mounted hat rack.

"Looks like he ambushed the poor guy from the back, presuming the COD *is* the broken neck. Pretty strong *muchacho* to be so quick and deadly.

"He made it away clean," the sheriff's detective continued, "before the Jupiter squad cars arrived. Fast and efficient. Definitely a pro."

"Looking at those marks on the floor," the doctor said, "it appears he dragged the body back here to keep it out of sight. That's probably when he noticed the phone off the hook. Maybe we'll find some DNA or prints on the vic somewhere, once I've got him in the lab."

"Good luck," the PBSO detective said. "Gotta get some guys in here and figure out what's missing." He snagged his sport coat, slinging it over his shoulder. "Emptied the cash register and snatched some costume jewelry for sure, but that hardly seems reason to kill the guy.

"I'll check the mall's office," Nogales said, heading out, "and see if they got any helpful footage from their parking lot cameras."

He turned to the Jupiter detective. "Hey, bud, ask your tech guys to pull any local store and street footage, too. See if we can get a line on this guy, or at least his vehicle."

"Good idea," the man said, toggling his radio to pass on the request. Finishing the transmission, he hooked Detective Nogales' arm as he was ducking under the yellow tape.

"My captain wanted to thank the PBSO for your help on this. We don't get many murders in Jupiter, and your M.E. and lab's got skills we just don't have."

"That's why we're here," the detective said, slipping on his sport coat. "The sheriff's office has been pretty much all hands on deck, helping Miami-Dade find their latest serial nutcase. But we can't ignore local needs, and what we got here seems pretty cold blooded. A killer is a killer, and we're gonna help you catch this guy."

"Thanks again. Our robbery unit's on the way. Detective Dupre'll be on lead. I'll give him your card. He'll get back to you, once he gets a handle on what's missing here."

"Swell. It's nice to work on something simple for a change."

But simplicity had aimed them in the wrong direction.

# 41

Shelly reviewed the items spread across her desk: her laptop, the notebook filled with a lined paper pad, three pens, plus a yellow highlighter, a digital TLR camera for better photos than she could get with her phone a thermos of hot coffee, and three chocolate/hazelnut granola bars.

Satisfied she'd covered any eventuality, she loaded all except her laptop into her spacious shoulder bag. She cradled the small computer under one arm and readjusting the strap of the now weighty bag as she headed for her employer's office. Two soft raps on the jamb and she stuck her head inside.

"Lois. I'm on my way. I want to thank you for letting me off early today so I can get started on this."

"You deserve it, Shelly. You've made all your arrangements?" the realtor asked.

"Yep. Got two appointments this afternoon at three and five, and then two more after dinner."

"A busy schedule, huh? You're not wasting any time finding a new place."

"Yeah. No moss growing on this rolling stone. I've really been looking forward to a nicer place to live, and you giving me this break has made it happen."

"You're who made it happen, Shelly. I couldn't be more pleased. You've accomplished more than any newbie agent I've ever seen."

"Thanks. It's been exciting, and I gotta admit I just got lucky with the Ingrams. Just being in the right place at the right time."

"That *was* luck, but finding the right property and making the sale ... that was good, professional work."

"I appreciate that coming from you, Lois. So, gotta run. My first appointment is in thirty minutes. I'm really excited."

"You know, with what you're clearing on these two sales you can afford to buy that townhouse, instead of renting."

"True, but I'm gonna rent first to see how I like the area. The first one has a buy option, so that'll be on the table if I'm still in love with it."

"Smart. So, good luck, and be careful. No more Croziers, I hope."

"Not likely." Shelly smiled. "All the listings are with established real estate agents, so I'm not worried." She waived as she disappeared from the doorway.

"No reason not to be careful," Lois called after her. It's a dangerous world out there, especially lately for young, attractive redheads.


Shelly slid a CD into the disc player of her Rav4 as she exited the parking lot: 'Scheherazade, by Rimsky-Korsakov. It was her favorite. They spelled the ancient storyteller's name differently than in "The Thousand and One Nights" her mother used to read to her, but it told the same story: a resourceful woman gentling a vengeful man with tantalizing tales.

Her kind of gal.

Her first appointment was with an agent from RE/MAX Realty, for a townhouse with two bedrooms, a den, and a modern kitchen. From the description and photos it seemed like her potentially best choice. She liked to leave the best for last, but schedule problems with the other three agents dictated against that. She'd see them all, no matter how alluring this one was.

She had fifteen minutes to make the appointment at three p.m. Plenty of time, even if there was a little traffic.

She hummed to the strains of the solo violin, portraying Scheherazade's voice, begging the emir to listen to her tale.

A woman wrestling with her fate.

A woman succeeding, just like Shelly.

# 42

"NMB Realty. This is Lois Howell." She was alone in the office, lingering late to tie up some files and balance the escrow account.

"Lois. I'm glad I caught you. This is Markos Panos, RE/MAX Realty."

"Oh hi, Markos. What Can I do for you?"

"I'm calling about your agent, Shelly Weitz."

"Ah, yes. She was to see a townhouse rental with you today. How did it go? From what she said, yours ...."

"That's the problem. She didn't show."

"What? She left in plenty of time to make your three o'clock date."

"No, not three. An agent from your office called and said she'd be delayed until five. Some sort of problem at home with her mom or something. Worked out great for me 'cause I was finishing another showing that was running late. But she never arrived, so I thought I'd better check to see if everything was okay."

"One of my agents called? I don't think ...."

"Yeah. A guy. I didn't catch his name."

"That's very strange because we talked just as she was leaving, and she didn't mention any change of plans. I think she was supposed to meet someone from Premier Realty at five. It's not like Shelly to mix things up. She's very organized."

"Well, that may be, but like I said, she never showed up."

"Listen, Markos, I'm sorry for the waste of your time. I know it's something we have little enough to spare. I've only got two male agents. I'm going to call them and see what's up. Either I or she will call to straighten this out, once we have the answers. Frankly, I'm a bit concerned. This is just not like Shelly."

"Okay," he said. "I'm not angry or anything. Shit happens. I just thought you should know."

"I appreciate that, Markos, and I *will* get back to you, once I have the facts. Someone owes you an apology."

She disconnected and immediately called Oleg Karlov's cell phone. He was just arriving home, but knew nothing of Shelly's schedule and never made a call for her to change the appointment. Lois spent five minutes soothing his ruffled feathers, assuring him he wasn't being accused of playing another gag on their newbie.

A second call to Clive Dipple produced the same results. He hadn't talked to Shelly since she researched a property for him, two days ago.

Scrounging around the girl's desk, the realtor found some of her notes scribbled on yellowed lined paper, nestled in her waste basket. She called the other three agents on the redhead's schedule, but got the same response ... two of them a bit peeved at a no-show wasting their time. They complained that a fellow realtor should know better.

Lois bit her lip, her brow furrowed, weighing her next move. After a few moments of pacing indecision, she called Helen Weitz to see if she'd heard from her daughter.

"Well, no, I haven't," she said. "She was viewing townhouses, looking for a new place to live. Said she was on a tight schedule so she'd grab a bite somewhere between appointments. I don't expect to hear from her until later."

"Damn," Lois muttered.

"Miss Howell? Is something wrong?"

"I hate to worry you, Mrs. Weitz, but Shelly never made any of her appointments." She wouldn't tell the mother about the mysterious change of time until she knew more.

"I hope she wasn't in an accident," the mother said. "We've had enough of those to last a good while. I'm going to check two local hospitals, just in case."

"Good idea. I have a friend with the North Miami Beach police. I'll see if he has any reports. I'll let you know what, if anything, I find out."

"Thanks. I'll talk to you later," Helen Weitz said, hanging up.

Two hours of frantic phone calls and an aimless drive around the area en route to Shelly's first appointment turned up nothing for the realtor.

It wasn't until the next morning that North Miami Beach Police discovered the girl's silver Rav4, stuck in the back of a Waffle House parking lot, six blocks from the first townhouse.

It was locked, with the keys nestled inside in a beverage holder. Her laptop was tucked under the rear seats along with her shoulder bag, still containing the digital camera and her wallet with fifty-seven dollars and a VISA card.

Nothing to indicate a robbery.

There was no sign of Shelly Weitz anywhere.

# 43

Smiley's audio bug in Shelly's SUV had alerted him to her plans ... a three p.m. scheduled viewing with a RE/MAX agent at a townhouse she was considering renting.

He placed a call from his car to agent Panos, using a burner phone.

"Hi. Our agent, Rochelle Weitz, has an appointment to meet you at three p.m., but she's running late because of an emergency with her mother. Does a change to five work for you?"

"Yes. That's actually better because I'm involved in writing up a contract," Markos Panos said. "Five should be fine. Is her mother okay?"

"Yes. Just recovering from an auto accident, but she's coming along. Can you reconfirm the address for the townhouse you're to show her?"

Smiley jotted it down, thanked the man, and disconnected. Everything was in place. The agent was filled with compassion for the poor girl, who was pretending to be this Shelly Weitz. So worried about her mother, also a phony since he knew Camille's real mother was in heaven ... or hell. Of this he was certain, as he'd sent the woman there himself, so many years ago.

He arrived at that sweet little townhouse thirty minutes before Camille's original appointment. The lock box on the door was immaterial. Deft use of his picks provided quick entry, and he'd left the door ajar for his love's appearance. His thoughts flittered to the last ersatz Camille, whom he'd ambushed in her lover's home.

He rued the damage he'd done to that unsuspecting Romeo, and the woman who'd proved to be another fake. Not empathy for the death and pain they'd suffered, but regret for the time and effort wasted on the wrong people.

Oh well. This time, it really *was* Camille. He'd never been more certain. Hurrying back to the street, he retrieved his Dodge Caravan. He backed it into the empty one-car garage and lowered the door.

A quick tour of the house familiarized him with its features. He would enjoy showing Camille around before convincing her to forsake this Shelly Weitz portrayal and come home with him.

Camille arrived on time, as he knew she would.

"Hello," she called, poking her head through the open doorway.

"Ms. Weitz?" he said, portraying Markos Panos, whom she'd never met. "Come in and let me show you this lovely townhouse."

"Thanks. Great location and sweet curb appeal. The master is downstairs, right?"

"Yes, with the second bedroom and en suite bath upstairs." He was pleased at how easily he flowed into the role.

"Perfect. My mom broke her leg in a car accident, so when she visits, she won't have to climb stairs. May I see the kitchen?"

"Certainly. This way." He guided her with a hand on her elbow, shivering with anticipation.

She glanced at him, gave a small head shake, and pulled her arm away. She strode toward the apparent entry to the small kitchen. The realtor followed close behind.

Shelly bit her lip, fighting a tickling tentacle of panic. This guy was a bit creepy. She hoped he wasn't going to be another

Crozier, having to defend herself against unwanted advances. He pressed so close to her, she was getting nervous.

Entering the kitchen she couldn't help but smile, thrusting away apprehension.

"Well, this is small but seems very functional, and so beautifully filled with almost new appliances. I love the molted granite counter and breakfast areas." She skimmed fingers over the smooth tan, brow, and gold-flecked stone surface.

She turned and bumped into Panos who was almost hanging over her. Eyebrows arched, she skipped back two steps and crossed her arms in front of her breasts. This guy was getting creepier by the minute.

"Excuse me," he said. "I thought you were going to go out the other way."

"No. I want to see the living room and the den. Then the upstairs. Okay?"

"Certainly. Right this way."

As she passed in front of him, he guided her with a hand at the small of the back, sending an army of goose bumps cascading down her spine. One more apparent pass, and she was going to make a run for it. She surreptitiously fingered the can of pepper spray in her pocket. She'd had enough of pushy men.

He followed her across the floor, a small frown creasing his otherwise almost plastic face. He was playing a game but she didn't seem to get it. Had he changed so much in eight years that she didn't recognize him? Time to alter that.

He'd intended to await their visit to the upstairs bedroom but couldn't stay his eagerness. Slipping closely behind as they entered the roomy den, he readied his cloth and chloroform bottle.

"Camille," he said, his voice soft and choked with passion, "this is not the house for you."

"Oh no, my name's not Camille," she spun around, "and your behavior isn't ...." She froze at the look on his face, eyeing the large white cloth he cradled in one hand. He snatched her arm, dragging her close. She was struggling to get a hand in her pocket, but his powerful hug trapped her arms.

Jerking her head back and forth she fought to avoid the strange-smelling rag he thrust over her nose and mouth

"Foolish girl," he whispered, as his left arm circled her back, drawing her supple body against his. "Of course it is," he muttered as his right hand pressed the chloroform-laden rag across her face.

She struggled futilely, kicking at his shins, an attempted scream muffled. She finally freed some sort of canister from her pocket, but it slipped from her fingers as she sagged against him.

"Foolish girl," he repeated, as he scooped up and pocketed the can of pepper spray. "It's time to come home with me, Camille. We have our prom to attend, even after all these years."

Smiley laid her on a handy family-room carpet that was a perfect size. He spent fifteen minutes wrapping and stowing his prize in the rear of his van. Then he wiped down anything he may have touched when his hands were uncovered by gloves. His DNA wasn't, to his knowledge, on file anywhere, but his fingerprints might be, from long ago and far away.

Moments later he pulled out of the garage, closed the door, and was on his way south, heading home.

Nearly an hour later, Smiley had backed into his garage, and after punching the button to raise the van's rear gate, he slid from the front seat. The Dodge's warning trill, signaling the opening gate, clashed with the screeching descent of the motorized garage door. He paused at the open compartment of his van, savoring his success.

*He had her*. Finally, Camille was back where she belonged. He gently unrolled the thin rug that encased his love, hiding her from prying eyes during their drive home.

Smiley brushed auburn hair from her still closed eyes, as she ventured through chloroform-induced sleep, surely dreaming of their coming time together.

It had gone perfectly. The master plan, flawlessly executed. Smiley was methodical and careful. Attention to detail was how he avoided problems.

He drew her into his arms, cradling her tenderly as he entered the house and headed for her bedroom ... *their* bedroom.

He actually smiled as he savored his success.

# 44

The buzz of his desk phone jerked Warner from the 'zone' he'd dropped into as he visualized what few facts he had on their killer.

"Homicide," he said, clearing his dried mouth.

"This Detective Warner?"

"Yeah. Who's this?"

"Dean Kracker, detective with North Miami Beach PD."

"Kracker, huh?" Warner couldn't squelch the chuckle.

"Yeah, and it's spelled with a "K." I've heard every conceivable Florida wisecrack there is, so save it."

"You won't hear it from me, Detective. So what can I do for you?"

"You're point man on this Prom Dress Killer, right?"

"Yes, I am." Warner tensed, grabbing a pad of paper and a pen. "You got something on that?"

"Yeah. I'm afraid it's probably your next victim. One Rochelle Weitz. Disappeared yesterday afternoon under very suspicious circumstances."

"Attractive redhead, mid-twenties to early thirties?" Warner jotted her name on the pad, with a three-stroke underline.

"You got it. She's a realtor up here and went off to look at some rental townhouses and never made it to the first appointment. The agent she was to meet got a call, supposedly from her office, saying she'd be two hours late."

"Sounds like a setup, and the perp knew her schedule," Warner mused aloud.

"Right. We found her car this morning in a parking lot, six-blocks away from the scene. There was an audio transmitter stuck under her dash. Someone was listening to her conversations."

"That may be our first break in this case," and it's about time, Warner thought. "Did you pull that agent's phone records? Get a location on the phone?"

"Yeah. Just got the info from Tech. Looks like a burner phone, so no trace on that. Call was pinged off a tower in NMB. No prints on the transmitter, either."

Warner sighed. "So we know he was probably tailin' her, but not much else."

"I'm afraid that's it, Detective. Anyhow, this is outta our league. We do mostly fraud and bunko up here. Thought you might want to come up with your team to see what you can dig up. You still got the Fibbies down there?"

"We do. A crackerjack team, too. Worked with 'em before. Give me your info and the location of the probable crime scene, and we'll be there within the hour." Warner scrawled phone numbers and addresses on his pad.

"You got the place taped hurt off, I hope?"

"Of course." A little twinge in his voice. "Got two patrol units sitting on it, too. I know this isn't one to take casually."

"Sorry. I didn't mean to sound condescendin'. It's just this case has been goin' nowhere, and it's damned frustratin' knowin' I gotta wait for his next vic to have any shot at catchin' this guy."

"Not a problem, Detective. I know you're the best we got on this kinda thing, so good luck. I'll stick around, to keep our department in the loop. Tag along where appropriate. This happened in our neighborhood, and we got a major interest in seeing this guy caught too."

"You bet. Glad to have you. We'll send a formal report on what, if anything, we turn up." Warner hung up, stretched, emitting a soft groan, and looked across the bullpen.

"Jack, where the hell are ya?"

"Here, Al." Jack Harris popped up from behind a partition. "What's up, boss?"

"Victim number six, most likely. He's moved north. Call Moe and send him to this address." He retrieved a sheet from the copy machine.

"Then grab your stuff, and we're outta here. I'll call Dalwin on the way."

"Where to, Al?"

"North Miami Beach. Let's hope he finally made some sort of mistake this time."

His tanned face set in hard lines as he retrieved and holstered his Glock and pocketed his badge.

*I hope this poor gal can work out what to do to stay alive until we catch this prick. So far none of his other vics have figured it out.*

He dial the BAU agent as he met Jack Harris at the door and filled him in on what little he knew at that moment. They would send a team to the scene too.

They were on the hunt again. He hoped there was a spoor to follow this time.

He damned sure didn't want to see another pretty redhead lying in some alley, all dressed to the nines.

# 45

"O-o-o-o-h-h." She flopped over onto her back, her eyes fluttering open. Her brow creased like tire tracks on a sandy plain as she squinted against the glare of incandescent brightness from a three-bulb fixture overhead. Tiny elves had taken residence in her skull, assaulting from the inside with pickaxes.

She gagged, trying to swallow, but there was no saliva in a mouth desert-dry and filled with the iron taste of long ago unbrushed teeth.

"Ugghh," she moaned as she planted her elbows and struggled to sit up ... a failed attempt. She collapsed and rolling onto her side, hugging her knees.

*What the hell...?* The last thing Shelly remembered was viewing a magnificent, modern kitchen in that lovely townhouse with that RE/MAX agent. And then ....

*He grabbed me from behind and covered my face with a smelly rag ... chloroform, I guess. He wasn't a RE/MAX agent after all. Duh.* She squiggled around and fueled by a surge of adrenalin, finally lurched partly upright.

She leaned against the bed's headboard, her legs sprawled out and struggled to recall those last moments. He had called her by a different name: Carole or Catherine, or something like that.

*He's mistaken me for someone ... Oh, shit!*

She noticed the hangered frilly pink and blue dress suspended from a hook on the back of the door.

# THE PROM DRESS KILLER

*What the hell is ... Oh Jeez! A fancy party dress. No. A prom dress.* A wave of chills scattered down her spine, as a fine dew of perspiration bathed her brow.

'Ohmygod," she mumbled aloud.

*I've been snatched by the Prom Dress Killer!*

She shuddered and clenched her jaw. Tears seeped from the corner of her eyes and eddied across her round cheeks, spilling in measured drips from her chin.

"Shelly, Shelly! How stupid," she whispered, her face buried in cupped hands. She's been kidnapped by this lunatic who somehow knew her every move. Knew where and when to find her, and then to portray the realtor. What happened to the real RE/MAX guy? She hoped this nut hadn't ....

Her head snapped up at the scrape of a key in the door. It had a deadbolt, she noticed. A shiver racked her body, raising the fine auburn hairs on her neck.

She was locked in prison with a delusional maniac.

*Oh, God! He's going to kill me.* She scrunched back against the headboard, stiffening her spine. She struggled against the terror inundating her. She mustn't show fear. Predators feed on that. Can't panic. Gotta think this through.

*He called me that strange name.* Her lips quivered as she battled for control. *Maybe he thinks I'm someone else. Someone he's been trying to find, but maybe doesn't quite remember.*

*Sure.* Her deductive mind whirling. *I bet he's been on a trial and error hunt, killing those other redheads when they turned out to be the wrong woman. He called me Carole, or something like that. Maybe those girls....*

The door creaked open and he filled the opening ... a short muscular guy with an almost plastic smooth face.

"Ah, Camille. I thought I heard you awaken." She followed his gaze to the nightstand. A baby monitor, like the one she used for her mom after the accident. She gritted her teeth.

*Camille. That's it. She was probably a redhead. That's my only chance. I've gotta be this Camille if I'm gonna survive long enough for them to find me. But why doesn't he know what she looks like? As long as he thinks I'm her, I may have an opening.* Shelly secreted her shaking hands under the bed's sheet and forced herself to hold his eyes.

"Has it been so long that you've forgotten me?" His attempt of a wry smile yielded only a grim slitting of his lips.

*Shahrazad.* She flashed back to her favorite tales her mother read her as a little girl. *That may be the way. Gotta be Shahrazad, placating him with stories about this Camille. Be strong, Shelly. You can do this. You are a clever novelist.*

"No," she forced her voice to be soft but firm. Her throat was parched, but she willed herself not to squawk. She sucked hard, drawing up saliva before continuing.

"But I've been away so long that everything is a little sketchy. How long has it been ...?" She arched her eyebrows, struggling to seem calm.

"It's Ron, darling. Ron Bachelor. It's been almost eight years since you failed to wait for me to take you to our senior prom."

"Oh Ron, I'm so sorry." She cast down her eyes as her mind dared frantically through one scenario after another, desperate to find the right story line. She *was* a talented writer, wasn't she?

"There must have been confusion about the time." He missed their date, so maybe he was late. "I waited and waited, but when you didn't show up, my parents ...."

"Yes, yes. They never liked me, did they?"

"Oh no, that's not...." She sensed a hard intensity in his eyes.

"Yes it was. And when I finally arrived, sporting a fine tux and carrying a lovely red rose corsage, they wouldn't tell me who

[164]

you went with. I used my very best persuasive manner, but they kept insisting you had left town."

"I ... I really don't remember. It's been so long ...."

"No need to cover for them now, Camille. I know they wanted to hide you from me, if it was the last thing they did." His chuckle was more sinister than merry. "Turns out it was."

"Was what?" Her eyes widened at what he was saying.

"The last thing they did, of course."

*He murdered her parents!* She quelled the cry of anguish hovering in her throat.

*He's an absolute sociopath.*

# 46

His stare, wide and devoid of emotion, swept over her, and he shrugged.

"But somehow you've arranged to have another mother? So resourceful. A girl *needs* a mother, I guess."

*Shit.* She forced herself to hold his eyes, unblinking. *This dangerous nut could kill Mom if I can't find a way to placate him.* She quelled tears, realizing he wouldn't expect this other girl ... Camille ... to be turning on the waterworks.

"Yes," her voice raspy. "Can I have some water? My throat is dry and so raw." She needed time to create a plausible story.

"Of course. How insensitive of me." He left, relocking the door behind him, and was back in moments with a cold glass of water.

Shelly took several small sips before she continued. "I met Mrs. Weitz when I was looking for a room to rent, and she sort of adopted me. She'd lost her only daughter," scrambling for something reasonable to say, "so it was convenient for both of us. I even took her last name."

"And Rochelle ... or Shelly? Where did that come from?"

"It was a name I'd always liked as a child." She folded her hands across her belly, her racing thoughts somehow calming her body. "So she gave me a place to live until I was able to get out on my own. A chance to start a new life."

*Easy, girl. Don't overdo it.*

"Ah yes. But why a life without me? Why? We were so in love."

She took another drink, still stalling. *Were they? Or was it all a psychotic delusion. Gotta be careful here.* She inched back, tucking her legs under her.

"I thought we were, but then ..." *careful* "... well, you didn't come for me. I ... I was *so* disappointed." The corners of her lips ticked downward, the vision of sadness. She was getting into the role she suspected she needed to play to survive.

"And so you moved to Florida?" His eyebrows arched.

"I didn't know what else to do. I thought you'd left me, and I just had to get out of town." *Now you're on a roll, Shelly, but don't overdo it. This is a delicate little skit you're playing.*

Hands clasped behind his back, he patrolled a ten-foot path, to and fro in front of her, but his dark-eyed gaze never left her face.

"And now you're a real estate agent, already successful. No surprise to me. You were always special. That's why I love you so.

"And I never abandoned you, Camille. I was just delayed that night by a wayward girl who needed to learn a lesson in manners. You should have waited for me." He paused, tilting toward her from the waist, scrutinizing her with a cold intensity.

She studied his bland face, her eyes wide with growing realization ... and returning terror. Was he already a psychotic killer as a teenager? She shivered, her hands fluttering in her lap. Can she really do this? Act out this charade with a homicidal maniac? She *had* to do it, and do it well.

"Cold, darling?" He edged forward, lifting her chin with his forefinger, locking on her eyes.

"Yes." She forced herself to hold his gaze. "And tired. I don't feel well, Ron. My head's pounding, and I have a bad taste in my mouth." She took more water, hoping to hold him off.

"An unfortunate aftermath of my ... convincing you to come with me. It'll wear off."

"Of course." She cleared her throat. "And I'm happy you finally found me. But I'm so tired, I won't be any company for you. Do you mind if I take a nap?"

"Certainly. Have a nice rest, and we'll have a late dinner together when you're up." He leaned in for a kiss, and she forced herself to respond, despite the gorge surging at the base of her throat. She kept her lips soft and slightly parted as he lingered against her. Iron will stiffened her body to avoid the shakes.

*I've gotta be the Camille this psycho thinks I am, but I need time to figure out how to keep him on a string until the cops ... or someone ... finds me. And please god, do find me ... before he realizes I'm not who he thinks I am. How long before I trip up?*

She skooched down on the bed, curling around the pillow in a fetal position, wishing him away.

"Rest now, my darling," he said and drew the sheet up over her shoulders. "We have plenty of time to catch up when you're recovered. Call me when you awaken."

He pivoted and left, with the ominous click of the deadbolt striking home.

*Well, so much for him trusting my love for him.*

Shelly snuggled deeper into the bed and draped the sheet more tightly around her, struggling against the crescendo still echoing in her skull.

*Gotta come up with a plan.*

Surprisingly, she dozed off.

# 47

Turning off NE 10th Avenue onto the towering palm and black olive shaded side street, Warner had no trouble finding the crime scene. Two black and whites were stationed in front of a row of modern ivory colored two-story concrete block and stucco townhouses, one of which was gaudily festooned with yellow crime-scene tape draped across its faux mahogany front door.

Warner slid his gunmetal-gray Dodge Charger close to the curb behind one of the squad cars, with Jack Harris arriving close behind in his tan Camaro. They'd trekked up from Miami in separate vehicles to be flexible, once they scoured the scene.

Both detectives exited their vehicles and hurried across the lawn toward a tall curly-haired bull of a man, parked on the top step of the sequestered unit. Warner reached for his badge, but the other cop waived him off.

"No need for creds, Warner. I know who you are." He extended a thick-fingered, calloused hand. "I'm Barry Rosenbach, the closest thing we got up here to a homicide detective."

"Glad to meet ya, Detective. This is my partner, Jack Harris. A frequent pain in the ass, but a damned good cop." The two men shook hands.

"I got one of those too," the bigger man said. "Don't know what I'd do without 'im." He gestured them toward the front door. "Best we can tell, this is where the girl went missing."

"Tell me what you know for sure first," Warner said as they entered the townhouse, "and then where that seems to lead."

"The apparent vic, one Rochelle Weitz, was supposed to meet another realtor, one Marcos Panos, here at three p.m." It took less than five minutes for the detective to replay the events as they knew them.

"So they knew something was wrong after Panos talked to Weitz' boss?"

"Yeah, and the proof was when we found her Rav4 the next morning, sitting in a Waffle House lot six blocks away, with a audio transmitter hidden under her dash."

"No evidence of a struggle here?" Warner asked.

"Nothing obvious. No one's touched anything without gloves since we've been on the scene, but this Panos guy was here first for awhile, and the house has been on the market and seen by several agents and clients, so it may be hard to use anything collected here as evidence."

"You're probably right, but I got my crime scene wiz, Moe Gold, on the way. If ya don't mind, I'll have him check it out."

"The Hawk? From what I hear, there's none better, so have at it. We don't get much high-profile murder up here, so I'm glad to have you guys."

"Okay. Jack and I are goin' to wander around. See if anything pops out. Moe should be along any moment." They'd already donned vinyl gloves and cloth crime scene booties, so as not to disturb any possible "trace" left by the killer.

"It's all yours, Detective. Just keep me in the loop. I'll stick around, and we'll keep the gawkers off." They shook hands, and as the North Miami Beach detective was exiting, Moe Gold came through the door, trailed by two of his techs.

"Getting a little far from home, aren't we, Detective?" he said, a grin tweaking the corners of his mouth.

"Just followin' our perp, Moe," Warner said, squeezing the sprite little man's shoulder. "And it looks like he's branchin' out."

"You're sure it's him, Al?"

"Yeah. Same vic type. Middle twenties, attractive redhead. Could be a copycat, but I doubt it."

"Okay. I saw the For Rent sign in front, so I suspect there's gonna be a lot of confusing shit to wade through. Lots of folks traipsing around the scene before the crime."

Warner stood, arms akimbo, gazing over the living room and the kitchen entrance. "Do the best you can, Moe. No one does it better. Just find me *something* that'll get me closer to snarin' this guy. We're gonna prowl around a bit, too." He motioned Jack Harris to survey the living room, while he worked his way into the kitchen.

"I'm on it, Al," the Hawk said, opening his evidence kit. His two assistants scattered in different directions, each searching for minutia that might lead to the killer. Every surface would be dusted, and there was sure to be plenty of material there ... possibly all unrelated to the case ... but nothing would be left undone.

The hunt was, once again, on in earnest.

# 48

Detective Nogales shoved through the swinging doors of the M.E.'s frigid lab, spying the tall angular MD scrutinizing a corpse. A quick glance told the detective this was not the victim he was there about.

"Hey Doc. Any news on our robbery vic?"

"I just finished dictating my notes, Filipe. Unfortunately, there wasn't much on the body. The tech boys are still examining his clothing for any form of trace. I believe they've found two hairs of uncertain origin. They'll pull DNA and run it through CODIS. Maybe we'll find something on that national data base."

"But you're not sure they're the killer's?" Nogales asked.

"No, but they aren't the victim's, so we'll see what we'll see. Any luck on your end?"

The detective pulled an ear lobe, pursing his lips. "Nothing solid. The parking lot cameras picked up a guy coming from the back, carrying what looked like a garment bag and a small satchel."

"He's your guy?" Doctor Magilly asked, straightening and backing away from the autopsy table.

"Can't be sure." Nogales cracked his knuckles and sighed. "No physical way to tie him to the crime. Looks suspicious, though, and he drove off in a beige Dodge Caravan."

"A plate number?"

"No such luck. The numbers were covered with mud, which definitely makes him a person of interest ... if we can find him."

"So?" The doctor gathered his tools and deposited them in a tray for cleaning. "You seem more interested than for simple murder during a robbery gone bad."

"Yeah. My gut tells me there's something more going on here. Maybe he killed the guy because he saw his face and could ID him, but that's pretty extreme for a robbery. Trading first degree murder for a few years in the clink, if he's even caught."

The doctor shed his latex gloves and tossed them in the trash. "I see corpses all the time as victims of a simple crime turned violent. Why d'ya feel this one is different, Detective?"

"I can see some punk holding up a store and acing the owner if he goes for a gun. The heat of the moment, ya know. But there's no sign the vic put up any kind of fight. The clerk's retrieving some merchandise, probably off a hat rack, and this guy sneaks up behind him and snaps his neck." Nogales shrugs. "That's just cold-blooded murder."

"I see what you mean," Doctor Magilly says. "I'll see if the lab can expedite the DNA results from the hairs, and the crime scene techs will let you know if they come up with anything else."

"Thanks, Doc. At this point, I got very little to work on. I'm waiting for Detective Dupree's report on what the Jupiter Robbery Division learns about what was taken. That may give us a lead."

"Still awaiting his family?" the doctor asked.

"Yeah. Jupiter PD located the son, due back tomorrow." He ran short thick fingers through his curly mahogany colored hair. "Robbery needs to get him into the store to catalog what's been taken. Maybe that'll steer us in the right direction. 'Til then, we're kinda dead in the water."

It was the doctor's turn to shrug and sigh. "So much unnecessary mayhem. I hope you catch this bastard, Filipe."

"Thanks, Doc. Meanwhile, I got other cases to chase. Let me know if your guys or CSU come up with anything good."

"Of course. Good luck, Detective."

He patted the shorter, burly man on the back as he exited the lab.

# 49

Her eyes fluttered open, her slitted gaze flitting around the darkening room, momentarily lost.

*What the ...? Where am I?* Then reality flooded back to her.

*Oh god!* Her mouth felt strewn with sand. It wasn't a dream. *I've been snatched by that lunatic killing redheads.*

She propped herself up on her elbows, wiggling onto her butt, leaning against the headboard.

*I won't be able to keep putting him off. What'll I do if he wants sex because he thinks we're in love? And what's with the fancy dress? Is he a pervert too, wanting to play dress-up?*

She shuddered. *Maybe he plans to take me somewhere, wearing it.* She sucked in a slow breath, trying to calm her throbbing heart. *That might be a chance to get away.*

Shelly knuckled her eyes and tried to suck moisture into her desert-dry mouth. She spied the glass of water from earlier, sitting on the nightstand. It was warm now, but still welcome.

She hugged herself, intent on quelling her shivering. She must control her terror, because unchecked, it could lead to a wrong move that might kill her.

Whatever his plans, she could try to slow them ... entertain him with stories, like Shahrazad ... but she realized she'd eventually have to accede to his demands. Panic loomed just under her emotional horizon, ready to engulf her if she weakened.

To survive, she'd have to eventually give in to whatever he expected from her.

*No. I'll have to do more than give in. I've gotta force myself to seem eager and willing to be his girlfriend ... and even his lover, if necessary.* Her hands shook like an epileptic. *God, can I really do that?*

*But maybe resisting him is what got those other girls killed.*

He loved this Camille and thought they were fated to be together. If she can be Camille, apparently a redheaded girl from his high school days, he'll care for and protect her. If she rebels, and proves he made a bad choice ... as he seems to have done four or five times ... he'll discard her and begin a new search. So far his mistakes haven't survived his displeasure.

Shelly clenched her jaw and resolved to be different. Whatever it took to survive. She'd try to become that Twelfth Century Arabian princess who wove tales for a thousand and one nights to forestall her deaths and placate her master.

Maybe he left clues ... trace evidence, according to research she'd done for her novel ... at the townhouse where he abducted her. The police must have *something* to go on. She'd read that great detective, Warner, was spearheading the investigation. He'd solved two other serial killers cases and that SIDS baby case. He would come for her. That was something to hold onto, when things got really bad.

She wondered if there were something she could do if this guy takes her out. He seemed obsessed with their Senior Prom, so she suspected there was a place they had to go.

Would there be some way to signal she needed help, even if she couldn't find a way to escape? But she'd have to be careful. Tiny rivulets edged over the swell of her cheeks. A quivering forefinger brushed them away.

One false move and she would die. She was sure of that.

# THE PROM DRESS KILLER

*God! What have I gotten myself into? Damn it, Shelly, it wasn't your fault. I've done nothing to draw this nut to me, other than look like his lost love.*

*I'm a clever girl. A talented novelist.* Clenched fists drummed on her thighs. *I can do this. I've got to do this.*

She twitched, her head snapping up at the scrape of a key in the deadbolt. A shiver rippled in cascades down her neck and back. She battled to steady herself. *Can't show him fear.*

The door opened with a soft groan, and he was there, his smooth face expressionless, arms set jauntily akimbo. He slid one hand into the pocket of his ivory cargo-style slacks.

"I heard you stirring, Camille. Have a pleasant nap?"

She swallowed hard, struggling to quell her shaking limbs and banish fear from her voice. The next few minutes would set the tone for survival ... or death.

"Oh yes, my darling." Her voice horse. "I'm still a bit groggy, but it's time we talk. I've got so many things to tell you." She sipped water from her glass. *I can do this*, she thought again.

"Wonderful. I'm eager to hear everything." He swung the door closed and an instant later, was perched on the edge of the bed, his eyes wide, the tip of his tongue darting across his narrow lips. A gentle waft of shaving cologne tickled her senses. Old Spice?

"Well, it's an eight-year adventure, so it may take some time," she said. She cupped one of his hands between the two of hers, battling rising gorge at the thought of his touch.

"We have a lifetime, now that we're together again," he said, as his fingers caressed her cheek.

"So, after the disappointment of missing the prom with you, I ...." She settled her mind on the story, willing the ever-present terror into a vault in the back of her mind.

And the game was on.

# 50

Moe Gold rapped on the open door of Al Warner's office, and peeked around the frame. Warner was hunched over scattered documents atop his scarred oak desk, a white foam cup of strong smelling coffee perched precariously on one corner of the top.

"I've got some prelims on the North Miami Beach crime scene, Al, if you got a minute."

"Sure, Moe." Warner waved the diminutive, almost dwarf-like forensics chief toward an armless wooden side chair. "Nothin' more important on my plate than catchin' this loony. What d'ya got."

"Too damned much," Gold said, running a hand over his balding pate. "The scene was lousy with prints from probably twenty or more people. Same thing with trace. Loads of fiber and hair and even a few skin cells. No way to tell if any of it belonged to our perp."

The detective eased back in his swivel chair, his thumb exploring the persistently itchy scar above his right temple, nestled under his thick blackish hair.

"So you're tellin' me you got nothing?"

"Not entirely," the Hawk, said. "We concentrated on any area that seemed wiped down."

"Smart. You figured only our perp would have reason to do that. So...?"

"Right. We worked the areas around the wipe downs and have several prints and two hairs we're concentrating on." He glanced at his notebook, flipping to the next page. "We've sent the hairs to CODIS, looking for a DNA match, but even if we get a hit, no way to know if it's our perp."

"And the prints?" Warner asked. He bounced out of the chair and circled his desk. "We need *something*, Moe."

"Always so impatient, Detective. Our best bet is one print ... fore or middle finger ... on the side of the switch for the garage door opener. It's only about a seventy percent partial, but seems likely to be your perp's because the rest of the thing was wiped down. I don't think there's enough for a positive match, but it might narrow the field. That's supposing we get some kind of hit from the national data base at AFIS. Anyhow, we're running it."

"That's it?" Warner rose and jammed his hands into his pockets, glaring at the smaller man, who chuckled softly.

"You got that I opened with this is 'preliminary,' Al? I know you'd like me to wave some magic wand and come up with a name and address for your guy, but it ain't gonna be that easy. We've got tons of stuff to process, and we're gonna do that as quickly and as carefully as we can. I'm not eager to see another pretty redhead waiting on an autopsy slab, either." He rose from the chair and closed his notebook.

"Yeah, sorry. But you know how I get when some nut's killin' women or kids on my beat. I'm just tryin' to get to Rochelle Weitz before she becomes his next vic."

"I got all my people on this," the Hawk said. "We're processing everything we can find. You'll be the first to know if we turn up anything even slightly probative."

"Okay. So don't let me keep you from it. All I can do is hope for the best, Moe."

The little crime-scene whiz nodded and hurried off, as Warner trailed him into the Homicide Department's bullpen.

"Harris. Olvida," he snapped.

"Here, Boss," said almost in unison, as Warner's two top henchmen materialized from behind glass-topped green office partitions.

"Gimme an update on any progress on the Weitz snatch."

Detective Rafael Olvida brushed back a persistent forelock of nut-brown hair and flipped open his notebook. "We got six patrol cops still canvassing the area around the crime scene, knocking on doors, looking for anyone who may have seen anything. So far, no joy." He flipped two pages over, and then glanced at his boss. "One woman, returning from shopping, said she thinks she noticed a brown or tan van of undetermined make and age, drive by. It's about the right timeline, but doesn't give us much."

"Two more boys in blue are working the Waffle House site," Olvida continued, "looking for someone who may have seen the perp drop off her Rav4. The parking lot's security cameras were inop, so there's no help there." He nodded at the shorter, wiry man next to him.

"CSU is still working the scene," Jack Harris said, scratching a short-stubbled chin, as he studyied his own notes. "For a change, we got a scene with too much to deal with, so they're in overload. I've been there every day with two other guys, looking for things outta the ordinary. The NMB detective, Rosenbach, has interviewed the RE/MAX realtor, Panos, and I sat in.

"Our best guess is the perp knew her schedule from listening to his bug, and delayed Panos with a phone call." He glanced at his boss and shrugged. "He then musta imitated him when Miss Weitz arrived. He probably knocked her out with chloroform, which he's used before, then bundled her up in his vehicle ... maybe the van the neighbor spotted ... which he already had inside the garage."

"We suspect that," Olvida piped in, "because of the wipe down by the overhead-door-opener switch and the door knobs, both inside and out, to the garage. But so far it's all supposition, and the only hard evidence we got is maybe the one fingerprint, and possibly the two hairs the Hawk found."

"And maybe a brown or tan van," Warner said, "which makes sense for easy transport of his vic. It ain't much, guys, but it's more than we had. So keep at it." He grasped Harris' forearm. "Is tech support checking the traffic cams and any nearby CCTV for the van?"

"Yeah," Harris said, "but tan, brown or even gold minivans are a dime a dozen. They're all over the place, so without a make or model and more detail, it's the proverbial needle."

"I know," Warner said, patting his ex-partner on the back, "but it's the only haystack we got, so keep at it. I don't want Rochelle Weitz to turn up dead before we can find this nut. Keep pushin' the interviews with neighbors and maybe something will pop up."

Unfortunately, there was little more at the crime scene that would help. But sometimes good things came from unexpected places, given a little time to ferment.

Detective Al Warner had capitalized on those little serendipities in the past. He hoped it was time for one now.

He just had to be alert enough to spot it when it trotted by.

# 51

Detective Nogales crouched near the curb, fingers filtering through scattered leaves and trash, searching for shell casings. The morning sun had raised high enough to bake the black pavement and send heat waves swirling up from the concrete walks.

His lips hardened into a grimace, and he shook his head. Drive-by shootings in Riviera Beach were often gang-related, which is why the sheriff's office was called in. Too frequently innocent bystanders were in the line of fire, and today a five-year-old African-American girl had taken one in the head.

Unfortunately, the twenty-year-old gangbanger that was probably the target had escaped with a grazed bicep. Nogales grunted and rose, not feeling guilty that he wished the situation had been reversed. He scanned the area, seeing only one news truck. Black-on-black crime was too common to make much of a stir.

He was jerked from his reverie by the vibration of his cell phone.

"Nogales," he said, after accepting the call from the PBSO M.E.'s office.

"It's Doctor Magilly, Detective."

"Yeah, Doc. What's up?"

"CSU's finished processing all the trace from the Braun murder in Jupiter. They pulled DNA from two light brown hairs found on the vic's clothing, and that's being run for a DNA match against the CODIS data base."

"Any useful prints?" Nogales sauntered off the pavement and into the cooling shade of a towering live oak.

"We pulled a partial from the side of the closed circuit TV video recorder. It doesn't match either of the Brauns but there's not enough to send it to AFIS. A CSU tech is using a new FBI program to see if they can enhance it enough to run it for a match, but so far, no go."

"Okay. Thanks, Doc. Let me know if anything turns up. Right now, I'm in the middle of an ugly drive-by in Riviera Beach."

"Gang related?"

"Yeah. Drug gangs warring over turf, it seems. Damned problem is, sometimes innocent little girls get in the middle. We got a street full of shell casings, and the only casualty is a pretty little five-year-old.

"I'll be finished here in thirty or so. Then I'm gonna call that Jupiter robbery detective, Dupree. See if he's got an inventory of what was snatched. Maybe give us a clue as to why *that* shop. My gut keeps telling me there's more to this than just a simple heist. Killing that shop owner just doesn't sit right with me."

"So you said," the doctor said. "You've great instincts, Filipe, so I'm betting on you."

"Thanks, Doc. Talk to you later." Detective Nogales flipped the phone closed, slipping it into his inside jacket pocket. He scanned the taped-off crime scene and spotted the local lead investigator. He trotted over to the man who turned to meet him.

"Anything more I can do for you, Detective?" Nogales asked. "Looks like you got everything in hand."

"Except the shooter," the black man said. "Amazing, with forty-six shell casings and a totally shot up house, no one saw anything. I come to these scenes because I hope by being one of them, someone will talk to me."

"They're scared, and with good reason. These thugs punish informers."

"I know. But if the community got some backbone and united against these bastards, they'd be cleaned out."

"That takes fearless leadership. Someone willing to risk his life. I don't see much of that anywhere." Nogales rubbed his chin and shrugged.

"Anyhow, I've gotta go. Another case I'm working. Let me know if the PBSO can help in any way, but you guys have plenty of experience with this shit."

"Unfortunately," the black cop said, shaking his head. "It's becoming a near daily chore." They clasped hands, and Nogales headed for his car, noticing that the one news van had already departed.

Using the Bluetooth in his car, he left a message for Detective Dupree to FAX or e-mail a list of missing items from the Jupiter crime scene. That was a case nagging at his subconscious. He was missing something there and couldn't quite put a noose around it.

As he headed for his office, he couldn't quell the image of that little girl's face, or what was left of it.

Damned trigger-happy punks.

# 52

"So when the Greyhound bus arrived at the Nashville station, I decided to get off." She sat on the end of the bed, so involved in creating this story for him, she had momentarily shed her angst.

*It must be late afternoon already. How long have I been here? Are they searching for me yet?*

Her captor slid his forefinger under her chin, tilting her head enough to capture her eyes. "Was that your destination? Nashville? Why there?" His touch rekindled the reality of the moment. Her throat constricted and she swallowed, willing her eyes to lock on his.

"Oh, no, not really." Resurgent panic was barely quelled by iron will as she struggled to keep her voice from cracking. She mustn't show the terror roiling at the barriers she'd erected against it.

"Actually, I didn't even have a particular place in mind." She paused and tried to marshal her thoughts. "I ... I was so disappointed missing the prom with you that I just wanted to get out of town." She forced herself to touch his cheek, lightly as the whisper of butterfly wings.

"I see." He intertwined his fingers with hers. "So what did you do in Nashville?"

"Well, the first thing was to call my folks. You know, to see if they heard from you."

"And what did they say? Your parents never liked me, did they?"

Shelly paused, dropping her gaze, an unforced tear trickling from the corner of her left eye. He'd hinted he'd killed Camille's parents, so he was testing her. He didn't trust her yet.

"I never talked to them," she murmured. "Some strange man answered the phone and started grilling me." Her gray eyes, moist with tears, found his. "He scared me, so I hung up. I never got to say my final good-byes to my parents. Something bad must have happened to them. I felt so alone, there in the bus terminal, so far away, in Tennessee."

"Yes, I believe something *bad* did happen to them." He rose and began pacing, hands clasped behind his back. "They wouldn't tell me where you'd gone." He halted, his thickly muscled back to her, shook his head, and sighed.

"Oh, Ron, they didn't *know* where I'd gone. I didn't even know where I was headed when I left." She realized the more uncertainty she built into this fairy tale, the longer she may be able to drag it out. She repressed the unlikely bloom, in the face of such horror, of a smug grin. Shahrazad was back. Shelly hope this time, nine-hundred-years later, it wasn't going to encompass a thousand and one nights.

"I just left. Ran away, really, from the disappointment of missing our time together. I ...."

"Ah, Camille. It's not you who must apologize." He slid back onto the edge of the mattress and took both her hands in his, firing a chill up her spine.

"It was my fault," he went on. "I allowed other ... business ... to delay me. To get in the way of what was really important."

"Yes. Our being together. Getting to know each other." How long *had* they'd known each other? Did they really have a date, or was it all a figment of a deranged mind? She'd better not get carried away until she separated reality from fantasy.

"Yes, our first real date. The beginning of a lifetime together," he said.

She quietly released pent up breath, quelling the need to sigh. She'd gambled and won ... this time.

*No time to get cocky. This guy is dangerous.*

"Yes, a lifetime." She demanded the corners of her lips to tilt up, much against their will, into what she hoped was a happy grin.

"So tell me more about your time in Nashville. Did you stay, or did you move on?"

"Oh, I looked for work there for several weeks. That's where I started training to become a realtor." *Gotta stick with what was familiar and realistic.*

"It was a struggle, though. All alone, with all my loved ones back home. I took odd jobs – a counter girl at a deli, a waitress at a sports bar, and even pumping gas at a service station." All things Shelly had actually done during her teen years. Things she was familiar with.

"Such menial work for a princess," he said, his eyes moist. It was his first show of real emotion.

"It wasn't so bad. It put clothes on my back and food on the table." She patted her belly. "Which reminds me, I'm hungry. You promised me dinner." *Gotta save some stories for later.*

"Of course. I got us take-out from a very nice Italian restaurant nearby. I hope you like veal in Marsala sauce, with spaghetti Marinara and garlic bread."

"Sounds delicious. And wine?"

"Certainly. Chianti should be perfect."

"Yum. My stomach is already rumbling." She slid off the bed and took his hand. "Lead the way."

Where were they headed? The dining room? Shelly doubted they were actually going out for dinner. She'd stay alert, checking for future opportunities to slip away, but from what she'd seen of this psycho, it seemed unlikely he'd be that careless.

After they ate, she'd feign exhaustion, promising to tell him more tomorrow.

She shuddered and bit her lip, hoping she could hold it together long enough to survive.

Just like Shahrazad, one night at a time.

# 53

One arm slung around her, Warner drew Eva against the hard, lean muscles of his chest. Her head snuggled into the crook of his neck, with a long leg draped over his, his senses awash with the perfume of her hair and the sweetness of post-coitus perspiration. Her magenta fingernail sketched doodles on his lightly-haired pecs.

Warner tilted her head and brushed her lips with a wispy kiss, his tongue teasing the corner of her mouth.

"These mornin' romps are makin' me late for work, babe. I'll get a bad rep."

"I'm sorry, Al." Her gold-flecked green eyes twinkled, the corners crinkling as she chuckled. "But not so sorry that I plan on stopping any time soon."

"Thank God." He grinned as his free hand began a tiptoed venture across her silky, damp skin. "I love bein' with you. Not just makin' love, but *bein'* with you. You energize my batteries."

"Me too. For me, it's not just making love with you. Or just being with you. It's that I'm in *love* with you ... totally, completely in love with you. I've never been happier."

"That's amazing. Wonderful, but truly amazing."

"What?" She rolled on top of him and stifled his response with her lips, her tongue seeking his, her athletic, lean body dancing against his. Sensing his response ignited her, feeding her once again growing passion. Her wiggling butt completed the task and he was quickly inside her. No foreplay or teasing was needed to fire their ardor.

Eva leaned back, her arms braced against his shoulders as she pumped slowly up and down.

"What?" she repeated with a throaty whisper.

"To be in ... love ... and loved ... by someone like ... you," he gasped as his fingers danced over her moist thighs and chest.

"Shhh," she murmured and leaned forward, her firm, full breasts teasing his skin. Her mouth engulfed his, her tongue a darting little saber, as her climax engulfed her, igniting his seconds later.

She slumped against him, his arms crushing her to him, as they wound down together.

Warner nibbled on the lobe of her ear. "I've only ever cared for three women, Eva," he murmured. "Just three, in my entire life. But there's never been anyone like you. Not Sharon, not Casey. I'm just gettin' used to actually needin' someone. It's kinda strange for me, but somehow, really beautiful."

"That's so wonderful, Al." She bracing her elbows and raised her head, her eyes finding his. "So what do people do, when they are so deeply in love?"

Warner's dark eyes slowly widened, and he snatched in a short sharp breath. "Uhh ... get married?"

"Boy!" she said, grinning. "For a super detective, you can really be slow sometimes."

"Married? You'd really marry me, Eva?"

"Was that a rhetorical question or a proposal, Detective?"

"A stunned proposal. I never thought ... will you marry me, Eva Guttenburg? Not exactly an on the knee ...."

She placed a finger across his lips. "What better place than right here, in each other's arms. And yes, I will happily marry you, Al Warner. With the proverbial bells on."

"You're sure ...?"

Her kiss was soft and sweet. "More than sure, if that's possible," she muttered, nestling against him. "Nothing big and fancy. I'd like a rabbi, but you can have a minister, too, if you want. Just a little ceremony with a few friends and colleagues. And soon, Al. No dilly-dallying."

"Okay by me. I'm not a religious guy, so whatever you want. Sounds like you've been thinkin' about this for a while. Got it all planned out, huh? I thought most gals want something big, at least the first time."

"This is going to be our *only* time, lover. And I don't need anything elaborate. Besides, our baby should be born a Warner."

"Baby?" His eyes flared, his hands cupping her head.

"A baby?" he gasped out again, filled with wonder.

"Yes, darling. We're having a baby." She dropped down, hugging him fiercely. "Do you want to know its sex?"

"You know that already? How many months ...?"

"I'm just into my third month. So ...?"

"God, this is unbelievable. Why did you wait so long...?"

"I have an irregular period, Al, and I've seen too many cases of false positives from worried patients. I wanted to be sure. So...?"

"Jeez, a baby. I never even considered ... Tell me, Eva—a boy or a girl?"

She settled back and straddled his groin, her hands resting on his chest. Her moist lips curled into a saucy grin, her green eyes crinkling at their margins as a giggle trickled out.

"A boy, Al. You're having a son. He'll be tall and brave, just like his daddy."

"Holy cow, this is amazin'." He drew her down, his lips consuming hers. "Marryin' a fantastic gal," he mumbled through the kiss, "and becomin' a dad, all in one shot. Wow."

She nestled against him, her auburn hair fluttering against his face.

"What d'ya think?" he murmured in her ear. "Do we keep this secret, or do we tell people?"

"What do you want to do, Al?" Scarlet lips brushed butterfly-wing kisses over his eyes.

"I wanna tell the world. Shout it from the highest hills, like in that song. Jesus, Al Warner's gettin' married! No one'll believe it."

"Okay by me. I may be on a media hot seat about how I was able to corral the elusive Detective Warner." She chuckled as she rolled off him and rose and started for the bathroom. "I've got a busy day of sessions but afterward, I'll start planning the wedding. But first I need a shower."

He lingered in bed, sprawled on his back, gazing blankly at the ceiling. A husband and a dad ... life-changing events he was surprisingly eager to embrace.

"I'll need a list of who you want to attend," Eva said as she returned to the room, fluffing her damp hair, buttoning her blouse, and tucking it into her skirt, "but let's try to keep it fewer than twenty each."

"No problem at my end. I doubt I can come up with half that many. Just some guys from the department, and maybe I'll even ask Mrs. Gerber."

"That's sweet, Al." She took his hand, drawing him to his feet, slipping inside his arms for a gentle hug.

"You know, I was thinking, that guy probably loves that woman, too," she said.

"What guy?"

"Your Prom Dress Killer. He's clearly searching for a lost love, and even when he errs, he treats his victims almost lovingly. They don't suffer when he kills them, and he dresses them with great care."

"Interestin'," Warner said. "So, if Weitz is smart enough to play into that, she may survive long enough for us to find her."

"That's what I was thinking. When I sat in on your interview of her mother, she said the girl was a budding novelist and loved story-telling. If she's clever enough to read this guy, she may use that skill to keep her alive."

"I hope you're right, lover." Warner had dressed and was slipping on his shoulder-holster and sport jacket.

"CSU and Forensics haven't come up with much new. This clever bastard's gotta make a mistake, and for Rochelle Weitz's sake, I hope we're on top of it when he does." He folded the tall copper-haired woman into his arms and brushed a kiss across her brow. He drew back slightly, his eyes locking with hers.

"I'm not dreamin', am I? I had lots of bad ones with the Angel of Death, but this is a whole new world for me. You *are* pregnant, and we *are* gettin' married?"

"You bet." Her fingers trailed across the side of his head, pausing momentarily over the X-shaped scars, hidden beneath a mat of dark curly hair. She shivered slightly, remembering their cause at the killing of the Angel of Death, and the aftermath.

"I'm marrying you, Al, because I love you ... desperately. Carrying your son is just a wonderfully happy bonus."

"It certainly is." He holstered his gun and offering his arm, as they started for the door together.

"I can't wait to tell the guys." His lips drew into a silly grin as they hurried down the steps of his townhouse, heading in opposite directions.

His hope for a break in the case may be just around the corner.

# 54

Nogales sat in his parked cruiser, studying his notes on the drive-by shooting he'd was investigating when his phone chimed.

"Nogales."

"Good morning, Detective. This is Pete Dupree, lead robbery investigator with Jupiter PD."

"Hi, Pete. I presume this is about the Braun theft and murder. You got something for me?"

"Yeah. We finally got through the store's inventory with the son, and I got a list of what seems to be taken. I can text it to your phone or FAX it to your office."

"FAX it, so I can get a hard copy." Nogales said. "But give me a quick rundown now, if you can. I don't need it item-by-item. Just an overview. I'm not going to be back to my desk until late."

"Okay. As you surmised from your report, there was costume jewelry taken ... 19 lots, according to young Mister Braun. Mostly Art Deco stuff, so more valuable than the usual baubles. He valued it at about 20G. The cash register was emptied, but he said they rarely had more than $200 to $300 in small bills in the register. There was $3,500 in the safe, but that was untouched."

Nogales rubbed his jaw, shifting the phone to his other ear. "That's it? Sure doesn't seem like something to kill over. It looked like a deliberate murder, rather than an act of panic."

"I agree," Dupree said. "But who knows what goads a nut?"

"Right. So let me know if anything else turns up. I gotta run."

Something was missing here, but he couldn't put a face on it.

# 55

Shelly struggled to lie quietly, fighting to quell her galloping heart and panting breath. She'd lurched awake from a suffocating dream of Ron Bachelor holding her underwater in a mossy pond, somewhere in a forest she didn't recognize.

If she could just remain still in bed, maybe he wouldn't realize she was awake. A small sigh seeped between clenched lips.

*What difference does it make? I'll have to face him eventually, and try to be a twenty-first century Shahrazad. My only chance is to become this Camille he's been searching for.*

She glanced at the digital clock on the night stand: eight a.m.. He'd be coming soon, whether she made noise or not. She tossed aside the black and white striped flannel blanket, she rolled into a seated position on the edge of the twin-size bed, straightening and smoothing the maroon silky nightgown he'd presented her the evening before.

Not yet fully self-indoctrinated on becoming his "lost lover," she never shed her lacy bra or flowered cotton panties. She prayed the cops would find her first, but was resigned to being an enthusiastic paramour if it came to that.

She stared at the lace-trimmed prom dress hanging on the back of the door. The grate of a key in the lock drew a small, soft groan.

She *had* to become Camille ... ardent, if necessary ... to stay alive. Anything sexual that occurred was a small tithe to pay to survive. She resolved not to end up discarded in a dank alley, clad in that ornate rag, another of this lunatic's failed ventures.

The door swung wide and there he stood, hands thrust into the pockets of his knee-length denim shorts.

"Ah, you're awake, as I'd hoped." His unlined plastic expression and lips, thin and as straight as a knife slit, sent chills scattering down her back.

*What does he want from me? Hard to believe someone so unemotional is searching for love ... for physical romance.*

"Yes," she said and forced a small smile to lift her lips. "I just woke. I'm still feeling a bit woozy, though. I'm not sure ...."

"Once you're up and around you'll shake it off. Now it's time to prepare, if we're going to the prom on Friday night."

"Prepare? A prom? What d'you ...?"

He'd retrieved the lacy pink and blue frock from the back of the door. "You'll model this beautiful dress for me now. We'll see that we have all we need to make a grand entrance." He thrust the hanger toward her.

"Try it on. Let's see how it fits."

"Of course." She plucked it from the hanger and laid it across the bed, drawing down the zipper on the back. Turned away from him, she slipped off the nightgown and stepped into the gown. She sensed his gaze sweeping across her body.

"You were always lovely, Camille, but you've grown into a very beautiful woman."

"Thank you, darling." Her arms were through the puffy sleeves, everything settled in place. "Will you zip me up?"

"Certainly." His finger slithered across her neck and shoulders, and then down her spine, eliciting a shiver she struggled unsuccessfully to contain.

"Something wrong, Camille?" There was hardness in his voice.

"Oh, no." Shelly forced breathiness into her words, battling the panic she really felt. It just dawned on her that all his victims were left dead, wearing dresses like this one. Was he going to kill her now, once she donned the frock?

"Your touch is so exciting. I've ... I've missed you." She gnashed her teeth, sickened at the role she knew she had to play ... and play *well* ... to survive. He kept talking about that damned prom, so maybe...? She inhaled in a slow breath, struggling to suppress the tremors that threatened to shake her apart.

"I was sure I knew your size," he said, "but this thing is a bit tight."

She sucked in her belly and said, "Try now. I think it'll fit." The zipper paused at the bottom of her rib cage, and then completed its trip up to the back of her collar.

"There," he said.

She turned to face him.

"Gorgeous. And the tightness just accentuates your tiny waist. How do you like it?"

"It's beautiful, Ron. And we're really going to a prom on Friday? What day is it? I've lost track."

"Thursday. I'll be busy most of tomorrow working with the committee, setting up the venue." Standing very close, his thick fingers trailed along her cheek, down her neck, lingering on her bare shoulder before venturing across her bodice.

Shelly strove not to flinch, then easing her clenched jaw, leaned in and brushed his forehead with a fleeting kiss.

"I'm so excited to finally be going with you," she said softly. Her mind was whirring as she searched for something to distract him from fulfilling the lust she saw in his eyes.

"You know when you didn't show up that first time, I thought about going alone."

"By yourself?" He stepped back, eyebrows raised and his recently busy hands now clasped behind his back. "How would that work?"

"Not easily." She sighed. "But I was so disappointed that I considered it." *Time for a tale.* "There is a story of a girl whose date didn't show up, and so she went stag. She learned later that he'd been injured in an accident, en route to picking her up.

"She felt terrible afterward when she learned the reason he hadn't come, especially since she had a very good time."

"Really?" he said as they settled together on the edge of the bed. He reached over to unzip the dress, and she hurried on.

"Yes. She was very pretty, and her mother had purchased her a fancy dress. But not as nice as this one, darling." She grinned, taking both his hands in hers now, hoping to stay their roaming.

"Anyhow, while a few of the girls resented her, most were gracious, allowing their dates to have a dance or two with her. Sherry ... that was her name, I think ..." *Shahrazad to my rescue, I hope* "... danced, drank punch, and had a surprisingly good time. At the end, she was shocked to be voted queen of the ball."

He bounced up and began pacing. "That's not right. She shouldn't have gone, with her boyfriend injured."

Shelly rose from the bed, and facing him, planted both hands on his shoulders to stall his prowling. She was amazed at the strength and cleverness she had mined, overcoming the terror that lurked in her heart.

"You're right," she said, trying to sound judgmental. "and when she learned why he hadn't come, she was devastated and riddled with guilt. She never attended another party. Her friends, who had originally saluted her for her moxi, disavowed her and shunned her for the rest of her high school days. She never got over the shame of having a great time while her love was in an emergency ward. The prom committee even revoked her crown."

He stared at her, and then glanced at his watch. "Just punishment. It's gotten late. Now I've got errands to prepare for tomorrow. You need help getting out of the dress?"

She shook her head, thankful for the passing of one more night. She'd modeled the dress and lived ... this time.

How long can she keep this up without cracking? Was she doomed to really become his lover, in some kind of Stockholm Syndrome?

She shivered, tiny droplets blossoming in the corners of her eyes.

She had to be strong if she were to survive and stay sane.

# 56

Palm Beach County Sheriff's Detective Felipe Nogales hunkered over his desk, studying a crime scene report, when he suddenly cocked his head, a darkened corner of his mind lighting up.

He snatched up his cell phone, scrolling down to calls from the previous day, and punched "call back."

"Dupree," answered on the second ring.

"Hi. This is Felipe Nogales, PBSO."

"Yeah, Detective. Something new on the Braun murder?"

"Still trying to put together a plausible motive. Something I just remembered, though. The parking lot cameras showed the probable perp carrying what looked to be a garment bag. No mention by the son of any clothing taken during the robbery?"

"No. And I do remember that now. Let me call him, and I'll get back to you. You think it's pertinent?"

"Just something nagging at me. Not sure why. Let me know what you find out."

"I'm on it, Detective. I'll get back to you, ASAP."

"Thanks," Nogales said as he hung up. He didn't know why, but his instincts told him this might be important.

An hour later, Felipe Nogales had just finished his report on the drive-by shooting in Riviera Beach and was about to leave when his cell phone rang.

"Nogales," he answered, leaning against the exit door frame.

"This is Dupree. Just finished with Braun's son. He was so distraught, he never thought to check the window displays. He went back and found there were a few pieces of retro clothing taken."

"Yeah? Anything specific?" Nogales returned to his desk, pulling over a pad of lined paper, making notes.

"A dress, a silk scarf, and some kind of artificial flowered hat," the Jupiter detective said.

"That's kinda strange. What type of dress?"

"Sort of a frilly party dress, from what he said."

Nogale's head snapped up, his eyes scrunching into narrow slits. "A party dress? Like what a girl might wear to a high school prom?" The nagging door in his mind blew open.

"Yeah, I guess. And the scarf ... holy shit! You think this was *that* guy?"

"The Prom Dress Killer? Could be. Miami-Dade's got a BOLO out for anyone buying one like that. It's how he dresses his vics."

"Jesus. It never dawned on me," Dupree said.

"Well, you're a long way from the crime epicenter. It's not exactly up front on your radar."

"Yeah, and I'm into robbery, not murder, but still ...."

"Don't sweat it, Detective. We're on it now. Get your CCTV video of that probable perp and his van down to Miami-Dade PD. Send it to the attention of Detective Warner. He's lead on the case. If Braun's son has a pic of that dress, get it to Warner too."

"I'm on it. I'll get his e-mail and send it as an attachment. Wow, this is really something."

"Damn right. I'm gonna call Warner now. I've dealt with him in the past. He's one tough, smart cop, and we might finally have a break on this case." He disconnected and then hit an autodial.

"Warner," the voice said after three rings.

¤ ¤ ¤

"Al, this is Filipe Nogales, PBSO."

"Yeah, Detective. What can I do for the Sheriff's Office?" He'd just returned to his desk from scouring the Murder Board, looking for some tiny nugget they might have missed.

"My turn to help. We had a recent robbery/murder in Jupiter."

"That's a long way from my beat, Filipe, but if I can help in any way ...." He sprawled back in his scarred leather chair.

"It's me that's gonna help, Al. I just got the inventory of what was taken. Hold on to your hat, Detective. One of the items was a fancy dress ... a prom dress!"

"What?" Warner jumped up from his desk, sending his chair skittering across the room. Jack Harris materialized at his door.

"Al, what's up?"

Warner held up a hand for silence. "Anything else, Filipe?

"A CCTV parking lot cam picked up the probable perp and his tan Dodge van."

A tan minivan, like what was reported by a neighbor in North Miami Beach. Warner was scribbling notes.

"The store's security tape was taken," Nogales was saying, "and the parking lot video didn't get a shot of his face. The van's plate was mud-smeared, but at least we got an idea of what he may be driving."

"You sure it's our perp?" Warner asked. His office had filled with a noisy sea of detectives and Captain Santiago. Warner waved them down.

"Not a hundred percent," Nogales said, "but the time stamp corresponds with the murder, and the guy's carrying a garment bag. It's gotta be your guy, Al."

"It's about time we got a break," Warner said, pumping his fist. "The video ...?"

"Detective Dupree, with Jupiter Robbery, is e-mailing it as an attachment, and maybe a pic of the dress, if the son of the store owner's got one. I hope this helps put the bastard away."

"It's our first solid lead, and we're gonna jump on it with both feet. Thanks for the good work, Felipe. I'm gonna check for that e-mail, and see what turns up. You get any forensic evidence at the crime scene?"

"Yeah, I almost forgot. There's a partial print. Not enough to run through the AFIS data base, but maybe it'll help."

"It's possible. We got a partial off our last crime scene. Maybe we'll at least get a confirmation this is our guy."

"Right. I'll have CSU send it to you, ASAP. Good luck, Al."

Warner turned to the mass of faces and thrust both arms into the air. Not a touchdown yet, but maybe a field goal.

Finally. Something to actually work with.

He hoped it would pan out in time to save Rochelle Weitz.

# 57

Moe Gold, Miami-Dade's forensics "Hawk," slid two slides into the comparative microscope, leaned forward on the stool, and examined the images. Fingers of his left hand drummed on the white lab counter as he studied the two images.

The fingerprint on the right was from the Jupiter robbery/murder scene. The other was from the North Miami Beach snatch of Rochelle Weitz. The bad news was they were both partials, too small to get a hit from the AFIS data base. The better news was they were both from different portions of what was apparently a right index finger.

The Hawk hummed softly as he adjusted the focus and maneuvered the images, studying the telltale swirls for similarities. By inching one to slightly overlap the other he was trying to create a more complete image that he might successfully introduce to a newly minted state-of-the-art FBI program, supplied by Agent Dalwin.

Al Warner was certain Rochelle Weitz had been taken by their newest maniac, and it was likely he was the same perp that had murdered the storekeeper in Jupiter and taken a prom dress.

But Warner wanted confirmation before they launched an all-out search for a four or five-year-old tan Dodge minivan with muddied plates. He wouldn't waste time and resources chasing a wild goose unless they were pretty sure it was the same perp.

Gold sat back and sighed, his heels hooked over the rung of the stool, and chuckled. Wild geese were common prey of hawks.

He arched back over the binocular eyepieces. Through meticulous micro-adjustments, he'd manufactured about three-fourths of a full print. He snapped a digital photo, slid off the stool and went about introducing it into the FBI's newest miracle program that was designed to enhance and reconstruct missing or degraded fingerprint swirls. It was more art than science, but Agent Dalwin swore it had produced some astonishing results.

If it worked, they might have enough to reintroduce to the AFIS data base, hoping for a match to their killer. He jotted his observations into his log, recorded his comments for the audio log. Then he flipped open his cell phone and punched an auto-dial number. Three rings before it was answered.

"Warner. What d'ya got, Moe?"

"Not as much as I'd like, Al. I examined the prints from both Jupiter and NMB. Comparing the parts that overlapped, I'd say there's an eighty-five percent chance of a match."

"Not positive though, huh?"

"No." The Hawk massaged the inner corners of his eyes. "But good enough to believe it's the same perp. I tried to meld them into one more complete print, and I'm running that through the new program Agent Dalwin got from Quantico."

"Good enough to run through AFIS?" Warner asked.

"Hopefully, but it's supposed to take a day or so for this FBI program to do its magic. You'll be the first to know if we get something worth pursuing."

"Good work. Keep me in the loop. I'm gonna hook up with Dalwin's team, and we'll start a search for that van. It's our first solid lead."

"Good luck, Al. I don't wanna see another pretty young redhead on the M.E.'s autopsy table again anytime soon."

"Me either, Moe," Warner said as he disconnected.

# 58

Al Warner pushed through the glass-paneled door of the squad's conference room, quickly surveying the small group of men seated at the oblong oak table.

"Where's Agent Dalwin?" he asked. "We're gonna need his team's expertise on this."

"He's on the way, Al," Jack Harris said. "He's rounding up the blond Amazon, Yeager, and I think Agent Ashkin."

"Right," Warner said, tossing a thick file onto the table. "He mentioned there's a new vehicle searchin' program he's got for us. Ina Yeager's their tech expert, and Harry is their crime scene specialist, and we're gonna need both their help on this."

"So the van is a solid clue, Boss?" Olvida asked.

"Looks like it." Warner studied the whiteboard, propped against a wall, filled with notations on time-line tracks depicting the progress of the case from the first murder to that very moment.

"The Hawk gives the prints from the NMB snatch site an eighty-five percent likelihood to be the killer's in the Jupiter heist," he continued, turning to the group. "Plus, we just learned that among the things he swiped from that shop was a classic prom-style dress. So it's his vehicle, all right."

"Yeah, but a tan or gold, four or five-year-old Dodge Caravan isn't much to work with," Harris offered, tugging at an ear.

"That's gotta be the most common minivan out there, and probably one of the most popular colors."

"But that's what we got for now ... and it's a helluva lot more than we had a few days ago," Warner said. He glanced up as Agent Dalwin pushed through the door, then he continued.

"Plus, if the perp doesn't think to clean the plate, that'll narrow the search field."

"We get any kind of ID off the print?" Olvida asked, then jumped from his seat as the other two BAU agents hurried into the room.

"I've provided Moe Gold with our latest software," Agent Dalwin said, in response to Rafael's question. "It's the newest thing from Quantico, designed to enhance and develop cleaner prints from partials. I think Gold did an excellent job piecing the two together, but it takes a while for the magic to happen."

"Yeah," Warner said, settling in a chair at the head of the table. "The Hawk said it's bein' processed, but it may take a day or so before he's got something he can send to AFIS."

"Meanwhile," the tall blond Agent Yeager said, "we've just borrowed a new program from Homeland Security that may help find this Unsub's vehicle. They use it for terrorism watches, but they've lent it to us for this case. We can plug in all sorts of parameters to help narrow the search."

"Like a mud-covered plate?" Warner asked.

"Yes, and even the model year and any noticeable dents or visible scratches. It can sort for twenty-three different features."

"Great. So we've gotta get it to all the tech centers and start monitorin' traffic cams and CCTV's."

"Already in the works," Agent Ashkin said. "We've distributed it to ..." he paused, dark eyes raised, one finger stroking the side of his prominent Semitic beak "... eight centers, I think, throughout the county. Yeah, and two in south Broward."

"They all know a young woman's life is hangin' by a thread?" Warner asked.

"They do," Dalwin answered. "We impressed on them that this is priority one. No one's taking this lightly, Detective."

"Okay then. Everyone stay on high alert and ready to go if we get a sightin'. We gotta be ready to move, 'cause this bastard's not gonna hang around, waitin' for us."

The room emptied to an undercurrent of muttered accents.

The hunt was on in earnest.

# 59

Struggling to calm almost constant jitters, Shelly pivoted left, then right, studying herself in the full length mirror on the closet door. The blue and pink party frock was actually quite pretty. Not exactly her taste, but she could see a teenage girl loving it.

*Are we're actually going to a prom. Can't imagine where there'd be one at this time of year, or how he expects to get away with bringing a prisoner. So is this all part of his delusion?* She shivered, her knees almost buckling. She snatched at the chair for support.

*And then what?* Moisture filled her eyes. *I gotta hope this prom isn't his end game … and that's when he murdered the other girls. He loves this Camille … or thinks he does … and should want more from her than just a night of dancing. I gotta hope I'm not gonna die ….*

The click of the lock drew her attention. Must be time to go. She sucked in a breath and tried to still her trembling hands and wobbling knees. She brushed away the tears, terrified at what might happen next.

*I gotta be his girl tonight if I expect to survive this horror.* Gritting her teeth, shoulders squared, chin high, Shelly bound up her inner strength. *I can do this.*

She pasted on the warmest smile she could manage as he strolled into the room, looking surprisingly dapper in a navy-blue tux. A maroon bowtie matched his cummerbund, and a white carnation decorated his lapel. His lips curled at their margins in his best but gruesome attempt at a smile.

"Ahh, you look so beautiful, Camille. The dress is perfect on you. Are you ready?"

"Almost. Can you zip me up?" She showed him her back, drawing in her abs to allow for the tight fit. His hands fluttered over her bare shoulders before attacking the zipper.

His touch caused a blossoming of tiny goose bumps rampaging across her shoulders and neck. He chuckled softly, clearly mistaking them for arousal instead of the panic that was their real author.

He turned her, slipping his arms around her waist, drawing her close. "At last, after all these years, we're finally together, my love."

He leaned in, and she did what was expected of her ... planting a gentle kiss on his narrow lips. His grip tightened, and she arched her neck back, placing a forefinger on his mouth.

"Later, Ron," she said, forcing passion into her voice. "I don't want to mess up my makeup or this lovely dress, and we've got a prom to attend. We missed our first, so we don't want to be late this time." She was stabbing in the dark, hoping it all made sense to his fantasy.

"Of course." He sighed. "It's time to go, and we'll have a lifetime together to enjoy."

*Jesus, I hope not,* she thought. *But I can't keep pushing him off or he may lose patience with me. God! Can I really do this?*

"Here, I brought you a corsage," he said as he pinned a small spray of red roses to her dress. She stared at the flowers, unable to remember if the bodies of any of his victims were decorated by a bouquet. She forced a smile.

"They're beautiful," she said, her voice a hoarse whisper, as she tried to control her shaking. She took his arm. "Lead the way."

It was her first view of the rest of the dwelling besides the dining room—a single story ranch house that looked to be about ten years old. She made mental notes, her realtor mode kicking in, evaluating any future escape possibilities. So far, that looked pretty slim, but perusing the surroundings seemed to calm her.

Maybe once they were on the road, or if there were a chance to signal any of the other people, wherever they were headed.

She'd stay alert, ready to pounce on any opportunity to flee, but she resolved not to do something stupid either.

She *must* keep panic under control, not allowing terror to push her into something futile, if she were to survive.

That was her primary goal.

To survive.

# 60

The ride in the minivan, tunneling through the night darkness along unlit streets, didn't provide the slimmest prospect to flee.

He'd seat-belted her in place and locked and disabled her door ... apparently a child safety feature. She surreptitiously tested the door handle while he was outside, confirming her fear ... there was nowhere to run. Even if she could get loose, there was no way to get away without the probability of him catching her.

She had little doubt what the consequences might be for a failed escape attempt. She visualized her icy body, draped in this frilly gown, propped in some dark alley. She vowed not to give him a reason to end her life that way. Maybe an opening would present itself once they reached the ball, or wherever they were headed, if there were other people there.

She would bide her time and hope for an opportunity. There was little else left for her than that.

Shelly eased back in the leather captain's seat and willed her taut muscles to relax, her thoughts racing through various scenarios. She hoped to be ready act, if the time came. She'd have no more than one slim opportunity at best.

She studied the houses speeding by as they hurried down the gloomy street. They were leaving a primarily residential area, heading into a more commercial zone, replete with warehouses and small businesses.

Why would a prom be held down there?

¤ ¤ ¤

Twenty-five minutes later, she realized she was planning in vain. They weren't headed for the usual prom venue, an auditorium or hotel ballroom.

Ron Bachelor's prom was a creation of his psychosis. He parked behind a small, darkened warehouse. He exited the van and helped her down, offering his arm ... a true gentleman. She actually needed his support, as she was wearing the two-inch heels she'd had on when she went to meet the RE/MAX realtor. It was a gravel alley and unsteady footing. The last thing she needed was a turned ankle if there were a chance to make a run for it.

Bachelor fished a red paisley bandana from his pocket. His lips twitched into a gruesome caricature of a smile.

"It's time, Camille."

"Oh, Ron. Don't!" Her knees buckled. "Please don't."

"It's alright, my love." He covered her eyes, knotting it firmly. "It's time to finish what we started."

*Oh god, he's gonna kill me now. Oh god!"* Only a strong arm circling her waist kept her from collapse.

The tinkle of keys was followed by the click of unlocking the passage door. Her legs like rubber, he half-carried her inside. Setting her down, he hung behind her, his hands resting on her shoulders, fingers lightly circling her neck.

"Ron, Ron. Please don't. I'm your ...." Tears cascaded across her cheeks.

"Shhh, Camille. This is our destiny. I've planned this for eight years."

*Oh, god. I don't want to die. This can't be ....*

She heard the snick of a light switch, and his hands slithered over her hair and down to circle her neck. His lips brushed the side of her throat, and then he withdrew the bandana.

She winced at the sudden cascade of bright lights in the cavernous building. The glare was accented by a spinning reflective ball, swirling the walls and floor with a scattering of shiny droplets of light. Waltz music suddenly echoed from several speakers surrounding the room.

Shelly blinked, eyes flared in surprise. It was, indeed, a warehouse, vast, but gaily festooned with crepe ribbons, dangling balloons and a suspended banner, proclaiming "Proviso East Senior Prom," apparently his high school.

A soft whimper escaped her lips, her eyes welling. She wasn't there to die. At least not yet. Instead, they apparently *were* going to a prom of his making. He was trying to recreate what they had missed, eight-years past.

The air was scented with the smell of lilacs, and she noticed an atomizer near a draped buffet table. It was host to several large floral bouquets, and well laden with chips, dips, a punch bowl and a platter of cut veggies. A tray of peeled shrimp nestled on a bed of ice, next to a plate full of hors d'oeuvres and deviled eggs. A bottle of Champagne rested in an ice bucket, with a pitcher of cold orange juice nearby, probably to make Mimosas.

A temporary, polished hardwood dance floor sat in the center of the room, and much of the surrounding area was covered by carpeting. A DJ table nestled in a corner, complete with a CD player and two speakers. A dozen formally dressed mannequins were scattered around, posed as if dancing together.

"Why the tears, Camille? I did this for you." He turned, taking both her hands in his. "It may not be as festive as the prom we missed eight years ago, but it will be more special. It's just the two of us, with no one to interfere with our pleasure."

"I'm ... I'm just so happy to finally be here with you." She brushed away the remnants of moisture, trying to force a smile onto numb lips. There's nobody to tell she was a prisoner, and nowhere to run. Her knees wobbled as she fought for balance. Repressed terror was swamped by a flood of relief.

*He's not going to kill me. At least not now. I've gotta play the part.*

"Are you okay, Camille?" His arm supportively circled her back. She steeled her backbone and struggled not to cringe.

"Yes. I ... I just lost my balance for a sec. It's these darned heels." An unrestrained shiver coursed through her at his touch.

"Are you cold?" he asked. "I have a shawl for you."

"No. No, I'm just so thrilled to finally make our prom with you." She fought to sound convincing, accepting reality.

*I'm alive! Thank god, I'm still kicking ... as Camille.*

She was doomed to be his lover for now ... an unwilling slave ... or surely die resisting. He might still kill here right there, that night. No! He loved Camille. She *had* to be his lost love, if she were to survive.

She'd do what she must. Play the role ... tell the stories ... be Shahrazad and live again another day. They'd come for her. That detective, the Hero of Miami. They said he never gave up. She'd hang in there, be strong and *be* Camille for this lunatic until the cavalry arrived.

*They're gonna find me. I've gotta believe that or I'm lost.*

"Okay then," he said. "We're finally here together, so let's have some fun. We'll dance. I've got Natalie Cole's recording with her father, singing 'Unforgettable.' That's not from our era, but my mom used to play his songs when I was a kid, and I love his smooth, clear voice. It's always been what I thought of as our song."

His razor-thin lips quivered into a grotesque emulation of a smile. "You've always been unforgettable to me." He took her by the elbow.

"But first some refreshments. Punch or Champagne?" He steered her toward the buffet table.

She stifled a groan. If she could drag this charade out long enough, she might be safe for another night.

He handed her a cup of gin-spiked raspberry punch. She dipped a large, cold shrimp into cocktail sauce.

"Thank you, darling. This is so wonderful ... that you did all this for me." She forced a warm smile onto her lips and pecked him on the cheek. She bit off half the shrimp and gulped several large swallows of her drink, hoping the liquor would relax her.

He sighed. "Nothing is too good for my one and only love." He took the partly empty cup from her, setting it on the table, and led her onto the dance floor.

Clicking a small remote he'd retrieved from his pocket, the warm, melodious strains of the iconic love song wafted across the room, a talented daughter harmonizing with her long-gone and beloved father.

He folded her into his arms and they began to dance. She commanded her stiffening body to relax and molded herself against him. She was his lover. She *had* to be his lover.

"My darling Camille." His breath in her ear set off a tiny rampage of goose bumps across her spine. She nuzzled against his cheek, her lips brushing a soft kiss against his neck.

She hadn't been with a man for nearly two years, but she was about to be his lover. His left hand pressed her very close, their pelvis' brushing. She felt a growing hardness there.

A soft breath seeped between her teeth, caressing his ear. They were soon to be lovers. She *must* live the part.

Somehow, she'd do this to survive.

Somehow.

# 61

Al Warner crossed his knife and fork in the large now empty bowl and pushed away from the glass-topped breakfast-room table.

"That was good, Eva. Nice to eat a light dinner for a change."

"Yes, and I'm starting to watch my diet. I've got a baby to consider."

"Yeah, a baby." Warner's lips curled into a whimsical grin. "Wow. Still tryin' to wrap my mind around that one." He reached across, covering one of her hands with his.

"Me, too, darling. I'd been thinking about that because ... you know ... being in my late thirties, I was running out of time. I know women even in their early forties can still have children, but the longer one waits the more problems can occur."

"That's why you stopped takin' the pills?" he asked.

"Well, if I'm having a baby, there's no one I'd rather have as the father than you, Al. So I threw the dice, as they say, and came up sevens."

Warner chuckled. "Nice metaphor, but I'm the lucky one. Who'd ever have thought ...?"

"Frankly, I never thought I'd get pregnant, or I would have told you I stopped taking the pill. You had a right to ...."

"Not a problem. I couldn't be happier. Never expected to be a dad, after all this time." He rose and pulled her into his arms.

"So," Eva said, her face nestled against his neck, "let's plan on giving this baby a proper name. I've talked to my rabbi, and he provided me several open dates. I'm going to check with a couple of downtown hotels to see which may have a small private room on one of those dates, starting in about a month or so, if that's alright with you."

Warner hesitated, his right thumb unconsciously finding the scar hidden under a mat of thick curly hair.

"I'm as eager to do this as you, babe. To marry you ... Jeez, it never even entered my dreams." He drew her mouth to his lips and brushed it with a gentle kiss.

"But I'd kinda like to hold off until we catch the crazy Prom Dress Killer. I want the most important moment of my life to have my full concentration, and that just won't happen with this nut still lurkin' around."

"I understand. It's going to be at least a month or so before I can arrange things, anyhow. Even a small wedding needs planning and invitations. Didn't you say you had a new lead?"

"Yeah, the first solid one. We've got a probable make on his van from that robbery/murder in Jupiter. We've got every tech available scannin' traffic cams and CCTVs. They thought they may have spotted it somewhere in south Miami, but it was one brief sightin' and it never showed up again."

"You've got the plate number?"

"No, just color, make, and probable age ... and a mud-covered plate. We're using a new Homeland program that that can scan and sort for a variety of variables."

"So you think you're close?" She rose and began clearing the table. Warner jumped up to help. She cooked, and he did the clean-up and dishes. He partnered with the woman he loved.

"I sure the hell hope so. The latest vic hasn't turned up in an alley, wearin' a party dress, so I wanna get this nut before that happens." He put the bowls in the sink, ran hot water into them, and soaped up a sponge.

"We got an idea where to concentrate now, so I'm hopeful ... for the first time in a couple of months."

"Okay. So what I'll do is try to arrange everything for about two months out. If you haven't caught this guy in six weeks, I'll postpone for a month. I don't want you under any pressure other than taking this deadly lunatic off the street."

"Sounds good to me. Be a helluva way to celebrate the miracle of marryin' the most wonderful gal, by puttin' this guy away."

Eva blushed. "That's so sweet. You've told your people about what we're planning?"

"Yep. I thought I was gonna need a back brace after all the congratulatory back slappin'."

"And your future son?" She slipped her arms around his neck, holding his eyes with hers.

"Uhh, no. I thought ... well, that seemed a little too personal at the time." He planted a soft kiss on her forehead.

"Okay. We'll keep that between us for now."

"Right." He finished stacking the dishes in the rack. "I'm goin' back to the office now. See if maybe they've got any new sightin' on that Dodge van. I should be back in a couple of hours, unless something hot turns up."

"Go get 'em, tiger," she whispered.

One heated kiss, and he was out the door.

Things were finally coming together.

# 62

They had danced for two hours, occasionally breaking to sip punch and Champagne and nibble on shrimp.

Shelly diverted him from conversation as best she could. She wanted to save story-telling for later, after they'd returned to the house ... her defacto prison. She hoped to put him off for another night, but knew in her heart she'd probably have to give in and have sex ... No. Make love to him ... soon.

She had to somehow hold on to the hope she'd find a way to escape, but so far she hadn't seen the slightest opening. Or maybe they'd find her before things got too intense. Tears crept into the corners of her eyes. He'd been doing this for nearly a decade and hadn't been caught. Rescue seemed remote.

And now, at midnight, it was time to leave. They were heading back to the house ... her prison ... and only God, and Ron Bachelor, knew what was in store for her. It was late, so she could probably stall the inevitable for at least one more night.

She struggled to swallow a large frog that had suddenly lodged in her throat as a new thought bloomed in her mind. Did he plan on killing her, now that she was wearing the dress and they'd gone to the "prom?" She shivered and battled to suppress the moisture that again threatened to seep from her eyes. Her heart pummeled her breast as she wondered what was next. Would he take her back or ...?

*Was this was what had happened with the other girls? Did he take them to this ersatz prom and then kill them? Like the Sultan did with all his wives after their first night together, before marrying Shahrazad.* She slumped against the wall by the door, her legs threatening to buckle.

*No! I gotta believe he loves this Camille, and if I can be her, I'll be safe.* She clenched her jaw, teeth grinding.

*I've got to be her.*

She pushed herself erect, as he secured the warehouse. With a firm grip on her elbow, Ron Bachelor, the Prom Dress Killer, escorted Shelly ... nee Camille ... to his van.

He was in control. There was nowhere to run, especially in two-inch heels and a billowing party dress. She brushed away the remnants of her tears, hoping he hadn't noticed.

*Stay alert, take in the surroundings and hope for a break in the next few days.* If she memorized the lay of the land, she might have a better chance, if she were able to slip free.

After installing her in the passenger seat and affixing her seatbelt, he slid into the driver's side, locking the doors.

"I was going to clean up our little club tomorrow," he said, patting her on the thigh, sending electric little tremors up her back. "But we had such a good time, I may leave it up. We can have a wonderful reprise next week. Won't that be fun?"

"Oh yes, if it's not too much of a bother for you. I loved having the opportunity to make up for our missed prom, Ron."

She struggled to quell a tremor in her voice, hoping she wasn't laying in on too thickly, but he seemed impervious to that kind of flattery.

And he was talking about their time together, next week.

So, for the moment, at least, she was still alive.

# 63

Al Warner was just backing his Dodge Charger out of his one-car garage when his cell phone trilled.

"Jack Harris," the pleasant female Bluetooth voice announced. Warner loved that feature on his Dodge coupe. It could even read text messages to him. He tapped the green "phone" button on his steering wheel.

"What's up, Jack?"

"Hey, Al. You know the Hawk finally got enough on that print to try AFIS again, and we just got a hit."

"What? Really? So do we finally have a handle on our perp? Something to help us nail this nut?" Warner shifted into "Park" and lingered in his driveway, actually holding his breath.

"Yes and no. No actual ID, like a name or description."

The detective's breath hissed out past clenched teeth, and he sagged back in his seat.

"But they were able to tie it to three homicides in Atlanta," Harris continued, "between two and four years ago. Not surprisingly, all redheaded young women. And the last two vics were dolled up in fancy party dresses."

"So it *is* our guy," Warner muttered, more to himself. "Get what you got on my desk, Jack. I'm on my way in, and we'll reach out to the Atlanta PD. See if they got anything to help narrow our search." He shifted into reverse, glanced over his shoulder, backed out and was hightailing for his office. He was still connected to Harris on his Bluetooth.

"You get any info on who was workin' the cases in Georgia?"

"Yep. Everything will be on your desk by the time you get here. I know you still like paper files, but I'm sending it to you computer, too."

"Great. Maybe we're finally gettin' a few breaks on this case." He switched on his siren and slapped a red and blue flashing light on his roof. The quicker he got on this, the sooner they might nail this lunatic.

"I'll be there in ten. Stick close, in case I got some questions."

"Gotcha, Al," Warner heard before disconnecting so he could concentrate on his driving. No time to get careless, when they were so close.

¤   ¤   ¤

Warner bounded up the stairs, three at a time, bursting into the squad room like a Brahma bull out of the gate. Jack Harris and Rafael Olvida, who had been clustered at the door, flanked him as he stormed toward his office.

"What d'we got?" Warner asked.

"Three murders in two different Atlanta PD districts. Two for sure our guy's MO, with the prom dresses and all," Olvida said.

"The third's the same vic type, but no dress," Harris said. "They had only partial prints, like us, but enough to tie all three together."

"They sent what they had to AFIS but never got a hit until Moe's enhanced print hit their data base. It was enough to tie theirs and ours together." Olvida was looking at his note book. "It's the same perp, alright. I got the referral info on the Atlanta detectives on the case."

"More than one, because of the two different districts?"

"Yeah," Harris said, as Warner reached his desk, settling on his chair. The two other detectives crowded in close.

"Makes sense," Warner said. "Did they know they had a serial killer?"

"Probably not," Harris said. "Apparently the districts are cross town from each other, and our perp only dressed up one vic in each territory."

"So they never made the connection?" Warner asked, and then looked up as Special Agent Dalwin knocked on the door jamb but didn't await an invitation to come in.

"It's not so uncommon, Al," he said. "The district with the two deaths appears to be the one with the partial that was in the AFIS storage base. When The Hawk's enhanced print lit the fire, they also referred it to the NCIC national base, and it tied everything together."

"So it looks like we weren't his first stop. Makes you wonder if there was something before Atlanta? We in touch yet with the Atlanta detectives on the cases?"

Captain Santiago had joined the group. "Not yet, Al. I thought it best coming from you. You're lead on this. They've certainly been notified by NCIC, so they're probably waiting for a call."

"Okay," Warner said, his eyes darting between his two top detectives. "Who's got the names and numbers?"

"Here, Boss," Olvida said, tearing a sheet from his notebook.

Warner snatched up his desk phone and made the call.

Thirty minutes later, two excited cops, Ambrose and Salazar, were gearing up for a visit to Miami, bringing their files and their expertise with them. The long-ago murders of pretty redheads hadn't gone cold on their case logs. They were eager to get in on this new leg of an old case.

And Al Warner wasn't too proud to take any help he could get. He only wanted justice for all the victims.

# 64

Shelly stirred, eyes fluttering open. She'd been in the midst of a pleasant dream, lolling on a sunny beach with her mom, when she woke. She was in mid-stretch before reality thundered over her, snatching out a plaintiff whimper.

That dream of happiness evaporated into the nightmare of reality ... her captivity at the hands of a homicidal maniac. She wiggled into a sitting position, her back against the headboard, her face cupped in her shaking hands.

*Jesus, what's next? I made it through last night alive, but how long can I keep putting him off?*

By the time they returned from the "prom," it was after one. They'd kissed, perched on the bed's edge, and his hands fluttered over her in teasing caresses. She moaned and sighed, feigning passion, but succeeded in earning one more day's delay by professing exhaustion. His final comment before leaving her for the evening portended what was in store for the next morning.

"Rest well, my darling," he'd said, "because tomorrow, when you're fully restored, we'll consummate our love and begin planning our life together."

She shuddered at that memory, tears pooling in her eyes, climbing across the swell of her cheeks. "Consummate" meant the time had come. Shelly sighed, knuckling away the moisture, and gritted her teeth.

She could do this. She *had* to do this ... become his ardent lover if necessary. Whatever it took to survive until they found her. She'd do what she had to do to stay alive.

Her lips narrowed into a grimace. Rochelle Weitz was a passionate young woman with a strong carnal nature she'd rarely had a chance to fulfill. Her life and designs for her future had been too busy to allow much time for men, and those few she'd slept with were passing dalliances. She had regularly satisfied her carnal needs alone, surfing in her fertile imagination. It was ironic she was fated to take a psychotic lunatic as her next lover. She doubted he'd tolerate any further delay, so now seemed the time. A soft moan echoed in her throat.

*I can do this. I* gotta *do this! No holding back, Shelly. Let it all loose.*

Almost as if he sensed the timing, the door locks rattled, and Ron Bachelor stood in the opening, wearing a paisley silk robe. His tight lips tilted into what she supposed was a smile, and the sparkle in his eyes portended what she'd feared but expected. His passion was an emotion not easily expressed on such a plastic face.

"Ah, I thought I heard you stirring."

"Yes, I just awakened." She battled to keep fear and tension from her voice. *I can do this,* she thought again, steeling her will.

"And you've made yourself ready for me? To finally consummate our long-delayed love?" He glided forward, tugging at the sash of the robe.

"Yes, my love." She forced husky passion into her voice. "Ready and eager, after so long a denial."

He settled on the edge of the bed, garment now open, revealing his bare torso.

A hand caressed her cheek, trailing down her neck and across her perky breasts. Tremors coursed throughout her body.

She choked down a lump in her throat, steeling her will, accepting what was about to happen.

"Camille, my love. I've dreamed of this, so long delayed by so many imposters. I hardly know how to begin." He slipped the straps of her silk nightgown off her shoulders, edging it down, baring her bosom. His fingers, as light as butterfly wings, tripped across the swells, tweaking erect nipples.

His eyes found hers, and shrugging off his robe, he leaned in, a hand gently cupping her head, his lips seeking hers. She tilted forward, her slightly parted lips brushing his, the pink tip of her tongue a teasing viper.

He edged closer, drawing her against him, his hand down her back, stripping away the flimsy nightgown. Her arms circled his neck, their mouths crushed together. She suppressed a gag, willing her tongue to take part, fencing – thrust and parry – with his.

They slid down, sprawled across the bed, their bodies clammy with heat, moving together in an erotic tango. His hands skipped across her skin as tiny mouse feet, moist lips venturing with carnal heat from breast to breast, then belly, and finally sliding lower to another set of lips, opened and damp with heat.

*I am Camille, finally with my lover. I am Camille. Write this story, Shelly. Be Shahrazad, the storyteller.*

*I am Camille.*

"Slowly, darling," she murmured. "Slowly." She forced her hands to caress him. She was relieved to find he was a tender and patient lover. She relaxed slightly, realizing this may not be the brutal rape she'd feared. He loved Camille, so maybe she could fake her way through this.

And as he finally entered her, she cringed, squealing softly, gritting her teeth, her eyes clenched closed. She wiggled against him, forcing herself to thrust back, willing her hands to trail across his back.

She steered her mind into the little fiction she had created, a passionate love story, trying to respond.

*I am Camille. Camille.*

*Camille with my lover.*

¤ ¤ ¤

They lay intertwined, slick with perspiration, totally spent, he on top, her head nestled in the crook of his neck.

"Camille. Camille, I've waited so long for this."

"As have I, Ron." She forced a calm huskiness into her voice, struggling to control her revulsion. He thought they were lovers, but in fact, she'd just been raped by a heartless killer ... and she'd survived by pretending to be his Camille. And she would do it again, if necessary. Send her mind off to a romance story, and live another day. And then another day, and then another? How long could she keep this charade up?

*Jesus. What if I can't escape, and they never find me? Will I be secretly his unwilling lover forever? Will I descend into that Stockholm Syndrome I've read about, and actually care for him? Love a killer? I don't ....*

He pushed himself up and rolled away, sitting up. Perched on the bed's edge, he trailed fingers across her still damp skin, and then leaned over, brushing lips against hers.

"Ah, Camille. I can't voice how happy you've made me. You relax now, darling. I'm going out to buy supplies, and you need a new wardrobe. I should only be gone a few hours. Then we can revel in our love again. It's so wonderful."

"Of course, my darling. I do need some clothes and some comfortable shoes." She rose, slipping into a robe he'd given her. Sometimes he talked as if he were in a "B-grade" movie.

"May I wait in the family room and watch some TV?" Maybe a chance to escape while he was out?

"No, not yet." He studied her, eyes hardening. "Work on your novel, and I'll be back soon. Then we'll relax together in the den later. I won't be gone long."

So she was his lover, but still not trusted. Better not push it.

He drew her into his arms and kissed her lightly, then picked up his robe, turning to leave.

"Rest, darling. I'll be back soon."

And he was out the door, locking it as he left.

So much for love.

# 65

Shelly slouched in the room's sole armchair, trying to work on the outline of her novel. Before he left on his shopping trip, her captor had provided, at her request, a pad of lined paper and two pencils. She needed the distraction, hoping it would be calming and prepare her for what was coming next.

Shelly suspected the story's ending would substantially change from her original concept, if she ever escaped this prison alive. She wasn't making much progress, though, stranded in writer's block, as her thoughts kept drifting off.

She plopped the pad on her lap and leaned back, biting her lower lip. She was terrified at what was happening, because a psychotic serial killer fantasized she was someone else ... someone he "loved" and wasn't going to ever let go.

Her choice was to continue faking being his enthusiastic lover whenever and however often he wanted, or surely die resisting, just as she believed the other girls had done.

How long could she carry on this charade before making a fatal slip on some detail that didn't dovetail with their history? But how much history was there, in reality? She suspected not much, so maybe she could bluster her way through any misstep.

What bothered her more was what if she never managed to escape, or were never rescued? And got pregnant? She'd have to make a life with him ... be his woman ... have his kids. Tears flooded her eyes and two wrenching sobs were ripped from her breast.

*I don't want to be his woman! I don't wanna die. I just want to go home.* She dabbed at the moisture with a tissue.

And if she were never found? If he always treated her as reverently as he had so far, gently performing loving sex, could she survive like that? Eventually acclimating to a life with him?

That scenario had happened more than once. She'd heard stories of women who'd lived with their captor for decades, and fought to protect him when he was finally caught. The Stockholm Syndrome, it was called. Would she ever be that kind of girl? She refused to consider that.

She brushed away recurring tears when she heard the garage door rising. Ron was back with her new wardrobe. All she had to wear up to now was the outfit she had on when he snatched her, and the silk nightgown and cotton robe he'd given her.

A few moments later, he was in the room, toting bags from Macy's, Bloomingdale's, and The Gap. He'd been shopping at the Dadeland Mall, according to the logo on one of the bags, so she had some idea of where she was ... southern Miami, maybe near Kendall.

"Okay, my love. Try these things on. You'll need a proper casual wardrobe, if we're to go out together."

Her heart fluttered with the beat of hummingbird wings.

*Go out together?*

Maybe a chance to escape, if he got careless. Unfortunately, so far that hadn't seemed one of his faults.

He perched on the chair, and watched as she unwrapped the packages. Not likely to have any privacy, but she was wearing her bra and panties from the day he took her.

There were tan shorts, gray slacks, a black skirt, ivory and beige blouses, underwear and a bra, stockings and two pairs of shoes ... sneakers and boat-shoe loafers.

She tried them on, one after the other, modeling them for him. Steeling herself, she acted coquettish, knowing he'd want her to be appreciative. She struggled not to cringe, seeing lust growing in his eyes, his tongue sweeping across his lips.

"Try the shoes, so we can move on, my love."

She had no doubt where he wanted to move on to, and had no idea how to safely postpone that outcome.

She opened the boat-shoe box, glancing at the label: size 6. They'd never fit. She was a seven-and-a-half. She went through the motions, but neither pair would work.

"Sorry, Ron. They're just too small. I'm a seven-and-a-half. Everything else fits fine, but I guess you'll have to return the shoes. I can go with you to try on new ones, if you wish." A stab at what she suspected was futility.

"No. I'll do it later. But now, watching you look so fetching, modeling these outfits, my love is overflowing." He rose, taking her hand, twirling her into his arms. He kissed her neck, then her ear, venturing across her cheek to her lips.

She let herself go. There was no other choice. She submerged her mind into the fantasy love story she'd devised. He took his time disrobing her, teasing and playing. Then they were naked, on the bed, and things were accelerating. She couldn't stifle a soft moan.

He chuckled, apparently thinking it was the sounds of passion instead of hopelessness. He would never have enough of her, and she would have to continue as if reveling in it. She dreaded the day when she might stop hating him for it.

Forty minutes later, they had showered together and were dressing. She donned the slacks and an ivory blouse. He was back in cargo shorts, a knit tee, and ankle boots.

"You relax here, Camille, and work on your book. I've got an Internet search to do on my computer in the next bedroom. Then I'll ride my motorcycle back to the mall to exchange the shoes. You shouldn't have another day without proper footwear."

"You have a motorcycle?"

"Yes. A Kawasaki Ninja ZX."

"Really? I didn't notice it in the garage last night."

"No. I store it in a small shed alongside the house. It's a fun bike, and I've got saddlebags and a removable rear storage box. Plenty of room for the shoes. I've got maybe an hour's work on the Web before I leave." He took both her hands in his.

"The returns and new purchases should only take an hour or so. Maybe I'll take you for a ride, after we get settled in. It's exhilarating." His lips brushed across her fingers before releasing them.

"Sounds like fun, Ron." *A ride on the back of a motorbike. Possibly a chance to escape.*

*Probably not, though. He's too careful for that.*

"I'll see you soon, Camille."

She lightly took his arm as he turned to leave.

"May I come with you while you work on the computer? Just a small change of scenery?" Maybe a chance to scout a way out.

"No." He stroked her cheek. "It's ... something personal. Work on your book. I won't be gone too long. I'm so excited that we're finally together. I'll be eager to be back in your arms."

She clenched her jaw, stifling a groan. She knew what *that* meant.

Then he was out the door, and she was alone again, locked in Hell with her thoughts.

# 66

Al Warner sorted through three files of recent murders, unrelated to their Prom Dress Killer. One was clearly a drug buy gone wrong. The second seemed a senseless shooting in Overtown. And the third a squabble over gang territory in Little Havana.

Warner needed to assign detectives to each, but his ranks were drastically thinned by the hunt for their serial lunatic. He'd have to pull some teams off that search to investigate these crimes. They can't be left without justice because of one high-profile killer.

He sighed, scribbling detective team names on Post-its and affixing one to each file. He'd have to fill the gap for their serial killer search with patrol teams. He pushed away from his desk and started out to assign the cases as Captain Santiago came through his door.

"Any news, Al?"

"On what? Our Prom Dress nut? Yeah, some. We got Olvida and his partner headin' three other teams, canvassin' Kendall, Coral Gables, South Miami, Pinecrest and the surroundin' areas, all armed with photos of the suspected van and pics of Rochelle Weitz."

"That's a big piece of Miami, Al."

"I know, Cap, but I got three other murders on my desk that need detectives to investigate. I can't ignore the rest of the city. I'm gonna try to get two or three more patrol teams down there.

Just hopin' to find someone who's seen the vehicle, or maybe even the girl. Try to see if we can narrow our search vector. We've concentrated all our tech teams in the whole southern regions, usin' the new Homeland program." He started for the bullpen, carrying the three new assignments, with his captain trailing.

"No new sightings since that first one?" Santiago asked.

"No, but I'm hopin' it's only a matter of time now. We got that whole quadrant saturated, monitorin' every traffic and CCTV camera we can find. Unfortunately, time may not be in Rochelle Weitz's favor, but if she's the clever gal her mom says she is, she may still be holdin' on."

"You're hoping she can stall him," Santiago says, taking Warner's arm to turn him.

"Yeah. Agent Dalwin's BAU team profiled him as lookin' for a long-lost love. If Weitz is smart enough to convince him she *is* that gal, she may be safe ... at least from dyin'. God knows what else ...."

"Hey, Al," Jack Harris yelled, jumping up from behind his green, glass-topped partition that passed for his office.

"What, Jack?" Warner's heart skipped a beat.

"Tech got a hit on a tan Dodge van with muddied plates!"

"Jesus, where?" He swiveled, thrusting the three files into his captain's hands.

"Kendall, off Ludlum Road and 104th Street. Might have been coming from the Dadeland Mall."

"Where's the SWAT team?" Warner met Harris at his desk.

"Coral Gables, but Ralph and his partner just left for Dadeland. He's the closest. He's heading over there with the photos." Harris was already holstering his 9mm pistol and pocketing his shield.

"Okay, let's go." Warner raced to his office to gather up his Glock and shield. "Will ya assign those cases, Captain? With any luck, we may have more detectives available sooner than I thought." He sped toward the exit with Jack Harris, his long-time partner close behind.

Warner and Harris sped southwest in his Dodge coupe, siren blaring and roof-top light-bar strobing. He wove expertly through traffic, some who failed to curb their vehicles at their howling approach. Warner muttered curses under his breath.

Eight minutes after departing, his Bluetooth chimed. The LED screen on his dash displayed Raphael Olvida's number. He trapped the green phone image on his steering wheel.

"Talk to me, Ralph." He gritted his teeth, swerving around another clueless driver.

"I think we got 'im, Boss."

"Where?" Warner concentrated on his driving, thankful for the hands-free benefits of his Bluetooth.

"We got several IDs leading to a ranch house in Kendall ... the 9500 block of SW 69th Avenue. We're on the way there now."

"Great. Wait for us. Jack and I are less than ten minutes out. Did you get a warrant?" He glanced at his partner, whose face split with a wide grin. They bumped fists.

"Talked to the ADA on duty. Said he'd have one sent to my phone by the time you get here."

"What about SWAT?" Warner asked. He made a hard turn, tires squealing in protest, onto SW 88th Street, heading west.

"They're still twenty, thirty minutes out. Boxed in and tied up getting around a big fender bender....

"May have to go without 'em," Warner said, muttering a curse. "You'll beat us to the scene, Ralph. No siren and lights, and hang back outta sight. Keep surveillance, and we'll figure it out when we get there."

"Hang tough, amigo," Harris chortled. "We're finally gonna nail this bastard."

# 67

Shelly studied her image in the full length mirror, pivoting slowly to see herself at every angle. She'd donned a pair of the shorts ... the *short* shorts that revealed all of her shapely legs ... and a light sleeveless knit blouse. She was wearing no underwear.

"What are you *doing*?" she muttered, uttering a soft wail, stripping off the outfit. This was overdoing the girlfriend thing. He obviously loved Camille in whatever sense he was capable of love, and she *had* to be that woman to survive.

She'd been without a man for so long, struggling with independence and a career, that she'd become nun-like. The last guy she'd made love to ... was it really two-years ago ... was handsome and self-absorbed, interested in her giving him pleasure, but with little return effort. It was once and done.

It shook her that Ron Bachelor, a serial killer who'd plied his trade in more than one state, was a tender lover to his long-lost Camille, no matter how much Shelly despised it. But that could ... no, *would* ... turn deadly if he discovered he'd chosen the wrong Camille again.

She was certain that's what happened with all the girls he'd killed in South Florida, plus the three he mentioned in Atlanta. And who knows how many before that.

She'd wiggled into silk panties and had snapped on her bra. She paused, uncertain what to wear. Shrugging, she gathered up the knee-length shorts and cotton blouse and began dressing again.

Didn't he say he was from suburban Chicago? How many corpses had he left there before moving south? She shuddered, suspecting there were more than one. All girls that probably resisted being Camille?

She groaned, rubbing away blossoming goose bumps on her arms. Her eyes welled, pools of fear, sending salty rills across the hills of her cheeks to puddle at the corners of her mouth. She backhanded them away, shaking her head.

*I've gotta get control. If I gotta be Camille to survive, then I've gotta act passionate.*

*Is this how the Stockholm Syndrome begins? By willingly participating? How terrifying.*

She stamped her foot and grunted. She wasn't there. At least not yet. She wanted to go home, see her mom, and resume her happy life. But would any of that ever be possible again, even if she were rescued?

If she was somehow set free, could she ever again be the person she was, before Ron Bachelor? He'd certainly fill her dreams with terror.

Those thoughts set her shaking again, tears gushing, crying openly. She slumped to the floor, her face in her hands, and bawled.

"I want to go home," she wailed softly. "I don't want to be stuck here forever. Please, find me. I want to go home."

She curled up on the floor, body racked by soft sobs. She had to get a hold of herself.

Ron shouldn't find her like that.

Because, in the end, she had to survive, no matter what.

# 68

Warner killed his siren and flashing lights when he was four blocks away. Hurrying south on SW 69th Ave, Jack Harris gestured at a blue Chevy Caprice, parked in the shaded umbrella of a large black olive tree.

"There's Olvida's Chevy, Boss." The house in question appeared to be in the next block. Warner slid his Dodge to a quiet stop behind the other sedan, and Harris and he exited his vehicle, approaching Olvida's car from both sides.

"What d'we got, Ralph?

"The house is the third from the nearest corner, on the west side. No activity there since we arrived."

"Not a busy street," Detective Michaels, Olvida's partner, said. "Three cars have gone by; two kids on bikes, probably playing hooky; and an older guy walking a mutt."

"No sign of the Dodge van," Olvida added. "He's either out, or it's in the garage."

"Any word from SWAT?" Warner asked, shading his eyes and looking down the street.

"They're still at least fifteen minutes out," Olvida said, exiting his car. "D'ya want to wait, Al?"

Warner rolled his shoulder and flexed his neck, dissipating tension. He crossed the street, a pair of binoculars in his hands, and examined the front of the house.

"The garage door's got a small window. Michaels, you saunter down there and take a peek. Thumbs up if the van's inside. If not, come on back. Don't linger. We don't want to get made."

"And if the van's there, Al?" Harris asked. He'd joined them at the curb, checking the clip in his 9mm Sig and chambered a round.

"We go. Don't want this bastard to have a chance to get away while we hang around, waitin' for SWAT and Dalwin's team. Far as we know, he's a loner, so it shouldn't be a problem."

The three other men all grunted eager accent. They each wanted a piece of The Prom Dress Killer, and none of them would regret putting a round or two in him, and worry about the paperwork and inquiry later.

Save the courts money and give the grieving families some sense of retribution.

Detective Michaels checked his own weapon, a forty-caliber Glock. He reholstered it under his sport jacket, and started up the street, hands in his pockets, trying to look like a casual stroller.

Ninety seconds later, he'd peeked through the garage door window and turned to his team. He gave two thumbs up, drew his weapon, and crouched near the corner of the building.

# 69

Warner caught Jack Harris's arm as he started to run for the house.

"Easy, Jack. Let's just stroll up the block, keepin' some separation, and act casual, just in case he's lookin' out the window. When we hit the front walk, Jack, you and Olvida hustle around back. Go on the far side, past the garage. Less likely to be windows there."

"Got it, Boss," Olvida said, checking his own weapon. "What's the signal to go?"

"I'll beep Jack's phone with a text. Go on a count of three after that.

"Listen up," Warner said. "While we'd all like to see this guy take his last breath, we really need him alive, if possible.

"Don't risk any of our safety for that. But we know he's killed in at least one other state, and there are families there who'll need satisfaction."

Warner searched their faces, getting varying levels of reluctant consent.

"Let's go get him." He nodded toward the house.

They started up the street, edginess quickening their pace. Tongues swept over dry, cracked lips, and breaths came in hurried gasps. Despite their considerable experience, they were all tightly wired, pumped with adrenaline.

As they neared the small ranch house, Warner glanced at Olvida. "You got the warrant, right?"

"Texted to my phone, Boss. We're legal."

"Okay, then." He gestured toward the garage, and Harris and Olvida slipped quietly around the far side of the house. Warner counted to ten, took a deep breath, and hit the SEND button on his phone.

His heart was jack-hammering his ribs as he counted to three. He nodded to Michaels, and snatching a tense breath, they rushed the front door.

Ramming it with his shoulder, the door jamb splintered from the powerful impact, and both men burst inside. Warner dropped to one knee, sweeping the room.

"Miami police," he shouted as the back door imploded, and Raphael Olvida tumbled into the kitchen, weapon up, searching for prey. Harris slipped in behind him, dropping into a crouch.

No perp visible. Warner jumped up, and a quick glance identified what were surely bedrooms, branching from a hallway to their right. He motioned to Michaels, who stood in the open doorway, to clear the living room and den, off to their left.

He froze as a thump echoed from the first bedroom, followed by a muffled clatter. Panting, his heart still doing the jitterbug, he darted to the corridor. Slipping quickly to the opening, his back plastered against the wall, he took a quick peek down the shadowy passageway.

Nobody there. There were two doors on the right side, and one, probably the master, at the end.

Then a voice echoing from down the hall, maybe from the second bedroom.

"Ron?" A woman, tense and quavering. "Ron? Is that you?"

Had they found her, or was it a trap? Warner gulped some air, clearing his throat.

"Miami police," he shouted again. "It that you, Miss Weitz?"

"Oh, god, oh, god. Yes, yes. I'm in the bedroom. Oh, god! You found me. Thank god you found me."

"Are you alone? Where's the guy?" Warner eyed the first door, hanging ajar.

"No, be careful! He's in the house." She was sobbing now. "I think in the next bedroom." She gasped, crying loudly. "Oh, god, I can't believe you found me." Heavy sobs echoed from the second bedroom, further up the hall.

"Hang on until we clear the house. I'm gonna get you outta there." He slithered down the passageway, back still to the wall, taking no chances. She had to be behind that second door ... the one with a keyed deadbolt.

The first bedroom was his immediate focus. He beckoned Harris to join him before bursting inside, crouching low, Warner sweeping left with Harris covering the right.

It was an average room, set up as an office ... and it was empty. A gentle moist breeze bathed his face with the combined odor of newly mown grass and faint trace of exhaust fumes, coming through an open window. A laptop computer sat on a small metal desk, displaying a Google search page. He eased over to the window, and peeked outside. Nothing but the fading whine of a distant motorcycle. Leaning out, he noticed a small storage shed, its door hanging open.

"He's not here, Al," Harris said.

"No. Gone through this window when we broke in, I'd guess. You and Michaels get out there, pronto. He may still be in the area. Check out that shed just outside. I'm gonna get the girl outta that room." As Warner strode quickly back toward the hall, he glanced at the lit up computer screen, jerking him to a halt.

He grunted and his eyes narroed, staring at the image there. It was a photo of him. The bastard was Googling him! *What the fuck*?

Warner hurried on to the corridor, placing a hand on the locked door. Time to set this lady free.

"Stand back," he called. "I'm gonna kick in the door." He glanced at Olvida coming up behind him, pistol at the ready.

"Cover me, Ralph."

Turning, he aimed a powerful kick at the lock. It took two tries to bust it open, shattering the jamb. He slid inside, back to the wall, his Glock ready, but all he saw was a pretty redheaded girl, dressed in shorts and a blouse, cowering on the floor at the foot of the bed.

"Miss Weitz?" He knelt in front of her. "Rochelle Weitz?"

She nodded. Tears streaked her cheeks, her arms crossed in front, hugging herself. She was shivering uncontrollably.

"I'm Detective Al Warner, ma'am." Her face was chalky. She was hyperventilating. "I've got you," he said. He took one of her hands, drawing her slowly to her feet. "You're safe now."

Still heaving with tears, she leaned forward, throwing her arms around him. He held her lightly, rubbing her back, like calming an edgy colt.

"Detective Warner." The emotional release choked her words. "Thank god. I'd almost given up hope you'd find me."

"No bad guy's perfect, miss. They all eventually make mistakes. This bastard was no exception."

"But I think he's been doing this for so long," she sniffled between panted breaths, "and not just in Florida. No one's ever caught him ... until you."

"Unfortunately, we *haven't* caught him ... yet. And we'll want to hear more about whatever you know. But first we gotta get you outta here and checked up by a doctor. How are you feelin'? You've been through hell."

"Hell, and then some," she muttered, as tears flowed again.

# 70

Warner continued gently stroking her back. "It's okay. Let it all out. You've endured a chillin' experience and have been incredibly brave. And you figured out what to do to stay alive. That's more than at least eight other gals have done. Take your time. I'm here to listen when you're ready."

She shuddered in his arms, hers wrapping him, her eyes, tiny faucets, in full flow against his shoulder. "Thanks. I was so terrified." She heaved a sigh, pulling back.

"I think there were more girls, somewhere else," she whispered through her tears.

Jack Harris appeared at the door.

"I called for Fire/Rescue, Al. Should be here in five or ten."

"Thanks, Jack." He stepped back, offering Shelly a tissue.

"I'll want to hear more about those other women, Miss Weitz. But you need to get to the hospital," he said, "and see a doctor. I'm gonna have Doctor Guttenberg check on you too." What she had endured went way beyond physical trauma.

"Meanwhile," glancing at Harris, "get CSU up here, and task the local patrols to start sweepin' the neighborhood north of here. I think he may have escaped in that direction on a motorbike. Let's find this bastard."

He glanced again at Shelly, holding her hands. "Any idea on where he might have gone?"

She paused, then sighed and shook her head. "No. As far as I know, he lived here." Her breathing was returning to normal. She ran a hand through her hair and smoothed her shorts.

"I've been trapped in this room except to eat, and to go to the prom, two nights ago."

"The prom? Really?" Warner's eyebrows arched.

"His idea of a prom, I suppose." Her voice quavered. She perched on the edge of the bed.

"Some kind of vacant warehouse ... a commercial area somewhere. I'm not sure where. It was dark, and I was scared he was going to kill me in that fancy dress."

"I understand. Tell me what you can."

"He either owns it or rented it, I guess. Decked it out like a ballroom. Even had one of those reflective light balls, a DJ setup, and a portable dance floor." She sighed, her unique gray eyes catching his. "We drank punch and Champagne, and danced to Natalie Cole's 'Unforgettable'."

A soft groan slipped between her lips, "I acted like I had a good time ... which wasn't as hard as I expected when I realized he didn't intend to kill me. At least not then. He thinks I'm Camille, a girl he loved in high school." She shivered, and Warner slipped out of his jacket, draping it around her shoulders.

"Thanks," she smiled for the first time that day. "Anyway, I guess they were supposed to go to the prom eight years ago, but he was late. I think he was delayed because he was killing another girl."

"At eighteen? Jesus. Where was this, d'ya know?" He crouched in front of her, taking a hand.

"Suburban Chicago, he said. Then I think he killed her parents because they wouldn't tell him where she was."

"Parents? Whose parents?"

"Camille's. But it's hard to know what's real with him and what's delusional. He seems totally amoral ... a complete psychopath." She shivered again, despite his jacket.

"You called out 'Ron' through the door," Warner said. "Is that his name?"

"Yes. Bachelor. He said he was Ron Bachelor."

"So, that's probably his real name, since you were supposed to be his girl eight years ago." Goose bumps trickled across his back. They were getting closer.

"I suppose. I tried to fake being this Camille, so he wouldn't kill me, but how does he *not* know who she is, if he's been chasing her for eight years?" Tears were again working their way out of the corners of her eyes.

"Boss, Fire/Rescue is here," Olvida said, appearing in the doorway. "No sign of the perp anywhere. But lots of personal things in the house that might help, including that computer. Kinda eerie, seeing he was researching you. What d'ya think that was about?"

"No idea. We'll see what Tech comes up with when they dig into his files. We'll get to that soon as we get this young woman into the hands of the medics."

Two EMTs hurried into the room, one carrying a collapsible wheelchair and the other a medical bag.

They set Shelly in the chair and took a quick check of her vitals, all of which seemed strong. They started to wheel her off, and she turned to Warner.

"Detective."

"Yes, ma'am." He was instantly kneeling at her side.

"I'm too young to be called ma'am," she said with a chuckle.

"Sorry. Habit. Shelly okay?"

"Perfect. Can you do one more thing for me? I'm kinda uncomfortable about this."

"Of course. What is it?"

"I had sex with that creep ... twice .... I had to do it, and fake loving it, because I was his Camille. But I sure don't want to have his baby. Can these guys get me a morning-after pill?"

"I'll ask 'em," he said, rising. "But you're gonna see Doctor Eva Guttenberg as soon as you get to Doctor's Hospital. She's a great lady. Even looks a little like an older version of you. Ask her, and I'm sure she'll see to it."

"Thank you so much." She squeezed his hand. "For everything. For finding me before that nut made me his forever." The tears were in flood mode again. "I've heard of women ...."

"That's over with, Shelly. You got to put your life back together and move on. I know something about how hard that is, too. Doctor Guttenberg is gonna help you with that."

"Okay, Detective, but thanks seem kinda hollow for all you did for me. All I can do is say, thanks, thanks, thanks."

"And I want to thank *you*," he said, grinning, "for easin' my conscience by stayin' alive. And if I'm gonna call you Shelly, you gotta call me Al. Okay?"

"It's a deal, Al. Now can I get a phone to call my mom? I was so busy getting saved I forgot she's probably been worried out of her mind."

"You can use mine from the ambulance," one of the EMTs said, "but let's get you going."

As they began wheeling her off, she looked back over her shoulder.

"Thanks again, Al. I can't ever say it often enough."

Warner's lips tweaked up at the corners, and he waved, and then sighed.

At least they saved one girl.

Now they've got to catch the bastard before he finds another Camille.

# 71

Ron Bachelor sat astride his Kawasaki Ninja motorbike, secreted on a narrow grassy strip between two ranch houses on the next block. His thin lips were twisted into an ugly snarl.

He'd slipped out the office's window as soon as he heard the doors crash in, and the cop screaming "Police." Luckily his Kawasaki bike was stored in the shed next to the house. He was racing away seconds later, roaring his anger.

*How in the hell did they find me? And Camille. They're going to take her from me if they can. She won't be able to fight them.* But *he* could, and he would rescue her. They belonged together.

He sped north for a half-mile and then made a wide loop, circling back. He'd donned his helmet, and he hoped they didn't know he was on a motorbike. For the moment he was safe, close by now, watching and waiting.

He growled when he saw Camille wheeled out to a red and white Fire/Rescue ambulance, his knuckles white from his death-grip on the bike's handles.

The fucking cops, always trying to interfere with his business. Now they were spiriting away his one love, finally found after eight busy years of searching. They were trying to keep her from him.

The bastards. Swarming all over *his* house. Taking his things ... things he'd spent years collecting. And taking Camille! The paramedics had finished checking her over, had transferred her to a wheeled stretcher, and now were loading her into the ambulance. As if he would have hurt her.

Well, they can't have her! He backed up the bike until he could turn it and idled into an alley. Once they started off, he'd chase them down and take her back. She must be terrified at being snatched away, after finally reuniting with him.

He thought of their tender yet passionate love-making. How he reveled in slowly igniting her libido. He'd never felt such intense carnal heat, and she'd willingly responded, thrusting against him, her legs locked around his, having orgasm after orgasm.

They were finally together, but now she was leaving again.

Not if he had anything to say about it. He revved the engine, powering down the gravel path and out onto the street.

She was his, and he was going to take her back. A couple of feeble paramedics couldn't stop him, but they might die trying.

Bachelor knew where they were taking Camille, so he sped down parallel streets for several block before falling in behind the warbling EMT ambulance, now two blocks ahead.

He accelerated the powerful bike, closing quickly. He'd make his move at the next traffic light. And there it was, less than a thousand feet ahead.

*Goddammit.* A patrol car was riding shotgun. They turned west at the light, and he saw another black-and-white in front. At least four cops providing protection. But it was *them* she needed protection from, not him.

Bachelor slowed the motorcycle, watching them disappear down the street. He had no chance to save her now. It was that damned super cop, Al Warner, who was fouling up all his plans.

They were surely headed for Doctor's Hospital at the U of M. The cops would probably provide security there, but that might not stop him from rescuing her later. He'd have to case it out ... make a plan. He was good at that.

He'd also learned where she lived, so that was another opportunity, if he couldn't get to her at the hospital.

Hmm. That Warner bastard might think she needed protection, even there. No one had ever succeeded in stopping Ron Bachelor from getting what he wanted, but that damned cop seemed as determined as he was.

Ah, but Bachelor also knew where her fake mother lived. Someone she seemed to care for. Grabbing 'Mom' could be the leverage he needed to get Camille back if he couldn't rescue her from that Detective Warner's grasp.

The hunt for his lost love was finally over, after eight strenuous years. Now it had become the rescue of Camille, reuniting them forever. It was going to take some planning and patience.

He grunted, thinking of his mantra over the last near-decade.

*Patience. Patience is my friend.*

# 72

Eva Guttenberg strode quickly down the brightly lit white tiled hallway, scanning room numbers. She weaved seamlessly through a parade of white-clad orderlies, pushing maintenance and food carts, and nurses and doctors in their blue scrubs.

Eva was a rare visitor to University of Miami's Doctor's Hospital, but as Miami-Dade County's designated shrink for the police department, she had privileges everywhere. Hurrying along, she spotted Room 205, the door slightly ajar. A uniformed officer reclined in a tilted chair beside the door. He nodded at her.

Peeking around the jamb, she rapped on the frame.

"Miss Weitz?"

"Yes." The voice was strained. "Come in, please."

Eva slipped through the doorway and approached the young woman. An attractive redhead that could have been her, ten years ago.

*I can see why Al was worried about me, with this nut on the loose.*

"Miss Weitz, I'm Doctor Eva Guttenberg," she said, offering her hand.

"Call me Shelly, Doctor." The small smile seemed a struggle. "Miss Weitz makes me sound so old." She accepted the woman's hand for a gentle shake.

"Okay. And I'm Eva. I feel the same way about most people calling me Doctor." She drew up a chair and perched on its edge.

"Detective Warner asked me to visit you. How're you doing?"

"Okay, I guess, under the circumstances. Being alive after living with that creep for almost a week is a definite plus." She made a weak attempt at a chuckle.

"I'm sure, and that's why I'm here. Are you settled in, okay?"

"Yes. They just finished checking my so-called vitals, so I was waiting for you to finish up my exam. I'd like to go home now."

"Oh, no. I'm not that type of doctor. I'm a psychiatrist. Detective Warner was concerned for your mental health, after what you've been through."

"Oh. He's quite a guy, isn't he?" Shelly said. "I knew his reputation, so I was praying he'd find me. He's a guy who never seems to give up."

"That's for sure. Someone special to have on your side. Anyhow, we need to talk. You've been through an unimaginablely traumatic ordeal. I know things must have gone on while you were his captive that may be hard to come to grips with. You need someone to help you with that. Someone to aid you in gaining understanding on whatever you did to survive. We need to talk, so I don't think you're ready to leave yet."

Tears welled in Shelly's eyes as Eva took her hand again, patting the back, trying to calm her.

"It … it was terrible and weird, and I *do* need someone to talk to about it." She sighed and closed her eyes for a moment. Then they popped opened, and she found Eva's.

"But first, can you get me a morning-after pill?"

"He forced you to have sex?" Eva squeezed her fingers.

"I'll … I'll tell you everything. I *need* to tell you all, but first I want that pill. I'm not having that psycho's baby."

"Of course. I'll be right back." She hurried from the room.

[253]

# 73

Ron Bachelor exited the office of the Best Western, twirling his room key. In the day of electronic keycards, this hotel remained old-fashioned. His motorbike was snuggled up behind some bushes, and the first-floor room he'd requested opened to the rear parking lot, which would allow him to sneak it inside.

The Miami cops were sure to have a BOLO out for the Kawasaki, now that they'd spirited away Camille and found out who he was and what he was using for transportation.

Of course, that wasn't going to tell them much, since he had no record anywhere, and there were no prints or DNA of him tied to a profile either. They may have something from one or more of his various past adventures, but nothing that would put flesh on those bare bones.

Shoving through the door to Room 126, he slammed it behind him and pitched himself onto the bed. He growled, pounding the mattress with clenched fists and short-booted feet.

Finally, after eight fruitless years, he'd found the real Camille, and they had snatched her away from him. He'd followed the ambulance for a half-mile but realized he had no chance to take her back. At least not then. He'd turned north, his own fury chasing him, knowing he had to put distance between him and that fucking cop, Al Warner.

On a whim, he'd charged across the Julia Tuttle Causeway and into Miami Beach. He needed a temporary haven ... someplace close by to go to reorganize and plan. The first thing he saw when he hit Collins Avenue was this Best Western ... an innocuous and inexpensive place to hunker down and set up a temporary shop.

He rose from the bed and slipped out the door, heading for his motorbike. He needed a new car. The bike was hot and it limited what he could carry. And he needed a more permanent headquarters ... a house in Miami where he could settle with Camille after he rescued her. He growled. If that proved impossible, there was always retribution ... something he was very good at delivering. That bastard, Al Warner, must pay for his interference and snatching his lover away. All in due time.

He needed to take a breath, ease up, and settle in. Rushing into things always proved counterproductive.

*Patience. Patience is my friend.*

The familiar mantra calmed him. He'd have to move fast, if he were to have a chance to save Camille now. The hospital seemed the most likely possibility. If that proved impractical, he'd been considering another option. But his first priority was to rescue his lover.

He needed some clothes and supplies. He always carried plenty of cash, but his first task after acquiring a new vehicle was a trip to his Brickell Avenue bank's lockbox to retrieve his stash before the cops got a photo of him into circulation.

He had no doubt that smartass, Warner, would force Camille to give a description of him, and they'd have an artist's likeness spread around. Warner may be clever enough to surmise he'd stored cash at a bank somewhere in Miami. Emptying his lock box was a chance he really should take now.

Yes, he'd risk riding the Kawasaki to a used-car lot to get a new set of wheels. Stealing one might point the cops in his direction, and he needed to stay under their radar.

He collected his keys and pocketed supplies from the dresser top and then retrieved the bike from its hiding place. He needed a car now and his cash that afternoon. Then a visit to Doctor's Hospital to see about retrieving Camille, and making them a whole couple again.

Nothing was going to stop that quest.

He'd spent the last eight years staying two or three steps ahead of those who would bring him down, and this is what he needed to do right now to keep that lead.

# 74

Bachelor eased his six-year-old white Toyota Sienna minivan backwards into a parking slot near the entrance of Doctor's Hospital Emergency Room. All had gone perfectly that morning.

The used-car dealer off Alton Road asked few questions for a cash sale, and Bachelor always had at least three different IDs with him to register the purchase and get temporary tags. From there, he'd quickly crossed the MacArthur Causeway into Miami and cleaned out his lock box at the Flagler National Bank.

Maybe none too soon, either, if the cops were on to that. With the motorbike in the rear, he made a quick side trip to the airport parking lot to ditch the Kawasaki. It was surely too hot to use again.

He glanced at his reflection in the mirror.

The wig ... slicked black hair, hanging to just above his shoulders ... the horn-rimmed glasses, body padding to add weight, and pencil-thin moustache, made him unrecognizable, even if they already had a sketch of him. Now he had to devise a way to get inside without raising anyone's suspicion.

He'd abandoned using the main entrance. There were too many police going in and out, and two cops seemed stationed by the doors, studying people entering. Were they looking for him? He wasn't going to press his luck.

He sat quietly for ten minutes outside of Emergency and watched the activity, awaiting the perfect moment. No cops to avoid there. He just needed the right opportunity.

*Finally.* He shouldered his leather satchel, loaded with all his necessary tools, and slipped out of the Sienna, adopting a prominent limp as he shuffled toward the Emergency Room entrance. Two Fire/Rescue trucks were unloading patients amid bustling medical staff. The air carried odors of a mixture of stale perspiration and anesthetics. No attention was paid to another patient arriving.

Once inside, he made his way toward the hospital wing but got confused and was unable to find any access. There had to be some way to get into the main building from Emergency. Teeth clenched, his normally placid face twisted into a snarl. This was not going as smoothly as he'd expected.

He spotted the stairway door, he edged in that direction, checking over his shoulder for watchers. Just as he was preparing to push through, an aged orderly strolled around the corner, pushing a lunch cart.

"Can I help you, suh?" the black man asked.

Bachelor forced his face to relax, noting no challenge in the man's demeanor.

"I'm tryin' ta get inta the patients' wing," he drawled, adopting a southern accent, "but I musta took a wrong turn somewhere."

"Those're on the second through fourth floors," the man said, "but ya kin only get over thataway on three. There's an elevator right up that there hall. Take ya there in a flash."

"Thank ya'all. 'Preciate the help," Bachelor said.

The man nodded, and then wheeled his cart away.

Bachelor hefted his bag and made his best effort at a smile. Things were starting to fall in place. He strode confidently up the corridor, but halfway there, he lurched to a stop, did a casual one-eighty and sauntered back toward the stairs.

Cops. At least four of them. Two entered the elevator, while the other pair lingered by the door, talking. He was uncertain if they were there looking for him or it was just a coincidence. Cops were often at hospitals because of accidents and crime victims. And that damned Warner thinks Camille is a victim.

His disguise was top notch, but he wasn't going to risk being stopped. He'd padded his body under his clothing to appear heavier, but he couldn't easily change his height.

The stairs appeared a better option. Three easy flights and then discover Camille's room. That orderly had stirred an idea that should work, with any luck. One thing he'd always been was fortunate.

He arrived at the exit door leading to the stairs. A quick check showed no one was watching, so he shoved through the heavy steel door. Leaning against it as it swung open, the latch snagged his jacket pocket as the pneumatic closer drew it back. Struggling to free himself, his hand got trapped in the jamb, smashing his left knuckles.

"God dammit," he hissed, jerking his hand free, leaving skin on the striker. Tears welled and the frustrated kick he delivered did more damage to his toes than the solid steel.

"Shit! Nothing is going right. Someone's going to pay for making this so damned hard." The Prom Dress Killer was not used to failures. He planned his moves meticulously, but everything was happening so fast, he was forced to improvise.

He sucked on his battered knuckles. Ironic. Emergency Room care was just outside that door, and he couldn't avail himself of their services ... unless he wanted to get caught.

And that wasn't in the deck he was dealing.

# 75

Bachelor started up the stairs, his hand wrapped in a white cloth from his satchel. Blood continued to ooze, staining the bandage His knuckles hurt like hell, but it wasn't enough to put a crimp in his plans. If he were to take back Camille, he had to do it today or lose the chance. He didn't know why they put her in a hospital, because he never did anything to hurt her.

He reached the third level and paused, peering through the small glass window. Nobody in sight, so he pulled on the horizontal bar handle ... but nothing happened. He scowled at it, and then pulled again, with the same results ... nothing.

"Now what?" He stepped back and studied the latch. He realized these were emergency exit stairs, designed to let people out of the building, not in. There was no lock on his side to pick, so he was stymied.

Maybe another floor, where the lock wasn't engaged. There had been no door at two, so he hurried up to four, but was frustrated by the same outcome. That was the last floor before the roof.

Smiley cursed softly and climbed the last flight to the roof exit. That one was unlocked, giving him access to the top of the building. *Something* had to work for him. He stepped out on the tarred surface and quickly skimmed the area, but he found little of any value.

The afternoon sun was darkening as a carpet of ashen clouds unrolled across the sky, shaking out a soft drizzle.

He pivoted at the sound of squealing hinges and saw the bulky metal door swinging closed. *Shit.* That might strand him there with no way back down. Smiley leaped forward, snatched at its edge and got a hand inside just in time, but his battered knuckles took another bruising.

"Goddammed sonofabitch," he said with a snarl. "This is that bastard Warner's fault. Why didn't he keep his fucking hands off my woman?" He rubbed his throbbing hand and grimaced, propping the door ajar with his shoulder.

He glanced around and confirmed his first evaluation ... there was no way down into the hospital from up there.

He stepped back onto the stairs and brushed off the light accumulation of rain before scurrying back down to the next level. He had to find a way inside without raising suspicion.

The Prom Dress Killer glared at the corridor through the door's wire-reinforced window, searching for a likely helper. Ten minutes passed before an orderly sauntered by, pushing a wheeled bucket and mop. Bachelor rapped on the glass with his keys, but the man wore head-phones and didn't hear him.

Moments later two nurses hurried by but they were talking too animatedly to notice the clicking noise his keys made against the glass. He growled and slammed the panel with the flat of his good hand. He turned away, clamping his hands over his temples, spewing a guttural string of curses and stamping his feet.

Ron Bachelor was not someone to be denied. Those who tried paid dearly. He sucked in a few deep breaths as his sing-songed his mantra spilled from his lips.

"Patience. Patience is my friend."

A few slow, cleansing breaths and he was back in control. He turned back to the door and pressed close to the small glass pane, determined to be heard.

It was several minutes before another orderly came into view, wheeling what appeared to be a meal cart. Bachelor pounded furiously on the glass with both his fist and the metal keys. The man paused and looked around, and Bachelor rapped the keys again.

The orderly left his cart and came to investigate, peering through the window. Bachelor waived, and the man's eyebrows knitted, and then he opened the door.

Finally, success.

"Thank God ya'all heard me," Bachelor said, shaking the man's hand.

"How'd ya get back there, mister?" the African-American man asked.

"I'm not sure. I was leavin' Emergency," he said, adopting his southern drawl. He raised his wrapped hand, the white cloth turned pink at the knuckles, "and thought I was leavin'. Obviously I made a bad turn somewhere. With all the commotion down there, no one heard my banging."

"Well, yer in the main hospital now. There's an elevator up that there hall. Takes y'all down ta the exit. Want me ta show ya."

"Thank ya. I kin find it maself. 'Preciate yer help." He patted the man on the shoulder and turned away. He watched the orderly wheel his cart off, and then started for the nurses' station.

He was inside. Now he had to learn where they were hiding Camille. Probably under her alias, Rochelle Weitz.

He wondered if Warner had posted guards.

# 76

Shelly placed the cup of water on her bed tray, the morning after pill taken. She sighed, and for the first time in days, the tension seemed to ebb out of her. She looked at Eva, her gray eyes misting, tears again sneaking out of their corners. She hitched up higher in the bed.

"After I woke up, locked in that bedroom, I noticed the fancy party dress hanging on a hook on the back of the door. I realized what had happened. I'd been taken by the Prom Dress Killer. I was terrified." She fidgeted.

"Was he going to kill me, like those other five girls, wearing similar dresses? Then he came in and called me Camille, and talked about our 'lost love.' And I began to realize that maybe he killed those other girls because they *weren't* Camille ... and maybe they erred by convincing him of that."

"Yes, I'm sure you were right," Eva said. "Somehow he doesn't remember exactly what she looked like ... just the auburn hair, age, height, and build."

"Right. I figured their mistake must have been denying that identity. So I was determined to be his Camille ... in every way."

"Smart girl. Your mom said you were clever and a good story teller."

"You met my mom?" Shelly struggled to sit fully upright.

"Yes. We interviewed her, trying to gain some clue as to where you might be. Of course, she had no idea, but was very worried."

"Yeah." Shelly settled back against the up-tilted bed. "Anyhow, not to drag things out, I started telling him stories that might fit in with our history, and listened for any clues. I figured I might be able to put him off with my tales for a while."

"Like Scherazade?"

"Exactly. I loved those stories from *The Thousand and One Nights* when I was a kid. They were part of the reason I started writing novels. It's actually pronounced 'Shahrazad' in that old book." She had crossed her arms, rubbing her biceps, a clear sign of hiding something.

"So what happened, Shelly? Don't be afraid to let it out."

"Yeah." She dropped her hands into her lap, her eyes gray pools. "Well, I couldn't delay things forever. The night after our ersatz prom, we had sex."

"Did he force you?" Eva gathered her hands for support.

"No. I figured if I showed any resistance he'd become suspicious. So I made myself seem like a willing, active participant."

"That was very brave of you. It must have been hard."

"I ... wasn't sure I could do it." Her eyes flooded again, rivulets coursing down her cheeks. "I went on autopilot, sending my mind away, living in an imaginary love story. I forced myself to actively participate ... to pretend it was wonderful, even faking orgasms. I was so sickened, I almost threw up, but I hung in there.

"He had no reservations about me being Camille after I faked such hot sex with him." She looked away, tears still wetting her cheeks.

"You did what you had to, to survive, a very brave thing."

"Maybe, but then we did it again, later that day. I was petrified I wouldn't escape or be rescued. I might be tied to him forever, if they didn't find me soon. I've heard of the Stockholm Syndrome. I'm so ashamed."

"You have nothing to be ashamed of. Fear and even pain can be powerful motivations. These are things you and I will work through together."

"When can I get out of here, Eva? He never hurt me."

"Soon, but you're not going home until Detective Warner catches this guy. It's not safe. We're relocating you and your mother into a safe-house."

"My mother?" She lurched upright, eyes wide, her tongue darting across her lips.

"Yes. With a psychotic, amoral killer like Ron Bachelor, she would be fair game, trying to get leverage for your return to him. Neither of you will be safe until he's caught."

"Jesus." Shelly knuckled away tears and settled on the bed.

"I know from our time together, he's plenty pissed off that I got away. He probably thinks you guys kidnapped me. He might go out and kill some poor girl just to blow off steam."

"That's a scary thought," Eva said. She cupped Shelly's face in her hands, "but you have no control over that.

"Dinner should be here soon. You eat and then rest, and I'll come to see you again later. We've got a lot to talk about to help you get back on a healthy path."

"Thanks, Eva," Shelly said, pulling the sheet around her neck. "I *am* bushed."

Eva turned to go, pausing in the hall to talk to the guards.

"Stay vigilant," she whispered to one of the officers at the door. "There's a good chance this guy may try to take her away."

"Yes, ma'am," he said, sitting up and dropping the novel he was reading. The other cop stood by the opening, his hand resting on his holstered 9 mm pistol. Their very lives may rely on being alert.

Because Ron Bachelor was far from done.

# 77

"Yes," the nurse said, typing on the keyboard. "Rochelle Weitz. Here it is – room 205. You're on the wrong floor, sir.  Do you have an appointment?"

"I'm supposed to do an interview," he drawled in his best Southern patois. His injured hand was in the pocket of his caramel-colored suede sport coat he'd donned for this charade.

She slid over a visitor's pass. "Well, you'll need this, but you may not be able to see her without an appointment. Doctor Guttenberg is up there now, and Ms. Weitz is being heavily guarded. She's the lady they rescued from that Prom Dress Killer."

"I know." Teeth clenched, he struggled not to react. "That's why she's bein' interviewed." He clipped the plastic covered card to his pocket and headed for the elevators.

He was inside, but how to get to Camille with guards posted and Warner's psychiatrist lover in the room? An unexpected visitor may trigger an alarm. And she might inadvertently give him away if she recognized him, despite his disguise.

He lingered by the elevator doors and mulling his options. Glancing at his watch. It was nearly dinner time. Good. That was what he needed. He snatched at the arm of a passing orderly.

"I'm new here. Where is the kitchen?"

"Level M1," the man shot over his shoulder as he hurried off.

An elevator's door hissed open, and Bachelor stepped in and pressed the proper key, relieved at the momentary absence of cops. A minute later he strode down a shiny white tile corridor, brightly lit by flickering fluorescents, heading for the swinging doors of what he assumed was the kitchen. Odors of cooking oil and garlic wafted out to him.

"Who's doing dinner for Room 205," he asked as he pushed inside. Five white-clad orderlies were filling wheeled carts.

"I am," an olive-skinned Latino said, lifting a hand. "Is there *un problema?*"

"I'm a nutritionist, new on the staff. Turns out she has some allergies," Bachelor said as he looked over her tray. "Come with me to storage, and we'll make some adjustments from stock."

"We should have everything we need here, Doc," said one of the cooks, looking up from a grill where he was sautéing chicken cutlets. "We do all the special meals."

"Yes, but there were some new supplements ordered I was told were in the storeroom," Bachelor said. "C'mon, let's move."

"*Sí*, but I gotta get goin'. I got eight other meals to serve."

"You want a patient to have an allergic reaction, and maybe even die, 'cause you were in a hurry." He clenched his teeth and struggled to remain calm. He had no tolerance for idiots.

*Patience is my friend.*

"This should only take a moment. I know what we need. You lead the way."

"Okay," the man said, sighing. He wheeled his cart from the room, and turned left, going through another set of doors, with the 'doctor' close behind.

"I believe what we need is on that upper shelf," Bachelor said, pointing to a wall rack.

The white clad man set the cart's brake and turned to the row of shelves. Running a hand along the boxes stored there, he said, "I don't see ..." which were his last words on earth, as The Prom Dress Killer drove a thin-bladed stiletto through the man's right ear and five inches into his brain.

Bachelor snatched at the sagging corpse, but his injured hand exploded in agony, the body thumping to the floor. The dead man's flailing feet slammed into the cart, sending it hurtling across the room, crashing into metal shelving.

"Hey! Everything okay in there?" came a voice from the hall.

"Yeah," Bachelor called back. "We got it covered."

"Need help, Rigo?" The speaker was approaching the doors.

"Nope," Bachelor poked his head out, the stiletto glinting at his side. This plan could blow up if he had to kill this guy too.

"All cleaned up. He's just reloading the cart. We'll be out of here in a jiff."

The paunchy Latino hesitated. "You okay, Rigo?" he called.

"Don't think he can hear you. He's just finishing up."

The orderly's gaze swept from Bachelor to the storeroom doors and back again. Then he shrugged and turned, taking control of his little vehicle, and started toward the elevators.

Bachelor's breath hissed out between tight lips. This was getting more complicated by the moment. He returned to the room and dragged the corpse behind a row of shelves, his left hand throbbing. That was the first time he'd ever been even a little hurt. He rose, adjusting his wig, and sighed.

Stripping the body, he quickly changed into the orderly's outfit, folding his own clothes and placing them, on a shelf, behind some bags of rice. He clipped the orderly's ID badge to his shirt. Lucky the kill wound bled little, and there were no stains on the white outfit.

Checking his reflection on a polished stainless steel panel, he nodded in approval. He was confident he could pass for Rodrigo Sanchez to anyone who didn't actually know the man.

Now he was ready to make his move.

# 78

Shelly stirred from her nap, scooting into a sitting position on the bed. She leaned into a lengthy stretch, and then slid out of bed and headed for the bathroom.

She adjusted her pajamas, studied her reflection in the mirror, and ran a hand through sleep-matted lustrous auburn hair. She loved that she'd inherited her mom's hair color. It frequently got her noticed by guys, but it sure got her in trouble this time.

She swished around mouthwash from a small plastic cup, washed her face, and emitted a small groan, before returning to her room. She wanted to go home. She had her fill of hospitals, but Detective Warner said she was still in serious danger until they caught Ron Bachelor. He was certain that nut would make an attempt to take her back.

Shelly jerked to a stop, her heart leaping into her throat at the sight of a man in her room. She relaxed as she smelled roasted chicken and realized it was an orderly with her dinner. His stare sent tiny feet tickling down her back. Something about him bothered her.

"Dinner, *señorita*," he said in a low, hoarse voice, as he removed a tray and set it on her moveable bedside table.

"Thank you. I think I'll sit in the chair." She perched on its edge, strangely tense, as he wheeled the table in front of her and lowering it. One of his hands trailed lightly over the back of hers, raising the fine hairs on the back of her neck.

"You don't look sick or hurt, *señorita*. And so many *policia*." He glanced at the door. "You like it here?"

"No, Mister ... Sanchez," she said, noticing his badge. "I don't like it here. I want to go home."

"Ah, to be with your loved one, no?" His tight-lipped attempt at a grin sent chills rippling through her, reminding her of another very different face.

"Yes." She sighed. "But I don't think ...."

"Everything okay in here?" One of the police guards filled the doorway.

"Yes. Thank you, Officer. I believe Mister Sanchez was just about to continue on his rounds."

"*Sí, sí, señorita*. I have more meals I must serve. I hope you get to be with your loved one soon. It is so sad to be kept apart."

Shelly watched the man shuffle off. As he passed through the doorway, he peered back at her.

*Strange man. For some reason he made me nervous. Hmmm. Sanchez. Wasn't her lunch orderly Sanchez.* This was a different man, but Sanchez is a very common Latino name.

She realized he brought to mind Ron Bachelor. Similar height, but much heavier, and different hair and a moustache. Somehow the face, though ....

*Relax, girl. You're starting to see that nut around every corner. That's something I hope Eva can help me get past.*

*But I sure can't wait to get out of here tomorrow. I hope they're done with all the medical tests, 'cause I feel fine ... physically.*

*Emotionally may be another matter.*

# 79

Bachelor exited Room 205, eying the two cops stationed at the door. He'd expected them to be bored and disinterested, but they seemed quite alert. They'd even given him a quick pat-down, but didn't discover the folding stiletto on his ankle.

There were too many people and too much traffic for him to make a move to take back Camille at that moment anyhow.

He mulled over Camille's situation as he strolled down the corridor, delivering the meals on the cart. Must not attract attention to an otherwise missing orderly.

Had she almost recognized him? He had sensed an intense gaze and agitation. She's clearly distraught at being snatched away from her lover, and said she longed to be with him again. He was about to reveal himself to her when the cop showed up.

*Patience.* Somehow he'd devise a scheme to bring them back together.

Finished distributing the dinners, Bachelor headed back for the kitchen storage area. He had to find a way to dispose of the orderly's body without raising an alarm. If he were just missing, they'd probably chalk it up to poor attendance. But if they found his corpse ....

He replaced the empty meal cart in its bay, gathered his street clothes, and stuffed them in his spacious satchel. He hurried to the nearby laundry room and returned with a rolling cart of dirty linens.

Bachelor hefted the body, tossed it into the cart, and covered it with soiled sheets. Then acting casual and bored, he wheeled the white basket out to the loading dock.

Five minutes later, his Toyota minivan was backed against the ramp, rear gate raised as he hauled the sheet covered corpse out of the cart and into the van. He had pulled away by the time the rear hatch automatically closed, and reparked in a nearby spot. He glanced back at the cadaver, swaddled in linens, confident no one would raise an alarm if it were noticed there.

He'd find a secure place to store the body later. Now he was preparing for Plan B ... the next act.

He'd return as the wayward orderly that evening and scout things out. Maybe just before the change of shift for the guards, when they'd be the most inattentive. With a friendly break, he could take her right out from under their troublesome noses. He had an excellent gambit for that.

If that seemed too dangerous, he knew she was being discharged in the morning. He could try to rescue her then.

One way or the other, he'd end the terror she surely must feel at being spirited away from him ... her one true love.

They'd be together forever, and no one could stop him, not even that interfering cop, Al Warner.

Maybe, with luck, he'd even have a chance to kill the bastard.

# 80

Warner hesitated outside the room, filtering the murmur of voices coming from within. He peeked around the jamb. Rochelle Weitz was perched on the bed, arms wrapped around her knees, peering at a sketch pad in the hands of a middle-aged, shaggy-haired rail of a man.

"Thinner lips," she mused. "Yeah, and a wider mouth." She shivered. "A thin-lipped mouth that didn't have a smile in it." She glanced at Warner, now easing into the room.

"Funny," he said.

"What?" Her eyebrows arched, and she showed her mouth could produce a grin again.

"Apparently that seemed to be his nickname in high school."

"What?" she repeated. "You've found out who he is?" She pushed herself erect and rolled onto her knees.

"Yeah. They called him 'Smiley' back in suburban Chicago. You know, like callin' a three-hundred-pound guy 'Tiny.' More about that in a minute." Warner paused at the base of her bed, feet spread, hands jammed into his pockets.

"How'r ya feelin', Miss Weitz?"

"Fine, Detective. And will you *please* call me Shelly? Miss Weitz is my mom."

"Okay, and remember, you're supposed to call me Al. Have the doctors cleared you to leave?"

"Yes, tomorrow." She sat back, swiveling so her feet hung off the side of the bed. She picked up the sketch artist's drawing.

"A little thinner eyebrows, slightly longer ears and a cowlick, and then you've got him." She glanced at Warner. "But if you know who he is, don't you have a photo?"

"Not so far. We've traced him back to his high school, but he skipped the photo session for the yearbook." His fingers had wandered to the bullet scars beneath his thick hair.

"From what you gathered, he's been doin' this for that long, so that may not be coincidental. Very damned calculatin' for someone so young to be so thoughtful."

She shuddered. "It wouldn't surprise me."

"Me either," he said, "and that's why you're goin' to have to be very careful until we catch him."

Her gray eyes, wide and moist, fastened on his. "You still think he'll try to come after me again? Even with your guys hanging around?"

"In his mind, you're his Camille. You apparently did a super job of convincin' him of that, and stayin' alive in the process. He's got no reason to doubt it now." He gathered her hands in his. "He thinks we've stolen you from him, and he'll want you back."

"Oh god! What can I do? And my mom? You said she ...."

"I had a patrol car pick her up this afternoon. She's on her way here, now. The FBI's got a nice safe house ... a big apartment, actually ... in Cutler Ridge, and they've arranged for you both to live there for now."

"Cutler Ridge?" She swiped at moisture pooling in her eyes. "What are we going to do there? That's so far from my real estate office, I won't be able ...."

"Look, Shelly." He sat on the bed with her. "I know this is a lot to process. I talked to your boss, Miss Howell, and she assured me you can take as long as necessary to get back to work. But until we nab this nut, your protection ... both yours and your mom's ... is my number-one concern."

She sat back and hugged her knees, rocking slowly as her eyes continued to leak salty rivulets.

"This is so scary." She sobbed, her voice choked. "How can we live like this, always looking over our shoulders?"

"You gotta face the hard truth here, kid. You won't ever be safe until we catch this guy. We were able to get a lot of information on him, and your sketch will help, but he's been clever enough to stay free, killin' women for at least eight years.

The good news and the bad news are the same news: he's found what he's lookin' for ... you." Warner was up now, pacing fitfully around the room.

"The reason that's good news is he'll probably stop snatchin' other redheads. And that's bad news 'cause his sights are gonna be set on you."

He paused his prowling and turned to looked at her

"You'll stay secure in that safe house, with plain-clothes cops inside and out, watchin' over you two. I'm askin' the boss for three shifts of four each, which is more'n twice what we've ever used before. But Mister Bachelor deserves our very best efforts."

She crawled out of bed and slipped into a white cotton robe.

"But what if you *don't* catch him, Al? We can't stay cooped up forever, living in fear."

"I know." He sighed, catching her by the arm, turning her toward him, hands on her shoulders. "If it looks like we lost him, at some point, we'll be forced to put you in Witness Protection."

"Ohmygod! You mean move somewhere across the country and change our names? Learn a new family history?"

"And do different jobs. If you remain in real estate, it gives him a path to findin' you. These guys are smart and patient."

She flopped on the bed and buried her face in a pillow, racked with tears. "How do I do thatand not go crazy?"

"I don't know, Shelly. I guess I'd just better go catch the bastard, and solve everybody's problems." He perched on the edge of the bed, cradling her hands in his.

The door burst open and a slender fiftyish auburn-haired woman limped into the room.

"Shelly," she yelled and rushed the bed. "Thank god! Thank god you're safe!"

"Oh mom," she said, sniffling, hugging the older woman. "It seems we're not safe yet."

They sat in each other's arms, crying.

*I'd better go fix that fast,* Warner thought as he left.

# 81

Bachelor picked up a copy of the *Miami Herald* as he exited the hotel's lobby, his parking permit in hand. The Toyota Sienna minivan sat in front of his room, all legal and sparkling clean.

He had zipped back across into Miami Beach, after liberating his lock box, followed by his abortive first attempt to rescue Camille.

Now, safely in his room, the thick wad of cash stuffed into his little in-room safe, he dropped into the desk chair and picked up the paper. His jaw clenched, his face muscles bulging as he read the headline:

### LATEST PROM DRESS KILLER'S VICTIM RESCUED

Camille's photo dominated a fifth of the page. He skimmed the article and saw Detective Warner given credit for getting her back alive.

As if he'd hurt Camille. She wasn't one of those pretenders. He scanned a brief sidebar on Warner, the so-called "Hero of Miami," and noticed he was getting married soon to the Department's shrink, Doctor Eva Guttenberg. He gritted his teeth.

*That bastard snatches away my one love but gets to have his woman. That's wrong!*

The one thing Ron Bachelor excelled at was setting wrong things right.

¤   ¤   ¤

Bachelor lounged on his bed and watched the evening news on NBC, seeking any information that might aid him in his rescue of Camille that evening. Things were not looking up on that front.

A photo of Al Warner flashed on the screen, followed by the female anchor's gushing praise over his heroics. There seemed excitement at his unexpected engagement to Doctor Eva Guttenberg. A head shot of the psychiatrist jerked Bachelor upright, his arms rigid posts, jammed down on the mattress.

*Unbelievable. She could be Camille, ten years from now.*

How unfair. Warner took away his love and then flaunted his own auburn-haired beauty, just to tease him.

He leaped up and began pacing. Time to put Plan B in motion to set things right. They couldn't be allowed to get away with this.

*Patience. Patience is my friend.*

That mantra calmed him and set his mind onto its usually methodical path.

He'd devised a way to get Camille back that very evening, and put these interlopers in their proper places. He'd return to the hospital later that night and scoop her up if all went well. If not, then she was being released in the morning.

That would be another opportunity, if security became complacent. If not, several other avenues had occurred to him: taking her from her home ... or an idea for leverage.

He slipped onto the desk chair, drew over a pad of paper, and began scribbling notes. The corners of his hard, narrow lips twitched upwards in his very best effort of a smile.

Plan C, if necessary, was developing into an exquisite course of retribution.

Even 'heroes' can succumb to properly applied pressure.

# 82

Detectives, plainclothes and uniformed cops, and FBI agents from the BAU and Miami Field Office milled around the squad room, chatting quietly. All eyes swiveled toward the door as Warner and Special Agent Dalwin entered, conversation sputtering to a halt.

"Okay," Warner said, as the small group crowded around. "This is where we are. We've got an ID on our perp ... one Ronald Bachelor: a five-foot-six white male, twenty-six-years old, light brown hair, stocky and muscular, last seen drivin' a Kawasaki Ninja motorbike. We've got a sketch of what Rochelle Weitz, who we rescued alive, thank god," to a small explosion of applause. "Thanks. Anyhow, she says this is an excellent likeness."

Jack Harris started passing out reproductions to each officer. "Use this as a guide, because he's probably changed his appearance by now." A murmur ran through the group.

"This guy is an even nastier puppy than we first thought," Agent Dalwin said, raising a hand for silence. "With what we retrieved from his house, we ran a full set of prints through AFIS, and DNA samples through CODIS. Those brought us a lot of previously unrelated hits off the National Crime data base, indicating he's been serial for nearly ten years. We've tied him to well over a dozen murders ... all but two being young women, but not all redheads ... in Greater Chicago, Indianapolis, Cleveland, Atlanta, and lastly here. There may be others we don't know of."

"Jesus," someone called from the crowd. "He started doing this as a *teenager?*"

"Looks that way," Warner said. "Even before he started his deadly hunt for his redhead, apparently one Camille Barry."

"The Chicago Field office has questioned people from his suburban Chicago high school class," Agent Ansel Whitehead added. "Bachelor and Miss Barry apparently sat near each other in classes, but according to those questioned, she was never involved with him. He transformed her politeness into romantic interest."

"Seems it was all in his mind," Warner said, pacing back and forth, "and you need to know this to understand how twisted he is. He began harassing her. Miss Barry's parents were worried enough about his stalkin' to send her away somewhere, causin' her to miss her senior prom." Warner paused his prowling, his face hardening.

"Apparently Bachelor killed her parents ... slowly and painfully ...." Rustling and grumbling echoed through the room "... tryin' to learn where she'd gone. We don't know where she is, but he believes he found her in Rochelle Weitz. His mind is so warped he doesn't even remember exactly what she looked like. We suspect the real Camille realized how dangerous this psycho was, and she's in hidin' somewhere."

"But don't mistake his psychosis for stupidity," Agent Harry Ashkin said, tenting his hands under his chin. "He's been clever enough to not only avoid capture, but to also blur his involvement in so many murders. Until Detective Warner's team was lucky enough to ID him, we had no idea who he was and what he was doing. He never came up on our 'radar' as serial until Miami."

"We're placin' Rochelle Weitz and her mother into protective custody after her release from the hospital tomorrow mornin'," Warner said, resuming his pacing. "We suspect that since he believes Miss Weitz *is* Camille, he'll stop snatchin' young auburn-haired women. That's the good news. The flip side of that will be his relentless efforts to take her back ... and kill anyone who gets in his way."

"Bachelor seems to have plenty of cash," Agent Anita Solto pitched in, "so we've notified all the local banks to be on the lookout for him. He may be using safety deposit boxes. We need to follow up on that."

"One more thing," Warner said, tilting forward, hands on his hips. "I'm the first to admit I'd love to put a couple of rounds in this guy's noggin, but we need him alive, if possible. Families of lots of victims want closure they won't get with him dead.

"But killin' him takes precedent over dyin' yourself, so don't take any unnecessary chances. This is one very deadly psycho who won't hesitate to kill anyone standin' in his way." Warner fought the subconscious need to rub the X-shaped wound under his curly mop.

"One way or the other, we need to take him down, dead or alive, and soon. Shelly Weitz and her mom will never be safe until that happens."

"Any logical killer, even a madman," Agent Dalwin said, closing his notebook, "would have fled the county by now, looking for less dangerous environs. But we think he's stayed close. He wants Camille back, so be careful out there."

"Right," Warner said, gesturing toward the doors. "So go get him. The clock's tickin', and the longer he evades us, the sooner we'll be back to square one."

The room emptied, the force dispersing on a mission that began looking fruitless.

Ron Bachelor seemed to have disappeared.

# 83

Shelly's eyes fluttered open at a commotion outside her room. Eleven p.m. She'd dozed off, watching the local news on TV. She wiggled into a sitting position, wondering about the disturbance. Maybe they'd caught Bachelor, and her troubles were over.

One of the cops stuck his head into the room. "Sorry to bother you, miss. There's a guy here with a wheelchair. Says you're due for one final test."

"What? Why? I was never hurt or anything. What kind of test."

The same orderly from dinner, Sanchez, appeared in the doorway, pushing the chair.

"For an MRI, *señorita*," his guttural voice again rousing goose bumps. Something about him continued to bother her.

"An MRI? Why in the hell do I need that?"

"For the *cabeza* ... the head ... *señorita*. They no tell me why. Just to get you."

"Jesus, so late" She slid out of bed, donning her robe. "Did Doctor Guttenberg order it?"

"*No se, señorita,*" the white-clad man said softly. "Just I bring you to MRI *ahora*." He entered the room, gesturing toward the chair.

"I don't need a wheelchair," Shelly said. "I can easily walk."

"Is hospital policy, *señorita*. *Necessario*." He pointed again.

Sighing, she settled on the chair, and he adjusted the foot rests. His fingers trailed across her calf, firing up goose bumps.

"Hang on a minute." The officer entered the room. "I sent my partner down to the nurses' station to check it out." He sauntered to where Shelley sat, crouching in front of her.

"It's probably fine, miss, but we were warned to be extra vigilant." He was unaware of the orderly looming up behind him.

"Who knows what this nut ...?" His voice was cut off as Bachelor drove his stiletto through the man's ear and into his brain ... his second victim of the day, killed noiselessly.

"The Shadow knows," he chuckled.

Shelly sat frozen, mouth agape

Before she could recover and emit a scream, he draped a chloroform-soaked cloth over her face. "Not a sound, Camille. I need you quiet if we're to escape."

"Ron? Oh God, Ron! Don't, don't ...." The quickly stilled words were muffled by the anesthetic rag as she slipped into unconsciousness.

"Sorry, darling." He sighed. "But in your excitement, you might give us away." He dragged the still twitching body aside.

He yanked the top sheet from her bed and knotted it around the woman to secure her in the chair. He quickly wheeled her into the corridor, glancing toward the nurses' station. No one was coming yet. Pivoting, he hurried toward the elevators.

He was heading for the loading dock, where his Toyota was parked nearby. Once he had her aboard, they'd be gone, and no one would ever find her again. Luckily, she'd be asleep and wouldn't be bothered by lying next to the deceased real Rodrigo Sanchez.

He'd dump that stiff once he was on the road.

# 84

Bachelor skidded to a halt when the elevator, fifty feet up the hall, emitted a nurse, a doctor, and two uniformed cops. That quickly became too risky an exit.

Wheeling right into a cross hall, he headed for the back of the floor, toward the freight elevators. That seemed his best route, less likely to run into interference. He moved purposefully without actually running. He needed to get off the floor before he was noticed. Camille tied in the chair with a sheet would certainly raise eyebrows.

As he pushed through the swinging doors, he spied his goal. Two orderlies, one African-American, the other Hispanic, were loading empty meal carts onto the elevator.

"Hold the door," he yelled, hurrying across the tiled floor. The Latin man's eyebrows arched when he saw the woman tied in the chair.

"She's in a coma," Bachelor said as the doors closed. "Being transferred to Jackson." He hoped they wouldn't ask why she wasn't on a stretcher instead of being tied in a wheel chair. He didn't want to kill anyone else that day.

"Whatever, *amigo*," the Latin guy said, pushing the button for M1, the kitchen floor. He glanced at Bachelor, pursed his lips, then shook his head and shrugged.

Bachelor waited for them to depart before punching "One." From there he could make it to the loading dock and get the hell out of there. He growled softly, angry at delays at every turn.

# 85

Bachelor exited the elevator and hurried the hundred feet to the loading dock. He parked his Camille near the edge of the ramp and locked the brakes on the chair. The unconscious woman was sliding down, despite the sheet restraints.

He grimaced as he struggled to right her, impeded by his aching left hand. After three unsuccessful attempts, he stood back and glowered.

"The hell with it. She'll be safe in a few minutes." He jumped off the platform and raced toward his Toyota minivan, nestled several rows back in the parking lot.

Bachelor beep to unlock the doors, slipped inside, and punched the 'Start' button. He backed out and wheeled around, heading for the open loading dock. Another few minutes and Camille would be his again, free from the meddlers who would destroy their fated happiness.

He spun the van around and as he began backing toward the ramp. he reached up to punch the auto-lift button for the rear gate. That's when he noticed motion in the dark shadows of the dimly lit area.

A man hurried onto the dock. Two now ... no, three of them. Cops! And a guy in white. He recognized the Latino orderly he'd just shared the elevator with, gesturing wildly. One of the policemen looked up, spied the van, and began shouting as he drew his weapon.

"Bastards," Bachelor shouted, pounding the steering wheel, as he shifted into "Drive" and sped off. He heard two pops from the pistol, but nothing struck his vehicle. They may have a make on his van, but he'd muddied the temporary plate, so they'd find it difficult to ID. White Toyota Siennas were numerous.

His lips curled into a fearsome snarl. Two more minutes and he would have been away free. Somehow that orderly had become suspicious. Maybe he knew Rodrigo Sanchez.

Whatever, he'd lost Camille again, but he still had a chance. Taking her tomorrow when she was discharged from the hospital seemed unlikely now. There would be extra heightened security, making it impossible, even for someone as clever as he.

But he had other options. They couldn't hide her from him forever.

Ron Bachelor was not someone to be denied.

# 86

Warner stormed onto the second floor of Doctor's Hospital, closely trailed by Jack Harris and Rafael Olvida. Room 205 was easily identified by the milling gaggle of doctors, nurses and uniformed police.

"Is she okay?" he snapped at a doctor who just exited the room.

"Physically, yes." He grabbed the detective's arm, halting him from charging into the room. "A bit groggy still, from the chloroform, but her vitals are strong. She needs to sleep now, Detective."

"I need to talk to her, Doc," Warner said, shaking free from his grasp. "We were seconds from catchin' that maniac."

"I know." The physician sighed, "But you'll get little from her now. It'll take at least a few more hours for the anesthesia to wear off sufficiently for her to be able to think clearly. Give her some time. She's safe now."

"Shit. That's what we thought until an hour ago."

Harris snagged one of the cops, Officer White, by the sleeve.

"Is it true he killed one of ours?"

"Yes sir," his voice hoarse. "Corporal Rio, sir." The man's gaze fastened on the tips of his polished shoes.

Warner joined Harris, his lips crushed into a twisted snarl, his brows knitted together over dark burning coals that were his eyes.

"What happened?" Warner squeezed the man's shoulder, offering support.

"Don't know for sure. Looks like the perp surprised him from behind. Stuck a knife or something through his ear and into the brain. Edgar never had a chance."

"He pretended to be an orderly," the other cop added. "Said she was scheduled for an MRI. We hadn't been given a heads up on that, so I went to the Nurses Station to check it out." He paused, choking back a sob. "When I returned, she was gone and Edgar was dead."

"Damn that clever sonofabitch!" Warner growled, unable to mask the rage in his voice. "So what happened then?"

"The main nurse's station got a call from an orderly," a second cop said, "saying he thought someone was impersonating an orderly, and he had a woman tied into a wheelchair."

"They called us," one of the doctors said, "and we notified your people."

"Right," White said, "so I raced back here, found Miss Weitz gone ... and Edgar." He sucked in a long breath and blinked moisture from his eyes.

"From what the guy reported, sounded like they might have been headed for the loading dock. Chris and I raced down there just in time to find Miss Weitz, looking drugged, in the chair and someone backing a White Toyota Sienna up to the dock. When he saw us, he boogied."

"I got off two shots," White added, "but he got away clean."

"No plate number?" Warner asked as he prowled back and forth, like a big cat in a cage with no way to get out. Olvida lingered back, out of his boss's way and took notes.

"Too dark," White said, "and I think it may have been obscured with mud. I called it in, and I guess there's a BOLO out on it."

"Yeah," Warner said. "No hits, though. He's slipped loose again, goddammit."

He snuck quietly into the room, slumping onto a chair. He'd wait for Shelly to wake up.

He stifled a soft groan and speed-dialed Eva. Helen Weitz was already set up in the safe house. They'd better move Shelly out that night. She was scheduled to go in the morning, but he wasn't going to give that ruthless psycho another crack at her.

Warner had devised a convoluted plan on how to evade Bachelor if he tried to follow them. They were scheduled to employ that scheme in the morning, but it was ready for operation that night too.

One thing seemed sure. Ron Bachelor wasn't going to yield this girl easily. Warner would need all his guile to protect her, and he didn't intend to fail that mission.

¤ ¤ ¤

The silver disc of the nearly full moon had only crept half-way across the black, star-sprinkled sky, when Shelly Weitz was spirited out of the rear entrance to Doctor's Hospital. She clambered into the back seat of a black Chevy SUV, and chaperoned by a cadre of vehicles, sped off.

Warner in his gray Dodge Charger and two black and whites led the way. Eva Guttenberg in her Jag, plus another squad car, and Harris and Olvida in Raphael's Chevy Caprice, brought up the rear. They hurried silently across Miami to Police HQ, where Shelly was hustled inside. No white Toyota van was seen, but they weren't taking any chances.

Twenty minutes later, six vehicles exited the building's covered parking lot; Warner's Dodge, Eva's Jag, Olvida's Chevy, and three SUVs driven by BAU agents. They scattered in every direction, and all side windows were obscured by taped-on newspaper. If Bachelor were waiting, he could only follow one, and each car took extensive precautions to shake any tail.

Only the one, however, driven by Special Agent Ina Yeager, shepherded Shelly to the FBI safe house in Cutler Ridge. And that Honda was shadowed at some distance by Jack Harris, double-checking it wasn't followed by their relentless psycho.

All went according to plan, and forty minutes later, Shelly's arms were wrapped around her mom, both consumed by sobs.

They were, for the moment, safe.

But the implacable Ron Bachelor was still on the hunt, and safety wasn't assured until he was caught ... or killed.

Shelly felt only slightly guilty that she was hoping for the latter.

# 87

Driving her gray XK Jaguar convertible, Eva Guttenberg swooped into the four-level parking garage adjacent to her offices, bypassing her reserved spot and finding an open slot on the second tier. She gathered her purse and briefcase, locked the car, and headed for the elevators.

Instead of descending to the street level as usual, she rose to the fourth level. Exiting there, she checked a note rubber-banded to a second set of keys and then scanned the alpha-numeric codes stenciled in front of each parking spot. Her gaze swept over the semi-lit floor filled with a phalanx of vehicles, but saw no one watching. Moving down the aisle, she pressed the "unlock" button on the key fob, eliciting two beeps and flashing lights from a dark green Chevy Caprice sedan.

Slipping into the driver side, she noted with satisfaction the darkly-tinted windows. If Ron Bachelor had followed her in hopes of getting a lead on where Rochelle Weitz was hidden, he wouldn't recognize her in this vehicle.

She fired up the engine, pulled out, and spiraled down the drive and onto the street. Several nervous glances in her rearview mirror showed no one on her tail. Warner had set up this hopefully fool-proof plan to confound that psychotic nut whenever she ventured out to counsel his last victim.

Thirty-five minutes later, Eva parked in the Cutler Ridge Apartment's garage and soon stood in front of Apartment 3 C. She knocked softly on the door.

"Who's there?" The voice was quiet and strained.

"It's Doctor Guttenberg, Shelly. I'm alone." She noted a change of light at the peephole, followed by the clicks of two deadbolts and the soft screech as a safety bar was withdrawn. This safe-house was designed to make a breach entry difficult, if not impossible.

The thick, solid-wood door swung ajar, pivoting on its massive hinges, and Eva was quickly inside, pushing it closed behind her. Shelly reengaged the locks as Eva moved into the living room where Helen Weitz was perched on the edge of a large green plush armchair.

"You're alone?" Helen asked.

"Yes. Detective Warner is out hunting Bachelor. With some hard work, and with a break or two, he'll have him off the streets soon. I know you won't feel safe until that happens."

"No," Shelly said, joining her on the cordovan leather sofa. "I won't feel truly safe until he's dead. I know that's a terrible thing to say, but ...."

"Believe me, I understand. Still, Al's hoping to take him alive, which he's seriously conflicted about. He really feels the pain of all the families ruined by this psychopath and would probably like nothing better than to see him dead. But there are a lot of families in places other than South Florida that need closure, and only Ron Bachelor can give them that."

"Doesn't change how I feel," Shelly said. "You brought it?"

"Yes. You finished the forms?"

"Here they are." Shelly handed Eva a small stack of papers. "Thankfully, Florida doesn't make this so hard to do."

"Well, we're a Stand-Your-Ground state," Eva said, accepting the papers. "The permit usually takes months to get, but with Al's help, we got it expedited. He knows a lot of the right people."

She withdrew a small package from her purse. "It's a forty-caliber Smith & Wesson nine-shot automatic. The 'Protection' model, so it's small enough to fit in your purse or pocket. Detective Warner said he'd make time to get you to a range and show you how to use it."

"Thanks. He's really a pretty special guy, isn't he?"

"In spades, as they say. He's a wonderful man to have on your side, especially if there's trouble."

Shelly, nodded, staring at the package in her lap.

"It's a Concealed Carry Permit, right? So I've got to keep the gun out of sight?"

"Right. But handy enough to get to it quickly ... and to be ready to use it without hesitation." Eva studied the young woman. "Are you, Shelly?"

"What?"

"Ready to fire without hesitation? Shooting someone ... even Ron Bachelor ... may not be as easy as you think."

"I've thought about it." She'd opened the wrappings and cradled the chrome-plated pistol in her hands. "I'm terrified at not only what he did to me, but what I was afraid I might be forced to become."

"The sex?" Eva took one of her hands in hers.

"It was more than that." The gun rested in her lap as she swept away tears. "For such a soulless, unemotional guy, he was a tender lover. He showered me with all the repressed passion I guess he'd saved up for Camille. I never before felt so worshipped by a man in my entire life. It sickens me that I understood it. I went along because I had to, but it could have been much worse." She sighed, her eyes misting again.

[291]

"I ... I feel *guilty* that it *wasn't* worse. That somehow I should have suffered more ... and I hate him for it. Hate him for making *love* to me, instead of forced, painful rape. Is that crazy?"

"Not really. But killing him won't wipe away what you may perceive as a stain on your soul."

"It'd be a good start," Shelly said with a wry chuckle.

"Well, that's why I'm really here. To help you deal with those feelings. In the few times we've been together, I've come to realize you are a very strong young woman. I suspect we can credit your mom for laying the groundwork for that," she said, grinning at the older woman, who'd settled back in the chair, watching them.

A small smile tickled Helen's lips in response.

"I've got an hour or so to spare," Eva said. "Pro Bono, as the shysters would say. So, let's talk and see if we can unravel some of the knots you've tied yourself in. Once Bachelor is finally gone, you'll need to be able to get back to your life."

"It'll never be the same," Shelly said, heaving a heavy sigh.

"No, you probably never *will* be the same, but with some work you can come out of this a stronger person. I have no doubts you can achieve whatever you aim for. You've proven how resourceful you are. You need to accept that is the real you. So, talk to me."

"Yes, let's. I'm really comfortable with you, Doctor. Both you and Detective Warner. And now that I've got some protection," she said, fingers trailing lightly over the pistol, "I feel like maybe I can get out of this prison for a few hours, here and there. Get some fresh air and sun on my face."

"I understand, but you can never relax until Al catches this guy. Bachelor's clever and resourceful, and despite all of our precautions to avoid being followed, it only takes one slip."

"Believe me, I'm not taking any chances, but I can't stop living, either."

"Okay. That being said, let's talk about your time with him. Tell me how you first felt and what you did to survive."

¤ ¤ ¤

Ninety minutes later, Eva was in the Chevy on the way back to her offices, talking with Warner on her car's Bluetooth.

"I think she'll be okay, Al. Changed but maybe even stronger. I'll see her several more times, but she's getting a handle on it. You definitely need to get her to a gun range, though, because I don't think she'd hesitate to pop Bachelor, given the chance."

"I plan on doin' that within the next few days. Our only new info on our missin' lunatic is, on the very day we discovered his hideout, he visited Flagler National Bank before they got the BOLO in their hands, and he cleaned out a big lockbox. He was toting a large duffle bag, so I'm guessin' he's probably got all the cash he needed to stay free."

*And continue his hunt for Camille*, Eva thought.

# 88

He hung back, keeping at least a hundred yards between his dirty brown eight-year-old Ford Fairlane and the gray Dodge Charger. Warner wasn't bothering with evasive maneuvers, so it seemed unlikely he was rendezvousing with Camille, wherever they'd hidden her.

Bachelor had purchased this second vehicle for cash at another used-car lot because it was too mundane to draw any attention, and the Toyota van had surely been made during his hasty retreat from the hospital. He growled softly, shaking his head.

He suspected Warner was alert to the possibility of being followed on his way to check on Camille, and this old Ford wouldn't stand out. He'd eventually ditch his Toyota minivan.

Bachelor had scripted a plan to relocate his love and take her back, but had been foiled at every turn. It had been a week since Warner and his henchmen had abducted her, snatching her right out from under his nose while he watched, helplessly. His return trip to the hospital that evening had been fruitless. Two minutes more and they'd have escaped into the dark. But fate had conspired against him.

He'd switched cars and returned in time to see them scurry out the back and speed off to the police building.

Shortly after she arrived at police headquarters, three cars and three SUVs exited the police garage simultaneously, all going in different directions. They were spiriting Camille away to a remote hiding place. He could only follow one, choosing Warner, but that proved a mistake. So now he was back to waiting, mulling his long-time mantra.

*Patience. Patience is my friend.*

He suspected either Warner or his fiancée would eventually lead him to Camille, but he was alone in this quest, so he could only follow one or the other.

He'd studied the auburn-haired Doctor Guttenberg, learning her habits and schedule. Three days before, he'd managed to locate her Jaguar in the parking lot of her offices and plant a tracker under the rear bumper. That allowed him to stay with Warner but be alerted if she took off on an unscheduled excursion.

Now pursuing Warner, Bachelor dropped back another hundred feet, sure he'd been unobserved but not taking any chances. He knew the rep of that damned cop ... smart and deadly. He watched as the sleek Dodge coupe pulled into a multi-story parking garage abutting Guttenberg's offices. It appeared that the detective was visiting his woman. Bachelor slipped the Ford into an open metered spot to wait.

*Patience. Patience is my friend.*

He deposited three quarters in the meter. He was wearing an excellent disguise and didn't intend to chance drawing any attention by doing anything even slightly illegal.

Three hours later, the gray Charger exited the garage, heading toward Police Headquarters.

Bachelor stayed with him all the way, frustrated that he wasn't getting any closer to locating Camille.

He couldn't know Warner had exchanged his coupe for one secreted there by Jack Harris to throw Bachelor off.

¤ ¤ ¤

Warner had driven off in a gold Honda Civic on his way to Cutler Ridge to gather up Shelly for a visit to a rural gun range in Florida City.

He was impressed, but not really surprised, at how quickly the young woman took to her new weapon. She practiced with grim determination and quickly became quite accurate with the big-bore pistol from within thirty feet. Warner had no doubt she would use that gun without hesitation if Bachelor tried to take her again.

He knew she had begun taking short walks, sometimes joined by her mother, and accompanied by a plainclothes cop. They often did some shopping in a small nearby strip mall. It housed a chic clothing boutique, a Dollar Store, and a vegetable stand.

The forty-caliber S & W was in her pocket, a round chambered and ready to go. He felt it was almost as if she were baiting him, hoping Bachelor would show up. His death might be the only thing to set her right again.

Eva still sneaked away to counsel her twice a week, very impressed at the young woman's mental strength. She admitted to Warner that she, too, had no doubts about Shelly's readiness to shoot Ron Bachelor if he made a move on her.

Both Warner and Eva had expressed hope Shelly would never have to face that challenge. Warner had warned her that the weight of killing another human being, no matter how vile, could tug on one's soul.

Warner and the FBI had marshaled all their efforts in their continuing hunt for the Prom Dress Killer, but so far Ron Bachelor had seeming to vanished from the scene.

# 89

Eva strode out the automatic doors of her office building, lost in thought. She was en route to what was probably her last session with Rochelle Weitz.

Shelly seemed to have a handle on her emotions. While she was still plainly nervous by the fact three weeks had passed without even a glimmer of Bachelor, she had managed to gain some perspective about her tangled feelings over their scary relationship.

Heading toward the adjacent parking garage, she was intercepted by a blue-uniformed patrol cop.

"Doctor Guttenberg?"

She paused, hands on her hips, regarding the dark-haired man with a bushy mustache and standard issue aviator sunglasses covering half his face. She glanced at his ID badge. She didn't recognize the name, but she rarely dealt with street cops.

"Yes," she replied.

"I'm Officer Tim O'Neal. Detective Warner tasked me to bring you to his offices."

"Oh? But I'm on the way to an appointment. Why ...?"

"The detective said that might be the case, but he insisted you come in." He grasped her elbow, guiding her toward the garage.

"Apparently they have a lead on this Bachelor guy, and Detective Warner's worried he may be looking to take revenge by attacking you. He wants you safe until they catch him."

"Really? Well, I guess if he feels it's necessary ...."

"He does. My partner dropped me off so I can drive with you in your car as further protection. That way, you'll have it available to use later. He'll follow in our patrol car for added safety."

"Okay, I guess. My appointment can wait if there's real danger." They had arrived at her Jaguar sedan, nestled in her private spot on the first level.

"Yes, ma'am. You're in *real* danger now," he said with a chuckle, as his strong arm snaked around her neck, yanking her back against him. He draped an acrid-smelling cloth over her nose and mouth.

Struggling, she managed to jam an elbow into his eye before the chloroform took effect.

"Bitch. You'll pay extra for that," Bachelor muttered.

"Your guy's taken my girl, and now I have his." He liberated the key fob from her nerveless hand, beeped the lock, and lifted her into the passenger seat, buckling her in. He snickered.

"Gotta be safe. 'Click it or ticket,' as they say." He bound her wrists with a zip-tie, then hurried to the driver side and started the car.

"Let's see if, after we get properly settled, I can convince you to tell me where you've hidden Camille. If not, then maybe the famous Detective Warner will want to make a trade ... his woman for mine. It's time Camille came back to me.

"One way or the other, by the time I'm done with you, my good doctor," he reached over, softly brushing fingers through her hair, "you're gonna be damaged goods."

He rummaged in her purse, retrieved her cell phone, and opening the back, removed the battery. He wasn't going to give Warner a beacon to follow once he realized she was gone.

He chuckled as he backed out of the slot and pulled onto the street. He'd rented a small house at the Doral Country Club. Interim accommodations until he had Camille back. Then they'd escape this miserable town and find happiness somewhere else.

He intended for Warner to find misery right there.

# 90

Warner's fingers brushed over his hidden scars. Maybe Eva was in session. She muted her phone when she was with a patient, but his call went to voice mail instead.

They'd scheduled dinner and a meeting with her rabbi to make final arrangements for their wedding ... if they'd caught Ron Bachelor by then. But he was having second thoughts about delaying the ceremony.

At the rate their search was progressing, they may *never* catch that clever bastard. A wedding date shouldn't have to rely on apprehending a homicidal maniac.

He hesitated, hand resting on his desk phone. Overcoming uneasiness at being too possessive, he dialed her office.

"Doctor Guttenberg's office," was the expected response from the assistant who answered for Eva and the two other doctors that shared their office suite. Each had their own phone lines.

"Hi. It's Al Warner. Will you ask Eva to call my cell when she's out of session?"

"Oh, hi Detective. Actually she's finished with appointments for today," the woman's professional voice morphed to friendly mode as she recognized her caller.

"Strange. Her cell's not on. She still in the office? Can you rap on her door and ask her to pick up?"

"Oh, no. She's left for the day."

"Really? And she didn't turn her cell phone on?" Warner's stomach tightened. Instinct waved a red flag.

"How long ago did she leave?"

"Just ten minutes or so. She may not have even gotten to her car yet. Maybe the doorman can catch her for you."

"Right. What's that number again?" He scribbled it on his desk pad, thanked the woman, disconnected, and redialed."

The call was quickly answered. "This is Plaza 52, front door."

"This is Detective Warner. Has Doctor Guttenberg left yet?"

"Yes. A few minutes ago. One of your officers picked her up."

"What d'ya mean, picked her up?" A shiver coursed through him, and he sucked in a quick gulp of air. His knuckles paled under the sudden tightness of his grip on the hand piece.

"A uniformed patrol officer. I heard him say you sent him because she was in some sort of danger."

"He said *I* sent him?" His breath struggled to make it past the bands tightening around his chest. This was very wrong.

"Yes. It was about the killer you're chasing. You didn't...?"

"No." He was up, holstering his Glock and pocketing his shield. "Did you see where they went?"

"They drove off in her Jaguar, sir. It did seem a bit strange, now that I think about it."

"What was?" He hunkered over the desk, leaning on his arms.

"The officer was driving, not Doctor Guttenberg. It seemed ...." The rest was cut off as Warner slammed down the phone.

"Harris," he bellowed, rushing to the door of his office.

"Here, Boss. What's up?" The wiry little detective popped out of his cubicle.

"I think Bachelor's got Eva." Warner raced toward the exit.

"What the hell ...?" Harris shouted, signaling to Rafael Olvida who'd materialized on the floor.

"Get Tech on this." Warner thrust a slip of paper into the smaller man's hand. "See if they can ping her cell. That's the number." He paused at the doorway, pivoting.

"Ralph, we still got that FBI traffic cam program loaded?"

"Yeah, Boss."

"See if they can pick up her Jag. It just left her office garage about five minutes ago. Call my cell. No radios, in case he's got a scanner. We gotta find her quick or ...."

"Shit," he bellowed. "That fucker's gonna torture her to find out where Weitz is. He wants revenge."

He raced down the stairs, leaving a milling crowd of angry cops, hurrying to begin the search.

Eva was in serious danger, and he suspected Bachelor might also be looking to make a trade. Warner was furious because he sure wasn't going to be a party to turning Rochelle Weitz over to that lunatic.

*Eva!* Their baby! What the hell should he do?

Catch that bastard, that's what. Nab him now, no matter what it takes.

He leaped into his Dodge Charger and roared out of the police lot, the growl of its 485-horsepower engine promising to close the gap in a hurry.

The gray two-door muscle car shot down the street, siren blaring, a kaleidoscope of blue and red lights flaring from its rooftop, as he expertly slithered through light traffic.

*If anything happens to her ....* His jaw muscles bunched into a demonic snarl. Ron Bachelor would pay for that.

*Hang on, Eva. I'm comin'. Hang on.*

He hurtled through a red light, blaring his horn as two cars spun into skids, narrowly avoiding a minor fender-bender. He'd worry about collateral damage later.

Right now, he had his woman to rescue.

# 91

Bachelor glanced at her, slumped against the door, her auburn hair spread across the window like a pool of dried blood. She still slept in the gentle arms of Madame Chloroform.

The corners of his lips tweaked up into his best attempt at a grin. Then a soft growl rumbled, echoing deep in his throat. That bastard, Warner, had his Camille, and now he had Warner's woman.

If he couldn't learn what he needed from her, she'd become trading material. Not something Bachelor was used to. He was always the one in command, doing as he wished. The others fretted and whined and threw up their hands in despair, all while he was having fun teaching wayward girls the necessities of good behavior and morality.

He'd given up finding Camille long ago and spent five years teaching morals to many lovely unwilling students. A soft sound slid past his lips … more a purr than a sigh … at the memory.

Then he'd seen a photo in a news story of a girl … a woman, now … in Atlanta he thought might be Camille. She was some sort of young executive on the rise, but she'd proved to be a pretender and paid the price for her charade.

As he became reenergized in his search, he stumbled upon one ersatz Camille after another … eight before Miami, but none to accompany him to their long-lost prom. He began sending them on alone, properly attired.

Then he found the real Camille here, in South Florida.

And now Warner had kidnapped her. His white knuckled stranglehold on the Jag's leather steering wheel eased as his gaze again swept over Doctor Eva Guttenberg.

If she didn't reveal his Camille's location, she'd become his bargaining chip. If Warner wanted *his* lover back alive, he would have to give up Camille. Whether that happened or not, he was going to teach this woman proper decorum.

They were headed for his new headquarters, a Mexican style three-bedroom ranch house he'd rented at the Doral Country Club. He'd already set up his "training room," properly sound-proofed and secure, where the beautiful doctor would learn her lessons. Those would be life-altering ... for her *and* Warner ... memories that would cling to them forever.

He wouldn't rush things, despite his eagerness to retrieve Camille. His tongue swept across his lips as he tasted the sweetness of it.

First, she would be taught who was her master. Forced sex ... frequent and rough ... would be his tool. He had an endless sex drive, rarely visited except in cases like this. And, of course, with Camille, to whom he'd made exquisite love.

He produced a real sigh, squirming in his seat as he revisited the wonder of their passion. Nirvana had been twice achieved with her before Warner had plucked her from his loving grasp.

He snickered, his hand flitting over Eva's breast, hip, and thigh. Those where delicious glories this woman would never give her lover again.

They may withhold Camille from him forever, but that meddling cop will pay a price he'll never forget. This beauty will suffer pain and disfigurement following the rough sex. Warner will get back a crippled shell of his lover.

Bachelor rolled his shoulders and flexed his neck, concentrating on driving this lovely sedan, eager to begin.

# 92

Warner's Charger streaked through traffic, siren resounding, lights blazing on his roof. He headed for an area north of Eva's offices because that's the direction the doorman said they went, but he had no inkling of Bachelor's possible destination.

He pounded on the horn, snaking between a pickup truck and a minivan, the screech of skidding rubber peppering him as the two vehicles spun out.

"Assholes," he muttered. "Doesn't anyone pull over when they hear a siren anymore?" His cell phone chimed, and a quick glance at the car's LED screen showed "Jack Harris." He punched the green button on the Dodge's steering wheel.

"Talk to me, Jack."

"No ping in her cell phone, Al. Traffic cams picked up what looks like Eva's Jag, heading north on SW 87th Avenue, just north of 24th. Not a positive ID, but it's the right model and color. They couldn't get a reading on the plate."

"Okay," Warner said, swerving across two lanes of traffic and changing his direction. "I'm headin' that way. Gotta break radio silence and hope he doesn't have ears on. Alert all the patrol cars in that vicinity." He took a quick peek over his shoulder before making another hard left, hurtling west as fast as 485-hp could take him.

"If a patrol makes him, they're to tail and report in, but are not ... I repeat ... not to interdict. Follow at a safe distance, try not to be noticed, and wait for me."

"Okay, Boss. Meantime Tech has the Jag's GPS signature, and they're starting the search. We get a hit there, he ain't getting away."

"Good work. Remind everyone out there he's got a hostage and isn't reluctant to kill. Get me a positive location on that car, Jack. Now!"

"Working on it, Al. I'll get back to you." The connection was broken.

A moment later, Warner heard instruction over his police band radio, alerting all units to be on the lookout for Eva's Jaguar, with admonishments to follow, report, but not to engage.

Warner grunted, hoping Bachelor hadn't heard the broadcast. Since he was in Eva's car, there was a good chance he didn't have a police scanner with him, but it never paid to underestimate a clever psycho.

"C'mon, guys," he shouted, pounding the leather-covered steering wheel. "I'm drivin' blind here. Give me something to work with."

Hunched over the wheel, arms stiff as rigor mortis, his jaw clenched hard enough to cramp, he dodged and weaved, hurtling northwesterly, waiting for more intel.

"If he hurts you, Eva," he growled, "I'll tear that sonofabitch from limb to limb."

His phone pinged again.

"Yeah, Jack. Where're they at?"

"Don't got that yet, Boss, but they should have a search for her GPS going any minute. Ralph and I are taking off to lend backup."

"Good idea," Warner said. "Sonofabitch." He veered hard right and laying on the horn, drove onto the sidewalk, scattering several people that leaped clear. He was circumnavigating three cars that had managed to tangle up, clogging the avenue. The

Dodge's bumper nicked a flower pot, flipping it, and sent several outside dining tables spinning into a restaurant entryway.

*Shades of a Miami Vice chase scene.* He ground his teeth as he swerved back onto the street, with no pedestrians damaged beyond heart palpitations, but the eatery's patio was a shambles.

"You guys head for the airport area," his heart doing the rumba as he continued his conversation. "I doubt he's gonna try to fly out with Eva, but at least that seems in the right direction for the moment. I'm less than a mile from 87th Avenue."

"On it, Boss. We'll keep in touch. Tech should have a reading on her car any minute, unless he damaged her GPS somehow. They're still scanning the traffic cams, too."

"Okay," Warner growled, snatching his fingers away from his X-shaped scars, "but we're runnin' outta time here. We don't snag this bastard soon, he may be gone, Eva with him."

"Ain't gonna happen, Al," Harris said. "We're gonna get him. Ralph and I are on our way now."

The whole of southern Miami was on alert. It seemed unlikely Bachelor could slip though, but they'd had him cornered before, and he still managed to disappear.

Warner refused to let that happen again.

He continued zigzagging northwest, awaiting more guidance.

Confusion and minor destruction was scattered in his wake.

# 93

Bachelor continued up SW 87th, mindful of the speed limit, not wanting to attract any undue attention. He wondered if the cops had learned he had Warner's lady. The snatch had gone without incident, just as his little abductions always had.

He glanced at the auburn-haired beauty slumped against the Jaguar's passenger door, his tongue slithering across his dry lips. She twitched and breathed a soft moan. She'd be awake soon.

He shrugged and concentrated again on his driving. Camille could easily be this woman in ten years. His jaw clenched. The reality was, from what he'd learned online about Warner, the detective probably was too stubborn and principled to consider swapping Camille for the beautiful doctor.

*No, he'll try to hunt me down. Take revenge for what I'm about to do to his lover. Good luck with that.*

No one had come close to finding him until Warner, and he wasn't going to give him that chance again. But what would he do without Camille? If he couldn't take her back, then ....

*Hmmm.* He tossed a fleeting look at Eva. *If I never recapture Camille, I can make this older version of her my substitute. Bind her to me. Make her mine. She'll learn to worship me, as Camille does.* He squirmed in his seat as erotic images flooded his mind.

*She'll resist at first, but I'm a talented teacher. She'll learn to revel in our love ... or pay a painful price. She's not Camille, but this may be an elegant solution ....*

Bachelor's musing was shattered when a glance in his rearview mirror showed a police car several vehicles back. Was it shadowing him or just a coincidence? He'd better find out before reaching his destination at Doral.

He took the next left off 87th Avenue, then another left, now heading south, away from his new home. Thirty seconds later, the black and white appeared, lingering behind four other cars.

No question now that they'd made him, but how?

Damn! If they knew he'd snatched the lovely doctor in her vehicle, they'd have a traffic cam search going. If in fact he was under surveillance, there may also be other patrols on the way. He'd have to shake this tail and find some other transportation.

There was his chance. The traffic light ahead had just turned yellow. Accelerating hard, he swerved around the one car in front of him and ran the light, speeding west. The cop car was stranded behind a line of stopped traffic. He turned north at the next intersection, and spotting a three-level parking garage, he whipped in. He hurried to the second level and backed the Jag into an empty spot at its rear.

The woman groaned softly and began to move. Not a good time for her to awaken, so he doused a cloth with a shot of chloroform and put her back to sleep. Then he slipped out of the driver seat, scurried to the street-side perimeter, and peeked out through the opening.

He was just in time to spy a squad car speeding by, silent and without flashing lights. It was soon followed by another, and then a third. They were hunting him for that bastard, Warner.

It was time for a change of plans and a new chariot. He hated abandoning the luxurious Jaguar, but he needed something more vanilla ... and right then.

# 94

Racing north on SW 87th Avenue with no definitive heading indicated, Warner was swearing to himself when his Bluetooth lit up, with "Tech" displayed on the screen.

"Warner," he barked. "Gimme something, will ya."

He was furious that a patrol car had picked up Eva's Jag on the avenue he was speeding along and then managed to lose it. He was hoping for better news.

"You got it. This is Officer Lightman. We've got a ping on the Jag on SW 17th Terrace and 89th. Looks to be a parking garage. No CCTVs on site, though, so we got no eyes on it."

"Right. I'm on the way. See if there're any traffic cams in the area, and keep an ear open in case there's any reported stolen cars in the vicinity. He's bound to ditch the Jag now that he knows were hooked into it."

"Got it, sir. I'll keep you posted."

"Okay. I'm goin' silent, so he doesn't hear me comin'." He switched off his siren and pulled in his flashing light from the roof. He was about five minutes away ... until he screeched to a halt, blocked by a two car collision, sprawling across both lanes.

"Shit! What's with all the damned accidents?" He flipped into reverse and glanced back, and then froze, bracing himself, growling his frustration.

The car following him barely stopped, nuzzled up against his rear bumper. The pavement behind him was quickly jammed with vehicles. He had no way to maneuver.

He was trapped for the moment. Swearing, he leaped out of his coupe and began directing the drivers to clear a path. By the time he worked free, ten precious minutes had flittered by.

Two patrol cars had already arrived at the garage where they found Eva's Jaguar, but she and Bachelor were nowhere in sight. Warner's sweat-slicked hands keyed his radio mike.

"Will someone report on what's goin' on there? I just got untangled from this fender bender."

"This is Officer Gomez, sir. No sign of the perp or Doctor Guttenberg, but we got a very angry lady that was carjacked."

"Was it our guy?" He idled his Charger, trying to decide what to do next. Tension set his whole body aquiver. He groaned. No sense in charging off until he had a destination.

"Probably. He cold-cocked her from behind, and she never saw him clearly. Said he was carrying somebody, though."

"Gotta be him. What kind of car?"

"A baby-blue Hyundai Elantra, brand new. We got her data to Tech, and they're trying to see if they can ping its GPS."

"Got it." He switched to his cell and called Tech Support.

"This is Warner. I need a location on that Elantra, *now*."

"Just coming up, Detective. Ahh, got it. Heading East on SW 12th Street ... now just turned north. Maybe heading for SW 8th. Calle Ocho is the fastest thoroughfare outta there."

"I'm on the way," he growled, squealing away from the curb, roaring north on SW 87th Avenue. Where was Bachelor going? The 826 Expressway? The Turnpike? Maybe even I-95 ... or back roads? With some luck, he may be able to head him off.

Eva would be counting on him ... she and their unborn son. Time to end this bastard's reign of terror. He gritted his teeth

It was *past* time to put him away, and Warner was the guy to do it.

# 95

Ron Bachelor hurried east on SW 8ᵗʰ Street, keeping to five over the posted limit, battling the urge to speed. He was eager to make it to the 826 Expressway and escape all this tumult, but he didn't want to chance drawing the attention of the cops that had flooded the area. They were clearly looking for him, but he doubted they had a make on this Hyundai yet.

Once away, he could work his way to North Miami Beach and the hiding place he'd established while preparing to free Camille from that humdrum existence. He had a cache of money there. Then he'd circle back to the hotel in Miami Beach.

He glanced at the redheaded woman, slouched against the door and still asleep. Fun and games would have to wait until things cooled enough for him to make it back to the house at Doral.

He'd have to buy another car, but he had the rest of his cash stashed away in his room safe at the Best Western, so that wouldn't be a problem.

*Thanks, Grandma. I don't know how I'd have managed without your inheritance.*

Too bad for the old biddy that she'd required so much convincing to give it up. He chuckled. She never needed it after cashing out that half-million dollar mutual fund, anyhow. He'd seen to that.

Luckily he'd decided to keep that hotel lodging on Miami Beach as backup. He always had at least three places to run in case of trouble.

He was almost to the expressway with its maze of high and lower entry and exit cloverleafs. He always marveled at the complexity of highway designs to accommodate the free flow of traffic. There, to his left, was the Mall of America, crammed as usual with shoppers, and ahead was the sign for 826 North.

He switched lanes, giving his best impression of a smile as he entered the lane leading to the circular ramp, soaring high above the road. It would be like a gentle rollercoaster ride as they descended to the expressway. He glanced in his rearview mirror, not seeing any cop cars in pursuit.

Good. He'd made it away, unscathed, as usual. His tongue swiped his narrow lips, tasting the pleasure he would have with the lovely Doctor Guttenberg. Then Warner would know what it was ....

"Hey! What the hell! Look out, dummy!"

A gray coupe shot past him, half on the shoulder, cutting him off, and clipping his left fender. He struggled for control as the Hyundai skidded sidewise, hurtling toward a concrete abutment. Bachelor tromped on the brakes and threw his arms in front of his eyes, bracing for the impact.

# 96

"Where's he at now, Lightman?" Warner shouted. "Gimme a target." He raced east on SW 8th Street, closing fast on The Mall of America.

"He's a hundred yards ahead of you. Looks like he's heading for the 826 North entrance ramp."

Warner zipped between two cars, slicing back into the left lane, cutting off a pickup truck. He needed to stop Bachelor before he hit the expressway, or things could really get dicey. High speed chases on a busy freeway were fraught with danger.

There! A blue Elantra, just edging left into the northbound entrance ramp lanes.

"Gotcha, you bastard." He clenched his jaw as he darted into the right lane, passed the two vehicles between him and his prey, and then shot across to the left shoulder, racing up alongside the Hyundai.

A quick sideways glance showed a mustached uniformed cop, looking nothing like the rendering Shelly Weitz had provided, driving the sedan. But then he got a glimpse of an auburn-haired woman, slumped against the passenger door.

*Eva!*

Gnashing his teeth, he accelerated ahead, then jerking hard right, cut them off and smacked the blue sedan's left fender a hard glancing blow. He caught a glimpse of the driver shouting angrily as the sedan spun out, spewing across the shoulder. It skidded sideways and slammed with a rending crunch into a concrete piling that supported a higher cloverleaf.

The force of the collision with the Hyundai tossed Warner's coupe back into the roadway where it was jolted on the rear bumper by the next car. Squealing breaks, the stink of burning rubber, and the din of colliding cars permeated the air.

Warner sagged, enveloped by the front and side airbags, stunned by the impact.

"Shit." He lurched up, rubbing his neck and struggling to disconnect his seatbelt. Once free, two hard thrusts by his shoulder were required to force open the door. He tumbled onto the pavement, landing on his hands and knees.

He snatched two deep breaths and heaved himself to his feet, leaning wobbly against the car. Shaking his head, he focused on the Hyundai, spying movement inside.

That murderous bastard was in there with Eva. Edging shakily around his crumpled Dodge, he lumbered unsteadily across the roadway, sucking in deep breaths as he regained balance and strength. He glanced back and noted what was about an eight-car pileup strewn across the ramp. The air echoed softly with the wail of distant sirens, fast approaching but still far off.

The cavalry was coming, but he couldn't wait. Reaching the Elantra's door, he heard scuffling and a hissing moan. Peering inside he saw the cop, surely Bachelor, leaning across the seat, wrapping the seatbelt around the unconscious woman's neck.

He was intent on strangling her!

Warner screamed. Three hard yanks on the door were fruitless. He snatched out his Glock, wishing it was his old steel Beretta 9 mm, and slammed the butt against the window to no avail. He couldn't shoot out the glass and chance hitting Eva.

He swore and leaped onto the hood, grunting as a bolt of pain sliced across his shoulders. He twisted onto his back, grimacing at the ache, gritted his teeth, and kicked both heels against the already shattered windshield. The second impact stove in the glass.

Warner slithered around on his belly, groaning as he swapped ends, and crawled through. He flailed at the man who had simultaneously tightening the belt around Eva's throat and was slamming her in the chest and stomach with short brutal jabs. Bachelor was brutalizing Eva, who sprawled across the seat.

Warner chopped at the killer's left collar bone with a stunning blow, interrupting his attack on the unconscious woman. Wiggling further into the car, spreading his legs to keep from falling through, he managed to lock a hand inside Bachelor's collar, yanking him backwards, kicking and thrashing.

Adrenaline fired Warner's powerful body as he heaved, scrabbling back, hauling the killer through the open windshield, both of them tumbling off the canted hood and onto the street.

Bachelor quickly regained his balance, coming up into a crouch, and charged a momentarily stunned Warner, who was balancing on one knee. As they collided, skittering across the pavement, Warner snaked an arm around the smaller man's neck, his thumb searching fruitlessly for a soft spot on the throat.

Though short, the Prom Dress Killer was a powerful guy. He peppered the detective's body with short, stinging elbow jabs as they staggered across the macadam. Still clutching Bachelor around the neck, Warner barrel-rolled and threw the man over his head.

Both panting, they scrambled to their feet, glowering at each other. Warner's Glock had been knocked loose and had found its way under the Hyundai. This was going to be hand-to-hand.

"You bastard," Bachelor shouted. "You took my woman, and now I've got yours. You won't want her back when I'm finished with her." A knife, a long-bladed stiletto, had materialized, lightly curled in his fingers. The five-inch blade glinted in the sunlight.

[316]

"I wanted to wait to carve up your lady a bit, but now it's your turn. I'll make her pretty later."

"Do your best, short stuff," Warner said, voice dripping with derision. "I'm not some poor little gal you can dominate."

Bachelor growled, feinting with the knife. He glanced at the car, then back at Warner, licking his lips.

"C'mon, little guy." The angrier Warner could make him, the more likely he was to lose control. That might create the opening he needed. The still far off squad cars wouldn't get there in time to help.

"Lucky your Camille isn't here, shorty. Her real name is Rochelle, but she hoodwinked you, didn't she? She told me how pitiful you are. A piss-ass poor lover. She was hopin' she'd have the chance to put a couple of slugs into your ugly puss."

Bachelor's eyes narrowed, and he roared, "She's my Camille, and she loves me. You can't hide her from me forever." Sweeping the glistening blade in short arcs, he charged.

Warner feinted right, and then dipped left, using well-honed judo skills to snag the knife hand by the wrist. Twisting and spinning, they both landed hard on the ground, the blade flittering away.

Locked together, they tumbled across the pavement, onto the shoulder, and then to the barrier at the edge of the roadway. Struggling to their knees, Bachelor locked powerful hands around the detective's throat, bending him back over the railing.

Struggling for breath, Warner staggered to his feet, still arched backward over the precipice, dragging the smaller man up with him. Bachelor was trying to break his spine, simultaneously strangling him. Warner clenched his rock-hard abs, and bracing his legs, inched away from the railing.

Gasping for breath, he locked one arm under the other's grasp and reaching over his back, grabbing a handful of shirt, he gave a powerful upward kick with his knee. He missed Bachelor's testicles, but caught him in the lower abdomen. The violent blow and a desperate yank with both arms, pitched the smaller man over his head, breaking his stranglehold.

Bachelor screamed as he soared over the retainer wall, hands flailing for something to snatch onto. He caught the narrow ledge, hanging over the abyss by his fingertips. Warner thrust himself over the rail, hooking his legs around a stanchion, and snatched for the killer's arm. Bachelor's onyx eyes glittered up at him, filled with hate.

He snarled. "Camille's mine, you bastard. You'll never ...."

Warner lurched for the man's wrist, but before he could get a firm grip, Ron Bachelor, The Prom Dress Killer, tumbled free. Spinning slowly in the air, he howled curses as he plummeted toward the curved exit ramp below.

A screech of brakes was followed by a loud thump, and then the metal-crunching din of cars colliding.

Warner struggled to his feet and peered over the side. Three cars were tangled together, with Bachelor's body pinned under the first. Only his feet were showing. A pool of blood was already seeping from under the wreckage.

Warner panted for breath, his fingers tracing over his badly bruised neck.

*Fuck, that was close. So much for taking the bastard alive.* His head snapped around, locating the crumpled Hyundai.

*Oh, shit. Eva!* He wobbled on new colts legs to the wreckage of the Hyundai.

He dragged his aching body back onto the hood and saw his lover sprawled across the seat, the seatbelt still circling her neck. He shimmied through the opening and was relieved to note her breast rising and falling to steady breathing.

Thank God, she was alive.

# 97

Warner sat by her bedside, one of her hands encased in both of his. He watched her steady breathing, frequently glancing at the various electronic monitors.

Eva had suffered no life-threatening injuries ... at least, not to her ... but there had been substantial trauma from the beating Bachelor was administering when Warner had rescued her. She'd been in a 'minor' coma, whatever that was, for three days. Warner understood that condition. He'd been there twice himself in the last three years.

Thankfully, she hadn't been aware of the various procedures she'd had to endure, once they had her at the hospital. But the outside world was returning to some semblance of normalcy with the violent death of the Prom Dress Killer.

Young auburn-haired women no longer needed to be more than normally careful in public.

He mused to himself. *Shelly Weitz and her mother are finally free to return home.* But her brief stint as Camille had surely left a permanent mark on her soul.

Warner had visited with Shelly twice since Bachelor's demise, and he sensed she had come out of this in more or less one piece, emotionally. He also expected the experience might have a positive impact on her novel writing career. Certainly her fame as The Prom Dress Killer's only long-term survivor would have a strong impact on her book sales.

Such are the quirks of life.

Warner had scrounged as much time as possible to visit his woman. The rigors of his job kept him more than busy, since killers hadn't taken a vacation now that Bachelor was gone. He swung by her hospital room whenever he could fit it in, hoping to be there when she awakened.

"Hi, baby. It's me," he whispered, stroking the back of her hand. "I know you need your rest after what that bastard did to you, but Buff and I miss you. So any time you want to ...."

He paused, noticing her eyelids fluttering. The docs said that can happen while in a coma, but ... her eyes blinked open. A tiny moan slipped between her lips.

"Eva? Can you hear me?"

Her head swiveled slightly, her lovely emerald eyes finding his.

"Al?" She blinked, and then a small up-curve tickled her lips.

"Yeah. Welcome back, sweetheart. Ya had me goin' there for a while."

"Oh, my ribs hurt," she murmured, followed by a soft groan. Then her eyes flared. "Bachelor?"

"Dead."

"You?" The smile widened.

"Yeah. I caught up to him tryin' to get on the 826. We fought, and he fell off the ramp and was killed. I woulda liked him alive to give closure to all those other families, but I can't say I'm sorry he's gone. Savin' you was more important than keepin' him breathin'."

"My white knight." She sighed softly, closing her eyes. "It's better that way. Him dead, I mean. Easier in the long run for everyone." A soft groan slipped between her lips. "There were a lot of families?"

"Yes. So far we've tied him to eighteen murders durin' the last nine years, mostly in six Midwestern and southern states.

More likely cases keep turnin' up. Lots of PD's are finally closin' some cold files."

"Wow," she said. "Good thing he finally wandered into the purview of the Hero of Miami, huh? The ultimate case closer."

She chuckled softly and then grimaced. "That hurt."

"He was beatin' you pretty hard when I dragged him outta that car." He glanced away, unable to look her in the eyes as reality dawned on her.

"The baby?" Her voice choked, eyes flaring wide.

"I'm so sorry, sweetheart. He ... he's gone, with all the punchin' that bastard was layin' on you."

Tears welled, turning her eyes into tiny green pools.

"Was there any damage ...?"

"No. No, the docs say you can still have kids. No permanent damage done."

"So we can try again? This time on purpose. We'll get married and start a family as soon as I'm up and around."

"We'll ... we'll talk about it later. Get better. Then we can make plans. I gotta run now. Got a drug-related killin' to chase down. I'll stop back this evening if I can. If not, tomorrow for sure." He leaned over, brushing her lips with his. She clutched his arm, pulling him closer.

"We'll be okay, Al. Won't we? Be okay?"

"Sure, babe. Just heal and we'll talk more soon. I really gotta run now. Killers won't wait." He rose and moved toward the door, paused, looked back, and waved.

She waved back. "Bye, Al."

A doctor and a nurse hurried into the room as he left.

"Well, Doctor Guttenberg. Nice you decided to join us."

They checked monitors and ran some test.

She sighed, easing back into the pillow.

Something was vexing Al, and that bothered her.

# 98

Warner eased her up the few stairs of his townhouse, steadying her with his grasp of her left hand and elbow. He unlocked the door, and Eva shuffled gingerly inside, making her way to his comfortable tan suede sofa.

There was a clatter of claws on the tile floor as Buff raced in, skidding to a seated stop, shoving his wet nose under her hands.

"Hi, beautiful." Eva chuckled, scratching the Golden behind his ears. "I missed you, too." The dog's tongue was busy washing her fingers. She leaned down for a wet kiss.

She sighed. Five days had dragged by since her rescue, and she'd had enough of hospitals.

"Can I get you anything? Some ice water, or maybe a hot tea? Mrs. Gerber made a pot of chicken soup too," he said.

"Tea would be nice, if it's not too much trouble. It's great to be back in your ... *our* home, Al."

"Tea's not a problem, babe. Just relax and get settled in. You've been through hell."

"And you, darling. How are you doing? You've lost a son too." Her eyes watered, trailing him as he moved around the living room.

"Yeah, I know." A barely audible groan echoed in his throat. "And I feel like I'm responsible ... for both that and the terror that bastard put you though."

He withdrew a cup from the beeping microwave and inserted a bag of Chamomile tea leaves.

"That's ridiculous," her eyes narrowed, her voice sharp. "How could you have caused what the psycho did? What you should focus on is that you saved my life and put an end to a string of senseless murders." So that's what was bothering him. He was the rare cop who took these crimes personally.

"Maybe. But if Bachelor didn't know about you ... that we are engaged, with all the media hoopla about the supposed Hero of Miami finally getting hitched, he never would have come after you." He settled next to her, taking her hands, kissing one.

"That's still no reason to blame yourself," she whispered and leaned against him, her head on his shoulder.

"No? I disagree. Being who you are to me, he thought he had a bargainin' chip to get his Camille back. Like a hostage trade." His arm circled her shoulder, drawing her lightly against him.

"He probably did see Shelly as our unwilling captive," she said. "In his psychosis, he thought she'd be an eager participant in a trade. That all they both wanted was to be together."

"Yeah? Well, I saw her yesterday ... her and her mom ... seein' they're gettin' their lives back to normal. Bachelor woulda been surprised to learn she *was* eager to see him again ... to put a slug or two in his head." He chuckled. "She wants retribution.

"She was almost hopin' he'd try to jump her again, 'cause she kept her S & W handy, a round chambered and ready to go."

Eva sighed. "I just hope she can get past what he did to her and what she did with him to survive. She's a strong girl."

"That's part of *my* problem, Eva."

"What, darling?" She sat up and pivoted toward him.

"I can't seem to get over what he was gonna do to you."

"But he didn't, Al." She caught his chin in her hand, turning his face toward her. "You saved me."

"This time." He cupped her face in his hands. "But what about the next time? What if I *can't* save you next time?"

"Next time?" Her eyebrows knitted together. "Why would there be a next time, Al?"

"Because you're my woman, and some psycho figures he can get to me through you."

"That's ridiculous," she said, shaking her head.

"Is it? I don't think so. Being married to me will always make you a target. And if we have kids, they would be too."

"Al, I hope you're not saying what I think you are." Tears leaked from the corners of her eyes, trailing across her cheeks.

"Yeah. We shouldn't get married, Eva." His eyes scrunched closed. "I shouldn't have kids with you, either. It's just too damned dangerous for everybody." He lumbered to his feet and lurched into erratic pacing. He paused, facing her, his chin sagging to his chest.

"Oh, Al." She pushed herself up on wobbly legs, grasping his upper arms. "Don't. Please don't."

"I love ya so much, babe. It's tearin' at my heart to do this. I *wanted* to be your husband ... father to our children. To have a happy, normal life." He drew her against his chest, a hand caressing her back.

"But it's a selfish delusion. There is no normal life wed to a homicide detective. It'll never be safe for you. And what if I'm killed, leavin' you alone, maybe with kids?"

"But you *will* be leaving me alone by doing this, and no one's managed to kill you yet, tough guy." Her mouth twisted into a weak imitation of a grin.

"Yeah? Already came within a single centimeter twice." His fingers traced the hidden scars on the side of his head.

"Look, I thought it through while you were in the hospital. This is the toughest thing I've ever done in my life ... and I've done some pretty rough stuff."

"Yes, the noble, self-sacrificing Detective Al Warner." Bitterness reeked in her words.

"Maybe that's true. Or that I'm just bein' selfish, 'cause I could never live with myself if anything ever happened to you because of me."

"I'm willing to take that chance," her voice soft and pleading, "because I love you. Don't I have a say in this?"

He stared at her, thick, dark eyebrows knitting, and he sighed. "I suppose that's only fair," he mumbled, again taking her hands. "So, what do we do?"

"Make love to me ... gently, because I'm still so damned sore. Make love to me now, and then we'll try to figure this out."

Without a word, he swept her into his arms, carrying her to the bedroom. His easy strength infused her with a sense of calm.

The special care he showered on her ... the near reverence ... and his determined effort to bring her multiple orgasms filled her with conflict.

She loved the passionate, powerful man beyond words, but in her heart, she feared love and words wouldn't be enough.

She sensed this would be their last time together. His moral insistence at protection at all costs ... even at the expense of his own personal loss ... was a constant in him not easily subverted.

Honor before self.

He was bidding her a lover's farewell.

# EPILOGUE

Six months had rolled by since the violent demise of the Prom Dress Killer, and Dade County had returned to a semblance of normalcy ... except for the lives of three people so deeply embroiled throughout that tense, dangerous time.

The follow-up investigation into the deadly career of Ron Bachelor continued for six weeks and turned up a total of twenty-one murders ... all but two were young women ... that could be tied to him. Police departments in six Midwestern and southern states were closing a multitude of cold cases, and relatives of those victims were provided some final semblance of closure.

No one came forward to mourn the death of The Prom Dress Killer. They learned that the real Camille Barry had reappeared, eager to resume a normal life after nearly nine years in hiding.

Al Warner shrugged off the media barrage that extolled the determination and bravery of The Hero of Miami. He went back to what he did best, catch run-of-the-mill killers: drug bangers, jealous lovers, and greedy pretenders.

The press did an "investigative" piece on the dissolution of his engagement to Eva Guttenberg, the second woman he rescued from Ron Bachelor ... and as usual, got many of the facts wrong. Neither Warner nor Dr. Guttenberg cared to set the record straight.

After convalescing for two weeks following her near-death, Eva Guttenberg threw herself back into her therapy practice, working long hours that seemed to preclude any sort of romantic adventures. Theories seemed unfounded that there was another man ... or woman ... that caused the breakup.

Eva and Warner maintained a friendship that was peppered with occasional coffee breaks, less frequent lunches, and rarer dinners. They'd talk together about their lives and activities, but assiduously avoided any hint of romance.

Some speculated about her attending a psychiatric conference in Chicago the same week he took some personal time to visit his mother, still residing in the town of Channel Lake, fifty miles north of the Windy City. Was it possible ...?

Rochelle Weitz was hard at work on a new novel, loosely based on her experience with The Prom Dress Killer. A major publisher had offered a mid-five-figure advance, but her new agent felt they could do even better by putting it up for auction. The "Big Five" publishers were all eager to handle the work of the now famous young woman.

She also was swamped with offers to publish a memoir of her terrifying experience. She was uncertain if she wanted to confess all that occurred while in Ron Bachelor's clutches. That was something to decide upon later.

The media and gossip columnists moved on to more current happenings. A dead romance between a famous cop and a beautiful therapist was so far on the back burners, it was slipping off the stove.

No one even took notice that Doctor Guttenberg scheduled a three-day vacation to view the cherry blossom festival in Virginia the exact dates that Warner was there to attend a FBI forum in Washington DC.

The two of them intended to stay off everyone's radar.

## THE END

If you enjoyed this novel and haven't read either of the two previous Detective Al Warner suspense novels, here is a brief excerpt from the second in the series.

# BORN TO DIE

## PROLOGUE

"Metro-Dade Police, Sergeant Avila."

Rico Avila rubbed his eyes and stretched, bored by a day full of checking in petty criminals and answering nuisance calls. Just thirty minutes left before he could bug out and hoist a couple of cold ones at La Isla.

"Detective Al Warner, please. This is Senator Ian Barker."

A firm, authoritative voice, laced with stress ... or maybe fear? Avilla hitched around in his swivel chair, sitting a little straighter, adjusting his headset over thick, curly hair.

"I'm sorry sir, but he's not ... uh ... available."

"When do you expect him?" The voice cracking, sounding desperate now.

"Oh jeez, Senator, he's still officially inactive, sir. On medical leave. Don't know when he'll be back."

"The Baby Butcher thing? It's been two months. I didn't realize he was so badly injured."

"Yes, sir. That bullet cracking his skull put him in a coma for six weeks. Can I get you his partner?"

"Who's that?"

"Acting Chief of Detectives, Jack Harris." Rico ran a finger down the directory, finding the right extension.

"I've got to talk to someone. I thought... well, Warner seemed the best...."

"Jack Harris has been his partner forever, sir. He's top flight."

"All right. He'll have to do."

"Yes sir. Just a moment, please." He put the call on hold and buzzed the direct line in Detectives.

"Harris."

"Jack, I got Senator Barker on the phone, looking for Warner. Sounds... scared."

"Well, don't keep him waiting. Put him through."

"Right." He switched lines. "I've got Detective Harris for you, sir," making the connection.

"Detectives. Jack Harris speaking."

"This is Senator Ian Barker."

"Yes, sir. How can I help you?"

"I'm... I'm not sure. I ... I think my daughter is missing."

*Terrific. Are you just guessing? And why are you calling homicide?* The wiry little cop clicked his ballpoint, sliding over a pad of yellow lined paper.

"Missing, sir? What d'ya mean?"

"My daughter, Ann. Eighteen. Supposed to start U of Miami this fall, but never showed up. We're worried sick."

"Wow, I see why you're concerned. When did you last see her?"

"Four days ago, when she left to move in on campus."

"She wasn't gonna commute, seeing you live in Miami?"

"No. She craved the full college experience, I guess. She wanted to make it, so to speak, on her own."

"Okay. Have you checked with her friends? Or maybe her potential college roommate, if she had one?"

"Yes, but with no answers. Her best friend, Willa Carpenter, talked with her the day she left, but thought she was at school. She didn't have a roommate on campus yet. At least none we know of."

"Any chance she just took off on her own? Maybe withdrew some cash from her bank account?"

*Kidnapped? Certainly a good candidate. A U.S. senator and a big-time real-estate magnate. Maybe our bailiwick after all.*

"I suppose it's possible. I didn't think to check the bank, but we just don't believe she'd do something like that without us knowing. As I indicated, she's quite independent. To a damned fault, I'm afraid."

"I'm not trying to be judgmental, sir, but do you mean rebellious? If I'm gonna help you, you need to be frank."

"I ... I understand. She is still a teenager, after all. Aren't they all rebels at that age?"

"I guess. Don't have any of my own, to judge. Mind if I ask why you waited four days to report her missing? We only require 48 hours for missing persons."

"We didn't want to create a public flap if it were something innocent. We try to keep our family out of the press, but now we're really scared."

"We'll be discreet, but I gotta know what I'm working with. Is she just a runaway, or did somebody snatch her?"

"Okay." A lengthy sigh. "I've got no other choice. Yes, she can be difficult. My wife and I are busy people. We've probably not paid Ann the attention she would have liked."

"I gotta ask, sir. Does she do any drugs?" *Why is this always like pulling teeth? They want help but don't give you anything to make it easier.* Harris doodled on the lined pad, dissipating his frustration.

"Uhh ... yes. A bit of Marijuana, and lately, some social cocaine. We sent her to a ... uhh ... clinic during the summer to dry out. I'm not sure that didn't make her angrier. You know, believing she'd been sent off as punishment. We were only trying to help, but ...."

"Yeah. So she may be a runaway?"

"Yes, I suppose. But that doesn't make us any less terrified something bad may have happened to her. Regardless, we want her back. We'll do whatever it takes to make things right with her."

Harris printed "<u>ANN BARKER</u>??" at the top of a fresh page, and then dropped the pen, with nothing else to add.

"Okay. If you can get me some recent photos, we'll distribute copies to all the patrol cops and the newspapers. Maybe we'll...."

"No! No press."

The detective suppressed a groan. "But the public can be one of our best tools, if she's just run off. Maybe a reward...?

"No press, I said. I keep my family private. I'll have photos for you this afternoon. Do your best with that. It's not just me I'm worried about. The publicity can ruin her life if she shows up in... uhh... compromising circumstances. I don't want that for her."

"Whatever you say, sir. I understand your caution. It just makes things harder for us. Get me the photos, and we'll get going. I'll do my best to play it close to the vest, Senator, but you gotta be prepared for a leak. I can't guarantee it won't happen."

"Yes, I know." An agonized sigh. "Do what you can. We want her home, safely and undamaged, if possible. She's our only child, and ... you know ...."

"I sure do. Meantime, if you learn anything else, or think of something, no matter how small, let me know. It's the little, seemingly unimportant things that often solve tough cases."

"I will. I'll call a messenger service immediately to send the photos. You'll... you'll keep me informed?"

"You bet. Keep your chin up, sir. We'll find her."

"Thank you. I hope you're right Detective."

Jack Harris massaged the bridge of his considerable nose after hanging up.

*We'll find her, alright. I just hope she's still breathing.*

He rang the duty officer.

"Avila, organize a meeting of the patrol officers first thing tomorrow. We got a missing celeb, probably a runaway. I'll have photos. Absolutely no leaks to the press. You got that?"

"Sure. I'll have everybody there. No mention of Ann Barker?"

"You eavesdropping again, Rico?"

"How else would I know what's going on around here."

They were chuckling as they hung up. Harris wished Al Warner *were* there. No one was better on the really tough cases. Warner was the sole reason that lunatic, Leordano, wasn't still killing children, but it almost cost him his own life.

*If I hadn't tracked him down in the 'Glades that day... Lucky I got there in time.* He sighed again.

Jack was already working two cases, but they were about to take a back shelf to a missing teenager. U.S. senators got priority.

# ONE

## TWELVE MONTHS LATER

The bawling had finally sputtered to a hiccupping stop.

Shellie Laughlin cracked the door, peeking into the room. The night-light cast fractured shadows across the bars of the crib. Stevie had been unusually quiet for two hours. Always hungry lately, the little man should be demanding his meal by now. The incessant crying was driving her crazy. Had he finally gotten over the break-in last month? Strange that a five-month old could sense the danger.

She tiptoed to his crib, never tiring of watching her new son, dreaming of his certain future in science or medicine. A little blonde angel, lying there on his back, so still.

Almost *too* still. She touched his forehead.

Cool. Good. All that wailing had flushed his ....

*Gee, that's strange.* She put her hand back on his face. Was he *too* cool? Dropping the side of the crib, she leaned in, listening, but there was no sound. She put her ear close to his mouth.

Still nothing. Shellie gathered him up, but he didn't wake. His body was strangely slack.

"John." She turned toward the door, her infant son clutched against her breast.

*"John!"*

She stumbled from the room, hurrying for their study, where her neurosurgeon husband was reviewing files. He would know what to do.

"Shellie, what is it?" He stood in the doorway, a cup of coffee in his hand.

"It's Stevie. Oh, God, it's Stevie.

"He's not *breathing*."

# TWO

*Not a single damned place to eat alone. Shoulda had lunch at home.*

Casey Jansson dropped her change on her tray and surveyed the cafeteria. Most of the white laminate topped tables seating four to six eaters were occupied by visitors or staff. The room rippled with quiet voices, the muted clatter of dishes, and the pungent smell of overcooked cheese.

Resigned, she approached a group of nurses and staff, clustered around a long, oblong mica table. Not eager to talk shop, she doubted it could be avoided. That's what they did at lunch. They would draw her in, regardless of any effort to remain aloof. Still, these were her friends; she couldn't just ignore them. She nodded to the two nurses, Rita from Delivery and Marcy from Pediatrics. Danny O'Brien, a second year resident, smiled through a two-day old red-stubbled jaw. His wrinkled blue smock, smudged with blood was a stark comparison to the nurses' starched whites.

"Hi, guys," Casey said. "Mind if I join you?"

"Join away," Rita said, patting the empty seat. The diminutive but voluptuous, dusky-skinned woman was an utter contrast to Casey's slim 5'8" Swedish blond looks.

"Always glad for some real company," Danny said.

"Hey." Rita gave him a friendly elbow in the ribs.

Danny laughed.

"You look bushed, Rita. Busy shift?" Casey couldn't help herself.

"For Sure. Lots of Palm Beach kids having fun."

"More yuppies, I bet," Danny said. "Waiting until it was almost too late before starting a family. Too busy with their careers."

"Yeah." Rita shook her head in mock wonder. "We had three like that last night."

"All a bunch of rich kids, huh?"

"Mostly," Rita said, "but there were some working class babies too."

"You always seem to end up with the celebs, though, don't you, Sanchez?" Jack, an intern, said, grinning.

"Just the luck of the draw." Rita twirled some pasta on a fork. "I was there for a bricklayer's wife this morning. Everybody gets equal treatment at St. Mary's. You know that."

"Sure, sure," Casey said. "Some are just treated more equal than others."

"Huh?" Rita, her mouth full of spaghetti, frowned at the tall blonde.

"Just paraphrasing George Orwell. You know... 'Animal Farm.' "

"Huh?" Rita repeated.

"Forget it. Not important."

"So, Casey," Jack said, "I heard you used to be in Pediatrics. You got seniority. Isn't Maternity a step down for you?"

"I like where I am." She brushed a lock of golden hair from her left eye, shifting on her hard plastic seat, suppressing the vision of Mikey, motionless and sprouting tubes and wires.

"I just thought...."

"Hey, drop it," said Danny. "Can't you see she doesn't want to talk about it?"

"It's okay, Dan. He doesn't know, is all." She turned to the intern, smiling sadly. "It's personal ... something I'd rather forget. Okay?"

"Jeez, I'm sorry," Jack said. "I didn't mean to ...."

"No problem. Let's just talk about something else."

Conversation stumbled to a nervous silence, like a pregnant woman awaiting the next contraction. Danny got things going again, but Casey drifted away. It was three years since she fell in love with little Mike Newman. Their five-month "affair" ended when he broke her heart, deserting her by dying after four weeks in a coma. Blinking away tears, she shuddered at the memory of his small six-year-old body, so cold and still. Her other love affair, with Mikey's father, Andy, quickly deteriorated. She couldn't bear to face him, and he never called.

She had *lied* to them. She just knew Andy blamed her.

Casey took a week's leave, returning to St. Paul to visit her family. After three days of moping in bed, her mother dragged her out, organizing a party for twenty relatives and friends. Casey was commandeered to help with preparation and cooking. Predictably, her father went fishing. A true Swedish iceberg, he left dealing with feelings or any family problems to his wife. Casey understood her father's reluctance to love openly. It was too easy to get hurt.

Life with her family settled into some semblance of normality for the rest of the week, but a subtle numbness pervaded her. Struggling with the empty agony of loss, she erected an outward façade of quiet reserve, burying her warmth and sensitivity under the appearance of a frosty, even snobbish Swede. In truth, she was shy. Once overcome by familiarity, she was the same warm friend little Mikey Newman had discovered. His father had learned she was also a passionate lover. But it all ended with the little guy's death.

Her heart got in the way of cool professionalism, and got shattered. After Mikey's death, she resolved to remain distant, never chancing getting close to a patient... or a man... again.

Maternity, where connections rarely last beyond two days, was the ideal solution.

***

She blinked at the sound of her name, climbing out of the black pit of her memories.

"Case? You okay?" Danny's ice-blue eyes regarded her with a worried intensity.

"Yeah, yeah, I'm fine. Just thinking."

"Well, quit it," he said, running a hand through fiery red hair. "You might hurt yourself."

"What's that, some kind of Irish wit?" She grinned at him.

"Just trying to get a little juice back into that smile of yours." They both laughed.

"You're good for me, Danny-boy." The others were gone, returning to their assignments.

"But not quite good enough?"

"C'mon, Dan. We both know that's over. You're still my best friend, aren't you?"

"Sure. You know I'm whatever you need me to be, Casey. But you can't blame me for still wanting it to be more. I'll always love you."

"Hey, you Irish rogue, cut the blarney. Life's tough enough without having to deal with that. Let's keep it the way we agreed."

"Yeah, sure. But for the record, it's the way *you* agreed. I didn't have any choice."

"Jesus." She chuckled. "See what happens when a woman falls for a younger man."

"Okay, okay, you got me. I'd better get back to the Ward before Dr. Scrooge sends his minions after me. Want to have dinner some night this week?"

"Sure. Got no plans. Give me a call."

"Swell. Maybe you'll see I'm more than just a serious medical-type."

"Oh, you nut." She shook her head, her wheat-yellow hair swirling like a golden halo.

His own special angel, Danny thought, as they went their separate ways.

¤  ¤  ¤

You can find the full novel, plus the first Warner suspense, *Death's Angel,* (which is also available as an Audio Book) as well as all of Bernstein's works at:

http://Amazon.com/author/georgeabernstein